THE
OLIGARCH'S
Wife

Anna Blundy has lived and worked in Russia on many occasions, doing a variety of things from singing in a blues band in the early nineties and making coffee for the ABC News Bureau, to interviewing Mikhail Gorbachev live in Russian on Radio Svoboda in 1998. She wrote a single girl column for *The Times* in her twenties and now writes a column for them about Italy, where she currently lives. She is the author of the critically acclaimed memoir of her father David Blundy (killed in El Salvador by a sniper when she was nineteen) and of five novels about war correspondent Faith Zanetti.

THE
OLIGARCH'S
Wife

ANNA BLUNDY

This paperback edition published by Arrow Books 2010

10 9 8 7 6 5 4 3 2 1

First published in Great Britain in 2009 by Preface Publishing

Arrow Books
20 Vauxhall Bridge Road
London SW1V 2SA

An imprint of The Random House Group Limited

www.rbooks.co.uk

Addresses for companies within The Random House Group Limited
can be found at www.randomhouse.co.uk

The Random House Group Limited Reg. No. 954009

A CIP catalogue record for this book is available from the British Library

ISBN 978 1 84809 084 2

The Random House Group Limited supports The Forest Stewardship Council (FSC),
the leading international forest certification organisation. All our titles that are printed
on Greenpeace-approved FSC-certified paper carry the FSC logo. Our paper
procurement policy can be found at www.rbooks.co.uk/environment

Typeset in Fournier MT by Palimpsest Book Production Limited,
Falkirk, Stirlingshire

Printed and bound in Great Britain by
CPI Bookmarque, Croydon CR0 4TD

For Alex, and for Jean in her unimaginable loss.

oligarch *n.* a member of an oligarchy; any of a small group holding power in a state. Also, an advocate or supporter of oligarchy. E.g. – the ageing oligarchs of the Politbureau.

wife *n.* 1 a woman; in later use esp. one engaged in the sale of some commodity. Now (chiefly Sc., freq. derog.) a middle-aged or elderly woman. 2 the female mate of a male animal.

'I would not be standing here tonight without the unyielding support of my best friend for the last sixteen years, the rock of our family and the love of my life, our nation's next First Lady, Michelle Obama. Sasha and Malia, I love you both so much, and you have earned the new puppy that's coming with us to the White House.'

Barack Obama

Chapter One

I t was on the news. A hard fact now, illustrated by short scenes, brightly lit and frenetically cut together to demonstrate, perhaps, the dynamism of the forthcoming police investigation, the dedication of the reporter bringing you the breaking news live as it happens, or even, perhaps, to reflect the violent horror of the man's death.

They showed the blue flashing lights of the empty police cars parked at frenzied angles and left running by the canals. And the still serenity of the ambulance that would be in no rush today. Nobody was under any illusions as to where Pavel Ivanchenko would be going this morning. They cut in a statement from a Kremlin official in Moscow denying that the Russian government had any involvement whatsoever in this regrettable incident and dismissing the very suggestion as ludicrous. Now over to the bridge where the reporter's hair blew across her face as she shouted above the noise. Then some stills of Pavel standing on the terraces of his London football club, Katya next to him, smiling the tight smile of the lavishly imprisoned. And back to the studio.

'That report from Serene Gosling in St Petersburg. Police spokesmen have confirmed that the body retrieved from the River Neva this morning is that of Russian tycoon Pavel Ivanchenko, who was reported missing on Thursday by staff when he failed to return from what he described as "an important meeting" in central St

Petersburg. Ivanchenko, who accused Russian President Vladimir Putin himself of being behind two previous assassination attempts, had been in virtual exile in London for six years and was wanted in Russia on charges of embezzlement and tax evasion, though he is thought frequently to have entered the country, unknown to the authorities.'

Mo breathed out. She wasn't sure whether the news made it seem more real or less real. Cobwebs seemed to surround her, slowing and tangling her every move, muffling sound and threatening to creep down her throat and stop her breathing. They had been there since she'd woken up on Friday (still, apparently, inhabiting her body but cruelly separated from every physical or emotional sensation). She wriggled her toes now, touching each one to the cork tiles under them and looking out at the magnolia tree, whose huge creamy artichoke globes were getting ready to drop, exhausted, to the grass below them. He was really gone.

The bracelet was heavy on her wrist, a twisted plait of diamonds and pearls, brilliant against her dark skin, the colour, he'd said, of chestnuts from the Siberian forests, shiny, glistening and brown as they burst out of their green cases. This was Pavel in whispering romantic mode, breathing the soul of his vast country into her ears. But really, had it ever been true?

It was strange, she thought, having absorbed the sight of the limp body being hauled, dripping, out of the water, how still death is. When that bestial, raging, choking struggle to live is finally over.

It had been worse than she'd thought. They should have given him the full dose, but Katya had been advised that that would make it detectable. Also it would taste bad. Mo, who knew nothing about poison, was reassured that even half of what they were giving him would kill an ox. Why an ox, she'd wondered, feeling sorry for this huge, gentle creature with a big wet nose who would topple sideways, tongue hanging out, lowing, not knowing why he was attacked

4

or by what. Sorrier, by far, for this imaginary ox with his broad hooves than she felt for their real victim.

As it turned out, he was stronger than any big-eyed ox. Katya, whose white mink was perhaps unsuitable for the occasion, realised something was wrong and tried to shoot him but she missed and hit a painting above the fireplace, an eighteenth-century gypsy dancing scene, a kind of *War and Peace* image of Russia from a time when stirrups gleamed and moustaches bristled and peasants knew their place in the mud. As he ran at her she shot him again and blood spurted on to her coat and into her face but he kept running, knocking her to the ground and falling on top of her, drenching her with blood that was so hot it seemed to steam as it flowed. A bowl of orchids had smashed to the floor. It was this that struck her most when she came into the room, just then, as it fell.

Mo, cold and clear as though she was standing in bright snow, tried to drag him off and plunged a large hunting knife into his back, feeling first the resistance of dense muscle and then the scrape of bone against the blade as she pushed. But he stood up, shouting, swearing in Russian, bellowing, hurling himself about until, unfamiliar, as if he were someone else, crazed with pain, perhaps, he threw himself out of the window, breaking the glass, sharp shards raining down on to the polished parquet inside, and crashing into the concrete of the courtyard outside. Mo ran to the window as he lurched out towards the gates, barely human in his agony, garishly illuminated by security floodlights.

Katya scrambled up and tore down the stairs after him, stumbling in her high heels, groaning and grasping at her bruised throat, the bodyguard standing there, inexplicably motionless. Mo followed now, out into the dark street to see Katya's coat fly out as she turned the corner towards the river, aware on some level of where he must be going. Both women stopped, fifty yards apart, as Pavel climbed the embankment wall, pulling himself up on a lamppost with a fish tail winding around it, and hurling himself, with a final roar, into the black water.

Katya had turned and raised her white hand, almost smiling. Mo nodded and then both women were still. Mo took a taxi to the airport and was in London again by dawn. The sky was pale blue at the edges by the time she turned the key in her front door and found that the flat smelt the same as it had when she'd left. Of toast and dust, of the apples that had been too long in the fruit bowl, of the paper record sleeves in the sitting room and the clean sheets she'd put on yesterday. She ran a hot bath with rose oil she'd bought with Pavel that time, and she put her clothes and shoes in a Tesco carrier bag to throw into the rubbish van as it moved, perhaps. She lay in the burning water staring at the cracks in the ceiling and wondering how she should feel, how other people had felt afterwards. She looked with detached interest at static scenes in her mind, flicking through a mental Rolodex.

It occurred to her how strange it is that when death happens, scrolling backwards through the life that has ended, it seems so inevitable, its manner and all the particulars. It seems as though that life was constructed in every detail to meet that death and as though time was always hurtling towards it. But, really, she need never have gone on that first trip to Russia. Katya need never have left Kirgask for Moscow. Her life, so swirling and chaotic, had not seemed, at any prior point, to be part of the design of Pavel's death. But now she and Katya had fulfilled their gruesome purpose and, for Pavel Ivanchenko, at least, time had stopped. Had it, she wondered, also stopped for her? Or had it really stopped when she first saw Katya, smoking a cigarette in the lobby bar of the Ukraina Hotel?

No, she decided. That, of course, was when it had started.

'We should live our lives as though Christ were coming this afternoon.'

Jimmy Carter

Chapter Two

Katya had not always been beautiful. Standing on the edge of the bath to brush her teeth, clinging on with her toes to balance on one gangly leg, she scrutinised herself in the small square mirror. White foam spilling out of her mouth, squinting dark amber eyes in the flickering strip of light, she practised raising one eyebrow, a skill which, if mastered, might impress Andriusha enough to make him let her fire his air rifle at sardine tins round the back of the House of Culture where they put the rubbish bins out.

Andriusha's dad had been kicked out of the Party for reasons unknown (though Katya had overheard her mum saying she was as sure as a salted cucumber that he must be Jewish) and had lost his job at the brick factory as a result. He sat around in their flat drinking vodka and singing sad songs to the blue budgerigar that lived in a domed cage on the kitchen table and could hang upside down by its scaly claws. Andriusha's mum was the nurse at school and Katya could only think of her in blurred close-up, peering into her eyes with an enormous magnifying glass, flattening her tongue with a fat wooden spatula, tugging at her knotted hair looking for nits or squeezing pouches of goose-bumped white flesh with her metal pincers to measure fat ratio which, if low, would be treated with an extra three dumplings at lunch, dripping in butter and steaming with the iniquity of poverty.

Katya's mum, whose beauty had once been spotted by a director from Mosfilm who came to Kirgask to stay with an aunt, said that, when she was young, bread had been so plentiful and the shops so full that one girl she knew even went on a diet like a Parisienne. Katya, who had inherited her mother's wide Tatar face and white-blonde hair, wanted to block her ears when she started talking about 'before'. Before, when salami and cheese apparently grew on trees and sugared buns hung from the hedgerows.

By the way her mother looked at the photograph of herself on top of the upright piano, Katya could tell that, secretly, when the dishes were cleaned and the only sound for miles was the train to Magadan passing in the night, she wished things had turned out differently with the director. He paid for her to go all the way to Moscow for a screen test, she said with a sad smile, and he promised to introduce her to Stalin himself, but, in fact, he had turned out to be a dirty goat. The words 'like the rest of them' were left hanging in the air, but no less loud for that. So, she came home with the golden domes of the Kremlin shining in her eyes and married Katya's dad, saying, as she so often did, that it was better to hold a pig in your hands than to look up at a crane in the sky. Katya was not so sure.

When her dad came home from work he would leave a line of bright orange brick dust round the edge of the bath that her mum would sponge off later, kneeling on the tiles, her felt slippers hanging off the backs of her feet. 'One day, Katiusha, everything will change,' he said. 'You be ready.' Having absolutely no clue what he might mean, Katya was sure she would be.

'I'm already ready!' she shouted, flinging her arms round his neck and jumping up to wrap her skinny legs round his waist. 'Andriusha's going to let me fire his gun.'

Downstairs the Svetlanovs were already arguing loudly. A plate smashed and the baby started crying.

Her dad nodded. After all, he'd been doing three hours of military training a week when he was seven. Even though he'd showered, the brick dust was still thick behind his nails and in the sworly holes of his ears where the black hairs sprouted.

'How's Dima? We miss him at work,' he said, sitting down on the divan and relighting yesterday evening's cigarette, a rare mention of Andriusha's poor father. He said it as though Dima had the flu or something.

'He sings,' Katya told her dad, standing on her head on the rug in front of him, her nightie shlooping up round her head to expose her bare bum.

'Shame,' he said, shaking his head and exhaling. 'What a shame.'

The smell of frying onions was already wafting through from the kitchen and hanging heavy in the stale air. Even with the windows open the air was still as fudge.

In the morning Katya ran to school, tugging the ribbons out of her hair and pushing her socks down to wrinkle round her skinny ankles. It hadn't rained for months and the dust flew up round her feet, the pale sun already hot and the tall birch trees parched and rustling. She stood outside Andriusha's building panting and flushed. She picked a little stone up off what was maybe supposed to be a lawn and threw it up at his window.

'Coming!' he shouted and she heard the door slam on the fourth floor, and the chaotic clatter of his feet hurtling down the dark stairway before erupting out into the bright courtyard, the pukh swirling through the air on a warm breeze.

Andriusha tore his red pioneer scarf off and shoved it into his pocket. His mum made him wear it even so.

'You can swap a horseradish for a horseradish but you're only wasting your time,' she said.

'Bastards!' Andriusha said, as he said every day when he took his scarf off, and he pulled one of his dad's cigarettes out of his satchel, lighting it nonchalantly with a thin match as they started to walk. He would sell them at school for twenty kopecks a piece. He would sell his own grandmother, Katya heard people say. Sometimes he even took a puff and looked at her importantly before he coughed. Sugar, salt and matches. The only things that weren't rationed. Even the Communists knew the people's limits.

'Look!' Katya announced, skipping backwards in front of him and raising her eyebrow.

'Firs and sticks!' he exclaimed, stopping dead in his tracks. 'OK. Tonight after orchestra! Fifty kopecks.'

Katya whooped and punched the air, sure that being able to fire a gun was essential for a girl of seven who was going to be ready when the time came.

It was a long day at school (especially as her teacher, Comrade Tarakanova, had given her a one in Revolutionary Studies and told her that her work was 'not worthy of a citizen of the Soviet Union') and an even longer evening at orchestra, scraping her bow across the strings in the stifling hall at such an angle as to make tuneful-ness impossible but perfectly facilitating a full view of Andriusha puffing his cheeks out to blow into his clarinet, a thin film of sweat making his forehead shine.

She stood out the back afterwards by the big steel rubbish bins and watched the night envelop the sky, shuffling her feet in the dirt, rocking backwards and forwards on her heels and practising useful facial expressions. She chewed her hair and started to bite her nails. The truth was becoming apparent. Tatiana, who played first cello and was fifteen, and Comrade Petrovich, who was the conductor and was forty, did not notice her standing there. He lifted Tatiana's skirt up and put his hand into her pants. She shut her eyes and moaned like her mum did when she got into a hot bath full of the bubbles Uncle Ivan had sent her from Leningrad.

Andriusha did not come and Andriusha did not come. When she got home, running through the night with the tears drying on her dirty face, her dad shouted at her and made her cry all over again. After he had gone into the bedroom and slammed the door her mum hugged her and told her she was her angelochik. 'Someone got hurt at the factory today,' she said, kissing her cheek. Her mother's hair smelt of lemons. For some reason this made Katya cry even more and when she got into bed she told Malyshka, her stuffed elephant, that they would run away to the circus together as soon as ever they got the chance.

The next morning she left her ribbons resolutely in and walked slowly down the path under the birches by the side of Kirgask's main road with her socks pulled up over her knees. She was so late that Andriusha was waiting for her out by the statue of Togliatti, the Italian Communist. He was eating a mushroom pie that his mum had wrapped for him in brown paper.

'I waited for you,' she told him as they walked solemnly to school.

Andriusha shrugged. 'I lent my gun to Oksana for her brother to use. She gave me a rouble and said she'd kiss me on the mouth,' he explained, as if it didn't matter a radish.

'I'll kiss you on the mouth,' Katya said, quietly, not looking into his sparkling black eyes.

'You're not pretty like her,' Andriusha explained, lighting his cigarette with a toss of his thick curls.

Katya laughed indifferently and bit the inside of her cheek until it bled.

'Where there is discord, may we bring harmony. Where there is error, may we bring truth. Where there is doubt, may we bring faith. And where there is despair, may we bring hope.'

Margaret Thatcher

Chapter Three

She was awake again, at her mum's. Dad said she had to go and she didn't really mind. What was the difference in the end? Nobody in the flat and the fear rising like writhing worms in her stomach. But this time it was different. For now, somewhere deep inside her, a place she imagined to be a bit like the one warm patch of sawdust fluff in the dark box where her hamster slept, Mo had a plan. She had had it, and she had kept quiet about it, since she went with her dad to the Zinns' house. Since she'd met Eli.

It started like a lot of days started whether she was at Mum's or Dad's: at about three in the morning. Creeping downstairs in the dark to put the chain on the door, she could smell the cigarette smoke from Mr Ferdinand's flat. There were still people down there, a few of them singing along to the record, like they felt they had to pretend they were still having a good time.

Her mum, who 'had her' for a weekend a month normally but this was a whole week because Dad had gone away, had got in fifteen minutes ago, arrival time marked in the dark red glow of the digital alarm clock, and she could tell from the muffled untidy footsteps and the way the keys hit the wash stand that she was drunk. Mo lay still, waiting and listening, hoping that Frances, which was what she called her mum, though others called her Frankie, would remember the chain so that she wouldn't have to get up in the cold herself, taking her now tepid pink rubber hot-water bottle brought with her from Dad's down with her.

Afterwards she lay awake the rest of the night, listening to the firemen talking round their brazier and waiting for the first W3, a double-decker and the herald of daylight and safety, to chug into action, its yellow headlamps fuzzy in the dawn mist.

It was the price you paid for being Frankie, Mo thought: a lot of late nights with strange men, a sweet smell of alcohol and the bitter choke of cigarettes.

'A man in the pub thought I was Debbie Harry!' her mum said in the morning, sucking in the cheeks of her reflection and mussing her hair thoughtfully. Mo wanted to go home where things were funny if Dad was there. Dad's flat was stark and clean. Stark because he didn't care about possessions and was hardly there anyway and clean because Mo cleaned it. Girlfriends would leave things like a pearly eye-shadow or a worn-down lipstick. Mo either threw them away, if she didn't like the colour or thought the girl might be dirty, or she kept them, clicking them shut in her jewellery box, the kind with a twirling ballerina, but it had broken ages ago.

Frances's dressing table frightened Mo. There was no order to it. Lipsticks lay on their side when Mo would like to have stood them up. A tube of brownish foundation was oozing on the glass and evaporated bottles of perfume accumulated in the back row, the sickly urine-coloured last drops caramelised inside, when someone ought to have thrown them away. The drawers, she knew because she'd opened them, were full of tubes, sponges and paper packets that Mo, without being able to articulate this, suspected had something to do with sex.

'I do think Debbie Harry is really bloody stunning, don't you?' Frances asked. Mo was bending over her hamster's cage and trying to coax it on to its wheel. She was allowed to bring it but she knew Frances somehow disapproved, pulling her face into a wordless wince every time she looked in its direction. Mo found the scratch of its claws on the plastic and the regular whine of each grinding rotation comforting in the long night, but she wished he wouldn't sleep all day. Last week her twin friends Karl and Mark's gerbils had eaten their own babies. This worried her in a way she couldn't pin down.

Confronted now with what she knew could never be an innocent question, Mo locked down, eyes to the floor, soft hands, still plump from childhood, holding on to each other for want of anyone else's hand to hold. She knew better than to disagree. 'Really? Why? Well who DO you bloody well think is half attractive then?' Frances might shriek, the tone disappointed and sharp, the suggestion, as ever, that Mo was perverse and impossible to please. To Frances, every contradiction was a highly personal affront, every breath of doubt in her omniscience a loud 'fuck you'. But even disagreement, Mo knew, was better than ignorance. 'Who's Debbie Harry?' Now there would be a textbook cue for a mock-horrified, utterly mirthless laugh followed by the unanswerable question: 'How can you not know that?'

And, of course . . . well, of course, the objects of her mother's admiration were always wispy blonde, always jagged thin, always red glossy parted lips a bit like, well, a tiny bit like . . . herself. Mo, in the cold isolating shadow of the other hand, was plump and dark. 'Coloured, darling. Coloured,' her mum told her, though she wasn't, actually, not that she would have minded. She envied the black girls' clique at school, their hairstyles shiny and immaculate, shoes always clean and unscuffed, sticking together, belonging, at the very least, to each other.

'Yes,' she said eventually, as she had known she must. 'Very.'

Her dad, it hardly needed saying, did not often take her anywhere. Normally, he picked her up from her mum's, drove her home joking and talking and offering the hope of togetherness, and then he went out. Work. Woman. Whatever. As soon as she saw him she ran outside from the smudgy, steamed-up patch of suburban window that was her lookout post. He rode the car up on to the kerb at a chaotic angle and flicked his cigarette out of the window where his elbow leaned. He got out and stood jangling his keys and shifting his weight from trainer to bouncing trainer. Other men, other people's dads, didn't wear trainers. Yet. Mo ran down so fast she sent an empty milk bottle rolling off the front step on to the grey pavement, but when she reached her father she stopped dead and looked up. It was a long way up.

They were going 'somewhere poncy' he'd said, so Mo put on the long patterned dress with a gathered waist that she'd stuffed into her overnight bag and she wrapped a lace tablecloth round her shoulders, fastening it with one of Frankie's big brooches, a heavy silver thing with a dragon on it. Not that she had any idea what 'somewhere poncy' might mean (in fact, on this occasion, it was a mansion in Hampstead Garden Suburb, where the lonely wife of an old school friend held occasional court). Her dad didn't do her hair, wouldn't have thought of it, and she was never quite sure what it ought to look like. She had tried to put it in high bunches like someone she'd seen on telly. The littlest girl in the Brady Bunch, actually.

'You look ridiculous,' her dad said. But somehow he said it with such fondness that it didn't make her stomach sink and her throat close up.

'No hug for your dear old daddykins?' he asked her, pulling an enormous doll in an enormous box out from behind his back, delighted by his coup. He'd obviously been abroad for the week, the long week she's spent with Frances. Abroad was somewhere that, in 1978, not many people went. It was before package tours and straw donkeys, before the expectation that summer means sun, sea and sex. And booze.

She took it and stared at the big brown plastic face that stared back at her. It was the first time she'd ever seen a brown doll. She wondered if he thought it looked more like her than the blonde ones.

'It sings the alphabet,' he told her, proud as a magician sawing his assistant in half. Enormous Dolly had come all the way from America, in fact, in a plane belonging to Freddie Laker, or his creditors, and packed into a suitcase with two hundred Silk Cut, a bottle of aftershave and some crumpled T-shirts.

Mo sat in the back and her dad smoked and listened to the news on the radio. Today he'd had the car cleaned (Mo wondered why, suspecting intrigue, deceit and something she wasn't sure she wanted to know about) and the smell of shampooed grey nylon and the spray they clean the dashboard with made her feel sick pretty much straight away.

'How's Frankie?' he asked. 'Has she been making that face?' He leaned round, the car swerving dangerously, and sucked his cheeks in.

Mo laughed. 'No,' she said, loyally.

'Karl and Mark died in a tragic accident at Priory Park paddling pool yet?' he joked. These were the only names he remembered from school, though she wasn't really friends with them that much.

'No,' she giggled, imagining a splash, stripy trunks, blood and screaming.

'Anyone told their parents the Revolution isn't actually coming?' he asked.

'No,' Mo said. She knew it was a joke but she didn't get it. She had got Enormous Dolly out of her box and discovered that she did, indeed, from the rigid confines of her broad chest, sing the alphabet. 'X, Y, Zeee.'

The car was swirling with the grey blue smoke of a thousand cigarettes when, hours later, they drove through some shiny gates and up a crunchy gravel drive that twisted through cool cypress trees to the house. And she had known, the moment she saw the house, dark pink with cream windows like a glorious dessert, with ivy creeping up to the battlements, that the world was not the place she had hitherto assumed it to be.

A boy with thick dark hair and fat-lensed glasses sat on the mossy steps between two smooth-faced lions, fiddling with his light sabre. Mo stayed in the car and looked at her shoes, but her dad got out and leaned on a lion, his sleeves rolled up. Slowly and carefully she undid the big brooch and left it on the seat with the lace tablecloth. She was not stupid.

'That's Mo,' he told the boy. 'Don't hit her over the head with that stick.'

Eli laughed, told him it was a light sabre and trundled over to Mo's window, swinging his weapon. He was wearing a thickly knitted red jumper, grey shorts and old white plimsolls with two thin red stripes round the bottom. 'Got poisonous tadpoles in the pond,' he said. 'And a chess set inside. I am a champion.'

'OK,' Mo nodded, getting out herself, tempted by the spectacle of dangerous wildlife and the offer of the companionship of a real champion.

Her dad went up the steps and across a lawn towards the door of the grand country-but-not-quite-country house, where a glittering woman in shoes as delicate as birds' bones and with dark frizzy hair piled on top of her head embraced him under an arch of cascading roses. Mo was used to people embracing her dad and used to going to their houses. This one was different though – obviously rich, probably married. She seemed to remember the latter fact suddenly, calling over to the children. 'Oh, Eli, darling. Do be careful!', lipstick-laughing, herself utterly careless, dripping with jewellery.

Mo already knew that she, for one, was never going to be careful again.

'Actually,' Eli said, blinking mole-like, his eyes strangely enlarged by his glasses. 'I didn't win. Sam Wasserman cheated and wouldn't put his queen back where it was. But I should have won.'

'I believe you,' Mo said, and she did.

'My fellow Americans, I'm pleased to tell you today that I've signed legislation that will outlaw Russia for ever. We begin bombing in five minutes.'

Ronald Reagan

Chapter Four

Pavel woke up and told himself he was lucky. The flat was freezing, the heating in their building had simply not come on this winter and his mum's fingers were going blue, as blue as the snow that stretched out forever in the dawn light, promising hardship. 'I saw things a person should never see,' his grandmother had told him when he was little, taking him on to her bony knee and coming so close that he could smell cheese and death on her breath. 'If you wake in the morning with a roof over your head, if breakfast isn't a cat's carcass or, God forbid, human remains, then you tell yourself you are lucky, boy. Lucky as a fox in a chicken coop.' Pavel obeyed her still, though she had died years ago, shrivelled back to the nothingness she'd come from. He had taken her seriously and knew himself to be the fox in the chicken coop, though he would contest that it was just luck that had put him there. His mother was awake already, smoking in the near dark.

Pavel woke his brother. 'Get up,' he said, and went into the kitchen, moving quickly (a fox has to move quickly) to get them breakfast. Instant coffee that he'd stolen from the big Gastronom on Leninskiy Boulevard, the only place in town that still had any, and bread and salami. He didn't need to steal, he had the money, but he liked to take what he could and pay only if he had to, a preference that would never leave him. He put his breakfast and his brother's on the kitchen table, the coffee steaming in the cold like piss on ice, the kettle settling back down on the rattling stove, and he took his mum's over to the sofa, putting it down softly on the rug.

'Thanks, dove,' she said, not looking at him. He wondered for a moment if she had heard about yesterday, but he knew straight away that he was being paranoid. She couldn't know that yesterday he had punched a woman and perhaps she wouldn't care anyway, God knows.

Once, before his dad blew his brains out and before she jumped, his mother had had friends, and the poor excuse for a human being he had hit had been one of them. But not any more. Nowadays, since the factory shut down, his mother lay still and her former friend, such a creature as she was, made vodka in the kitchen in a huge glass vat like an old diving bell he'd seen in the museum once in Archangel. Every day when he called she knelt scrubby knees on her cracked and stained lino floor to open the tap and let the samogon flow out. She bottled it up herself in old sasparilla bottles, shoving corks into the necks and pushing them down with a dirty thumb. Her face was puffy and swollen, the wrong colour for a face, her eyes small and watery, disappearing into the transluscent flesh. Because, of course, she drank the stuff herself. Her apartment hadn't been cleaned for years and in winter (it was almost always winter) there were frozen patches on the walls where the damp came in, and she shuffled around in felt valenki and a loosely knitted grey woollen shawl that she pulled up over her head, the oven on with the door open, all four hobs blazing for heat, but really just a useless blue flicker in the ice-brittle air.

He'd been in fights at school, Christ knows, but it was only when he started selling the vodka that it got serious. He had to do something, his mother and brother so useless, everyone looking to him for food, for clothes. You had to be tough, that's all he knew, all he'd known since his dad first pummelled him and left him bleeding on the bathroom floor. That's what he said when he'd finished, washing his bloody hands in the sink. 'You have to be tough.' He must have been eight. You didn't have to do it with women though, not normally.

'The secret to women, Pasha,' his mother told him, laid up with her withered stick legs stretched out in front of her while he cooked supper for her and his brother in the heavy black frying pan, thinly sliced potatoes fried in oil with whatever he could find chucked on top, sometimes a bit of salami or cheese, 'is to pay them a compliment – a specific one, mind: choose an item of clothing, a scarf, shoes, their hair, anything – and to be interested in them. Really interested.' She looked at her nails often, as if the main reason she lamented her survival after her jump was that her nails had suffered. Her advice was theoretical, of course. Whenever Pavel mentioned anyone from the outside world to her, she, confined to the sofa, waiting for the rest of her body to wither like her sorry legs and her love for her violent and dead husband, would say, 'That bitch deserves a good kicking.'

He was late yesterday because he'd taken his brother to a rehearsal after school and the tram broke down, the driver climbing up on to the roof in a cloud of driving snow to try and fix it, her overalls immediately drenched, sparks flying from the overhead wires. He and Gleb climbed up to help too, but Gleb slipped and hurt his arm, lying there in the gutter in a pool of grey slush crying and clutching his violin case to his chest. Pavel hated him at that moment more than he'd ever allowed himself to hate him before, his helpless little slug of a brother who sucked and sucked the life out of him, providing nothing, always trying to seem different, be different, only taking, even from their ruined mother. But he pulled him up and took him home without saying a word, feeding both his dependants before going out again.

Last night he banged on the woman's door and shouted but nobody came. It was dark inside. If he didn't bring the order they'd break his arms – he saw them break Oleg's from up at the flats, so he knew they were telling the truth, as if he needed proof. It was cold and Pavel had stopped wearing a hat, hoping to be taken for a foreigner, the men from America who shuffled round the scientific institute, skidding in their smooth sunny-soled shoes, looking powerful with their bare heads next to the richly furred Russians whose hospitals couldn't cure pneumonia if they got it, whose homes were perhaps not warm either, who dressed like bears because their lives were no better than a bear's. Pavel knew who he wanted to look like, whose side he was on in life's vicious game, even if they dismissed him. He heard someone explaining to them, gesturing over to him as he scuttled the pavement: 'They aren't really children. They're animals.' Perhaps this was in response to a pitying comment: 'The poor rats, running the streets with armfuls of bottles when they should be at school.' The suckers, he thought, the weak like my brother, they are at school. Not me.

Lips chapped and blue, the dark street below already obscured by the blizzard, he took a step back and kicked the door in, knowing nobody cared, nobody would call the police and that, if they did, no police would come. Not to this flat. He flicked some lights on, shouting the woman's name, walking angrily round until he found her, collapsed drunk on the divan, snoring loudly. She had pissed herself and Pavel found that bile was rising in his throat though he'd never thought of himself as squeamish before. He wiped his own mother's arse, everyone knew. You had to be tough.

'Get up!' he shouted at her and she sat up, bundling herself together, clearly no idea where or who she was, what was going on. She started fawning, apologising, promising, calling him 'young master' and 'comrade' and weird old-fashioned stuff he'd only heard in books. He was repulsed by everything about this life and he suddenly knew what would make him feel better, what women who let him down deserved but rarely got, swimming in their own piss and excrement. He pulled a fist back and punched her hard in the face. She fell slowly, as if deflating, and Pavel bottled the vodka himself while she lay there clutching at her head.

It was only yesterday, he was still fifteen, he still lived with mother and brother, still breathed the same acrid air as they did, but he knew things had changed, that he was now somebody who could punch a woman and come home, do his chores, take his brother to school, all as if nothing had happened. Somehow it was a bigger deal than when he'd lost his virginity – a big sad disappointment that was.

He thought about girls all the time. When he still went to school he used to look at the bottom of the girls' skirts and imagine touching their legs, slipping his hand up between their thighs, feeling their knickers over their pussies. He watched their necks when they pushed strands of hair back, golden tendrils that slipped from their ribbons, and he imagined the bliss of being held in the wet warmth of a girl.

But it wasn't like that. Boris the arm-breaker told him there was someone he could fuck, that he shouldn't go round a virgin, you can get beaten up for that, he told him. Pavel was keen, standing at the tram stop in the freezing slush waiting for Boris, trying to imagine what it would be like, his hard-on in place as it basically had been for two days since Boris first mentioned the girl. Liubov was her name, Liuba, and there was a part of Pavel still left whose heart soared at the sound of the name, meaning Love. He imagined her flesh as white as the snowdrops that used to come up at his granny's dacha, her eyes blue as cornflowers, her body as soft as freshly baked bread torn from the loaf.

Boris turned up with a couple of the others, hunched behind him, their bodies trying to keep out the cold with whatever contortions were necessary, all of them smoking, all of them older than him. Boys big enough that the real commuters – the people whose tram journey would take them back home to a hug and a kiss, a warm radiator and laughing children who knew nothing of this life — moved out of the way, eyes down, letting the bull-shouldered teenagers with grazes on their faces and vodka on their breath go past.

Liubov's building was out of town on a huge new estate of vast grey high-rises planted in deep mud that was now puddled with porridgy ice. Wet black-brown snow lay piled at the sides of the road. The building stank and there was a heap of shit in the lift.

'Was that you, Seriozh?' Boris barked, punching his dumb-eyed crony hard in the stomach while everyone laughed, including Pavel. He was not stupid — Boris paid him more than twice the average monthly wage every week to do the pick-up and deliveries. He was so rich that he planned to go into Tomsk soon to buy an electric heater from the one shop that still, rumour had it, stocked them. Liquidity wasn't Pavel's problem, availability was.

A guy in his forties opened the door on the seventeenth floor. He could easily have been sixty, teeth brown and rotten, grey stubble, thin vest, blue flip-flops, clearly drunk. He stood under the bare bulb in the hall and welcomed the boys into the oppressive heat of the flat. They took their boots off with something bordering on respect, jostling slightly in anticipation, the man blowing smoke inadvertently into all their faces, his expression that of someone lost and confused, his smell distinct as that of hunting dogs. Pavel folded his coat over his arm and waited, his toes twitching in his socks, feeling the warmth of the lino under them. Boris scrumpled some notes into the man's hand and told everyone he was going first.

'She's in there,' the man said, waving at a doorway off the hall with a thin hand. 'You boys want a drink?'

He led them into the kitchen while Boris slipped through the door into the girl's bedroom.

Pavel and the three others stood round the kitchen table under another bare bulb and took turns swigging from a vodka bottle that the man opened with a combination of penknife and teeth. Pavel looked out of the window at the view of other tower blocks, a churning grey sky and light drizzly snow and tried not to burst into tears.

By the time his turn came, last because he was the youngest and a virgin, he was quite drunk, his muscles relaxed and head blurred with the thick tepid liquid. The man hadn't provided any bread to go with the vodka and Pavel felt the alcohol slopping about in his tight stomach. The others were pulling on their coats and boots as Pavel opened the flimsy door to Liubov's room. Her name had been prettily scratched and then coloured in with paints in swirling letters on the door, by a woman, a long time ago. Liubov, Love.

'Hurry up, OK?' Boris said. 'We'll see you downstairs.'

The room smelt of sweat, of sex and the air was unpleasantly dense, coating the inside of Pavel's nostrils with the taste of semen. The curtains were shut, thin curtains with a Felix the Cat pattern on them that looked as though they had never been opened. There was a dressing table with two naked dolls sitting blankly on it, their chubby plastic arms and legs glistening in the heat, an old bear next to them with sad eyes. Liuba lay naked on the bare mattress with her legs open, her eyes shut and her arms limply by her side. Between her legs her cunt was swollen and wet, dripping with the other boys' come. Pavel stood in front of her, squinting in the bright yellow light from a bedside lamp, the kind with pink frills around it. He didn't move, revolted but strangely aroused, wondering why she didn't have a sheet or a blanket on the bed, wondering if he would know how to do it.

Liuba opened her eyes and propped herself up on one elbow. She was perhaps twelve or thirteen, with the wide moon face of the kids that mostly go to the home, eyes blank, glazed, without expectation or hope. She had long mousy hair and the beginnings of breasts swelling on her chest, bruises on her shoulders and round her emaciated hips. He thought perhaps her nose was bleeding a bit but he didn't dare look too closely.

'Come on then,' she said, peering at him as though he had come from another planet or was a dog or a horse. 'Or do you want me to turn over?'

Pavel opened his mouth to speak but nothing came out immediately. He coughed. 'No. No, that's fine,' he said, undoing his zip and climbing on top of her. Pleased that he was doing what was expected, she lay back and shut her eyes again, her whole body dying under him.

He pushed into her and came immediately, clambering off and turning away. She didn't open her eyes, speak or move and Pavel, filled with horror and shame, went out into the corridor for his boots and coat, closing the door behind him.

He heard the man approach from the kitchen, the plastic of his flip-flops slapping the floor. 'I hope the bitch was lively. Gave you a good one,' he said, his cigarette ash falling to the floor from the butt in his mouth.

Pavel nodded enthusiastically, though nothing could have been further from the truth.

'I might have a go myself,' the man muttered, pushing Liubov's door open. 'Take her a drink too.' He was holding the bottle of vodka they had nearly finished in his filthy hand.

Pavel caught a glimpse of Liubov, still lying where he had left her and realised that this man was her father.

Outside in the corridor he vomited against the wall, pure vodka that stank of bile.

Boris hit him between the shoulder blades with his clenched fist as they walked away back towards the tram stop, wading through the mud and slush. 'Now you're a man,' he said.

He hadn't felt like one then but now, now that he had punched a woman to protect his own flimsy arms, he knew that any pretence of childhood he had ever had was over.

'I like Mr Gorbachev. We can do business together.'

Margaret Thatcher

Chapter Five

Katya had learned to separate her lives. There was the life that came with Dad's friend Konstantin playing his guitar over at their flat with a papirosochka stuck in the side of his mouth while Mum stood and danced in the gap between the chugging Zil fridge and the Formica kitchen table – a life of laughing and weeping and huge emotional truths that could be borne only with the requisite amount of vodka – and there was the real life that paid for it.

Real life was the queue for the Salyut they drank, a dark red champagne that tasted of the blackcurrants they picked up north, shrouded like Muslim girls against the dark clouds of mosquitoes. You could only get more than your allocated one bottle of it if you showed an invalid's or a war veteran's pass. Seven hours she'd stood in the shallow slush on the marble floor of the dully chandeliered shop with her dead grandfather's pass in her hand, chatting to the woman behind her who was divorcing her pig of a husband and who was no way going to let him have the dacha where the pear trees he had planted when they were students in love were still producing pears so juicy you could die.

But what a night it was when they drank the Salyut, the real life of the queue the price for the happy delirium, with snow billowing into the hot room through the open fortochka and the candles still glowing with pale light even at two o'clock in the morning and

Konstantin with his songs about the steppe and the girls who'd never love him now.

Katya could see why the girls had loved him then though. He had deep lines around his eyes, eyes as white-blue as Siberian ice, from laughing so much at the injustice of it all. It didn't matter, in those days, that he wore thin jeans with metal studs in them from Ruslan, the only men's clothes shop in Kirgask, to be found directly opposite Ruslanka, the only women's clothes shop in Kirgask. It didn't matter that he bathed just once a week at the bath house, kept chickens on his fifteenth-floor balcony or that his teeth were crooked and, if she were honest, a little stained. He knew poems by Blok and Mayakovsky and would declaim them if asked (and if not).

Her mother made a dish that night, a dish she described as 'Chinese' and who knew it wasn't? Three tins of rubbery white calamari fried up in oil with rice she'd got from the boot of someone's Lada Samara round the back of the House of Culture – where everything happens. And mushrooms bought dried from round the neck of an old woman and soaked in hot water until they were the texture of marshmallow, salted and stirred in with sliced cucumber and dill. And Konstantin also knew forbidden poems that he would tell only in a dark whisper when sweet black tea had been served in the white china cups with pink roses on that her mother said she'd bought in Moscow that time. The one time.

But later, when Katya went back into the kitchen to fetch her hairbrush from the shelf, the first birds singing in the birch trees in the courtyard and her father snoring in bed already with the brick dust in his ears, she'd found her mum kissing Konstantin on the sofa. Real life was back, and this time it was back for good one way or another.

Things were changing in that imperceptible way like when winter starts. For months you wonder when it is going to snow. A few flakes in October but not really snow. The trees lose all their leaves and

33

stand spindly and nude in the grey sky but still no snow. And then, maybe in November, there will be a big blanket overnight that hides and muffles the streets and houses, but it melts away to slush the next day and the sun comes out again. By New Year it is impossible to imagine that there were ever flowers or grass or soft earth or that there ever will be again. The world has been white and hard for as long as you can remember. But you can never remember when it changed or understand why you didn't notice.

On the way to school she told Andriusha about what she'd seen that night. He said she should bribe Konstantin by threatening to tell her dad, and Katya was shocked. He was becoming obsessed by money, had twice now smelt of vodka on the way home from school and he had a new friend, a dangerous-sounding friend who didn't go to school at all and who traded vodka. 'That's illegal,' Katya said, immediately feeling foolish.

'It's business, Katya. It's life,' he said in his new voice.

They walked in silence for a while and the snow lay deep at the side of the road and hung like huge bear's paws from the heavy branches of the trees. Snowflakes sparkled on Andriusha's eyelashes as he talked, his cheeks red and his breath a billow of white smoke. The ground squeaked underfoot and, though it was nearly eight o'clock in the morning, it was only just getting light, the pinpricks of stars fading into the paling blue of the sky, a tram grinding past, its lights yellow in the freezing dawn mist, huddled shapes of passengers inside, steaming up the windows. Masha from their year with the lazy eyes was squashing her face up against the window to amuse them. And then Andriusha, holding a letter he had forged that would exempt him from the ostensibly optional but actually obligatory patriotic poetry class (he was an expert forger) told her a joke.

'So, Gorbachev's late for a Politburo meeting,' he said, catching her eye to make sure she understood the daring subject matter, more

34

daring than any story she could tell about her mother's stolen kisses. She, for her part, raised one eyebrow.

'And he's running to the car but the driver's flustered and drops the keys. "Oh, get in the back, I'll drive," Mikhail Sergeievich says. So the driver gets in the back and Gorbachev is speeding down Kalininsky towards the Kremlin. He gets pulled over but doesn't get a ticket. The traffic cop's colleague says to him, "Who was that?" And the traffic cop says, "I don't know. But his driver was Gorbachev!"'

Andriusha's conversation had become more and more risqué since his dad died, since they had stood, still against the cold, at the side of his father's grave and thrown red carnations down on to the coffin, at night, illegal, an owl hooting in the woods to mark the end of a non-Party member and a Jew. Now there was nobody to sing to their budgie any more and, after a few days of hanging upside down and waiting for Dima to return, it died too.

Andriusha lit a cigarette and waited for her response to his joke, a western brand that he'd got for a whole term's Soviet Studies essays from Gorik who was captain of the ice-hockey team and had a cousin in Leningrad.

Katya laughed but felt kittens scrabbling in her stomach, and Andriusha was satisfied. They fell in behind a crowd of their friends who'd just jumped down off the tram into the deep snow, talking and jostling. Katya wasn't sure why the joke was different from other jokes, but it was. He hadn't whispered it. That was one thing. Also, it wasn't political, exactly. It wasn't like the jokes her dad might have told late at night, leaning in towards the company, glancing theatrically over his shoulder as though the knock on the door could come any moment. It was just a joke, as bold as a cow in a pig sty.

She sighed and linked arms with Olya whose mum made herbal medicines from things she found in the forest and whose clothes were always infused with smells like lavender and moss from all the vapours coming off the strange bubbling brews. She believed in the secrets of the Kirgask mushrooms as though Lenin himself had prescribed them.

Today the deputy mayor would be talking to the older girls at school and everyone was supposed to be on their best behaviour. Katya had been chosen to present him with a small bouquet and a welcome speech that had the word Comrade in it. A lot. She wasn't nervous. Since Sasha Kuznetsov, who was two years older than her and had blown his little finger off with a grenade he found at the rubbish tip, had fallen off his bike craning round to watch her walking to the river in her mum's old shorts last summer, she had realised that her dad, his eyes wet with tears of love and pride and his hands rough on her burnt shoulders, had not been lying. Her long brown legs were not like a stork's, as she had feared. Her wide face did not make her look like a Chukchi who sewed bloomers out of reindeer hide with a bone needle. Or, if it did, then this was a good thing.

For Katya was fourteen now and it wasn't so much that Vasily Vasilich had promised anything – at least, not in words – but she was familiar by now with that open-mouthed, dry-lipped, palm-sweating look that meant a man would promise pretty much anything. Katya, after all, was becoming a realist who knows that a canary who lives in a cage dies in a cage.

Vasily Vasilich Komykin, there could be no doubt, stood firmly planted in real life and he was proud of it. Second deputy mayor, he was in charge of promoting Kirgask (even though he had actually been born in Tomsk), its life-giving fungi, its beautiful girls and its talented youth as paragons of Soviet virtue. Though promote would not have been a word he would have chosen. In charge, he would say, tapping his flat laminated world so that it quivered under the force of his fat finger, of putting Kirgask on the map. For the better the news about Kirgask, he thought, wiping his hair across his head and pulling up his trousers, as the centre of all good things

Communist, the more likely an invitation to Moscow for the eager Vasily Vasilich. And, the Lord knows, he had waited and waited for the opportunity to present himself to the powers that be.

The thing about Vasily Vasilich, the thing that he most liked to point out, the thing that represented the source of most of his ideas and ideals and the source of the souvenirs that perched in the glass cabinets of his brutally lit office, the thing was that Vasily Vasilich had been to Brighton. A plastic model of the Pavilion sat on his desk, dusted by himself, always with a furtive little look towards the door, using the small paintbrush he kept in his top drawer for the purpose. The certificate of mutual appreciation from the Brighton mayoral office hung framed on his wall and he spoke of the visit, now ten years ago already, with a reverence and fondness that most people reserved for memories of their earliest childhood, for speaking of the texture of their mother's dress and the smell of it as you pressed your cheek to it, clinging with both arms to her back as she cycled along the boulevard with a box of apples on the front of her bike.

For it had been in Brighton, with its creaking wooden pier, the capitalist paint peeling shamefully off under his socialist shoes, that he had eaten fish and chips, deep fried in front of him and carefully wrapped in waxed paper by a girl no older than his own daughter. It was in Brighton that he'd watched that girl shake the fat plastic pot of vinegar over his chips, her breasts wobbling visibly under her white apron. It had not occurred to him before then that a western woman might hold such charm for him. It was the smile she'd offered him as he handed his money over, dropping a ten pence piece, yes, the big silver one, in his confusion, a smile directed at him, the Russian delegate with the KGB stooge (that bastard Mikhail) standing behind him, a smile that reminded him of a time when he'd been hungry and handsome, when he could make a girl giggle with a sly wink. It was that same Brighton smile that had led him, hours after the fish and chips had settled in his capacious stomach, to accept the furtive knock on the door that evening in his room at the Grand Hotel, the prostitute's knock that came every evening, usually ignored.

He quickly drank a whisky (decidedly inferior to good Georgian cognac, he was satisfied to note) from the mini-bar and paced the royal-blue carpet that would be held for ever in his reverent memory before he opened the door. Oh, he knew perfectly well that it was not behaviour worthy of a Soviet citizen. But the girl who knocked, in her sticky leather skirt and white pointed shoes, was sweet and pretty and smelt of beach pebbles and the honey from his father's beehives. He devoured her as though he were spooning pink blancmange into his mouth, as though he weren't half bald now, overweight, God knew, and old enough to be her sugar daddy. Though he was a bit short on the sugar, he would admit. The next day he packed the absurdly tiny mini-bar bottles and all the peach-soft toilet roll into his suitcase to take back to the USSR.

And, the morning of the day they left, when the delegation was taken to watch the Miss Brighton finals 1979 on the pier, Vasily Vasilich had quite a swagger in his step, felt almost like the jet-haired, oil-eyed demon he had once been. No sterling currency left, no. But a swagger. And the girls were lovely. Not a patch on the Kirgask Komsomol beauties, to be sure, but lovely, shivering in their swimsuits, soft goose-pimpled flesh pudging over the elasticated waistbands of their bikinis, smiles strained against the sea breeze.

It had taken years of tireless campaigning. It had gone all the way to the Supreme Soviet in Moscow. Perhaps Gorbachev himself had reviewed the proposals. Vasily Vasilich couldn't decide whether to cringe with shame at the thought or to puff with pride. He brushed the top of his pavilion and blew the dust from his brush whenever the idea troubled him. Whenever, in fact, any idea troubled him. He looked up at his framed portrait of the man, the fourth new portrait in as many years as General Secretary after General Secretary had dropped ignominiously dead, and he surprised himself with the wave of utter quivering loathing that swept over him and through his office in the Town Hall where Svetlana Alexandrovna in her white blouse and the tight grey skirt that covered her fat knees would soon bring him a glass of tea on a tray with a doily and three wrapped sweets, a lemon, an orange and a pineapple. Pineapple! Always three.

And then one day, one glorious day when he had just bitten into a poppy-seed bun and was wiping the edge of his mouth with a worn handkerchief he'd bought at Marks & Spencer in Brighton, the sludge-green Bakelite phone on his desk rang with approval. The Miss Kirgask Beauty Contest was authorised to go ahead. His beauty contest.

'Firs and sticks!' he exclaimed, putting the receiver down gently as though it might leap up and bite him on the nose like a stoat, cruelly changing its mind.

Katya stood up from her chair, curved tubes of hollowed steel with faded canvas stretched across, the kind of chair that screamed on the parquet when you moved it and always laddered the thick 'flesh-coloured' tights the girls wore. Nobody had flesh that colour, Katya was sure. The hall was quiet but shuffling. She could hear the white cotton shirts brushing against each other as people moved close enough to whisper, the chairs creaking with anticipation, the vast and boiling radiators lining the sides of the auditorium and creating a deep and shimmering heat haze up near the ceiling, bubbled and gushed.

She walked up the steps to the stage and welcomed Comrade Deputy Mayor Vasily Vasilich, handing him a wilting bouquet in a sealed plastic wrapper and shaking his swarthy hand, which was doughy and damp. She felt her forehead glow in the overhead stage lights, only two of which were actually working and, on her way back down the steps, she stumbled slightly on account of having been stage blinded. Her comrades in the audience drew in their breath to gasp as one, but exhaled gently as she recovered her balance and sat down.

'He was looking right at your tits,' her friend Olga whose mum made herbal potions hissed into her ear.

'Don't be stupid. I haven't got any,' Katya hissed back, having a quick look at Olga's which were already swollen and large like rising loaves of bread.

'He was looking anyway,' Olga insisted. This was true.

Their teacher, Comrade Tarakanova, scowled at the girls from the end of her row and they changed their expressions from frivolous to earnest in an instant with a sincere flash of the eyes towards the vast banner of Lenin that hung, its corners curling, behind the speaker on the stage.

It would be a heroic deed, Vasily Vasilich insisted, to volunteer for the contest, to show the world, people in New York, Beijing, Paris and Brighton (the words themselves trembling with the excitement of far away) that Russian women are the most beautiful in the world. The winner would accompany him to the final in Moscow, he said, saving this news until last, as though any of them needed that extra little persuasive push. Moscow, after all, was further and glittered with more promise and grandeur than anywhere any of them had been so far. The news, Katya knew, could not have been bigger. Somehow it was linked, hooked like a burr on a woollen scarf, to Andriusha's joke, and to the kiss she had seen in the hot kitchen, the windows steamy and the kettle wailing. To change.

The news was, to wrap it up in muslin like soft cheese, that it was now officially a patriotic duty to put on make-up (where would they find any?) and pretty clothes (worse). They were now positively supposed to look like the women in Irina's magazine. Everyone had seen Irina's magazine, exchanged with an Italian tourist for a beaver fur hat in a Volgograd hotel three years ago, full of daring photographs of girls in silk and chiffon, lace and fur, in high heels and with toes and fingernails painted purple, their lips glossy and their eyes dark and brooding and covered with six different shades of shadow. The page about multiple orgasm had been translated by someone's brother who was doing a Modern Languages diploma and was training to be an interpreter and it had been passed round the school so many times that it disintegrated. Katya lent Irina her grandfather's veteran's pass in exchange for three days with the magazine (for this he had defended the Motherland against the Nazis!). She looked through it with her mother and her mother had actually wept, turning the pages with thin bony fingers as though *Cosmopolitan* were a priceless and ancient document in a museum, the kind you have to wear cotton gloves to touch, her colour high and her breath short, sitting on the edge of the divan in her apron and slippers. It was snowing so thickly outside that you couldn't see the trees in the courtyard.

'Don't be silly, Mama,' Katya said, nudging her in the ribs with a sharp elbow.

He mother shook her head, wiped her tears with the back of her hand and smiled. She put her arm round Katya's shoulders and said, 'Well. It's too late for me. But maybe you will dance. Maybe there will be a party yet on our street.' They were looking at a picture of a girl walking towards the camera on a platform with an audience gazing up at her as though she were a violinist. She wore a pale pink silk dress and roses in her hair. That, in short, was what they were now supposed to look like – it was a patriotic duty!

Katya told Andriusha about the contest as they plodded their way to school in a snowstorm that threatened to extinguish the very lights of their eyes. He was talking, as he'd started doing a lot lately, about military service.

'I heard of a guy who got a friend to smash his kneecaps with a hammer,' he said with his chin to the wind, daring her to advise him against such an extreme course of action.

Katya had heard these stories too. In fact her father had a cousin who had pretended to be insane. Had run around shouting and babbling and saying anti-Soviet things so that they put him in hospital. He was gentle, Dad said, like a bear cub, and they would have killed him in the army. Everyone knows about the initiation ceremonies, the bullying, the suicides. His parents had encouraged him, had told the authorities that, yes, he had always been unstable. A lady psychiatrist with dyed orange hair set in a meringue on her head had advised incarceration in a secure unit and a straitjacket. Medication. Bad enough, but then, without warning, they operated. 'And now he sits in the unit still, by the window, gazing out at nothing because he can no longer move or speak. It happens,' Dad said with a shrug.

'I'm going to enter the beauty concourse,' Katya said, changing the subject as they approached Togliatti, a petrified snowdrift today, his thin Italian suit of bronze no protection against this. Andriusha spat his cigarette into the snow where it sizzled and went out. His walk was becoming a swagger and Katya thought it must be the influence of his new friend, the vodka-seller from town.

'If you want to prostitute yourself, I guess,' he mumbled, hunching his shoulders.

Katya froze, letting the wind blow her and the snowflakes melt on the tiny patch of exposed skin around her eyes. Andriusha didn't notice that she'd stopped until she shouted, 'Hey!'

He turned, a shape in the swirling white under the trembling mirage-like glow of a streetlamp. 'What? You OK?' he said, trudging back to her.

When he arrived she slapped him in the face. Or, at least, her glove slapped him in the scarf.

'You are completely unlaced!' he said.

Her chest burned with anger, but she walked on beside him. 'Vasily Vasilich said it was a patriotic duty!' she shouted, though even shouting was soft in this weather.

'Who cares who you're prostituting yourself to?' Andriusha argued. 'You think it's better to show off your zhopa for the Communists?'

'I will show it to whoever I want to show it!' Katya spat, running ahead of him with enormous effort, dragging her feet through the snow and angling her body against the bitter wind.

In the end it was only Vasily Vasilich, for the time being, who actually got to see it. Everyone said they knew she would win, but they only said it afterwards. Well, everyone knows who was going to win afterwards, don't they, she thought. There's nothing clever about that. A fisherman can see another fisherman from miles away. But, the day before the contest, when he told her he had the casting vote, that the judges were split, that he could help her win, she had understood him. He called her to his office in the Town Hall and invited her with an imperious gesture to sit on a tight red leather armchair that the backs of her legs stuck to. His secretary turned out to be a friend of her mother's (Fatter. Was she pregnant? At her age?) and she had smiled gently, perhaps apologetically, at her and brought her a cup of tea and a strange sweet with a pineapple on the wrapper that tasted like the smell of urine. It had made Katya need a wee and she distracted herself by looking at the strange ornaments Vasily Vasilich had collected in his office. A big plastic children's toy stood on his desk, all pink and white with little domes and fences. It looked as though you were supposed to put animals or puppets in it, she thought.

'But the concourse hasn't happened yet!' Katya objected. 'Respected Vasily Vasilich, how can the judges be already split?'

'My little dove,' he said, smiling a bit and then coughing. 'The entrants are already . . . well, they are already known to the panel . . .'

Immediately, Katya grasped the situation like a peasant grasps a chicken round the neck.

Andriusha laughed when she told him. 'The goats. Just like everything else. The wolves are all full up and the sheep are still breathing. Typical. So, who's going to win? Oooooh. Let's see. The mayor's daughter or the Duma deputy's? Tough call.'

He had a cassette of an American singer – Joni Mitchell – and they were listening to it, turned down as quiet as it would go so that the neighbours wouldn't hear. Andriusha had taken the bedroom now and his mum, with her starched white overalls and her stethoscope, had moved on to his old divan in the living room. He had made a collage on the wall of flattened cigarette packets arranged in a pattern like a picture by Matisse, *The Snail*, and some of the weird sculptures he was always making from coarse grey clay littered the surfaces like a petrified dinosaur park. 'The wind is in from Africa . . .' Joni sang, and the friends could almost smell the dark orange earth and the salt and the coconut groves . . .

'Tanya's not entering. Her dad won't let her,' Katya said, taking a tiny puff of his cigarette. They both sat on the bed with their backs against the wall and hugged their knees in front of them. Outside the birds were arguing their way to sleep, Katya thought. 'No! That's my branch!' 'No! Mine!'

'So that would leave the mayor's daughter then.'

'Or me.'

Andriusha laughed and choked on his smoke. 'Did he say what you'd have to do?'

'No,' she told him, looking down at the tops of her knees and resting her chin on them. 'But Svetlana Alexandrovna told my mum that he always used to stroke her bum before she got fat and

44

once he said he'd fire her if she didn't wear a see-through blouse, so . . .'

'Right,' he said, and, putting his cigarette end into an empty vodka bottle, he moved round so that he was kneeling in front of her. He leaned down, took her face in his hands and kissed her on the mouth. Katya, who hadn't been expecting it, pulled away, coughing, and clambered up so that she was standing, awkwardly, on the bed. She jumped off it and on to the floor and ran out of the flat, down the stone stairway that smelt of cats and cabbage and out into the street below without her outdoor clothes.

The next day she saw him from the stage, lurking there with his eyes blazing as she smiled and threw her hair back over her shoulders with a haughty flick. Varvara was shocked not to win, and Katya was as surprised as she was. Vasily Vasilich gave her a little nod, a sign that it was to him she should be grateful for the wire crown perched on her head, the tight shoes and the flowers in her arms. And in truth, she was. Grateful.

Her mum saw her off at the station. It was spring and you could smell the mud through the melting snow, feel the warmth coming up through the earth. The dusty green train stood on the platform and a blackbird perched on the roof of Katya's carriage, its head cocked to one side. 'Look,' said her mother. 'It's a good sign.'

'Don't be silly, Mamotchka,' Katya told her, throwing her arms round her neck. 'Be kind to Papa.'

Her mum flushed a little and hushed her. 'Of course. Of course. It was a mistake,' she said, still holding her tight. Her hair always smelt of lemons, as if scented by some Sicilian grove she'd dreamed of and would never see.

Konstantin, naturally, had not been round since. Even Dad hadn't mentioned him. Katya had watched for any untoward happiness in her mother, any extra attention to her appearance, any singing or smiling to herself, but there had been none. Just a slightly tenser edge to the cleaning and the scrubbing after work as though, thought Katya, the stain on her soul had seeped into the plastic shower curtain, behind the divan and on to the broad gloss-painted window ledge where the herbs stood in pots.

She had packed her a whole chicken, torn into pieces and wrapped in foil. Three boiled eggs, a jar of preserved tomatoes, a bottle of fruit compote and half a loaf of black bread.

'It's only sixteen hours,' Katya complained, looking at the tear-furrowed face of the woman next to them, clutching a shaven-headed teenager to her chest, and at the broad-shouldered men with ham hands and steel teeth, dragging luggage through the heavy doors to their carriage, harangued by the carriage lady, who was stuffed into her dark green uniform, in charge of the samovar and the heating and disapproving of everyone.

When the train creaked and heaved itself out of the station, her mother running alongside it waving, Katya, shamefully dangling her threadbare elephant Malyshka from one hand (well, it had seemed a pity to abandon him now that they really were running away to join the circus), watched Kirgask break apart, from the solid structures of the town centre, the House of Culture, the Town Hall and her school, to the scattered wooden cottages that spread around the outskirts like crumbs broken off an Easter cake, and, finally, nothing but fields, brown and wet and patched with grey puddles of melting snow and trees infested with dark crows. And perhaps all the little pieces of experience and love and hate that made up Katya broke apart too. Or, she thought, perhaps they were only just coming together.

'Women only!' the carriage lady shouted at Vasily Vasilich as he dragged himself into the narrow corridor. She had been squirting boiling tea into an engraved glass and did not shift out of the way to let him pass. The chattering women, who had changed into slippers, flip-flops and even felt valenki and were unwrapping their food, laying it out on the little tables and pouring vodka into paper cups, were silenced, staring at the fat apparatchik who had invaded their carriage. Vasily Vasilich put a five-rouble note into the dyezhurnaya's hand and she nodded, painted lips pursed, and backed into her compartment. Shoving his way past and around the other women, his pale eyes fixed on Katya, he stumbled as the train shook and lurched and, eventually, gasping, he almost fell on top of her. Just in time he spread his arms, one either side of her, grabbing the wooden rail and pressing his chest against hers so that she could smell his sour sweat. He dropped the sugared bun he had brought her. Katya had not known he would be on the train.

'We need to discuss protocol,' he said when he had righted himself and picked up the bun, pushing it, dust-blackened, into her hand. 'For Moscow. Not here, in this gaggle of geese. I have a private compartment.'

Well, he would have, Katya thought. And it wasn't even that bad, really. He didn't have to say anything as demeaning as, 'Do it or you're going back to Kirgask for the rest of your life like your poor mother.' Nothing like that.

He just said, 'I think it would be best if we' – he said 'we' – 'if we could get a look at you naked.'

She shrugged and he leaned past her to bolt the door to his compartment where everything was neat and put away and smelling of soap.

She dropped the bun into a steel bin and took off her clothes in a measured way, as though she were spooning out flour for a raisin cake. She folded them up and put them down on the couchette where the sheets were printed with pale lilac silhouettes of the Moscow Kremlin. She stood there, bare feet on the linoleum floor, and looked Vasily Vasilich right in the eye. He had gone bright red and was wheezing. Perhaps he will die of a heart attack, she thought, imagining him writhing, rolling on the floor like a walrus, going purple, his eyes rolled back in his head, his tongue lolling out.

Apparently unable to speak, he gestured to her to turn around with a rotation of one fat white hand. Katya turned around to face the door. On the door was a printed sign with a hammer and sickle in the corner that said, 'To the glory of Marxism-Leninism'.

Vasily Vasilich put his hands on her bottom and squeezed hard, letting out a groan as he did so, his dick prodding against her side. Andriusha was right. She was prostituting herself. But not to Communism or to Vasily Vasilich. But to life, as her mother hadn't dared do. And it would pay her, she was as certain as the thunder after lightning. Katya bit the inside of her cheek until it bled.

'Why don't you get a ball of wool and go and knit yourself
an iron curtain?'

Letter to Brezhnev

Chapter Six

It was still dark and the heating in the flat hadn't come on yet. At Frankie's, which was how Mo thought of the place, it was either much too hot, an integral part of the noise of the television and the smell of an Indian takeaway and too much booze, or it was like this, bitterly cold and somehow empty, deserted. Mo understood the word 'close' for hot and humid. The heat and noise in the flat contained her and Frankie and concealed the unspoken abyss of nothingness that threatened to consume them both, pressing it down. But sometimes, at night, in the stale cold air, when even the fire engines across the road were still, Mo felt as though she was huddled, injured and shaking, in the corner of a vast abandoned farmhouse in the middle of nowhere with wind whistling through broken windows and rats scurrying in the cellar and no help to be found.

Her dad had taken a job in America and sold his London place, the place that she thought of as home, or, at any rate, where she usually put her stuff and where her letters came. She was supposed to be joining him there but Frankie said, delighted, that there was 'fat chance' of this, though Mo chose to believe in the chance, fat or thin. She got dressed by the orange glow of the streetlamps, pulling on snapping underwear, a polo-necked jumper and short skirt, pushing her toes into the sharp points of her shoes as though hiding herself in an elaborate costume.

She crept past Frankie's room and into the kitchen where she switched the light on and waited as the fluorescent strip flickered, flashed and steadied itself to a buzzing white glare. She made herself a cup of tea and ate some Ritz crackers out of the box. Frankie always said, inhaling deeply on a cigarette and looking disdainfully at her, that she'd get fat, but the puppy fat, as Frankie had seemed to enjoy calling it (as if there was something inherently repulsive about puppies, contrary to popular opinion) was long gone; she knew she wouldn't get fat now.

Perhaps, she thought, Frankie hoped she'd get fat. The power Frankie had once wielded, as a mocking sexual being who flaunted her clothes and make-up and the raggedy men these props won for her, was gone and she was, Mo thought, scared. It had suited Frankie to have an overweight, dark-skinned child to hold up against herself – blonde, skinny, pissed and available. She had liked to think that Mo longed to be just like her, ached with desire to attain such levels of allure as she could never hope to achieve. But it hadn't turned out like that.

Today she was meeting Eli for tea after school and she ran out of the gates as fast as she could to get to the tube station before any of the other girls got there and started hassling her about where she was going and why and was she a lesbian. She kept Eli a secret because she knew she wouldn't be able to explain him to anyone, a champion chess player (he did win the contest six years in a row after his ignominious defeat at the hands of that cheat Wasserman), a prize-winning mathematician whose mum still got up at five every morning to help coach him. She'd never been to his big posh school before and all she really knew about it was that everyone called him 'yid' and that all they did was wank on biscuits and force whoever came last to eat the biscuit. This sounded apocryphal to Mo but Eli insisted they really did it. He also told her they stole pineapple rings from supper when they had gammon (which they made him eat) and put them round their dicks because it made wanking better.

So, with all this in mind, she had, she supposed, pictured a café somewhere in town for tea, the kind of place where 'the Nazis' didn't go and where there was ketchup and vinegar on the table and where grease and cigarette smoke vied for dominance. But, as it turned out, he meant tea with the anti-Semites at school and so they sat 'in hall' up a short wooden staircase in a far corner of Westminster Abbey where a tiny cobbled courtyard is hidden away behind an arched gate and where a dark panelled dining hall echoes with rowdy voices at about four forty-five on a weekday. The long tables are made from the remains of the conquered Spanish Armada and minstrels once played in the gallery to accompany the first nights of Shakespeare's plays performed to Queen Elizabeth I. Eli did not know this and nor would he have cared if he had known, holding everyone who had ever been at the school personally responsible for every pogrom ever inflicted on his people, basically equating public schoolboys with Holocaust. Not that he was scared of them. He shoved a befuddled-looking, probably stoned and certainly much taller blond boy out of the way to get to the toaster. 'Ladies first,' he said, as the stoner staggered aside.

'I knew you were a bit camp, Yiddo, but does Matron know about this?' the boy said, jostling back for toaster position.

'This is Mo, you dicksplash,' Eli explained, and the boy, clocking a real bona fide female as though for the first time ever (Hey, Mo thought, possibly for the first time ever, nannies and matrons notwithstanding), blushed deeply in bright splodges on his downy freckled face.

'Nice to meet you,' he said, standing deferentially back, away from the toaster, and letting Eli shove four slices in.

'Hi,' Mo said, aware that she appeared composed and wanting to tell him that girls actually prefer circumcised dicks, not that she had a preference herself or, indeed, had ever seen either kind.

'"Small Jew Triumphs Over Big Spotty Evil",' Eli muttered to himself.

They ate bright pink square cakes from metal trays and drank copper-orange tea from thick-rimmed mugs, slopping clots of jam on to their toast from medical vats that lined the middles of the tables. Eli complained about his mum's lover who threatened to destabilise the family (ostensibly, as far as Mo could make out, because he was posh and Gentile and because of the way he pronounced Covent Garden, waistcoat and forehead – she mentally corrected herself – Cuvvent, wistcut and forredd). Mo sympathised (what else could she do?) and thought about, but didn't mention, her mum's lover(s) who would do well, in her view, to pronounce anything much at all. Somehow Eli's interloper was all part of the eccentric grandeur of enormous wealth and the comforting belonging of Jewishness that, though Eli complained, this Gentile would probably not seriously affect. Hers was part of the grim squalor of dank mediocrity. This much she knew.

'God, this place is incredible,' she said, mainly to deflect attention from her own thoughts.

'This? Well, if you like billion-year-old decay, I suppose . . .' He shrugged, glancing around as if something as trivial as the room he happened to be in hadn't really struck him before. 'They stole my clothes and stuck them up on that balcony last week. It was supposed to be amusing.'

Mo ignored him, faintly assuming he was lying. Surely if he was really bullied he would tell someone?

'I would do anything to come to a school like this,' she said, meaning it, but smiling, unconsciously, in a way that gave it the light brush of a friendly joke.

Eli looked genuinely stunned. The idea that anyone would

actually harbour such a perverse desire had never once crossed any area of his ramshackle mind. 'Would you?' he asked, stuffing a cake into his mouth whole and punching the boy next to him who had reached out for it before him. 'It's dog eat dog,' he explained, spitting crumbs.

'Fuck you, Yiddo,' the boy said.

'Toss off, Goebbels,' Eli spat. 'Get your own.'

'Well, it's better than my school,' Mo sighed, picking up flecks of pink icing from the empty metal tray by pressing down on them with one finger and then putting it in her mouth to suck the sweetness off. 'Last week in geography this boy in my class got up and pissed in the teacher's briefcase.'

'No way!' Eli grinned, clearly liking the concept.

'Seriously,' Mo confirmed. 'He said, "Sorry, sir, I was desperate," and the teacher just sort of burst into tears.'

'I wish you would come here. We've got a Russia trip next year. It might be OK if you came,' he said, running a hand through his tumble of black curls in an attempt to straighten out the sheer, knotty stubbornness of some people.

'I thought maths was supposed to be your bloody forte. I mean, shalom? My mum is on the dole, my dad is totally absconded and I am not on the game. Yet.' Mo laughed, mocking his inability to understand the basics of a free-market economy.

'Doesn't cost anything. Get a scholarship,' he told her, flicking the explanatory tails of the flimsy black gown he wore over the black woollen suit. 'Ha!'

'Anyway, I couldn't possibly . . .' She started trying to explain, wrapping her hands round her empty mug.

'You're such a fucking Cassandra. Apply for the Lower Fifth, get a scholarship and Bob's your proverbial uncle.'

Mo wasn't sure if she wanted to kiss Eli for believing that his own omnipotence might extend to her, or if she wanted to kill him because she knew so well that it couldn't. This fantasy was from the same stable as her dad transporting her to a glorious house in Vermont or her real parents coming to find her in a big blue Volvo with dogs in the back (she was not, in fact, adopted, which made her chances particularly slim).

'What are you laughing about, fat face? You said you wanted to come. So, come,' he shrugged. 'Don't want to come? Don't come.'

A justlikethat life, the idea of which made Mo reach out and brush Eli's hand with hers in the hope, perhaps, of being infected. For Eli, emotionless rationale was paramount, action key. Otherwise the bastards might get you.

So she shut her mouth and filled in the application forms Eli shoved in front of her face when she went round to his house the next time, wondering at the kitchen roll that matched the units and the enormous preponderance of onyx. She scribbled as Eli's dad flicked through the television channels, occasionally pronouncing, 'He's one of us.' His tone suggested more that he was naming and shaming paedophiles than rejoicing in the achievements of his fellow Jews.

She had waited in at Frankie's hoping she would hear the dipping wing of celestial salvation hit the tiles in the grotty shared hall downstairs, the salvation being an interview, a chance.

'You have to actually have Premium Bonds for your numbers to come up,' Frankie told her when she noticed an air of anticipation hanging heavy in the sworls of yesterday's smoke.

'Good point.' Mo nodded, taking a cracker out of the box.

'You'll—'

'Yup.'

'I'm just saying.'

'I know.'

Eli phoned her up before the letter came. 'So I broke into the staff room last night to read the list of interviewees and you're on it. I was going to stuff your name on the end if you weren't. I need an ally here, if you know what I mean. Anyway, it's in the bag – tell me I'm a genius. "Eli Zinn, Boy Genius, Triumphs Again".'

'You're a genius,' she agreed. 'But you didn't actually do anything since I got an interview anyway.'

'True. True. But I swear I nearly had a heart attack in there.'

'No, you didn't,' Mo laughed. Eli was always having heart attacks.

So she walked, hands clasped in front of her, her heart pounding, into a sixteenth-century library to be faced by a man in a pumpkin-coloured three-piece suit, a suit that announced a delicious cocktail of deep respect for the establishment, a colourful eccentricity and a twist of flirtation. He threw his arms out at the glooming books that stretched up to the ceiling, most of which could only be reached by ancient cherry-wood ladders on brass rails, i.e. accessible only to those with the requisite equipment – intellectual as well as physical.

'Well . . .' he paused and looked down at the papers in front of him. 'Sorry! Had no idea who you were for a minute!'

This stunned Mo. She had been taught to pretend to know everything – an admission of weakness equals an open invitation to attack. Was he stupid? Or were these different rules? Or were there, more terrifyingly still, no rules at all?

'Well, Mo! Do sit down!' he shouted, waving his hands wildly at the chair in front of his desk, suggesting that, though it might seem mad to sit on such a piece of furniture, she must nonetheless do so. It was dark in here, but Mo could see the dusting of snow on the cobbles of the yard out of windows.

The low winter light fell sharply on the side of the man's face, emphasising decades of sparklingly irreverent hilarity and, Mo understood, a sexiness of which he was very aware, slightly camp academic thingy aside. 'So! You can see, can't you, the role books play in MY life!' he shouted, arms outstretched to display his library as though she might not have taken it in before, might not have noticed that it contained, by and large, books. 'What part . . . Mo? Yes, Mo . . . do they play in yours?'

Mo could hear her cheeks throbbing feverishly and was aware of a feeling rising to her throat that she feared she could not possibly contain. It might, she supposed, have been unadulterated joy, though it was not dissimilar to the need to vomit. 'Well,' she said, pupils swimming with inky adoration. 'So far, books, to be honest, are my whole entire life. I read while I'm walking along the road, I don't sleep very well so I read all night long, I read on my lap in lessons at school, I . . .'

Mo realised that she might have overstepped a mark (don't gush, don't show off, don't embarrass yourself, people might think you are arrogant, rude, awful, ugly . . . her mind reeled from the internal assault) and she paused, stricken with embarrassment, while Dr Hepburn laughed.

'Do you know Daniil Kharms?' he asked, leaping up, his eyes bulging out of their sockets.

'Um . . . not really . . .' she apologised, gripping the sides of her delicate chair with both hands.

'God! Honestly?! You *must* read these short stories, anti-Stalinist samizdat! You will love it,' he declared, running, loping over to a tower of shelves and dragging a book out, flicking through it and then tossing it on to his desk in front of her with a thud that threw dust up into her face. Breathe in the ages, he seemed to say. 'Take it! But bring it back!' he said, sitting down again as though recovered from some neurological attack after which he was, at last, able to relax.

'"And did those feet"?' he asked, his mind again seized, humming the tune.

'Um . . . I'm sorry . . . I . . .' Mo mumbled.

'"In ancient times?" Did they? "Did the Countenance Divine shine forth upon our clouded hills?" Do you know why it's at the back of the hymn book?'

'I honestly don't,' she admitted, relieved that she was at least able to say something in reply.

'Because the answer, of course, to all those questions is . . . ?'

'Is?'

'Not on your Nelly, mate!'

Mo laughed and Dr Hepburn twinkled at her, looking, if she was honest, though she preferred not to be if there was an option, as if he might kiss her.

'Right!' He looked down at his papers again, second seizure over. 'You like . . . Tolstoy . . . good good . . . and . . . Nabokov! For God's sake girl, you *do* need an education! We must get you in here as soon as possible. But throw that rubbish away. Burn it! Nabokov!' He shook his head, appalled, trying to free his mind from the contagion like shaking water out of his ears.

'I just . . .' Mo said, leaning forward into his shaft of milk light.

'Don't even tell me. Oh . . . and you must sign up immediately for the Russia trip. Nabokov! Christ alive,' he sighed, and he shook a handful of papers at her as if shooing away a fly – perhaps the papers were her own exam results or perhaps someone else's? – and he stood up, chasing her as she ran, terrified, skidding on the polished wood, out of the library.

An eager girl with short blonde hair was perched on one of a row of chairs in some ecclesiastical rays emanating from the cloisters outside. Mo erupted out of the doors, dishevelled, breathless. She hugged her rough canvas bag to her chest and tried to straighten her hair, but she felt like a dog, escaped from near drowning, feebly licking its drenched fur.

'How did it go?' the girl asked her, smiling shyly.

'Um, OK, I think,' Mo smiled back, certain that he'd been joking about the trip, that her ejection from paradise was incontestable. She waited until she was on the tube, hemmed in by sweltering humankind, to let the hot, fat tears of ignominy roll down her hot fat cheeks.

Perhaps Frankie had been right all along. 'Shit,' she muttered. 'Shit. Shit. Shit.'

Eli phoned her up that night. 'How did it go?' he asked. 'Although you should be asking me how it went. I am half drowned. All bloody day in the river for some bollocks our eight was never going to win.'

'Sorry. How did the race go?' she asked, laughing at the thought of him, tiny and coxing a boat of broad-shouldered thugs. She was eating Cheeselets out of the box.

'It was shit. Anyway, so, I went in to see that Nazi, Hepburn,' he told her.

'I thought he seemed nice,' she said. 'I mean, a nutter obviously, but not a Nazi.'

'You are a shiksa and don't notice,' Eli assured her. 'He's a Nazi. Dr Death himself. Anyway, I persuaded him to give you a scholarship. Promised him you'd shag him.'

'It would be a pleasure,' she chomped.

'You wouldn't?'

'I might.'

'You couldn't?'

'How do you know?'

'God.'

At first, Frankie refused to be defeated. 'We can't afford it, darling,' she said, stroking the side of the Robinson's strawberry jam in mock sympathy.

'I got a full scholarship,' Mo explained, not meeting her mother's eye but reaching across the Formica to take the jam and opening the lid with a triumphal pop.

Frankie was rigid with horror for a brief moment, her cigarette shaking almost imperceptibly in her long fingers. Then she coughed and relaxed, taking a long sip of her coffee. A spoonful of brown granules still undissolved on the surface.

'Yes, but, Mo, the uniform, the extras. I'm sorry, darling, it's not going to be possible . . .' she tailed off, fixing her cloudy eyes on the bins in the back garden, the numbers of the flats daubed on the sides in white paint.

'I asked Dad,' Mo said, getting up with a mouthful and swinging her schoolbag over her shoulder.

Frankie's voice chased her down the hall. 'You did what? He'll never pay you know. That bastard . . .'

Blah, blah, blah, Mo thought, certain now of her escape route.

In her first Russian lesson, in one of the rooms whose windows, in early summer, were brushed by thick branches of cherry blossom, Hepburn drew a letter of the Russian alphabet on the board and turned to face his seven pupils, knowing that this initiation ceremony was as steeped in significant solemnity as a coronation. Eli passed her a note from the other side of the room, written on a Rizla and depicting Hepburn as a giant penis with a swastika on his forehead. A girl called Saffron, who was also on a full scholarship and impressed everyone by living on a proper housing estate in Pimlico, opened it on the way and coughed a crisp up laughing.

'Zh,' Hepburn said, smiling at them and trying to ignore the commotion which, he had no doubt, involved someone drawing obscene pictures of him, probably Zinn. He scratched the side of his nose, anxious that they might have missed his point, which was, surely, as plain as the nose on his face. 'Zh.'

Then he wrote two other letters next to the beautiful, complicated zh.

'Zhook,' he said. 'It means beetle and it also means bugging device.' The class laughed but Mo could feel every part of her wrapping its tendrils round the shape of the 'zh', welcoming the distant, curvaceous beauty of the alien thing that could only be better than the sharp, sour, antipathetic sounds of English. She fiddled with a packet of cherry-flavoured sweets from the tuck shop.

'Give me one of those,' Hepburn said, noticing them.

'You shouldn't, sir. You'll get a sugar high,' she told him.

'Hand them over or I'll confiscate them,' he laughed.

She popped one out of the packet and took it over, plonking it down on his table in its wrapper, sulkily.

'You know, Mo,' Hepburn said. 'I think you've got a bit of a soft spot for me.'

Having managed to keep her image intact for the whole lesson so far, she suddenly blushed deep pink, down her neck. Eli was sitting right there and he knew she thought Hepburn was hot. Now she was totally exposed.

Afterwards Saffron came up to her in the girls' loos where they were all having a fag.

'So, do you really think Hepburn's hot?' she asked, taking a purple lipstick out of her make-up bag. Everyone said that when Saffron forgot her make-up bag she pretended to feel ill so she could get the tube back home to get it.

'He's OK.' Mo shrugged, beginning to blush again.

'He nearly got kicked out for fucking a girl in the sixth form last year. She denied it but everyone said she was pregnant.'

'What are you trying to say? That if he fucked her he'll fuck me? I'm sure it doesn't work like that.'

Saffron laughed, smacking her newly purple lips together. 'Oh, I'm quite sure it does,' she said.

'Hmm, you're probably right.' Mo smiled, blowing a smoke ring and impressing everyone.

'The future doesn't belong to the fainthearted. It belongs to the brave.'

Ronald Reagan

Chapter Seven

By the time the Russia trip actually happened Mo had started leaving her hair down every day, had bought an Aran sweater, a pair of flat suede shoes and a handful of silver rings with Saffron at Portobello, and she got stoned every Saturday night round at Eli's house, though he never smoked. His parents were always about to get divorced according to Eli and Mo had once been there as Mr Zinn (who funded whole West Bank settlements with his unknowable wealth and had to run all his mail through a metal detector as a result) choked his way through the Friday night 'woman of worth' prayer while Mrs Zinn (who always liked Mo, perhaps because she'd once liked her father) winced as though someone was trying to squirt lemon juice into her eyes.

Every weekend Eli bought the hash, he rolled the joints with fierce concentration, handed them round but didn't smoke them, like one of those casino magnates who have never made any kind of bet in their lives.

'Subdue the Nazis and there won't be a pogrom,' he whispered to her in explanation of his abstemiousness, and then he leaned out of his bedroom door to shout down to Imo, the live-in Filipina maid, asking her to bring up some more cans of beer and some smoked salmon.

'Right, Eli,' Mo nodded, now used to the lengths to which his paranoia took him.

* * *

'Things have changed in Russia,' Hepburn said to his class, squinting in the brutal airport light. 'But don't go mad. I mean, we're not going to get followed around by the KGB any more, but I don't want you buying dope off the fartsovchiki or smoking on Red Square, OK, guys?' He winked at Mo, as if it was bound to be her breaking the law and getting them all thrown into a gulag.

Everyone laughed because, as Mo had quickly learned, things said seriously were treated as a riot of hilarity and jokes were met with nods of grim sagacity. It was easier that way – a posh thing.

Mo sat next to Eli on the plane.

'My mum's going apeshit about this trip, isn't yours?' he asked as the back wheels left the ground with a grinding roar. The English drizzle slapped against the windows like slanting tears, and the plane shook as it hurtled upwards through the dense grey cloud that had shrouded London for months, and out into the miraculous blue of freedom. 'She wants me to go round visiting refuseniks and waving the bloody Israeli flag. It hasn't crossed her tiny Yiddishe mind that I might actually be interested in Russia and its culture.'

'You're not, are you?' Mo laughed, taking a chewing gum off Saffron from across the aisle. She unclipped her tray table and laid her hands, palms down, on top of it, to steady herself.

'No, but I'm not all just maths maths maths more maths and chess,' he moaned. 'And Hebrew lessons. Anyway, how come your mum didn't bring you the airport?'

'Oh, I'm ashamed of her and won't let her meet any of my friends. That's why you can't come to my house either,' she said, knowing that total honesty was the best disguise. Nobody ever believed a word she said.

'No chance of a shag?' he wondered idly, looking around ('Call this a business?') for the instant service he expected. 'In Leningrad, say?'

'None,' Mo confirmed. 'It's the Isro. But you're lovely.'

He often asked, more on the off chance than anything else, having resigned himself inwardly to a lifetime of virginity, not realising the cachet that intelligence and money would have in just a few years' time. After all, they wouldn't be callow teenagers for ever.

'Right,' Eli nodded. 'Fair enough. What's wrong with the Isro?' He shook his mass of tight curls and Saffron laughed.

'You look like Jimi Hendrix, man,' she said, her eye make-up so heavy it seemed to make her eyelids actually droop.

But all the silly bravado aside, Mo's heart fluttered when they entered Soviet airspace, pounded as they descended into Moscow's Sheremetyevo airport and almost burst when the customs boy, after a three-hour wait, glowered into her face from behind his protective glass, demanding to know the purpose of her visit.

'Escape,' she wanted to say. 'Please let me stay here for ever.'

For she had already seen hundreds of miles of white obliterating landscape, ice deep enough to freeze any loss, frigid enough to chill any unwelcome emotion. She had seen flanks of armed soldiers in fur hats emblazoned with hammers and sickles marching towards her across a frozen runway, and she knew they would protect her from the iniquities of . . . well . . . capitalism or something. Here she would be western, romantic, glamorous – Mo the Magnificent. They would feel that it was she who held the promise and the escape while she knew full well it was the other way round.

'Doesyourarsefityou?' she asked the passport-control woman. Apparently, it meant hello.

'Zdravstvuitye,' the lady replied, a kiss of smile appearing at the edges of her cat's bum lips.

That morning Mo had dragged her I'm-a-western-teenager costume on in a London suburb and by evening the performance had led to the very steps of the Bolshoi Theatre, under the same pink and white portico where tsarinas had stood, where horse-drawn sledges had pulled up and spilled their fur-clad passengers out into the elegant crowds, where taffeta dresses had dragged through the slush, where Nureyev and Pavlova had scurried in late for work on prancing tiptoe and where she, Mo, gingerly stamped her arrival in the USSR by treading soft footprints in the snow with her entirely inappropriate suede shoes.

'Come on, Momix,' Eli said, nudging into her and trying the new nickname again, his hands thrust deep into his coat pockets. 'Hepburn'll do his nut if we miss the overture just because you're out here making a fucking snowman.'

The man in front of them took off his black fur shapka and brushed it off carefully with the flat of his hand.

'Do you think it's still alive?' Eli muttered, his breath hot on Mo's cheek, the smell of his last cigarette, Dunhill Lights bought at duty free with a fifteen-year-old swagger, bitter in her nostrils.

She smiled, taking Eli's bony hand in hers and they walked through the doors into the swirling red and gold fantasy that is the Bolshoi's interior as the audience stood and the heart-soaring national anthem boomed from the orchestra pit.

'You are so hot for me,' Eli commented, leading her weaving through the crowds to their assigned row, his curls bobbing with coiled enthusiasm.

Later they walked back to the hotel with Saffron, dodging the others, heads down against the cold, pale ghosts of snowstorms chasing each other on the broad grey pavements, the buildings vast silhouettes against the sky that dwarfed the city's last hurrying, bundled-up people, brittle with determination to be home, wherever that might be. A few stray cars were still adrift in the six-lane roads, chugging slowly through town, their faint yellow headlights making no impression on the vast black night. The silence was almost total and the colossal placarded commands to build a better Communism would have to be obeyed tomorrow. There were no bars, shops or restaurants, no flashing signs promising the immortality of eternal consumption, no invitations to spend in return for scant comfort. Mo found a truth in this blank darkness that she had not expected.

For Pavel seemed almost to appear out of nowhere. Of course, that's just how it seemed to the westerners who didn't know the city, didn't know that black marketeers slouched on all the street corners near the big tourist attractions, mocking up chance meetings, idle conversations that might – nearly always did – lead to a profit. Pavel had, in fact, sniffed out the foreigners like a wolf, emerging chance-like from the dark, eager and ready to pounce. He pounced.

'Khai. I'm Paul,' he announced, reaching out to Eli with a broad friendly hand. He wore a ski jacket and no hat, short blondish hair, wild blue eyes, and it wasn't clear at first that he was Russian though his skin was dun, exhausted. 'Where you from?'

Mo said London.

'London! Big Ben?' he said. Then he put on a 1940s *Brief Encounter* accent and trilled the words, 'This is a gramophone.' Everyone, including Pavel, laughed like mad. 'Me, I am from Siberia. Near Tomsk. Siberian man!' he exclaimed and punched his own chest. He shook the girls' hands too. 'You want to try a Russian cigarette?' he asked, reaching bare hands into his pockets and producing a flat cardboard box. The three English leaned over the box and Pavel flicked it open. The cigarettes had an inch of tobacco at the top in thin paper and then a filter that was a long tube of cardboard.

'Looks more like something you'd shove up your minge,' Saffron commented.

'Sorry? You have to speak slowly, my English isn't so great,' Pavel said with a big smile and an American accent.

The English laughed but didn't repeat what Saffron had said, instead tugging their gloves off with their teeth and taking a cigarette each from the box.

'Like this,' Pavel explained, speaking in a low voice and standing very close to them. He took Mo's papiroska from her hand and pinched the cardboard, making a kind of mouthpiece.

'You got American cigarettes? Lucky Strike?' he asked and Eli, realising he'd had a swap in mind, pulled out his Dunhills and gave three to Pavel.

'Dunhill?' Pavel was interested; he held the packet in his hand with reverence. 'I never saw these before.'

He gave it back to Eli, putting the Dunhills carefully in his box, and he shuffled his feet. He was wearing purple loafers. It must have been minus fifteen.

'What hotel are you staying at? The Mezh? Kosmos? Rossiya?' he asked, eyes sparkling, the black night colossal around them.

'The Ukraina,' Saffron offered.

'Really? That's unusual. I'll walk you back,' Pavel suggested or, perhaps, commanded, striding off down a small street that Mo feared might lead to certain death or, at least, arrest.

'Don't worry,' he said, looking straight back at her as though he'd read her thoughts. 'Paul knows the streets like the back of his hand.'

Eli raised his eyebrows at the girls.

As they walked Pavel cut deals. 'You got jeans? Make-up? You girls got Tampax?' he asked. So he would have understood Saffron's joke, after all. 'I give you army hat, army belt, badges, bust of Lenin. You show me what you got and I bring you tomorrow to the hotel, OK? You got cameras? For a camera, how about army greatcoat?'

At one point Pavel leaped into a dark doorway and told the English to wait.

'I'm scared,' Mo said, again employing her total-honesty-that-nobody-believes policy.

'I think he's gorgeous,' Saffron said.

'Oh great. I get two girls to myself for five minutes and

68

Mr bloody He Man with a crucifix round his neck comes and muscles in.'

'If anything, he's a Communist not a Christian,' Mo nudged him.

'Hey, when you're as foreskinless as me there isn't a difference,' Eli pointed out.

'Honestly. Think about something else for eight seconds,' Mo commanded.

'Other than my willy? How?'

At this point Pavel re-emerged. 'Had to call a friend,' he said.

'Do you live here?' Mo wondered, amazed that such looming, glooming darkness could contain residences for humans.

'Unfortunately, nyet. This is very prestigious. Central, near to theatres. No, a friend of mine.'

Saffron fell in with Pavel and Mo and Eli walked together, smoking the disgusting papiroski, quickening their pace against the freezing, brooding darkness.

'Hepburn definitely fancies you,' Eli commented as he quite often did.

'Everyone fancies me,' Mo laughed, swishing her hair accordingly and pouting at Eli.

'I don't much but I'll shag you if you really want.'

'No, you're all right,' Mo told him.

But as they walked, Saffron deep in sales talk with the Russian, Mo imagined their teacher kissing her, pressing her up against the side of a dark corridor in one of those ivy-green Russian trains as it trundled through forests where wolves lurked in the deep snow between the trees and where dissidents were shot by KGB stooges in long leather trench coats, a quick bullet between the eyes, hands tied behind the back and a dull slump into a snowdrift as dark blood leaked into the virgin white. He would have his warm hands firmly on her waist and would look into her face as she shut her eyes in soft surrender. It was true, he did fancy her, but he'd never dare do it, never dare to kiss her throat softly and put his hands through her hair, she thought.

Someone else in their party might though . . . you never knew.

They flicked the cardboard butts over the railings of a bridge and looked at the hard ice of the Moskva a hundred feet below them, both imagining a fall, their hair swinging in front of their eyes. A Metro train rattling now across another bridge further towards the bright red star of the Kremlin, one single figure hunched at the window of the last carriage.

'Shall we?' Eli suggested, cocking his head towards the petrified river. 'A joint pact? "Public School Toffs Die in Ice Tomb Suicide".'

'Seriously. I want to go back to the hotel. It's about minus forty,' Mo complained, sliding around exaggeratedly on the pavement, jumping up and down a bit, chivvying Eli along.

'Come on, you guys!' Pavel shouted loudly as they passed a traffic policeman staring blankly out of his booth. Pavel could have been arrested for talking to foreigners and was making sure he was taken for one.

'Shall we go to the bar?' Pavel suggested/commanded when they burst out of the revolving doors into the heat and light of the Ukraina Hotel lobby where two grey-uniformed guards glared at them, standing quickly to attention. They'd been hunched playing cards and smoking behind their hands. If they'd asked for Pavel's documents he would have been hauled off immediately, but his disguise and his accent worked this time and the westerners swept in together, indistinguishable one from the other with their money and strange clothes. Later they would have him, but for now he was in.

'Bar,' Eli read from the sign above one of the labyrinthine corridors that led away from the echoing airport enormity of the main lobby and down a narrow strip of maroon carpet on dusty parquet towards a curved brass bar in the area that separated the banks of lifts

70

from each other. There were no windows here, just a few plastic garden chairs and tables arranged on a big green rug, the steel doors of the ten lifts, five on either side of the wide central shaft of the hotel, and the bar structure itself with a few cans of eastern-European-looking blackcurrant drink on the counter, some small cans of Heineken, some plates showing slices of white bread with grey fish arranged on top of them, a single bag of crisps, a shelf of Soviet champagne, a shelf of vodka, some thin glasses with orange stripes round the top and a bored-looking barman in a dirty white waiter's jacket. Behind him on the wall a television was blaring white noise and a scrambled blue fuzz from its bracket.

Pavel seemed to know the place well, though he wasn't relaxed here – he was tense, excited, whispering. He went and shook hands with two young Arab men in thin leather jackets who were smoking and leaning close to each other, their arms surrounding an empty bottle of vodka and two shot glasses. Their eyes were bloodshot and they were both unshaven. A big laundry bag sat on the floor next to them, spilling over with packets of tights and stockings. Also on the floor next to them was a guitar in a case. One of them gave Pavel something small which he shoved into his pocket. Pavel returned the gesture with something equally small and similarly secreted. Mo was aware of being in another world where an apparently random meeting might mean everything.

Katya was getting pretty annoyed with the evening. She got pretty annoyed most evenings but she wasn't stupid. She liked the money and she found she could switch herself off from the violence, just like she switched herself off from Vasily Vasilich and his revolting assault on the train. She concentrated on the life the cash would one day buy her and she imagined the men as revolting animals, her body as an item for sale. She was still stuck, a potato in frozen earth under a mountain of snow, she thought, in the flat out at Yugo-Zapadnaya, living with Vasily Vasilich's contact, Sasha, who kept four girls like flies in honey and actually wasn't too bad, considering that he was a low-life specimen. His grandmother lived upstairs and came in with pies and jars of pickles and tried to mother them a bit and, in any case, her best friend Olga had soon turned up from Kirgask having begged Vasily Vasilich for the opportunity.

'You are an idiot!' Katya screamed, hugging her friend and bursting into tears right there at the bus stop in the rain one grim grey autumn day when winter was already threatening to obliterate everything.

'Now we can be idiots together,' Olga confirmed, settling quickly into the routine of picking up clients in the Rossiya bar and taking the last metro home to Sasha's at night, handing over what was supposed to be half but was never more than a third of the cash.

To Katya, it had been as obvious as a bee on a rose from the outset that the guy she had picked up tonight was going to drink himself into a stupor before any cash was handed over, and she would like to have ditched him, but she was supposed to meet this mysterious 'friend' of Andriusha's, so she dragged the drunk old toad along just in case nothing better turned up.

'Please, Katenka? I owe him my life,' Andriusha whined, but he needn't have done because actually Katya had quite wanted to meet this Pavel character since he'd taken Andriusha's life over back in Kirgask, with the vodka trade and the dark cash and the mysterious cuts and bruises. Owe him his life? Maybe. To Katya it looked more like Stockholm Syndrome.

She hung around the Rossiya lobby waiting, staving off approaches from the drunk Finns who were on some kind of football tour and who she wouldn't probably have taken even if she wasn't busy, and finally, her shoes pinching her toes painfully (her outdoor boots were in a carrier bag in the cloakroom), she went to the booth to call Andriusha long distance to check what was going on.

'Thank God you called. Change of plan. Pavel's got a job on. Go to the Ukraina Hotel, Kutuzovsky Prospect . . .'

'I know where the Ukraina is, Andriusha,' she sighed, hanging up.

Great. Andriusha'd sounded drunk too and she was worried about him, or at least she would be if she didn't have enough to worry about, God knows. Her dad was ill, coughing the brick factory cough that everyone got in the end and her mum said she thought it wouldn't be long. And now here she was, waiting waiting for this probably fictional friend of Andriusha's, the one she'd been hearing about for years. He lived in Moscow now, apparently, and he might be able to help her.

Well, help she needed.

So now she was sitting in the bloody Ukraina next to a dribbling apparatchik and waiting for this Pavel to emerge. Some foreign kids came in, her age she supposed, but children nonetheless, and the guy kept looking at her as if he was considering an approach, but he was too young, she thought, the babies never dare.

She already had a contingency plan for when her date collapsed as she knew he must. She'd go over and join two Iraqi students who she'd seen around before, buying and selling small stuff, mostly grass from Afghanistan. One of them would probably pay her and be quick, but they would have to go into the toilets because they definitely lived in the hostel and not at the hotel and she always hated that, leaning her hands on the cistern and trying not to look into the bowl in case she threw up. Olga, who was the one girl out at Sasha's who seemed to actually enjoy the grated carrot diet, the pretence that they were models and the incessant encouragement from Sasha to spend their money on cheap nose-jobs, had got a Japanese with a Kremlin-view suite tonight and he had, in fact, offered to take them both. Katya was beginning to regret not snapping him up, even though she couldn't work with another girl, couldn't look her in the face again afterwards she didn't think. Still,

73

she would probably have been back at the flat by now if she'd gone with them, snuggling under the blanket and counting up the profits in her head. It wouldn't be long before she and Olga could afford to rent a flat and get out of the whole hotel thing. You just needed to be clever. And careful. Katya bit the inside of her cheek.

Mo was transfixed. At a set-back table, under the bright overhead lighting that, perhaps intentionally, precluded intimacy, a young girl in scuffed high heels, a neat skirt and a silvery-shiny blouse was flirting with an old man in a suit. A girl, in fact, who would be the other half of the biggest drama of Mo's life, one day far in the future when this moment was almost forgotten. Katya smoked a very thin cigarette with a picture of a butterfly on its filter and occasionally she sipped at a cup of dark yellow champagne that sat in front of her on the table. The bottle was nearly empty, as was the vodka bottle that stood next to it. Her companion was red in the face and sweating, the worse for wear. Some of the buttons of his shirt were undone and his face seemed swollen with booze.

'Daddy?' Eli suggested under his breath as they approached the bar, trying to make a claim on the intimidating space with a confident gait. '"Young Girl Has Innocent Drink with Father at Moscow Bar".'

Mo laughed and they pointed, together, at a bottle of champagne in the hope of being understood. The barman, without meeting their eyes, used a grubby finger to tap a sign on the counter that said 'Hard Currency Only' in two languages. Eli rummaged in the pocket of his jeans and brought out a twenty-dollar bill – the currency of choice that they had been told to bring. The barman shrugged, took the money and put the bottle in front of them on the counter, a challenge of some kind or, perhaps, a statement of profound resignation. Mo pointed at the glasses and said, 'Pozhaluista. Please.' This was almost more than the barman was able to cope with, but, sighing, he provided these too and slumped back into his low chair, utterly defeated.

'No change then,' Eli shrugged, picking up the bottle and glasses and going over to an empty table. It must have been after midnight by now. Standing up, Eli opened the bottle and poured out the champagne so that it fizzed out over the top of both glasses and on to the table, where it gathered, foaming, round the half-full ashtray – everything was going to overflow this evening and, on some level, they both knew it.

'Bollocks,' he said, sitting down. 'Cheers.'

'Na zdorovye!' Mo said, grinning. Saffron, who had been waiting around for Pavel to come back to her side, gave up and came to join them.

'Do you think he knows that tart with the corpse?' she asked. 'He said he liked my top. Four quid, Camden Lock.' Mo hadn't quite labelled Katya as 'tart' yet.

'She's beautiful,' she muttered, but Saffron wasn't listening.

Pavel didn't know her, not yet, and he soon came back to his foreigners, back to his business deals and possibly some sex, he thought, if they weren't too frigid.

By the time they opened the second bottle half an hour later, Hepburn had appeared, snowswept with the rest of their class.

'Christ alive, where WERE you?' he shouted, cheeks livid pink, fists clenching and unclenching in an effort to unfreeze his hands. 'We looked everywhere! I thought you'd been hauled off to the Lubyanka!'

'"Reds Execute School Trip Strays!"' Eli shouted in welcome.

Stripped of the automatic authority that comes with standing in front of pupils armed with the potent gift of information, Hepburn – or Spencer, as he had shyly suggested he might be known for the duration of the trip – looked not so much different to the rest of them, mussing his hair with one hand as he took off his hat, smiling broadly, unsure whether he would be accepted into the group or banished on grounds of advanced age.

'Well, I'm happy to see they haven't.' Dr Spencer Hepburn laughed, turning to the rest of the group, standing in a huddle of uncertainty. 'Come on, everyone. Let's warm ourselves up a bit.'

One of the Arabs picked up his guitar and, head bowed reverently over the strings, started playing 'Let It Be', as the bloke who quite categorically wasn't the young girl's daddy collapsed on the floor unconscious with his flies undone.

Mo noticed that the girl, invited now to join the Arabs instead, went, carefully picking up her bag and cigarettes and smiling. As she passed the table of English schoolchildren and their teacher, long-legged, dark blonde, high-cheekboned and radiating sexual confidence, Mo thought she might be even younger than she looked and began to feel a bit sorry for her, cheap lipstick drying on her mouth and unfashionable pearly blue eye-shadow smeared high on her lids. Nonetheless, Mo knew that girls that looked like that, had that composure and easy sexuality, those were the girls people killed for. Murdered for.

Nobody made any effort to help the drunk lecher, least of all the barman who, in any case, looked as though he'd been in a deep coma since Brezhnev died.

It was the teacher who spoke to Katya first, in good Russian, joining the table with a bottle of champagne and some fresh cups. Katya could see that he was interested in the dark-haired girl, his student she supposed, but she was being dominated by the weirdo with the glasses and a blond guy who looked slightly out of place, perhaps not quite one of them. Might he even be Russian?

'Who's that? Do we know him?' she asked Khaled, blowing her smoke out carelessly. 'I saw you talking to him.'

Both guys shrugged but looked shifty if you asked her, so Katya kept her eye on the 'foreigner' in the purple loafers – pederast shoes – just in case.

The teacher's name was Spencer (though he coughed and admitted 'Dr Hepburn' unable to keep up the charade) and he wanted to know all about where she was from, what her parents did, what she was doing in Moscow. Katya slightly glazed over because she had heard all this bullshit before. The foreigners always liked to pretend there was some kind of rapport and that really you fancied them like mad and only wanted to be paid because the conditions here in Russia are so hard. The Russians just asked what she would do and how much: blow job, straight sex, anal, slap the money on the bedside table and get on with it. Not that many Russians could afford her these days the society she had grown up in, the pioneer camps, pickled mushrooms and peace rallies had disintegrated around her.

Spencer chatted and she answered monosyllabically, her mind drifting and hating this bar, the plastic cups and strip lighting, the windowless, airless hell of it. She thought she would soon go back to Kirgask, to see her dad, to check up, after all, on Andriusha and to get away from this life for a while. She hated the western men and their stupid presents that they thought were generous but were really a way of making themselves feel less sleazy, thinking they were like a boyfriend with their bottles of perfume and silk under-wear all bought at duty free. What they didn't understand was that Russian boyfriends stood meekly in the snow outside metro stations with three carnations wrapped in plastic, walked you home and put hot lips on your cold cheek. They didn't take you into some room that smelled of carpet-cleaning foam and fuck you up the arse, sweating and groaning.

'Have you read Kharms?' Spencer asked, his eyes bloodshot now with the champagne, chatting a girl up the only way he knew how.

Christ, what was he on about? Nineteen thirties satire? This he thought was foreplay though he didn't even light her cigarettes? She would never understand the English.

'Daniil? Sure. We passed it round at school under the desks,' she told him.

'No!' Spencer exclaimed, apparently finding this romantic or something. Why banned books thrilled foreigners so much she would never know. Surely it was easier to read *One Day in the Life of Ivan Denisovich* in a normal book than on scrags of typed paper that came a week apart so the thing took a year to get through? Well, they wouldn't like it so much if they lived here, she thought.

'Mo, Eli, Saffron! Come over here! This young lady has read Daniil Kharms!'

The three kids glanced at each other and laughed, but they picked up their stuff and came over, leaving the bloke who might be Russian and the rest of their class at the table on the other side, though he didn't take his eyes off them; he had the room covered, like a hawk over a meadow.

Katya was glad that the dark girl was coming over. She was always glad to be approached by a woman, let's face it. Whatever it was she might want it couldn't be as bad as whatever a guy was going to want. Not that she minded, not really, not unless they turned nasty which, of course, they sometimes did. Keep your mind on the money, she told herself, feeling like a long-distance swimmer covered in grease, focused solely on the faraway shore. For Katya, the faraway shore was a place of her own and she was nearly there.

There was a warmth about this English girl, Katya thought, a plum-pie-straight-out-of-the-oven warmth, all flushed and excited, laughing and expecting to be adored, listened to, touched. It was how Katya would like to have been, would have been perhaps, if she had never won the contest, never become one of Sasha's Yugo-Zapadnaya girls.

* * *

Khaled, now sensing an opportunity through his alcohol fug, got all his tights and stockings out to show Saffron, and Tariq, his friend, was still strumming his guitar drunkenly.

'These ones with little hearts on them are so wicked!' Saffron squealed, immediately ready to cut a deal.

'For twenty dollars, two pairs . . .'

Katya, staggered at his gall, took her last cigarette out of the packet and was about to crumple the cardboard up when Mo stopped her.

'No!' Mo insisted, taking the packet from her hands and tearing little pieces out of the sides before bringing the top right down over the bottom to make one tiny little box.

'Da-daaaa!' She laughed, giving it back to Katya in the form of a gift.

Katya met her eyes and smiled. 'Spasibo,' she said. 'Thank you.'

'Any time,' Mo offered and Eli, who was a bit embarrassed to be smoking and drinking in front of a teacher and so had been quieter than usual, explained that she always did that.

'She'll have to make a career out of it because she's crap at everything else,' he offered.

'Bumazhku dai,' Katya said to the table in general. Nobody responded. 'Paper?'

Spencer brought a notebook out of the pocket of his jacket, blue-lined, ring-bound, and ripped a sheet out.

Katya, head bowed over her work, produced an origami swan and handed it to Mo.

'OK, that's a lot better than mine,' Mo beamed, genuinely moved and delighted by her gift.

'I think we can safely say you've been trumped, Momix,' Eli helped, taking a big slurp of his champagne and scrumpling up the plastic cup afterwards in a show of something that might have been manliness. '"Britain Pipped to Post by Mighty USSR in Oregano Battle".'

'Origami.'

'Oh. Yuh. Well . . . No need to get all Adolf Eichmann on me.'

'So, basically, anyone who doesn't grovel to you in all your spasmodiousness is a Nazi henchman?'

'Ve havv vays off mekkink you grovel,' he nodded, his curls shaking.

At some point in all the drinking and laughing Katya took Mo's address on another sheet of the notebook and imagined a house with a picket fence, a father in a bowler hat with an umbrella and a corgi running about on the lawn.

'It rains in England?' she asked, looking at the address as if to exact its secret, thinking that the rain must be clean and not like the toxic stuff here in Moscow.

'Yes, a lot,' Mo admitted, herself thinking how funny that that's all anyone knows about England in the rest of the world.

'And fog? Smog?' Katya wanted to know, imagining characters from Charles Dickens emerging from the thick gloom with capes and silver-topped canes.

'No! Not any more!' Mo laughed and she and Eli started miming making their way through a pea-souper to each other's arms.

Katya looked at Mo with a smile that gleamed solidarity and sorority, never mind the iron curtain. Or, at least, this is how it appeared to Mo in her already very drunken state. Mo was never sure whether the world seemed more benign when she was drunk, or whether it *was* benign but it was only when she was drunk that she could allow herself to see it. Perhaps it was the siege feeling of the bar, friendships lost and won in an instant.

She asked Katya how old she was, one of those questions that she'd been taught how to ask, like 'What is your name' and 'Where is the cinema'. Katya looked around as though it was a secret from someone who might be lurking behind one of the columns, then she held the palm of her hand up like a gorilla signalling friendship and scrunched it into a fist: one, two, three. 'Pyatnadsat' lyet,' she said. Fifteen. Christ. And yet, God knew, fifteen years probably felt like an eternity in this Godforgotten place. A lot of the girls working might be even younger. (They were.) Mo drew her breath in, tasting the significance of the confession on her tongue and tried to imagine being at school with Katya somewhere in Moscow with big red ribbons in their hair, laughing about a teacher, sharing a sandwich at break time, giving the shaven-skulled boys heading for their national service scale-of-one-to-ten attractiveness ratings.

Pavel was teaching Eli how to drink a whole shot of vodka in one gulp without even wincing (all to do with when you breathe).

'Now *this* is fun,' Mo heard Eli shout a few shots in.

'Hey. Mate. You're not seriously called Paul, are you? What kind of name's that for a Siberian vodka fiend?' he spluttered, wrapping an arm round his new friend.

'Pavel.' Pavel smiled, gently removing the offending arm and shaking hands again in his new, slightly more real, personality.

Katya leaned forward to Mo, smelling of lemony soap (she had discovered her mother's secret in a plain white packet one day, looking for antiseptic for a cut) and whispered, 'He loves you, because you are so confident and happy.' She said it in Russian, pointing at Eli and throwing her hair back and beaming to imitate Mo. This was not how Mo would ever have thought of herself but, she decided, she would try to do so in future.

Perhaps because it was all they could do to demonstrate unity in the Ukraina Hotel's bleak lift-shaft bar with a drunk on the floor, or perhaps because they were extremely pissed, they started laughing. Katya curled up on her chair, almost burying her face in her bare knees, her whole body shaking, trying violently to rid itself of all the things that really were not funny at all. Mo held her stomach, looking as though she might be contorted in agony; tears started to spill out of her eyes and her cheeks hurt.

'You girls seem to be having a nice time,' Spencer commented, moving his white plastic chair to muscle in between them, breaking the developing intimacy he seemed to fear or to desire, slopping more champagne into their three glasses. The two girls looked blankly at him, not knowing what to say. He rolled up the sleeves of his baggy white shirt and leaned his elbows in the sticky swill of the table.

'Christ, look!' Mo said suddenly, touching her teacher on the shoulder in amazement. The unconscious man was crawling on hands and knees towards the lifts and Pavel was coming over to whisper something in her ear.

'I have been watching you. You have very beautiful skin,' was what he whispered. 'I would like to touch it.'

Later, Mo found herself (or, rather, lost herself) staggering along the corridor towards her room on the twenty-third floor, holding her heavy room key. The woman who seemed to guard the lift and the rows of swinging keys had handed it over grudgingly, shouting incomprehensible commands from beneath her tangerine caramelised hairdo. Mo wobbled and leaned her hand up against the flocked wallpaper, catching her breath and laughing. The world was not stable tonight. Pavel supported her with one arm round her waist and, without pausing to consider it, Mo turned to face him as he pushed her up against the wall and kissed her as though breaking a vow of silence he hadn't wanted to take.

'Oh God,' he murmured, pulling back to look at her, smiling as if, for him, this moment was mystically predestined and meant to be, his eyes boring into her soul in the hope of finding, or in the belief that he had found . . . salvation? 'Mo.'

Kissing him back and pressing her body against his, Mo pulled his shirt out of his trousers behind him and ran her hands up his back. Swimming blackness filled her brain and she softened every

82

part of herself to let the ultimate oblivion sweep over her. But he wouldn't let her go.

'Don't you want to?' he said, looking down at her face again for reassurance that she was who he thought she was, that there was no mistake.

'I did turn fifteen last week,' she whispered, breathless, mouth open, eyes wide, limbs draped around him. She was telling the truth as the absurd joke she felt it to be, wanting to reassure him as much as he wanted to be reassured. Couldn't he see, after all, that she was really as old as the hills, that her age was merely a part of her brilliant disguise? She longed to collapse with him into the dark tonight, the first night of her new life, to make their rebellion against the frozen river and the empty streets complete.

But Pavel's eyes flashed amusement and he pulled away from her to take her in properly. 'Well, I am seventeen . . .' he began and would surely have continued, but the floor shifted under Mo's uncertain feet and she lost her balance once and for all and fell over with an eloquent thud, a drunken schoolgirl in a Moscow corridor, helped back to solid ground by a concerned new friend. Where, she wondered, a creeping awareness that the grotesque dream was not about to recede into her swirling mind and that she was lying on the floor about to have sex with a Russian, was Eli?

A door opened with a sharp click and she and Pavel both looked round, realising (she with a penetrating shame) how they appeared, how obvious it was what fumbling was going on out here. Mo also knew whose room that was, even in the blur of her general twattedness – it was Spencer's and the onlooker was Katya, her hair a mess, her face flushed and her handbag gaping open on its clasp. She shut the door quickly behind her, looked without recognition at the couple she'd been singing with less than an hour earlier and ran down the corridor, shoving a hundred-dollar bill into her bag.

But she didn't finish her run, turning back suddenly to face the pair, a flash of understanding on her face.

'Ty Pavel?' she asked. 'Are you Pavel?'

Pavel drew his breath in, straightened and looked at her. 'No,' he said in English. 'My name is Paul.'

Katya turned and went, Mo shouting 'Goodbye, Katya! It was lovely to meet you! Write to me!' after her and then Mo heard the dyezhurnaya scream insults at Katya as she got into the lift. Sobering up fast, she could imagine what they were.

'Why did you lie?' she asked Pavel, still sitting on the brillo-pad-type hall carpet.

'Because I was supposed to meet her. But I don't want to fall in love with a whore,' he said, and, helping her up he guided her back to her room, held her hair while she threw up in the loo, brought her a glass of water and rested his hand on her forehead while she let her eyes slide shut in the dark on the single bed next to Saffron and Eli who lay, fully clothed, in a childish embrace on the other one.

'Spokoinoi nochi,' Pavel whispered before he left. 'Goodnight.'

She had taken his phone number, but it would be years before she used it.

'You can build a throne out of bayonets, but you can't sit on it for long.'

Boris Yeltsin

Chapter Eight

Katya went home soon, after the night at the Ukraina, the night when the teacher had overpaid her as she'd known he would. Back to Kirgask. Something about that night, some burr of anxiety, had latched on to her and sent her running. Her dad was terribly ill, it turned out, and Andriusha was really in trouble, something to do, there would be absolutely no doubt, with the stupid Pavel guy who never showed up, and Katya, after all, dreamed of escape from the Moscow life like a bear dreams of winter. She put the little box Mo had made her on the desk in her school-girl room and she sat on her bed by the window looking out into the courtyard and chewing the end of a pencil, letting the smell of onions from the kitchen, the fading blue ribbon of a swimming medal that hung on the mirror, the comforting shape of her school shoes on the floor and the distant grind of the factory seep into her. She tried to write to Mo in English, the unfamiliar script jerky on the page, and it was hard to imagine that these words might come alive with meaning for someone so far away.

She found herself ignoring how and where they'd met, the other life that, she supposed, had become real life, and writing only about Kirgask and swimming in the lake in summer with Andriusha, about her mum who had nearly been a film star and about the budgerigar that had died of grief hanging upside down on its perch. It wasn't that she was ashamed of what had happened in Moscow, of who she was there, but somehow it didn't seem relevant to who she was here, when she could hear her mum and dad (now with this cough) talking quietly in the kitchen and a dog barking outside, children in the rusting climbing frame where she'd climbed herself not very long ago. She took the letter into town to the Central Telegraph and queued a long time for the stamp, watching people write out telegrams with the glutinous ink in the wooden pots at the top of slanting desks. Even then, she nearly ripped the letter out of the envelope and scribbled out the request for help, for a visa, for an invitation to London. But she didn't. Whatever anybody else might think, she had her pride.

And it can't have been more than a day or two after she'd posted the letter that a man called Mikhail came round.

'Good afternoon,' he said, in a harbinger of doom way that made her shiver.

Her mum, who loved a visitor, even one like this, made him tea and Katya recognised him and remembered, as he leaned forward nervously with his tea cup held to his mouth directly over the saucer to catch any dribbles, that he had been with Vasily Vasilich, lurking behind him, that day at school when the Beauty Concourse had been announced. 'Tea should be like a kiss. Hot, sweet and strong,' he said, an old saying that everyone knows and that nobody finds funny but they all laughed anyway.

Mikhail (he didn't give his patronymic) was very thin and tall, his skin stretched tight over his skeleton as though it was only temporary and wasn't going to settle in – we would all soon come to dust. Mikhail was probably instrumental in having brought a few people to dust come to think of it, KGB man that he clearly was.

Her mother gave Mikhail biscuits, sukhariki, very dry curls of unsweetened biscuit from a big plastic packet, and he dipped one in his tea though he kept his leather coat on, belted tightly at the waist.

'I love the simple biscuits,' he said, clearly indicating that he was used to a more expensive variety.

He coughed before he began, clearing his body of the phlegm of responsibility for his reprehensible actions. 'I must ask, as a matter of grave importance to the security of the motherland, who you know in London and what is the name of this contact?'

Katya's mum laughed with a giddy twinkle, clearly glad that someone suspected her of having foreign connections. Her dad didn't laugh though. He clenched his unwashed fist on the table and lowered his voice. Katya could see how hard he was finding it not to punch Mikhail, knowing the man's background and what his job entailed, holding him, in fact, personally responsible for all the evils Communism had inflicted on the Russian people, for his illness, for the deaths of so many of his friends.

'If I ever got a word out of this living hell to someone on the outside, do you honestly think I would tell you about it, you pathetic piece of dog turd,' he said slowly, carelessly, every word, in fact, a punch.

Mikhail blinked furiously, but both men seemed aware that things had changed over the past few years, that the balance of power was shifting like melting ice on the lake. 'It's just that we have heard about your letter,' he said.

Katya, who was stirring an old white pair of trousers around on the blazing gas hob in a huge vat of black dye and at whom Mikhail was determinedly not looking, realised, screwing her eyes up in the steam, that she was the issue here.

'I sent it. It was a letter to my English pen pal.' She turned, smiling eagerly, using the English words 'pen pal' so that Mikhail didn't have a clue what she was on about. 'She is studying Russian. I am trying to improve my English.'

Forced now to shift his position on the low wooden stool that he was far too tall for, Mikhail took on the appearance of someone who might choke to death on his tongue like an epileptic.

'She lives in London. Mo is her name,' Katya went on enthusiastically. This was not going to be difficult. The man was an apparatchik of the most depressingly familiar type.

Mikhail tried to swallow and, in the effort, he dropped the cup and saucer he'd been holding so carefully. It shattered on to the lino in front of him, his body now under her control, not his own. The black dye boiled and spat noisily.

'Oh, firs and sticks. Let me help you.' Her mum leaped up and started cleaning up the embarrassing fluid at Mikhail's feet, her back curved painfully over as she collected shards of precious china.

'I will need you to write me a report detailing any conversation you may have had with this person. Your letter will be sent to London only when it has been carefully studied by my colleagues and only if it is found to be . . . shall we say . . . safe,' he explained, nervously chewing the edge of his biscuit, moving his huge feet (rudely, but making his point, he had left his shoes on) this way and that to avoid the swoosh of the tea-mopping cloth.

Katya slunk towards him, swaying her hips. Her father had his head down, eyes to the plastic tablecloth with a print of bright lemons on it, both fists now clenched.

'Vasily Vasilich Komykin took me to Moscow. That's where I met her,' Katya told him, causing Mikhail's face to fall as though it was his bureaucratic power that held his features together, the fact that others feared him. Now not only did his features seem to disintegrate at the sound of his boss's name, but his whole manner changed and he shuffled, apologetic, flustered and stooping out of the apartment, his size suddenly inappropriate. He tried to shrink himself by pulling his arms in and bending his head down, folding like an accordion.

'Bastard,' her father said, standing up and kicking his stool over with a clatter when he'd gone. 'I know him. He had Dima sacked. As good as killed him. Bastard.' He had tears in his eyes at the mention of Andriusha's father and he wiped his sweating palms on his overalls.

Katya went over to him and hugged him tightly, looking up over his shoulder away from the pain to the china samovar on the top shelf, some blue and white Gzhel figures and a big laquered bread bin with painted strawberries on it, all dusty and forgotten.

'It's all right, Papa. He can't do anything to us,' she said, aware that having been to Moscow put her in the role of protector to her own parents, of provider and, at fifteen, of the only adult in the house.

He hugged her back with a squeeze that forced the breath out of her lungs and then pushed her gently away, his eyes brooding under his sprouting eyebrows, a wildness left untamed.

'But I can do something to him,' he said, and he ran heavily out of the door and down the stone steps, his last act of brave defiance against the now crumbling regime that had crushed his colleagues and himself.

When he came back her mother washed his hands in a bowl of soapy water on the kitchen table as he coughed violently, rubbed purple iodine into his knuckles and bandaged them, weaving the long strip of material under and over as though she was making a tapestry. The windows were open and the evening filled the flat with deep yellow light as the birds sang in the birch trees.

The KGB stooge was hospitalised, they said, whispers in the queues in town, and, however diminished his power was in these changing times, Katya knew it would be hard for her stay around here. The visit from Mikhail and her dad's shredded knuckles remained, linked in her memory to her father's death which actually happened some weeks later. Perhaps because it was his last big spurt of energy before the pathetic decline that tore out her insides as if she were a gutted fish. Thin, weak and increasingly colourless, he slipped away from them as though death was trying to strip down the physical being to nothing before it finally devoured the soul itself. Not that Katya believed in souls. She held his hand for the agonising final hours when every crackling, rumbling, bubbling breath must surely be his last, nurses snapping around the crowded ward under flickering light, helping those who stood a chance.

At just sixteen, Katya did try to find a job in Kirgask. She asked around about secretarial work (though God knew she wouldn't have had the first clue how to do it) and she even went to see Olga's mum and offered to help her with all her remedies and potions, teas and poultices. She'd be glad of help, she said, but she couldn't pay. It was the same everywhere: people looked at her with fear in their eyes after the Mikhail incident (though he was out of hospital in no time – a corpse that wouldn't die). Andriusha, who now drank vodka at breakfast and had too many friends that ordinary people were frightened of, at first said he could help her. He had contacts, he said, good contacts from Pavel in Moscow, this guy again, who was making a lot of money and leaving the Tomsk and Kirgask side of things increasingly to him, he boasted, puffed up like a cockerel. He suggested that he was powerful in his own right, that one day Pavel might answer to him. Katya called his house every day, sometimes going round to the flat and ending up drinking tea with his mum who still worked as the school nurse and said that Comrade Tarakanova, who was now the headmistress, had gone quite mad since they had been officially instructed not to use the word 'Comrade' any more. Andriusha's mum delighted in calling her Ludmilla which was, after all, her name. But the contacts, the job never materialised and Andriusha was anxious, twitchy about a 'very big' favour for Pavel that was coming up, that would change everything. Well, it did.

Katya headed back to Moscow after some idle months, her savings down to nothing and her heart aching for her dad, back to doing the hotels with Olga and saving money so that one day she might stop and do something more worthwhile, though, as time went by, any other way of life seemed distant and unlikely.

As the years passed and the Russians got richer, first matching then far surpassing the wealth of visiting foreigners, the scarred and swaggering men with cash in their pockets and gold watches flashing at their wrists became regular clients and the better-looking girls left the pimps and hotels for flats of their own, could afford to have fewer clients and still pay the rent. Nobody could stop them – they were holding hard currency and they were rich. Really rich. Katya worked hard to make absolutely sure that she and Olga were among those girls. She wasn't stupid. When you were making real money the prices in roubles were laughable. You could buy a whole block of flats for a year's worth of men. And so the Moscow life that she'd made a feeble attempt to escape from became, at last, inescapable, partly because of the letter and the KGB guy and her dad beating him up. Moscow life that wasn't all work, after all. They had their gorgeous apartment, she and Olga, they went to the clubs and danced until their feet were sore and their voices hoarse. At least, Olga did. Katya tried to enjoy it, but found the seething mass of people, the noise and the lights oppressive. If anything made her long for a cool swim in a big lake it was Titanic nightclub and the phantasmagoria that had people paying insane money for a big purple drink that made you simultaneously drunk and wired. They had been there the other night to support a friend who danced the cages (at midnight the girls were lowered naked in cages into the screaming crowds and they danced their arses off for an hour while men reached in, red-faced, sweating, wet-eyed until the cages were hoisted back up into the ceiling and the girls drank bottles of cold water and smoked until the next lowering at two) and Katya danced, or tried to. One night Katya noticed someone watching her in the suffocating nightmare of the club, music pounding, lights flashing, girls with vodka bottles on their hips pouring shots like rounds of ammunition, armed men strutting around her, but she couldn't now remember what he was like. Short, tall, prison tattoos or army, shaven-headed, beard? She had no idea. She woke up with a card in the back pocket of her jeans though and assumed it must have been him, a P. D. Ivanchenko, TomStal. Well, join the queue if you can afford it, she thought, tossing the card into the garbage under the sink.

'Hey! I'll have him! Don't throw work away!' Olga wailed from her lair on the sofa, but she didn't bother to get up to fish him out.

Katya picked her keys up off the table and slung her bag over her shoulder, off to meet Andriusha at the station. She caught herself in the mirror, hardly recognised herself for a second. Fiddling around for her purse, taken aback by the sight of this slick, hard-faced woman in the mirror, she wasn't sure how it had all come to this, how she had become this person who offered help and sent money home in fat envelopes, a woman with a car and a nice flat who shopped with all the scruffy foreigners (why do they go out with holes in their jeans?) at the hard-currency supermarkets stocked with things there weren't even words for in Russia, all from Finland, credit cards only. Years ago, when she'd first arrived in Moscow, she had expected rescue herself.

But, actually, if someone had been logging her life's trajectory it would not have seemed as baffling as it seemed to her, for it would have been easy to chart what had happened and why. Russia, after all, was changing, and she had always vowed to be ready. Ready she was.

Katya pushed her hair back out of her face and set off – for today Andriusha was coming to Moscow for the first time, to check in with his boss, to stay with Katya. Why he couldn't stay with the creep who employed him, who knew, but Katya was glad. She held the keys to her Mercedes in a hot hand and turned round to look at the flat, hoping he wouldn't judge it, judge her, hoping it would be OK. Olga glanced up at her from the cream leather sofa where she was taking refuge from her hangover in a tub of blueberry yoghurt.

'Are you going, or what?' she asked, stretching out her long lazy legs and flicking on the TV. She had a tattoo of a butterfly on her ankle.

'Get dressed, can you? You haven't got anything today, have you?'

'Not a turnip,' Olga confirmed happily, licking her spoon.

Olga's mum thought she was selling her herbal potions in Moscow but they, of course, sat in boxes in the closet. Every month, though, Olga sent her a huge sum of money that she said she'd made from sales to big stores.

Olga would smile, filling the envelope and kissing it shut. 'She'll die as happy as a sow in mud. But richer.'

'I mean it,' Katya said, opening the sliding door of a vast white fitted cupboard in the hall where more than twenty fur coats hung. Arctic foxes, minks, sables and seal, some with a hood, some with a belt, some long, some short. Katya pulled out a short brown mink and shrugged it on, switching on the spotlights to check herself in the mirrored wall on the right. A vase of tall lilies stood on a bookcase next to her.

'Hey! That's mine! The bloke with the car factory – you know, Grisha – he gave it to me.'

'Arkasha. So what? You're not going out anyway.'

'True.'

'Get dressed. He's a country boy.'

'He never remembers me.'

'He remembers you.'

'He never remembers me.'

'Well, he hasn't seen you for five years. Just put your clothes on and it will be fine.'

'Put your clothes on. Take your clothes off,' Olga muttered to herself, spooning more yoghurt into her mouth. 'OK. OK. He's your Chukchi boyfriend.'

'He is not my boyfriend and he is not a Chukchi. He's just . . . You know. He prefers to stay in Kirgask where he can do some good and—'

'Some good like selling the stuff you send him and buying vodka with it?'

'That is *not* true, Olya. What you just said is *not* true. He just . . . you know. Military service was hard for him . . .'

'Every sandpiper praises its own swamp.' Olga smiled, knowing she had hit home but wondering why she needed to. Without Katya she wouldn't have a wardrobe full of furs, a flat with a view of the Kremlin (if you craned your head round a bit), a Jacuzzi bath in the beautiful peach sunset colour they'd chosen together and, most wonderful of all, a woman, Zuza, who cleaned every day, changed the flowers and took all the linen to the cleaners up on the corner of Kutuzovsky in a bundle. No. Without Katya she would be running a herbal remedies kiosk on the main drag in Kirgask outside the derelict House of Culture with its shutters hanging off the hinges and rats in the old cinema. The Mayor's office would have her shop bulldozed every six months and she would also have continued to be fucked by her mum's new boyfriend, Pyotr.

Katya screeched up at Paveletsky Vokzal and clunked the car to locked with a click of the key fob. She waded through slush to the station entrance and pushed her sunglasses on to the top of her head, glancing up at the huge arrivals board and holding tight to her pale blue kidskin handbag. An old man, a bomzh, was urinating on to the floor right in the middle of all the crowds that surged blindly round him with suitcases, bundles and purpose, unthinkingly creating a space in which he could perform like those blokes in Gorky Park who paint themselves gold and stand very still.

Andriusha looked lost. She spotted him immediately, standing on tiptoe to search for a familiar face, his bag slung over his shoulder as the passengers spilled off the train, tumbling down into the outstretched arms that swept forwards to cling to them on the swaying platform. The train still creaked and groaned, recovering from its arduous mission to bring Andriusha to Katya in faraway Moscow. Announcements roared into the cavernous station and bands of barefoot gypsy children, their owners waiting darkly in the shadows, tugged at the clothes of those more fortunate than themselves.

Katya rushed up to him, surprising him out of the milling people as though she'd emerged right in front of his face from a fog. He was startled and, when she tried to kiss him on both cheeks, he recoiled, unfamiliar with the metropolitan greeting and she stumbled forwards, turning the attempted kiss into a big hug. He brought his arms round to try and hug her back but his bag fell off his shoulders and, in the end, they just stood facing each other in the raging sea of commotion.

'Hi! Hi!' Katya said, happy to see him, looking him up and down to see if he really was as brittle and as skinny as her hands had already told her. 'Welcome to Moscow! Sorry, I didn't have time to buy flowers.' She knew as sure as chickens were counted in autumn that he would have brought red carnations to greet her at a station, as tradition dictated, even if he had become a bit . . . well, bandit-like.

'You think I'm so provincial I need wilting flowers to show I've arrived in the big city, do you?' he said, slinging his bag into place and looking around for the exit.

Katya laughed. 'Don't be silly!' she said, leading the way to the car, walking a few steps in front of Andriusha and twisting back to talk to him. He avoided her eye and shambled along, shoulders hunched, fringe flopping into his face. He trod his thin trainers straight into the pool of slush surrounding the car without comment and then slumped into the passenger seat, reaching over to unlock Katya's side, not understanding that it was centrally locked.

'I'm not that rich, really,' Katya smiled at him, watching him light a cigarette with shaking hands. He didn't offer her one and she noticed he was smoking Belamor Canal so she wouldn't have taken one in any case. She zhuzhed down the window to alleviate the intense cheap-tobacco-smell situation. 'I just . . . well, a friend bought it for me.'

She backed out of the space, hitting the horn hard as a taxi pulled over, blocking her.

'Fucker!' she said, leaning now on the horn until the car moved, bent all the way round to see out the rear window.

'Bought what?' Andriusha asked, looking at her for the first time, his face wan, eyes dull, hair greasy.

'The car!' Katya said, laughing. She screeched out on to the main road, pushing her foot down hard on the accelerator and swerving violently round a chugging Lada Zhiguli making slow tracks in the grey slush that turned the whole city into a shallow lake. She reached forward for her own cigarettes, Marlboro Lights, nestled with a slim gold lighter in the walnut box behind the handbrake. Easing into a traffic jam she lit one, flashing her eyes at Andriusha and smiling again. 'You're so funny. You know you've always wanted a Mercedes Benz. You know? Like the Janis Joplin song?' she said, about to sing it, genuinely delighted to see him but worried that he might sneer at her apartment, at the flash city style he was about to encounter at a time when she knew from her parents what things were like in

Kirgask, even if he himself had been raking it in illegally for years. God knows where the money went because he hadn't spent it on clothes, that was for sure. Mum's friend Svetlana had actually fainted from hunger at work last week and everyone was living off the pickled dacha produce. Most shops weren't even bothering to open and the black-market traders were making a killing, flogging German Food Aid unpacked in Moscow.

'Rooster today, feather duster tomorrow,' he said, blowing out a big billow of smoke and pulling his thin jacket closer.

Katya considered being hurt that he thought her to be a rooster and, indeed, that some part of him was looking forward to her becoming a feather duster. She reached out and touched his arm, gently. 'Yes. True, of course. You're always right.' He was definitely being very weird.

Moscow was shades of grey today with the snow melted and the streets awash, the cloud low and the wide pavements crowded with people whose only ambition was to be somewhere else. Crows the colour of slate hopped heavily from spindly branch to crumbling balcony above the muddy courtyards and exhaust fumes hung thickly in the air.

'I know it looks awful. I wanted you to see Moscow different,' she sighed. She had always imagined him coming in winter when they would walk arm in arm through the deep snow at Novodyevichy Monastery, their breath white in the icy air and the gold domes gleaming their magic in a sharp turquoise sky. Or, perhaps, he would come in summer and they might sit outside at a boulevard café under the lime trees with ice-creams or ride the ferris wheel in Gorky Park and laugh above the rooftops. But that was before, when they were just starting out, before they both changed and, in the end, he had come now, into the dark grey seething city and the low light that left no flaw hidden, and it was flaws, after all, that Andriusha must surely have come to seek out.

* * *

Olga had changed into jeans and a T-shirt that said 'Look But Don't Touch' on it in English and she answered the door with bright pink latex washing-up gloves on and a cigarette in her mouth, squinting to avoid being scorched by the smoke.

'Oh, hi! I was just going to do my roots,' she said, pulling one glove off and taking the cigarette from her lips.

Katya rolled her eyes accusingly at Olga and came in, tugging her coat off. Andriusha mooched past her and into the main living room where he stood, apparently transfixed by the deep white carpet.

'What did I do?' Olga asked, annoyed that she was supposed to be on some sort of fictional best behaviour for this low life vodka-trading thug from Kirgask whom Katya inexplicably idolised.

'Just . . . you know. Pretend to be normal,' Katya hissed, fixing a smile back on her face and shoving past her friend to deal with Andriusha who was clearly adrift. 'Hey . . . yes, well, it's . . . we're going to have it redone,' she explained, embarrassed, feeling his contempt for her taste, suddenly tacky when seen through his eyes, vulgar, overstated when understatement was clearly the thing.

'We are not,' Olga said.

'Well. We . . . you know . . . we should talk about it . . . Maybe it's a bit much, you know . . . I mean, people are really struggling in Russia at the moment . . .'

It was true. She sent boxes of tampons home for her mother to sell.

Olga plonked herself down on the sofa and crossed her legs, cocking her head to one side. 'So we should have some peasant-style apartment in sympathy?' she wondered. 'It would probably cost more to put all that kitsch in.'

'Um . . . Andriusha . . . you remember Olya?'

Andriusha, who was standing very still on the edge of the room and seemed to be shivering, raised his eyes with what appeared like effort to look at Olga. His face stayed blank as though his brain was slowly transferring the data on to a disk for closer perusal.

'He never remembers me,' she said. 'Hi, I'm Olga Davydovna, Olya,' she waved her hand at him, trying to raise him from coma. 'We screwed in Ivan the cripple's shed after Toma beat you up? Remember?'

Katya dropped her car keys and when she bent down to pick them up her sunglasses fell off her head. 'What?' she asked, straightening up to face the unpleasant truth. Truth, she always found, tasted like raw horseradish. Perhaps that was why she smoked.

'Didn't he tell you? No. Well. It didn't last long, did it, Andriushochka?' Olga said. 'And you never remember me.'

He smiled weakly and seemed to collapse into the sofa opposite his tormenter, bones turned to noodles by her mocking laugh.

'You look different,' he said, pulling his cigarettes out of his pocket with a tug as if needing to touch something from home, something that was his to suck on for comfort in this stark world of spotlights and white furniture from Finland or God knew where. America itself, perhaps.

Katya noticed, now that he was against a background of dairy cream leather, how incredibly dirty his hands, fingernails and hair were. He appeared to have brought the actual soil of Kirgask with him. Perhaps he had rolled in it like a bristly pig before screaming slaughter.

'I look exactly the fucking same,' Olga complained. 'A cat always knows whose meat it eats.'

'It was a long time ago,' Andriusha said, looking around the room to avoid Olga's eyes, resting them on shining objects whose purpose he seemed not to able to fathom. A vase, a cocktail shaker, a pewter Maserati, a big porcelain female nude in semi-erotic pose, the bronze eagle whose outspread wings held up the coffee table.

'Exactly!' Katya agreed enthusiastically, padding softly over to the kitchen area and flicking the kettle on. 'You always hit the nail on the head, Andrei. I'll make us some tea, or . . . Have we still got that champagne Lyova brought?' she wondered, vaguely asking Olga but opening the enormous gleaming fridge and pulling the bottle out without any answer being forthcoming. 'Ah ha!'

Andriusha flicked his head round to look at her, the mention of another man galvanising him slightly, his eyes suddenly bright and focused as though he'd needed this shot in the arm to bring him to.

'Is Lyova your boyfriend?'

'No,' the girls said in unison, looking at each other, Katya in badly concealed, over-smiling panic.

'Yes! Yes. He's Olya's boyfriend.' Katya nodded, correcting herself, righting the situation, pulling three slender glasses out of the cupboard and bringing them over to the smoked-glass table in the hope that Andriusha would approve a proper welcome cere-mony. That, she thought, must be what was lacking: no flowers at the station, no drinks on the table.

'I'm sorry. I didn't make food.' She blushed, bending towards her old friend with her arms outstretched. Black bread and red caviar would have been right, would have been simple but plenty. 'Could you?' she asked Andriusha. And she so wanted to hear about home.

He tore the foil off with his teeth but then he wasn't able to untwist the wire because his hands were shaking and the bottle kept slipping from his grasp. Katya looked away, willing herself to trust him, trying to concentrate on the clouds out of the window and the little girl's piano practice in the flat below. She remembered orchestra after school at the House of Culture and how tight her ribbons had been, how hot the hall. She could picture where Andriusha had sat, three along from Masha in the second row, and how he might turn to wink at her when nobody was looking.

But Olga got up with a deep sigh, took the bottle from him,

popped the cork in a flash and poured out three glasses of champagne while Andriusha peered slowly round for an ashtray, his eyelids heavy, eventually tapping the burning ash into the foil he held scrumpled in his hand.

'Oh, no . . . let me . . .' Katya said, rushing to the kitchen and bringing back a pearl-effect ceramic Tatar chieftain whose lap was the receptacle. She thought Andriusha would find this funny (they had always laughed at things . . . hadn't they?) but he didn't react at all, preferring to stare into his drink as though it were the entrails of some sacrificed animal.

Katya, hoping to woo him with sincerity, tossed her cornfield of hair over her shoulders and rooted her stockinged feet strongly in the deep carpet as though she were about to perform a difficult yoga pose. 'I've known you a long time, Andriusha,' she began in a low voice. 'I loved your family and I hope you loved mine. We walked to school together every day, summer and winter and we . . .'

She wished she was able to say the words without seeing their feet planted on the pavement in front of the statue of Togliatti and without smelling the dumplings, he would bring wrapped in foil, mushroom, cabbage or ground meat. And for some reason, as she began to describe their friendship without really saying anything, Katya found that tears rushed to her eyes like a pack of dogs that had been silently waiting to be called and had finally heard the whistle. She wasn't expecting them and the hairs on her arms stood up as the sky seemed to darken outside and the room became cold as if someone had opened a fortochka in another room.

'Um . . . sorry. I'm not very good at this . . . but . . . welcome to Moscow, dear friend, and here's to us!'

Awkwardly, perhaps too urgently, she pulled Andriusha up out of his seat so that some of his champagne slopped on to the sofa and she grabbed him in a tight hug, weeping as she did so, hoping that her love for him and for the children they had been would somehow osmose into him through her touch. He put one hand round her back, more for balance than anything else, and in the other he held his cigarette and his glass. She felt his poor body skinny and rigid, not responding to her touch or her tears – not, perhaps, even aware of them. His smell was rancid, like the sour cheese they sold at the market, peeling off the muslin to reveal the wet white mound, slicing shards off it and holding them out to taste on the blade of a long knife. Letting go, embarrassed, Katya backed away and sat down next to Olga, cradling her glass, defeated, and pulling her knees up under her for protection.

'Sorry,' she said, her eyelashes lowered and wet with tears.

Andriusha was left standing, steadying himself. Without warning, he said, 'Here's to us,' in a gruff growl. Then he tipped his champagne back in one, blinked and looked baffled, an owl in torchlight.

Katya laughed, relieved. She nodded. 'Quite right.'

'Jesus,' Olga sighed, exhausted by the rigmarole, and taking a demure sip. 'To us.'

When the phone erupted in a sharp ring all three of them twitched at the unexpected intrusion into their tangled thoughts.

'Yup. Listening,' Olga stated, matter of fact in her bare feet with the nails painted dark purple. 'That's right. Yes, he's here . . .' She put her hand over the receiver. 'Andriusha. It's for you.'

Shuffling over to the phone, Andriusha had a short conversation and made an agreement. 'Pavel,' he said reverently, his eyes flickering.

'Ah, Pavel the Great,' Katya mocked. 'You know he never turned up that time. At the Ukraina? Years ago. Maybe six, seven years ago.'

'He did,' Andriusha said, slumping back down into the sofa. 'He just didn't like the look of you, he told me. I need to see him later but first he wants to meet you on business. Said he saw you at Titanic the other night, dancing. Sure it was you. Anyway, I promised him you'd go. For my sake? Please?'

'Sure.' She shrugged. Work was work, she supposed.

Hauling himself to his feet like an eighty-year-old, swaying there slightly and then gazing round the room, again looking for the exit, Andriusha said, 'I'm going to lie down.'

'I'll show you where we've put you . . .' Katya immediately agreed, putting down her glass with a gentle clink and thinking that perhaps he just needed a rest after his journey, that perhaps the real Andriusha was hidden by the shroud of four time zones and the grime of travelling. 'You'll soon be a cucumber again!' she said.

This cheered her up and she led him happily, gold bracelet and slim watch chiming softly together, to his room – her room in fact, with an en-suite bathroom in pale pink with gold taps, chosen from the brochure the size of a whole hod of bricks, all the way from Stockholm. 'Da-daaaaaa!' she announced, an expression she'd borrowed off Mo, the English girl in the hotel, and used regularly ever since.

But Andriusha made no reaction, except for walking over to the circular bed with its vast embroidered bedspread, dropping his shabby rucksack on the floor with a flump and lying down, his eyes already shut as though they had resented the strain of being open, his shoes on and his jacket hanging open around him, abdicating himself completely from the present, from consciousness, from life itself.

'Right . . . well . . . have a good sleep,' Katya whispered, shutting the door with a soft click.

'He's shattered,' she explained to Olga with a stretched smile that betrayed her.

'Yuh,' Olga sighed, opening *Cosmopolitan* which was on its

second ever Russian issue and used a whole vocabulary that the girls normally found hilarious but today looked flat and meaningless. 'He's fucked off his face. You going to meet this Pavel?'

'Might as well,' Katya admitted, picking up the phone. 'You can ride two horses with one arse.'

Olga laughed and got up to put her rubber gloves back on. 'It's you *can't* ride two horses with one arse,' she said.

'Oh. Well. I can try!' Katya smiled, her Moscow personality re-forming around her as though she'd been a boiled egg without a shell, and she dialled the number.

She arranged to meet Pavel Ivanchenko at the Amadeus Café in the Slavyanskaya. She parked in the lot by the old ruined Moscow house that the American chain had failed to get permission to pull down. It sat forlorn on a patch of grass, the panes of its windows smashed jagged, the plaster flaking off it like a hideous disease, its useless decrepitude exposed by the gleaming new western cars that pulled up around it to park in neat paying lines and by the fifteen-storey hotel that had shot up behind it, mossy reflecting glass hiding the creatures within and their revolting, dripping wealth that threatened to ooze out and engulf the whole city in a hedonistic swamp.

Katya said hi to Oleg, the 24-hour-a-day parking attendant. He had a gun in his blue holster and a gruesome scar across his throat. The Slavyanskaya sentry box was his home and he was grateful, took his job seriously, sent the pay back to his wife in Magadan. He directed Katya to the space behind the beige taxis, exclusive to the hotel, hard currency only and over a hundred times the price of a Moscow street cab.

'You take care of yourself, love,' he told Katya and she beamed at him so that the whole city seemed to warm up in imaginary spring sunshine.

'Will do, comrade,' she joked, pushing her shades back on to her head and gliding into the space.

Inside, past the security and the bleak marble reception area she could see just two other girls sitting at the Amadeus. Svyeta was alone, pushing an obscene slab of chocolate cake around her plate in her hungry-history-student-who-saved-up-enough-money-to-come-here-for-the-lovely-western-food-act, not that she'd ever dream of eating a bite. Dashenka, an old friend of Katya's, had scored and was giggling at the attempted joke of a neat Japanese man who swung a large black wallet from his wrist. Katya waved discreetly and was glad from the bottom of her Kirgask heart that she wasn't working the hotels any more.

And that, over there behind his copy of *Kommersant*, must be Mr Ivanchenko. She went straight over to him without hesitation.

Right, she thought. A fool doesn't keep his money for long. All the awkwardness of dealing with Andriusha, the rollercoaster of feelings and anxiety, had no place here. She was in work mode, protected by the empty eyes and neat smile of her professional life, ready to strike a deal and keep her side of it.

'Hello. I'm Katya, Andriusha Klyzhenko's friend,' she said, standing by his table, her weight on one spike-heeled foot, her car keys still jangling in her hand.

Ivanchenko lowered his newspaper and looked up, his eyes chips of bright blue Siberian ice. She knew him from somewhere. Perhaps the nightclub, but perhaps . . .

'And how is the most beautiful woman in the world today?' he asked, putting his newspaper on the table now and gesturing to Katya to sit down opposite him.

Katya laughed. 'I don't know. If I see her, I'll ask her,' she said, sitting down and beckoning to the waitress, who wore a frilly black and white French maid's uniform, a humiliating declaration of subservience, and who had always been apocalyptically rude to her. 'A glass of champagne, please.'

Ivanchenko, seizing control of the situation, wrested from him by Katya's joke and confidently lavish order, changed the order to a bottle of champagne and smiled, victorious in the dim light.

He drew in his breath as though he would need it all for the import of what he had to say. He fixed her in his gaze and said, 'Never turn down a compliment, Ekaterina.'

It annoyed her to know that he was right, that to flick back a person's attempt at friendliness was defensive and stupid. She smiled.

There were no windows to the outside world in here; nobody wading in black galoshes and felt valenki through the slush around Kievsky Station, hauling their huge bundles of belongings, grim-faced and stinking of despair, could see into this other world of cake and coffee and killing time. And nobody inside could glance out from their foaming cappuccinos and see the real, struggling, grinding, screaming world of poverty and desperation and want to weep.

'I've been thinking about you for years,' Ivanchenko said, leaning forwards. 'And then when I saw you at Titanic . . . well, I never go to nightclubs, but I had to meet someone discreetly, so . . .'

'It's a disgusting place. A friend of mine dances in one of the cages, so . . .'

'Poor girl,' he shook his head.

Katya shrugged. 'You do what you have to do.'

'Do you do what you have to do?' he wondered, pulling back slightly, less sure of himself now.

'I do what I want to do,' she said, smiling reassurance at him.

'Good.' he nodded. 'But your eyes . . . You aren't speaking to me with your eyes.'

Oh, please. Did he want to get laid, or what, she wondered. Or was he hoping to be her pimp? No thanks.

'That will take time,' she smiled.

Ivanchenko took the bottle from the waitress's hands and poured out the champagne himself, pushing a glass towards Katya across the sterile table. 'Listen,' he said, crossing his arms across his chest.

'Listening,' she replied, taking a sip of her drink and raising her eyebrows at Svyeta who was staring across at them.

'Listen. Don't treat me like some apparatchik you had to fuck to get yourself to Moscow, OK? I see where you came from and what you're doing. I came from there myself and I'm doing the same thing with my own God-given gifts, OK? You're from a country town where you left a boy who loves you. Your parents think you're modelling and you're sending Tampax back for your little sister and food for half the village. You probably don't work the hotels any more. You probably have a few boyfriends who keep you and a girl-friend in a nice flat with enough fur coats to be a pension for you both. You think I don't know this stuff? You think I didn't scrabble in the fucking dirt myself?'

Katya's mouth had fallen open and she was staring at Ivanchenko now as though he'd stripped himself naked and stood up, dangling his genitalia in front of the whole lobby.

'I haven't got a sister,' she said, pushing the words out like flies that had got into her mouth.

'I see you in there past your mask, country girl with your stork legs,' Ivanchenko said. 'But if you're going to show me some high-class hooker personality then I'm not interested.' And he got up out of his chair and walked away across the grey marble towards the smoky glass of the revolving doors, pulling some keys out of his pocket as he went.

Svyeta put her fork down. She was wearing a neat black wig with a long fringe.

'You've lost him. Shame. Looked rich,' she said, laughing in the expectation that Katya would come and share the champagne with her instead. It always looked better to be sitting with another girl.

'Not yet!' Katya muttered, leaping to her feet and running after the man as though he was Lenin himself. 'Not yet.'

Pavel Ivanchenko turned back and glanced over his shoulder.

'Today is the last day of an era past.'

Boris Yeltsin

Chapter Nine

Eli tried to psychoanalyse it, of course.

'You're projecting,' he said, passing her a joint he'd rolled for her, throwing his eyes up behind him to the poster of Lenin she'd bought for him from her favourite shop on the Charing Cross Road. She got the tube there every Saturday and spent all the money her dad sent her (though the accompanying letters and calls had long since evaporated) on books and tapes in Russian, anything to feed her addiction. She knew she was a junkie, though the polite word was Russophile.

'You're using a superpower as your superego. You're pretending the whole socio-economic edifice of the Soviet Union is your father and will protect you,' he explained, ignoring his mum's pleas from outside the bedroom door that just this once he might accompany them to *shul*.

'Tell him, Mo!' she cried.

'I do try, Mrs Z,' Mo shouted back. Eli would not unlock the door.

Eli continued. 'You are hoping to use a country – no, not a country, an idea, an ideal as container for your Bionian contained, your crushed hope, your attempts to reach out for a reverie you never had.' He took a big slurp of his hot Ribena. 'Ouch!' he hissed, burning his lip and slopping the boiling purple liquid down his 'Fight For Your Right To Party' T-shirt. 'I mean, you can't equate psychic flow with an autocracy.'

'Eli?' Mo breathed from deep in a corduroy bean bag the size of a hippo, eyes glazed, joint poised between thumb and forefinger.

'Da, darling?'

'Shut up.'

'Sure.'

She had, it was true, gone back to England after the school trip obsessed, addicted, possessed, any superlative would be appropriate. She plastered her room with posters of Stalin, Krushchev, Gorbachev without his birthmark (the only posters available), bought books way above the level she could understand just so that she could have shelves as full of Russia as her head was. She watched the news about summit meetings and short-, medium- and long-range nuclear missiles and she wrote letter after letter to her new friend behind the iron curtain, but Katya, now bizarrely built up into a strange peasant worker fantasy figure straddling a tractor in a red headscarf, never wrote back. Mo, newly inspired, with her life's direction as clear to her as black oil on a polar bear, worked her arse off at school and Eli said she was becoming nearly as square as he was. She was going to go to Moscow and be a . . . gymnast. No. Journalist. That's right.

And, in fact, when the time came, and the idle, slightly frightening blank time at the end of university finally arrived and Eli said, 'Sarita dumped me. Let's move to Moscow,' Mo was pretty much ready to go. 'Er . . . OK,' she agreed. 'How?'

'Oh, come on! We're twenty-one. World. Oyster. Pavements. Gold. "Oxford Graduates Make Good in Muscovy." What are you waiting for?'

Mo, who was at that particular instant waiting to be handed her Big Mac, fries and apple pie in the McDonald's on Victoria Street after getting her passport processed, shrugged in agreement.

'Poyekhali!' She smiled, popping one chip in. 'Let's go.'

* * *

There was a letter in Mo's clanging metal post box that day, at the bottom of the dirty stone steps that the man with one arm so uselessly swept.

She had never had a letter here before and only Frances actually had the address as far as she knew, though she may well not have known she had it, given the state of her half the time. Moscow was harder work than she'd expected, actually, remembering only that school trip and the night at the Ukraina when the Russian boy had kissed her and Dr 'Spencer' Hepburn had gone to bed with the prostitute. But now here she was living here, working in telly for Americans and listening to Eli's endless angst about girls who did, didn't or might fancy him. He had a proper job, of course. He was working for a law firm, the law somehow more proper than news in both their minds, perhaps for its less ephemeral quality, perhaps just because Eli was a bloke and what they do is supposed to be more proper.

'I mean, law is the foundation of society, of civilisation,' Eli said, putting six sugars in one small glass of tea. 'What? That's how they drink it here. Christ, it's like living with fucking Mengele.'

'Wasn't he the doctor who experimented on twins and stuff? How is my raising my eyebrows at your sugar intake anything like living with Mengele? If I was Mengele I'd have chopped your plums off by now and fried them up for some delicious pelmeni filling,' Mo pointed out. It was a conversation they had often.

They were both slightly hungover from staying up too late last night and drinking kiwi liqueur from the kiosk. '"British University Graduates Poisoned by Alcoholic Kiwi",' Eli said as they finished the bottle. This was the morning after.

'Hey!' He raised one finger at her and his glasses tipped down his nose slightly. He was in a huge electric-blue dressing gown his mum had sent him 'to keep warm', little knowing that Moscow flats are so overheated that it's keeping cool that's the problem. He was sweating brightly but refused to take it off. 'It's a slippery slope is all I'm saying. One minute you're getting a little bit over-authoritative about someone else's cup of tea, and the next you're rounding children up in the ghetto.'

'Oh, I see.' Mo nodded, going over to kiss the top of his head fondly. 'But surely if nobody reported the things that needed seeing to then nobody would even know what laws might want adopting. So, really, news is the foundation of society.'

'But news is just salacious gossip that can be manipulated.'

'Law can be manipulated. Do you even know anything about the Third Reich?' Mo sat down at the kitchen table, digging in for the argument.

'Know anything about the Third Reich, Momix?!' Eli was outraged. He straightened the lapel of his dressing gown. 'There is not a single book with flames and a swastika on the front written by some public schoolboy with fuck all better to do that I have not read, so there. And, more importantly, you know . . . fuck you.'

'Ah, yes. Stunning advocacy. You will be an amazing barrister. Hey, did Charlotte phone you?' she asked, remembering the latest thing, the office secretary with the redneck boyfriend who was keen as mustard on his right to bear arms.

'Yes, but I think she sees me as a friend. I fainted that time at the Bolshoi and she just feels sorry for me.'

'You didn't faint.'

'I nearly fainted.'

'You didn't.'

'Well, I felt very dizzy. Oh! Hey! That freak with no legs came up to say there's a letter for you "From Abroad".'

'No arm. Really? That's weird. I'll go down.'

The corner of it was poking out of the box and the woman from upstairs with all the cats was staring at the American stamps as though the letter box was stuffed full of dollars for the taking.

'Good morning, Praskovya Dimitrevna Kolbasova,' Mo said loudly. Nobody ever said anything loudly in this country unless they were on a rostrum or, worse, already holding a microphone, and she particularly liked greeting the cat lady in full because her surname meant salami.

'Good morning,' the cat lady mumbled, averting her gaze from the letter and scurrying out into the slush.

Back inside Eli had gone for a shower and to transform himself into mega-successful man in pin-striped suit and cufflinks and Mo sat down to read. It was already clear who this thing, an intercontinental ballistic envelope, was from and she had butterflies in her stomach and felt sick. It was the first time she had heard from her father in thirteen years. She tore open and unfolded the thin blue airmail paper.

Dear Mahogany (do people still call you Mo?),

I'm sorry it's been so long. I wanted to start a new life with no links to the old and that included Frankie. Not you, of course, but I thought it would be better for you if I didn't interfere any more. Please write and tell me what you are doing and who you have grown up to be.

I have just got married to Terri (see photo!) and our beautiful baby boy Zane (also in the pic) is now five months old. I thought you would like to know.

Love, Daddy (Dad? I don't know any more!)

PS. Sorry not to write more but after all this time I don't know what to say.

Address but no phone number. That's how much he wanted to hear from her. The letter had gone to London, posted three months earlier, before making it here – Frances had been in a dynamic mood, obviously. Mo put the letter and the photo down on the table and exhaled very deeply, realising that all those long evenings when she had waited for him to call, to call for her, all that time she'd told everyone at school and Frances herself that she was moving to America, all that time he had been doing something else, thinking about something else, not missing her at all, not really. It was a realisation that made her insides empty out in a flash like a vacuum, leaving nothing behind.

Eli came in naked rubbing his hair with a towel. 'Sorry. Don't be too turned on. I can't find my pants. What's the letter? Whoa!' he saw the photo. 'Trailer park city! Who's that?'

'Terri and Zane,' she said with withering contempt. 'It's my step-mother and stepbrother. My dad got married and had a baby. I am so devastated I might throw up,' she stated. She was doing the total-honesty-as-lie thing that she was good at.

'Yeah, don't blame you. And look at the state of her. Blonde as Eva Braun too.'

'Eva Braun wasn't blonde,' Mo pointed out, pleased to be back on familiar territory.

'Wasn't she?' Eli was crestfallen, and still naked.

'Actually, I'm not sure.' Mo laughed. 'But it doesn't matter because she was definitely a Nazi.'

'That's for definite,' Eli agreed and they both laughed.

'Anyway, can you please be responsible for making sure that I never mention, call, write to, forgive or . . . you know . . . give a single thought to my dad henceforward and as long we both shall live?'

'I will. Alleged dad.'

'*Very* good point.' She smiled. And she kept to it. Nearly. She had an audition for a band later and didn't want to be too messed up for it.

Mo went across to the Slavyanskaya, submerged herself in the hotel pool and let her fingertips graze the textured tiles at the bottom. Her right lung hurt when she swam, stabbing her with a pointed reminder that her life was polluted, especially since vile letter from bastard man. She winced and came to the surface, pushing her hair back off her face and gasping at the chlorine-dense air. It always knocked the edge off a hangover, to swim. Perhaps she osmosed some water into her parched body from the pool, or perhaps the vodka seeped out, bleached and sterilised by the chemical atmosphere. It cooled her burning eyes and made her feel at least not corpse-like alcoholic unhealthy.

After ten reluctant lengths Mo dragged herself out of the pool like someone who had been thrown in against her will wearing all her clothes. She felt heavy and lumbering, paddling up the tiled beach and out of the overheated water, too shallow to dive and too hot for strenuous exercise, looking at herself in the reflection of the mirrored windows that hid the outside world from view. She knew people in here thought she was a prostitute just because most of the pretty girls were, and she kept her eyes down to avoid any possibility of being approached. Membership of the hotel gym came with her honorary membership of Americanness through her job. The US was a nation, she thought, that liked to keep fit, liked to provide perks and keep its employees happy in return for their souls. This was fine by Mo, to whose soul they were more than welcome.

Mo looked at the actual prostitute showering next to her, at the strange Mohican of her pubic hair and her silver painted toe- and fingernails. She wondered if you always showered between clients and assumed you must do, but then what if you had a busy day and there wasn't time? She hated the idea of those men (all, presumably, married or wouldn't they go out on the pull in a more normal manner – or is the prohibition and power the thrill?) paying to be allowed to touch these girls, pretending to themselves even that the girls really were the fantasy they were projecting on to them: eager nymphomaniacs desperate to suck an old man's penis just for a taste of the West. And she hated the idea of the ensuing secrecy and lies back home in Pennsylvania over supper with the family. 'Fuck any prostitutes while you were away, darling?' 'Why, no, my love, not a one.' Why, she wondered, is *that* everyone's secret? The only secret – I did things with my genitalia that someone else wouldn't want me to have done. That is the secret. How boring and how distasteful. And she wondered, as she often did, what happened to that prostitute she'd met that time and whether she might be one of the girls in here, transformed by grooming into someone unrecognisable.

Mo shook the thought off and took her soft neat pile of clothes out of her rattling locker. Her theory was that if she could keep her clothes, her hair, the flat, the trappings of her life in some sort of order, then perhaps the chaos in her mind would follow. Clean clothes, clean life. Except it didn't seem to work like that.

She was going to be late now. She would have to run across the bridge and up the slope in front of the jagged Gothic horror of the Foreign Ministry where the slush seemed to collect in pools of grey slop with knobbly lumps of ice in them as if in protest at foreign policy or, perhaps, rather in support of it. She dashed through the hotel, her wet hair flailing behind her, past a tart in a strange black wig chatting up a Japanese guy at the Amadeus Café and out into the murky day which hung low over the city, pushing people's spirit out of them from above like a malign deity.

By contrast, Mo was always delighted to walk into an office where the lights were bright and always on, where the phones thought they were in New York and where television screens, shining constantly with perfect picture, showed bright-eyed people in glistening make-up punching the words in upbeat, off-beat casual American English.

118

They shipped the coffee in from Manhattan in air-locked slabs and they talked about themselves and each other as though it really mattered.

An old woman shouted at her on the way, 'You have to cover your head, dear! You'll catch a cold!' Personally, she quite liked head freeze and she walked into work steaming.

The office, installed in the gutted centre of an old Muscovite stately home's stable block, was open and whirring, buzzing and bouncing beams off satellites, twenty-four hours a day, and it made her instantly happy. It was important to her, even when she wasn't working nights herself, which she loved to do, to know that while she was curled up in her boringly perpetual ball of fear and dread, sweating into the thin sheets their grubby landlady had provided, the office was light and bright and someone was working, someone in new trainers who thought life would probably turn out just fine. 'Ciao,' she said to the room in general when she walked in.

The office manager looked up and smiled through his huge walrus moustache (obligatory, apparently, for ex-pat Poles), carrying on his phone conversation. One of the translators, both of them KGB, was whispering into her receiver in Russian, holding her hand up to further obscure what she was saying. She was forever on the phone to her son who was a ballet dancer and very neurotic, and the urgently spoken pep-talks he got always left the office phones covered in a smear of fuchsia lipstick.

'Hi, Tanya!' Mo shouted, and Tanya stretched her lips across her teeth almost as though she was smiling. She would prefer to have been addressed as Tatiana Dimitrevna, but the Americans would brook no formality.

Walrus finished his call and beckoned Mo over. 'Listen, New York wants a piece about the new rich Russians, the entrepreneurs who are collecting up the country's resources, you know? Those guys with the cars and the guns? Do you know anyone?'

Knowing people for the bright-toothed correspondent, Diane, to go and interview was Mo's job. She was bad at it, having basically fairly few Russian friends since she mostly sat around talking global anti-semitic conspiracy with Eli. But she pretended and it usually worked out, even if she had to accost people in the street and drag them into the office. 'This is Irina. She was a card-carrying Communist, but when her factory shut down she had to start up a small business selling jam from her dacha.' Exactly the sort of story the channel loved: encroaching capitalism as unavoidable human reality.

'Um, well, there's someone I could try, I guess,' she said, digging her nails into her palms. Because, in fact, Mo had a little secret. Well, not a secret exactly, since she'd shown the picture to Eli, but she had seen, she was sure, a big photo of Pavel, the boy she'd kissed, in *New Times*, a Russian magazine. He was supposed to have cunningly accrued half of Siberia's steel industry in the privatisation that was going on, and had become mega-rich. The story hinted at 'foul play' but Russian magazine articles always hint at foul play. And in her handbag, in her ragged address book that she had never changed, lost or thrown away, was Pavel's phone number, written in that handwriting they teach Russians at school, written using Dr Hepburn's green Biro. Of course, there was no way he still lived there, but . . . It would be quite a coup at work. It wasn't a Moscow number. Mo punched the keys.

'Da?' someone said on the other end.

She apologised for calling out of the blue, took a cup of coffee from the Russian door guy with a wink of thanks, and explained that she had been given this number by Pavel Ivanchenko many years ago and she wondered if by any chance . . .

'He lives in Moscow,' the man said. 'I can't give his number out.'

Mo took a sip of her coffee and began, at last, to feel the kiwi liqueur tang receding.

'I quite understand that. It's just that I am making a big television programme' – a lie, it would be a two-minute piece at the end of the nightly news at best – 'about Russians who are taking advantage of the new freedoms and actually being dynamic in the sense that . . .' She went on and on in this vein until the man, Gleb was his name, said to call him back in ten minutes.

Mo went into the producer's office for her morning flirt. 'Hi. Learned any new words in Russian today, Bob?' she said, shutting the door behind her.

Bob gave her a blinding grin and held up his coffee spoon triumphantly. 'Lozhka!' he said. 'Learned any more ass wiggles?'

'I will do you for sexual harassment,' Mo told him, sitting down at his desk as if to take notes, ostentatiously crossing her legs.

'Me? You will call me for harassment? Girl, you have been harassing me since you sashayed in here with that ass six months ago.'

Mo timed the ten minutes and called Gleb back. 'Hi, it's Mo from the Moscow bureau of—'

He interrupted her. 'Five one one two one zero four,' he said, and hung up.

Slightly breathless, Mo called the number straight away, simultaneously writing it down on a yellow post-it and sticking it on the base of a metal standard lamp. The office lights were too bright, the electronic whirring sometimes deafening.

'I'm listening,' Pavel said. 'Slushayu.' It was astonishing that she had reached him, that she was hearing his voice. It's not often you phone up foreigners you've randomly snogged, unless you are a character in a film trying to work out, for plot purposes, what it is about you that nobody likes. And it must be far less often that, upon attempting to contact aforementioned snogee, you actually succeed. She grinned to herself.

Mo did not mention that she had met him before, but simply

gave the pitch for the piece and asked for an interview. He could come into the office, she said, or they could do it at his apartment, which would be better since it would make him seem more . . . human?

Pavel agreed, six o'clock this evening. Mo put the phone down and went over to Walrus with her news.

'That's amazing, Mo! Ivanchenko? You know him personally?'

'Well, not really . . .'

Agreeing to meet Diane and the crew later at Ivanchenko's flat, Mo went to her audition feeling invincible.

She'd seen the advert up in the Metro station, tags with someone called Dima's phone number hanging pathetically off the bottom and the only one torn away had been taken by Mo, the first and only applicant. 'Band needs singer', it said, glued onto a dun tile, written by the band member who had the nicest writing and kept chickens on his twentieth-floor balcony. They probably hadn't expected a westerner in a short skirt with dark skin and big tits. But that was what they'd got.

Mo got the Metro out there to the audition at Prazhskaya, fifteen stops trundling into the outskirts like a desperate person, willing to travel even here to be in a band, here where people carried cardboard boxes of small scurrying animals and pulled frightening bundles that might be dead children along on makeshift trolleys. Fifteen years ago the hall they'd borrowed had held eight hundred people for a local Party meeting that ended in some kind of vote but nobody could remember about what. There was a stage at the front and black stage lights hung from the ceiling, but somehow they hung a bit too much and it was obvious they didn't work, dangling defunct, Mo thought, like a flaccid penis or old empty breasts, all over now, not needed.

She was nervous, having never sung in public before. These few shambolic, apparently drunk blokes stood around, one in cowboy boots, another holding a jar of beer, waiting for her to sing. The microphone was standing on the shiny wooden floor, the lead worming away across the room and under a swinging door marked 'Exit' where the power point must have been. A tiny amp and a speaker stood right next to it in the dim light, demonstrating very clearly the absolutely minuscule impact of technology on this bleak, cavernous world. Huge plastic ice cubes that might once have had bulbs in them covered the ceiling, but the men and Mo stood in the near dark of a pale twilight. There was a strong smell of urine. Mo couldn't imagine being able to fill the auditorium with her voice.

'Nu, davai,' Dima, the band's foreman, said encouragingly, shifting his weight from foot to foot and hearing his mother in his head telling him to keep still, may she rest in peace.

'You've changed,' Mo sang. 'That sparkle in your eyes is gone . . .' She shut her eyes and swayed, imagining Frankie and the sitting room at home, the crackle of the record player, black cigarette burns in the grey nylon carpet, cans of lager on top of the television and water pouring through the ceiling like a giant's tears.

It turned out that Mo had enough pain to fill the hall twice over. Dima was wiping his eyes on his shirt sleeves by the end.

'Practise these songs,' he said, handing her a cassette. 'First gig's on Friday, Arbat Theatre. Be there at six to rehearse.'

'Cool!' Mo grinned, her second big success of the day so far, the letter pushed into the mental abyss like everything else unwanted. A singer.

When she got back to the office the camera crew, four enormous Polish men, all with the crucial walrus moustaches and wives in Warsaw, were loading up the van with vast metal crates of equipment, customs cleared and labelled, state-of-the-art technology for capturing the idiosyncrasies of a foreign culture for the folks back home. Mo had once seen Diane, the correspondent, teaching a producer how to do a piece to camera. It was a big favour and

Brigitta, the protégée, born in Sweden but now an enthusiastic US citizen, had been absurdly grateful ('You can't imagine how much this means to me.'). Diane stood by the cameraman and adjusted Brigitta's stance, showing her how to turn very slightly sideways and then bring her head back to centre so that she didn't look fat, and putting her hands in her pockets so that she could bring them out in a gesture of emphasis at the key moment. And then she hit her with the advice: 'Think of the dumbest person you know, look into the camera as if you're looking them right in the eye and then explain to them, using as few words as possible, what is going on here in terms they will understand.' It explained a lot, Mo thought, about television news.

'Hey, Mo,' Tomek the Polish sound man shouted, spitting his cigarette on to the pavement. Most people didn't understand names for women that didn't end in an 'a'. It confused them and they said Mo with a hard 'o' like in lock. 'You translating on this steel guy?'

'Absolutely. I set it up,' she confirmed, stepping from kerb to gutter and back again to keep warm. 'Hey. I just got into a band.'

'Brava. Can we come to the concert?' Tomek asked, lifting a vast metal crate off the pavement. The armed security guard flicked his gaze up and down the street.

'You have to.'

Normally Mo answered the phones for twelve hours at a stretch, transferring incoming ones to people who were sitting less than three metres away from her or, if they happened to be getting coffee or going to the loo, they might need paging on the office's brutal loud-speaker system that shouted commands as if to bedraggled and confused prisoners who expected to be shot for the slightest mis-demeanour. When she was on the night shift she would take earnest messages, writing neatly on notelets designed for the purpose that offered helpful courier-fonted prompts – *time of message*, *message from*, *message to*, *content of message* – just in case. Not today. This was her story and she couldn't wait to see Pavel, hardly believing, even though she'd seen the photo, that it was really the same guy. Would he remember her? Would he remember that she'd fallen over? Oh God.

'Let's go,' she said, getting into the back of the van and putting her seatbelt on. This always made the Poles laugh. They found it endearing that she laboured under the impression that having a seat-belt on might save her when Voitek ploughed the van into six lanes of oncoming traffic on Leningradskoye Shosse. She didn't know how to explain to them it wasn't naïvety about life's risks that made her do it, but rather that it was about as close as she was able to get to holding someone's hand. If she had said it they would have laughed even louder, assuming, as everyone always did, that she was joking.

Diane came running out of the sparkling bureau, the invisible (but nonetheless authentic for that) Stars and Stripes waving proudly over the doorway. Pulling on her slim beige coat and drag-ging her handbag through the air after her like an unruly dog on an insufficiently strong lead, she leaped in beside Mo. 'Hey there,' she said. 'Howareyou?'

It went without saying that she didn't want to know. In fact, she didn't even require an answer. Her lipstick today was mid-brown and matched her nail varnish.

'Does anyone know where the fuck we're going?' she asked, smoothing her hair and laughing. Voitek claimed he did and they lurched off into Moscow to find 'the steel guy', leaving a dry rectan-gular patch of road behind them and a trail of billowing white exhaust fumes.

As they passed Dyetsky Mir – Children's World – up by the Lubyanka, Diane turned her head to face Mo, showing her thick make-up and the fine sad lines it was intended to cover in dis-concerting close-up, and said, 'What's Russian for vagina?'

Mo was very taken aback. 'Vlagalishche,' she said. 'But . . .'

Diane laughed. 'You know, that kind of sounds like one,' she said, pulling back her sticky lips and rubbing her teeth with her finger.

'But that's very medical . . . I mean, it's not an insult . . .' Mo tried to explain.

'What? You wouldn't say: Get out of here, you vlagalina?'

'Vlagalishche. No.'

'So what's the insult?' Diane asked, not interested any more, perhaps not interested in the first place. They carried on up Sretenka, past the blue and white water-and-war-stained palace on the right and back out towards Prospect Mira, throwing up tides of slush on either side. There was a man selling pears out of a turned-up box by the Metro.

'Pizdyets,' Mo announced. 'It's masculine. The word is pizda. Then pizdyets is like "oh fuck" and I suppose for a person it might be . . . I don't know . . . pizduik?'

All four Poles were practically crying with laughter by now, their private buzz of incomprehensible conversation halted at Diane's first question. Russian and Polish were similar enough, though they were too proud to admit it, to cause extreme hilarity when a foreigner attempted to pronounce their most nerve-shatteringly unacceptable obscenity.

Voitek, still laughing, drove up on the kerb and started hauling the equipment out of the back while Diane and Mo approached the grim old apartment building and walked into the overheated and humid dark, up the first wide flight of steps around the broken cage-like lift that ran up the centre of the building. The letter boxes hung open on their hinges; the caretaker, a moon-faced man who didn't speak to them, watched them go, broom in hand as though he had been standing there since Beria was shot, and the smell in the air reminded Mo of the early seventies: sour and thick, uncleared rubbish and people who still only bathed once a week. She had cobweb-tangly dreams where the light was like this – just light enough to see the shapes of things but too dark to find your way.

'He just bought basically all the steel in the world,' Diane told her on the way up the stairs, assuming she knew nothing about Ivanchenko, unaware that he was her contact. 'Young guy. Really obscenely grossly young. Got everyone to sell him their vouchers. Probably had to torture them out of half of them. But he's going to be a gazillionaire. Pucker up.'

Diane seemed to assume that everyone in the world was looking for a rich man to marry. Perhaps, Mo thought, everyone should be. It was probably naïve to imagine these things weren't crucial.

Mo was wearing, for it seemed important in retrospect, a tailored peacock-blue coat with huge buttons and shoulder pads, a striped woolly hat with her curls boinging out the sides (as Eli liked to put it), tall black patent-leather boots with grey astrakhan fur round the top and big metal Cyrillic letters down the sides. Pavel, who opened the door himself, was wearing a pale pink Ralph Lauren shirt, jeans, a black belt and brown leather slippers, the kind that dogs hold in their mouths in adverts.

'Dobro pozhalovat.' He smiled, sending out a shaft of light to fall at their feet as though the sun shone out of his flat. 'Welcome.'

The lady across the hall leaned her head out of her own grandiose doorway into the thick dark. 'I'll report you for having foreign visitors!' she shouted at the steel guy.

The steel guy laughed. 'Good morning to you too, Mrs Abramova,' he said and she slammed the door, sending a pocket of rancid litter-tray air out of her world and into theirs.

The steel guy raised his eyebrows and stood back to welcome them in. Mo had seen a lot of Russians do this, side with foreigners, one westerner to another, accepting with good humour the bizarre habits of the inscrutable natives type of thing.

'Pavel Ivanchenko,' he said, shaking Mo's hand, obviously not recognising her and mistaking her for the correspondent; after all, she was the most telegenic of the two women standing in the hallway of his Moscow home and, in Russia, you couldn't be too young. It was only as Tomek was setting up the lights for the interview, plugging cables into sockets above the glossy skirting board, that Mo noticed the gun-toting thugs with their backs against the wall. And perhaps it was the lurch of fear, the sudden sobriety that came with the sight of big guns ready to be fired, that made her remember something. She looked at Pavel's hands, clasped together, expectant, waiting for the interview to begin, and she felt one of them touch her forehead, thought she remembered him stroking her forehead as she went to sleep, like a guardian angel. Or, more obviously, a kind father, entirely unlike the bastard one she had heard from this morning. She coughed and pulled herself together, standing slightly behind Diane who was making small talk.

'Great place,' Diane barked, glancing around without taking it in. It was an old kommunalka, converted into one vast flat with huge leather sofas, very varnished floors, heavy new chandeliers and a glass table.

Pavel looked at Mo. 'I love your hat,' he said. 'Was it you who called me?'

'Yes. I did. Thanks. I love this hat. It's the only thing that ever controls my hair.' She smiled and, as she smiled, she could see that he recognised her.

'Take it off,' he said, holding out his arm in command.

Mo pulled it off and shook her hair, laughing, showing that she too knew it was him.

'I'm really embarrassed I fell over,' she said, truth as lie.

Diane spun round angrily. She did not like having her thunder stolen, or lightning, or whatever it was that people steal off you in American self-help books.

Pavel smiled as if he'd been in prison for twenty years and was now out, staring up at the blue sky. Or, at least, that's how it seemed to Mo. 'Yes! You did! Well, a young girl shouldn't drink like that. It's good to see you. You never sold me your camera,' he remembered, scowling, a deep scar above his eye not falling into the expression.

Nobody really looks like this, Mo thought, like one of those propaganda posters Mayakovsky used to paint: chiselled Soviet youth, azure-eyed, sharp-jawed warriors equally at home picking potatoes or bayoneting capitalists. But Pavel did look like that.

'You never came the next day,' she said, the Poles by now all boggly-eyed in amazement. 'I know him,' she told them. 'We met in a hotel years ago on a school trip. He wanted my camera.'

'I'll bet he did,' Diane snorted, getting her hairbrush out and dragging it angrily through her perm.

Pavel sat down in a leather armchair and looked deep in thought. 'Hey! I will tell you why! I got arrested that night. I got arrested leaving the hotel. It cost me a hundred roubles – which was a lot in those days – to get out. I had to go home to Siberia for a long time.'

Mo laughed.

'Which is where you bought all the steel,' Diane butted in, ready to begin.

'Not quite all.' Pavel laughed. 'Not yet. I love your shoes,' he told her and Diane looked down at them, surprised.

Mo had forgotten Pavel's American English, which had improved vastly, and she was entirely superfluous at the interview, watching as Tomek unfurled the gold reflector upon which Diane insisted (it made her look younger, pinkifying the light), listening as Pavel explained how important steel was to Russia's economy and how Yeltsin's enormous wisdom had enabled him, and others like him, with the will to succeed . . . blah blah blah . . .

He talked about how he had always been a capitalist, trading vodka and hard currency on the street as a schoolboy when the others were in their Soviet propaganda lessons. He made it sound pioneering, romantic, snow-swept, his rise from Oliver Twistish beginnings to the flash brutality of Moscow.

'And is there a special someone with whom you'll be sharing your new-found riches?' Diane asked him at the end with a glutinous smile.

'Well, not yet, but I met someone today with whom I could certainly share something,' he said, looking straight at Mo so that she blushed deeply like she used to do at school.

Afterwards, Diane used his phone to call the bureau and the Poles packed up, chivalrously helped by the armed thugs who had obviously decided that there would be no bullets flying in the next ten minutes at least.

Pavel made his way over across the shining parquet to Mo and stood in front of her, staring so openly that she couldn't look up at him.

'Look at me,' he said. 'Please.'

When she did they both started laughing again. He reached out and tucked a curl behind her ear. 'I want to see you again.'

'I'm singing in a band on Friday at the Arbat Theatre,' she told him. 'Come if you like. It starts at nine. It will be rubbish. We're not even rehearsing. I just have to learn these songs off a tape. I mean, I've never even sung in public before and they've put an advert in the *Moscow Times* so it could be extremely embarrassing. I mean, obviously if you're busy . . .'

Pavel interrupted her by putting his hand over her mouth in a way that made her knees buckle. 'I'll be there,' he said, turning her round with his strong hands on her shoulders and pushing her out of the door after her colleagues.

* * *

Eli wasn't impressed.

'The bloke from the hotel back when Duran Duran were cool? Who gave us the papirosi and took half my Dunhill?'

'Duran Duran were never cool. But, yes, you know. I showed you that thing in *New Times*. He's completely minted now, has all these bodyguards and stuff,' she explained, getting a packet of biscuits out of the cupboard. 'You've eaten nearly all the biscuits,' she said.

'The key thing here is the nearly. Eat the remaining biscuits and rejoice.'

'OK. Anyway, he's coming on Friday to this gig.'

'What gig?'

'My new band. Do you ever listen to a single word I say? The blokes out at Prazhskaya. We're playing in some theatre on Friday.'

'I can't. It's the Sabbath.'

'No, it isn't.'

'It is nearly the Sabbath.'

'This has never arisen before.'

'Fine, I'll come, but if I get struck down . . .'

'I'll strike you down if you don't shut up.'

While they were doing the sound check that nerve-racking Friday Mo went to the theatre's small office on the first floor and called Eli on the avocado-green plastic phone on the manager's desk. A small portrait of Lenin still hung on the wall as though forgotten there, not significant enough to take down or replace, just a picture of someone you'd hardly notice any more, gathering dust, dimming, yellowing round the edges. The manager, a long-haired bloke who did performance art and was from Belarus, gave her a beer (not the real manager, not the person who'd hung the picture, of course, but the person who had broken down the doors to squat the beautiful art-nouveau theatre with the swirling curved metalwork and carved wooden stage front now that the KGB probably didn't care any more and nobody could afford to go to the theatre anyway). The first drink of the evening, for she started drinking even before she painted her mouth bright red and her eyes black, before she pulled on her sequinned mini-skirt and perched the bowler hat Eli bought her flirtatiously on her head, fag in mouth, hopping around on the scabrously peeling grey lino backstage on one fishnet-stockinged foot looking for an errant shoe while Andrei plucked at his bass.

'Eli, you are coming aren't you?' she whined slightly. 'Not that you need to. I may not go on.' When she needed reassurance it was to Eli she turned.

She put her cigarette out in the manager's ashtray and he offered her another one, but she didn't think she could stomach it. They were doing ten songs, all blues standards that she could sing pretty easily in front of the bathroom mirror, even when Eli was shouting at her to shut up, rounding off with 'You've Changed', her audition song.

'You will go on, Momix, and you know I'm coming. I'm bringing half the bloody office.'

'OK, just checking.'

She was drunk by the time they did indeed go on, not quite drunk enough not to be nervous, a lot of people in the audience, from her work, from Eli's work, Eli himself, his glasses glinting reassuringly in the gloom, all very smoky and dark, the crowds seething in front of her, faces blurring into each other, arms reaching out at the stage. She saw Tomek, the cameraman, kissing Diane, his moustache wet with beer foam. Diane nearly toppled over with the force of him, his bulky Timberlands, rough jeans and soft lumberjack shirt. Mo, her mind whirring even as she sang into the breath-wet microphone, felt sorry for his wife in Warsaw. She knew nothing about her except that her name was Pavla and she imagined a straw-blonde, strawberry-cheeked woman with a soft bosom and embroidered skirts, stirring honey vodka in an earthenware pot and producing sweet dumplings from a hot oven for a bevy of plump children. This was in contrast to Diane, a brittle spindly thing with sharp edges, a loud voice and a solid fan-base back home. It wasn't that she disapproved of infidelity in any moral sense, but it always made her sad, something she would have to deal with later though she couldn't know that now. After all, she was still young.

She was partially blinded by the flashing colours of the stage lights and sometimes a pale hand would put a shot of vodka by the front of the stage, or a bottle of beer, and suddenly her set was over, her throat sore from singing in the stinging clouds of smoke and her head pounding with the beat of Volodya's drums. Pavel didn't show up.

Afterwards, when Eli had left crawling after the big-bottomed Charlotte (rumoured in the office to have such powerful orgasms that towels were needed to mop up her come. How they knew this Eli had no idea, but it excited him. A lot.) Mo set off to walk home, wanting to sober up in the cold night, to have the wind slap against her face and tighten the skin on her scalp, to deal with the disappointment. She watched the piece they'd made of the interview, less than seventy seconds of an hour's interview, and somehow, on TV, Pavel looked like any other boring young entrepreneur with money on the brain. Mo knew there was more to him than that though, something powerful and damaged.

The back streets she walked through were empty, the snow banked up at the sides, frozen solid, a few cars glooming by the pavements, most people's bedroom lights extinguished now in all the old flats with crumbling balconies that made it possible to imagine a past of impassioned piano playing and austere lace tablecloths. But, out of nowhere, a BMW swung round a corner. A boy leaned out with a gun, shouting, music blaring, and she froze, terrified, as the car screeched at her, mounting the pavement. She knew what she was supposed to do. Sit down and kick, then they couldn't get you in. The boy jumped out of the swinging door laughing and jeering at her; she was already on the ground, kicking out, her hand on her rape alarm – as if it would do any good. He pointed his gun at her, not seriously, but he was drunk and her heart was pounding, throat closing. She shut her eyes but nothing happened. The music was still playing loudly and the driver was leaning over shouting at his friend, suddenly sounding frightened and urgent. She opened her eyes again, feeling her fingers pushing through her gloves into the ice on the pavement, and saw that the boy was being held round the neck by someone else, a gun to his temple; his face was screwed up and his legs had collapsed so that he was held up by the choking arm. By Pavel.

'Get in the car and fuck off,' he told him, calmly.

'OK,' the boy agreed, climbing back in, childishly, flailing, the car squealing off into the night.

Mo couldn't fish any words out of the densely weeded, tangled swamp in her mind as she sat there, gasping with terror, her coat and gloves wet, her mind sinking and soaring in a nauseating fashion.

'Sorry I was late,' Pavel said, putting the small black revolver in his pocket and turning towards his car, a Mercedes limousine that was parked discreetly on the corner, two bodyguards standing by it, both still aiming their weapons over to where the botched attack on Mo had taken place. Pavel turned to them. 'OK, guys,' he said, reassuring them that it was safe, though Mo was sure that was supposed to be their job.

'I fell over again,' Mo said at last, smiling at Pavel.

He reached out and hauled her up to standing so that she fell into his arms. 'Yes. I am used to it now.'

She looked up into his face. 'Only twice in a decade, actually,' she argued, though she was in no position.

'I'll take you home,' he said. 'And then, tomorrow night, I'll take you out for dinner.'

'OK.' Mo nodded, as obedient as the gun-toting boy, wondering how it was that his offers had always sounded a bit like orders.

And in the car he held her very close, putting his hands round her ribcage inside her coat, and he kissed her in a way that was strangely shocking.

'Blessed are the peacemakers, for they shall inherit the earth.'

Bill Clinton

Chapter Ten

P avel woke up and told himself he was lucky. True, he was
lying on the floor at the bottom of a back staircase at the
Ukraina Hotel with a broken finger, a swollen head, bruised
ribs and blood dried on to every bit of his body he could currently
locate, but he was alive, he was inside (unlike a lot of people they
beat up in here, turfed out afterwards to die of exposure overnight,
dug out of the snow in spring – podsnezhniki, snowdrops) and he
hadn't been taken to the cells.

And not only that, but he'd kissed the glossy girl whose mouth
tasted of strawberries and who came from another planet where
people don't wipe their father's brains up off the floor when they
are seven years old, where mothers don't leap from ten-storey
windows and brothers don't tell people who want to kill you where
you've gone.

They came up to him, a pair of them, KGB, and whispered in
his ear, walked him slowly to the back stairs and down into the
hotel cellars. One of them jumped up and down on his head so
that his face was pulped to this strange doughy consistency, his
eye socket ripped, and the other kicked him in the genitals over
and over again. He paid them, he remembered, trying now to get
to his feet as a hotel waitress walked past him (ignoring him as she
knew she must), a hundred roubles not to kill him. Finally, after
a couple of attempts, he felt conscious enough to haul himself up,

immediately nauseated, and stagger out into the street where everyone took him for a drunk, gave him a wide berth and a look of revulsion. He got the Metro back to the friend's place where he was staying, a friend he was in business with, dealing currency, making a killing. He climbed the stairs with difficulty, feeling his way in the dark, fumbling for his key with messed-up hands, one finger hanging loose. But his friend was gone, the apartment ransacked, everything stolen.

He remembered, looking round at the chaotic shreds of his first Moscow life, that he'd held the girl's hair back while she threw up. He didn't know why, what had softened him. Really, he'd gone to meet Andriusha's prostitute, to offer her a deal. He meant to take her on as well, move her into a little apartment, but he knew when he saw her that he wasn't ready. You had to be tough, yes. But you had to be ready, and he would be.

At that point he was ready to lie low in Tomsk for a while, let the 'arrest' blow over. It turned out to be the best thing he could have done. He saw the opportunity and he took it, building up a business so successful even his mum would be proud of him. Well, maybe that was a stretch too far.

You see, when the time came, he knew the Party bosses already because he'd bribed them, man after man, to leave his vodka business alone, a business that in less than a year involved kiosks along every street in Tomsk and all the towns around, including Kirgask. He paid for the cheap corrugated-iron construction, he had boys to protect his kiosks from rivals (the kiosks all painted bright yellow with his dad's nickname for him, 'Pavlik', daubed on the front) and he got the boys' wages paid by sending them out 'offering' protection to other vendors. He wasn't a gangster, even if that's what his mother shouted from her rotting sofa, what his brother whispered in the dusty halls of the Tomsk conservatoire where they had their minds on higher things. He was providing a fucking service.

Obviously, anyone who didn't want the protection got their business torched, but business, after all, was business, and Pavel was soon past getting his own hands dirty. The vodka was delivered on time and went out to the kiosks on time and if there was a problem the boys went round and sorted it out. It wasn't complicated.

And then, falling into his lap like a whore for hard currency, there was the steel. He, Pavel Ivanchenko, who everyone said would come to nothing, he was the first person in town they came to when the privatisation vouchers were issued. They came to him because they knew he had the money, or could get the money. The morons on the steel company board, apparatchiks their whole lives, thought they could get rich quick, and they did, but they couldn't see the bigger picture.

Maybe a year, maybe two after his flight from Moscow, once his own business was up and running and the competition (such as it was) crushed, he went to a meeting at the company's headquarters, in a kind of makeshift trailer on the vast expanse of a half-defunct steel plant where the fat pigs sat at desks and ran the business into the ground without a care in the world, Soviet to the last. One of them had a plastic ivy plant on his desk, the tendrils brushing the dirty lino on the floor, and Pavel fought the urge to ram it down the guy's fucking Communist throat. They got a bottle of Georgian cognac out of the cupboard and had a fat woman in tight clothes bring in glasses on a tray with a doily on it, like that made them civilised, wooing him like a virgin Komsomol leader.

The workers, they explained to him as if he were a goat in a meadow, had got shares, privatisation vouchers now, and they laughed, laughed because the workers didn't deserve anything, deserved to eat shit for being what they were – everybody's equal except us. These people, the workers, people like Pavel's father, people like everyone, were desperate, slaving their lives away in grinding jobs for which they now hadn't been paid for a year. And, of course, they sold their sparkling new capitalist vouchers for virtually nothing to the factory bosses who were now, they told him, their puffy faces flushing with excitement, willing to sell them on to him, to Pavel. He could see by the bloating behind their eyeballs that they'd all be dead within a decade.

'All the vouchers?' Pavel asked, reaching out for a boiled sweet in a wrapper from the ornate dish.

'All of them.'

'How much?'

'A million dollars, US.'

'A million dollars?'

They laughed, knowing they were being audacious, that they couldn't get this lucky. He imagined them rolling around like elephant seals in a tart-infested sauna, red and sweating their good fortune away. A couple of hundred thousand dollars would keep them swimming in cognac for as long as they would last, cognac and girls, unimaginable money. But Pavel imagined more.

'Done,' Pavel told them, swigging the cognac down and getting up to leave.

'Cash,' one of them shouted after him.

'Give me a month,' Pavel confirmed.

In fact it had taken less than two weeks. He must have driven forty thousand miles along desolate grey roads where other cars were a big event, where he bought fuel in metal tanks from the real old country guys who kept a few in their old Ladas because the nearest petrol station was five hundred miles away. He ate meat from the roadside barbecues, never sure what meat exactly it was, and the lonely gypsy salesmen were hardly going to tell him, squirting cheap imitation ketchup all over the charred carcass and slapping a slice of black bread on to the paper plate. Fine by him. He didn't sleep, taking the speed pills he bought in brown glass bottles from the chemist, army issue and slipped under the counter for hard currency, and smoking feverishly. He knew he could do it because he knew his sales pitch. It was easy. 'We will all be very rich.' He had been in business practically since he was born and he knew how to do it: manage it well, have a tight loyal team and treat them like gods, always making it clear that everything you give can quickly be taken away again. He wasn't running a fucking co-op. Every bandit he knew from the Arctic Circle down chipped in. He sat in cellars doing shots with cauliflower-headed maniacs, born in places where the sun never rises, where there is ice on the ground in July, born to fight, all of them with prison tattoos on their ham hands and across their backs, all of them in thin leather jackets with gold chains round their fat necks. A hundred and fifty of them signed up in all, men with businesses importing cigarettes and liquor, cars, new and second-hand, property even (buying and selling flats the government technically owned by getting the old and dying to sign over the property to them in name in return for sustenance that rarely came); he promised a share in the profits equal to their contribution, a deal that he explained would make them multi-million-aires, in dollars, all of them, something that the factory bosses seemed not to have grasped. He was good at it, giving the storyteller in him some air space, describing the beaches in the Caribbean with white sand and azure seas, the girls who would be fighting to suck their dicks, the yachts . . . But he would keep a controlling share, he made that clear, he didn't lie. At first he planned to buy them out one by one, honestly, when the money started rolling in as it surely would when TomStal was working at full capacity, supplying steel to the ship-building industry around the world, to the military industrial complex, to . . . Well, in short, the sky was the limit.

Maybe he would have bought them out. Maybe he would. But when a bunch of thugs with hardly human faces tried to kill him on his own patch, right on the streets of Kirgask, his own dicksplash of a brother telling them right where to find him, probably pissing himself with fear, well . . . That was that. And he didn't harm anyone. Not personally. It was a gradual process, accidents happen, nothing was ever written down and there was nobody to miss the Arctic underclass of violent criminals who'd been destroying the fabric of society from the inside out . . . after all. When it's all mine, he told himself, I'll move back to Moscow and they won't be able to touch me.

Pavel Ivanchenko woke up and told himself he was lucky. This morning it was truer than ever. He was in a broad bed the size of his grandmother's whole dacha, under a feather-filled blanket from Sweden and it was a bright Moscow day with a laquered blue sky. He was twenty-four years old. He pushed his feet into his leather slippers and pulled the duvet round him, padding over to the phone in the living room where his tea would be waiting. He thought about the girl from yesterday lunchtime. The girl he'd waited so many years to meet. She chased him out of the hotel, her hair flying, her cheeks pink and eyes lively, and he knew he had her, knew she could see what he needed just as he could see what she needed. He tried not to let it happen but he couldn't help it. He tried hard not to let the chink of hope open up in him like a wound, the hope that he might be able to lie down with a woman and shut his eyes in safety, her cool fingers on his face. Not the bitches and cunts he had in here most nights, cheap little sluts gasping for a faceful of come and a purse full of cash. Not them. Someone who knew about the grey expanse of landscape and the sharp black trees, the endless sorrow of out there, out there where old men fall bleeding into the ice clutching a handful of coins, where women drink vodka and let their children starve, where fathers sell their mongoloid daughters for drink. Someone like Katya.

He thought now as he did often of the mongol girl, of Liuba, though he couldn't bring himself to visit her. He'd sent Andriusha round to deal with the father, one shot right between the eyes, and had him take the girl to the same sanatorium as his mother, up in the mountains. He pumped money into it: indoor swimming pool, Turkish baths, doctors and nurses, great restaurant. A manicurist for his mum, all the treatments. He slapped his name on it and got the manager from a good hotel here in Moscow to go and run it, but he never went there. Never read the letter Liuba wrote him — or perhaps a nurse wrote it for her, who knew? — chucked it straight in the stove where it belonged. Gratitude made him want to vomit, not that there was any danger of his mother offering any, God rot her. But now, maybe he would take Katya there, maybe she would light up Liuba's sad face with her golden smile? Maybe he should shut the fuck up and not even let himself think like that?

He drank his tea, enjoying the burn to the inside of his mouth and throat. He liked it hot, wincing with the sensation that bordered on pain. But Pavel knew pain and this wasn't it. It was six fifteen and he called across time zones to check in at the office, to get the figures, to reassure himself that his Cayman Island bank account was continuing to bulge at the coffers. Then he called Andriusha, the cretin he'd called urgently to Moscow. The cretin who would need to be taken in hand. The cretin who had, it was true, introduced him at last to Katya. Part of Pavel didn't want to lose him but he wasn't worth anything in the state he was in, that bruised-eyed look of an alcoholic, an addict, probably drowning in remorse. The ones who do the dirty work often get like that. He'd been great to start with: charming, clever, skinny, no obvious threat to anyone, and he'd seemed to enjoy the power of life and death over Pavel's rivals, the street scum who dared to try it on. Now Pavel wasn't sure what to do with him.

He was, however, sure what to do with Katya.

He glanced back at the girl still lying curled up in his bed. He sent the boys in to the Hotel National late last night, this morning perhaps, after he dropped Mo home, just a kiss. Leave them wanting more. The boys knew what his type was: clean and under eighteen.

'Wake up,' he told her, though he suspected she was already awake, waiting to see if there was more work, more money to be made. He never fell into this trap. They always tried to charge for another night if you did it again in the morning and, in any case, he'd had her by then and wasn't interested. 'Your money's on the table in the hall. The boys will see you out.'

Today was going to be a good day. Last night his face had beamed on to television screens across America, an example of Russia's new capitalist freedom, a lesson in how things should be done, a real rags-to-riches story of a poor Communist boy with nothing who, by sheer hard work and determination, had become perhaps one of the richest men in the former USSR. He knew how it sounded and he smiled to himself, thinking that they could never know, these westerners, what it was really like. It would scare the shit out of them.

He smiled to himself again when he opened his wardrobe, loved the smell of the dry cleaner's and the bunches of lavender that Varvara hooked on to the hangers. When he was dressed he splashed his face with cold water, ran his wet hands through his hair and pulled on his black cashmere coat, silk-lined, sent from Jermyn Street. Boris was slumped on the floor against the door and Pavel felt a flash of fear like ice in his stomach that Boris was dead and that a bandit lurked on the stairs, but the beast burped, farted and stumbled his way into life, shoving his pistol into his belt, checking the knife in his boot and smoothing his jacket. Pavel regretted not using Boris instead of Andriusha all this time. Andriusha had been acting a part for him, he knew, was sensitive underneath it like a girl. That made him good, above suspicion, safe. But Boris was a proper bull-bandit, a moron, a sportsman. Boris who had once, could you believe it, employed him, Boris the arm-breaker, Boris who had taken him to

Liuba in the first place. It was a long time ago and now Boris was the most grovellingly loyal servant he had.

'Let's go, Boris,' he told him. 'A woman is waiting.'

'No good last night? We picked the best one ...' Boris whined, following him downstairs, worried he had displeased his boss.

'She was fine. Thank you, Boris. No, not that kind of woman.'

He meant it. He knew she was a hooker, for Christ's sake, but what woman wasn't when it came down to it? This one had fire in her eyes and he wanted that fire for himself.

The English girl might have to wait. She was fantasy, escape and everything he knew wasn't real. Katya might even perhaps be the answer for his scarred and tattered soul.

He stared out of the window at Moscow as they drove, despising the poor struggling people with their shopping bags and bowed heads, wondering what he should bring. She had a cupboard full of furs from men who thought they were romantic, that he could be sure of. Jewellery? Either of these things would have done for Mo, he knew, a girl who had probably never been treated properly by a man. But Katya, Katya had an apartment stuffed with expensive gifts she didn't give a shit about. And suddenly he knew.

'Stoi!' He ordered the driver to stop the car and turn it around. 'Ptichii Rynok,' he commanded, and the Mercedes swirled round in the slush drawing pathetic honks from the lesser vehicles sliding about the road, and accelerated hard the other way. When they got there he refused to allow Boris to get out of the car with him. This was his gift and he wanted to choose properly, without distraction. Nobody, he was sure, would try and wipe him out here. And who, after all, was left to try?

Along the kerb were the old people who had been edged off the main drag by the hungry young, women with boxes full of new-born chicks, yellow, fluffy and peeping, a tramp with a whole litter of kittens clinging mewling to his coat, a lady in furs with a parrot in a cage, probably the last thing she had to sell before her coat and hat. Pavel edged through into the main area of the market, almost smelling his way to the dogs. Adult dogs, well trained and sold as guard dogs or hunting dogs, sat obediently by their owners exhibiting their skills of stillness and biddability. These weren't for him. Then the cages of puppies, some sedated, some scrambling about yapping, some lying exhausted in their own shit.

The black one, sitting fine and alert but composed in the corner of its cage, alone but not afraid, caught his eye. He pointed at it and a woman with a whole row of steel teeth rushed forwards.

'Yes, sir, a fine dog this, sir, pure Labrador, sir, a gun dog he could be, sir, but they were originally bred in Labrador to catch fish, sir. He'll be a right little prince for you, fine sir,' she said, babbling, twittering, desperate to make the sale.

'How much?' he asked as she reached into the cage for the puppy, putting him in Pavel's arms as though now he would never be able to resist. He felt the warmth and strength of the tiny animal as it pushed its black nose up to his face, licking his cheek with a bright pink tongue.

'Fifty roubles for you sir. Just fifty.'

'Thirty,' he said. He couldn't help it. Fifty roubles was a paltry amount: the average monthly wage for those still getting paid at all, but only amounting to about ten dollars at the current rate.

'Forty,' she said, her lips pursing. 'He's a fine dog, sir. A purebred.'

He handed her thirty-five roubles from his coat pocket and walked away with the puppy nuzzling under his coat.

'My momma always said, "life was like a box of chocolates . . .
you never know what you're gonna get."'

Forrest Gump

Chapter Eleven

Going out with Pavel wasn't like going out with anyone else, anyone English at any rate. There was no sitting around watching videos and getting stoned, no going to the cinema just for something to do that didn't involve talking, and no hanging out with friends in a group drinking or, for that matter, eating. It was more like having won a prize or an award: Roll up! Outings with amazingly handsome and charismatic Russian man! Here, now!

They didn't argue, he didn't criticise anything about her and he never ever turned up without a gift. Oh, and when he stopped the car he ordered her to stay in her seat while he came all the way round to open her door and help her out, whether or not he was driving. He wouldn't let her light her own cigarettes, he walked on the outside of the pavement with a protective arm around her, and he always opened doors for her unless it was a crowded place that might conceivably be dangerous and then he would go in and hold the door open for her from inside. He came to nearly all her gigs and stood watching at the side quietly, giving her a safe lift home afterwards and, on the odd occasion when he didn't make it, he sent a car. He was like a fantasy dream date.

'Unreal,' she explained to Eli.

'Exactly,' Eli confirmed with deep and snarling suspicion.

Dream date except on that first night, the night he promised to come and take her for dinner after the gig. He didn't show up and she sat at the kitchen table with Eli, mascara and lipstick on, foolish in a short black dress, drinking sweet champagne from the kiosk instead, expecting until at least ten thirty that there would be a ring on the door, but there wasn't.

'"University Graduate Stood Up by Russian Bandit Saviour",' Eli said, but Mo was annoyed. That was twice now that he had kissed her and buggered off, twice that he had helped her to standing and dumped her in eight years.

'Bollocks,' she said, slumping down into no-longer-expectant-posture at ten thirty-two. 'He's not bloody coming.'

'That's about the size of it. He's probably beating some poor little Jew to a pulp round the back of the Ministry of Defence as we speak, the Giant Gentile Beast,' Eli agreed, slopping more booze into the thin glasses that came with the flat.

'Honestly. What's wrong with you? He's not like that at all. He's nice. Kind. You'd like him.'

'I don't remember liking him all that much when I last met him and "nice" and "kind" are not usually words applied to the low-life street thugs taking over the country in the privatisation frenzy.'

'It was a low-life street thug who was about to kidnap me and take me off to be gang-raped out at fucking Bagrationovskaya. He rescued me.'

'What are you? Some sort of nineteenth-century heroine whose horse is lamed on the moors at dusk and is about to despair when the Lord of the Manor comes galloping by on his noble—'

'Mercedes.'

'Exactly.'

'Maybe I am,' Mo decided, raising her chin. The trouble with liking the masculine power that, frankly, most English men don't have, certainly not her uncertain university boyfriends with their angst and facial hair, is that it makes you seem very anti-feminist.

Personally, she hated that most male-female relationships she'd ever seen were mildly abusive towards the female, that the act of sex involved a degree of passivity on the part of the female and attack on the part of the male, that men talked loudly in restaurants and waved their arms about while the women sat still, that men all assumed the woman would wash their socks when it really came down to it, and yet . . . Well, she was, she supposed, a mammal after all.

'I am a mammal, after all,' she said.

'What is that supposed to mean? That you're about to give birth to a live young and suckle it? Get over yourself. In any case, you're always so cold even when it's boiling hot outside that I am given to slightly suspect you of not being a mammal at all, but of being a lizard.'

'No, I just mean—'

'You mean you want him to knock you about a bit, get you in line?'

Mo sighed. 'I tell you what. You have got really annoying since Charlotte agreed to shag you.'

'Ha! Jealous! Seriously, the whole bed was soaking—'

'Enough.'

But the next day, in the morning before she left for work, there was a knock at the door. Mo opened it in her dressing gown and saw an old lady in a headscarf, bundled up against the cold so that she was almost spherical.

'You Mo?' she asked.

'Yes,' Mo confirmed, speaking into the cabbagey gloom.

'Wait here,' the woman said, and went downstairs again, only to return with a metal bucket full of red roses. Then she went down for a bucket full of pink roses. Then a bucket full of yellow roses. Then a bucket full of white roses. When she had finished she handed Mo an envelope and rolled away, job done.

Pavel had neat handwriting. *Sorry. I had work to finish. I will pick you up at seven today. P.*

She knew it was a cliché, she knew it was just money, but, honestly, it was the nicest thing that had ever happened to her. She thought this stuff only happened in films.

'Creepy,' was Eli's comment. He sneezed and didn't stop sneezing until he left for work.

'Shit, I'm really sorry, I'll leave them on the balcony . . .' she offered, but he waved the offer away, as though his suffering was but a trifle in the light of her happiness. He was, she assumed, being sarcastic.

Pavel took her, that first night, to Kropotkinskaya 24, which was about the only real restaurant in Moscow in those days, the only place that didn't have a weirdo playing disco covers on a synth under disco lighting and a strip act that would appear without warning, bored teenages taking their clothes off and spreading their legs before scuttling back off to get dressed again in the kitchens, the women watching with frozen expressions, the men trying their best to look lustful and butch in very adverse conditions.

When he came to pick her up he stood braced outside the door with a big thug behind him and declined her invitation to come in and say hi to Eli, her flatmate.

'Your boyfriend?' Pavel checked, looking less like a Soviet propaganda poster now and more like an Aquascutum advert. No westerner would ever turn himself out as well as this. No westerner would have that much grief in his eyes.

'No. Friend. We share the flat.' She smiled, grabbing her blue coat from behind her and shouting goodbye. 'He's a lawyer.'

'I should get his number,' Pavel said. He took her arm and escorted her down the smelly steps to his car which purred outside. At the restaurant the doorman knew him and the maître d' fawned embarrassingly. He gave them a table against the wall and another one nearby for Boris. There were heavy green velvet curtains, a spindly old violinist taking cash for requests and white starched tablecloths that reached the floor. The cutlery was pre-Revolutionary and gave the whole place an air of historical grandeur.

'I should have worn my tiara,' Mo said.

'No. You would look like a provincial beauty queen.' Pavel laughed, leaning forward to look at her more closely. 'Maybe a crown of wild roses.'

'Then I'd look like some sort of druid getting wasted at Stonehenge.' She smiled, screwing up her face. She knew he meant it to sound romantic but she was uncomfortable being idealised like this. Pleasantly uncomfortable.

And, after about ten pleasantly uncomfortable evenings during which she received a ruby on a gold chain, pushed into her hand across the table without comment, a bottle of Yves Saint Laurent Paris perfume that he said smelled like her (well, it did now), a white mink stole that made her feel like Grace Kelly, wrapped round her shoulders as he walked her out to the car one night in thick wet snow, and more flowers than Eli's allergies could ever be expected to handle (all banished in the end to freeze on the balcony), Pavel suggested they take a trip to Tomsk.

'You are going to Tomsk with a murdering mad Russian?' Eli asked, but it wasn't really a question, it was a sigh of defeat.

'Well, if we don't consummate this thing soon we're going to end up being friends or something.'

'The worst.'

'Exactly.'

'Well, if you see any pogroms out there, don't join in, OK?'

'I don't think there's anyone left to have a pogrom against, is there?'

'Good point. But you know what I mean . . .'

'Not really,' Mo admitted, stuffing some things into her much-too-big suitcase. She hadn't really brought any weekend-away type stuff from London and nor was she quite sure what a weekend away in Tomsk might entail. Though, actually, it would take a whole weekend just to get there.

Pavel had booked them first-class compartments and one for Boris. Mo found it strangely easy to ignore Boris, accept him as Pavel's shadow and not think too much about it. She would have expected herself to be trying to make friends with him because she always chatted to people's cleaners and stuff, probably naïvely. I mean, they weren't doing the job to make friends and be treated as equal, after all. They were trying to get the house clean. Well, now she was getting the hang of it and said 'Good morning' and 'Goodbye' to him but not much else.

They caused a stir on the platform, rushing through the crowds, Boris trying to surround them and lead them, checking around constantly at the same time, but the carriage lady had been warned they were coming and she welcomed them in smiling, shutting the vast green door behind them with a satisfied pull of the lever. Mo realised they had the whole carriage to themselves and that this lady had been lavishly remunerated for all the cancellations she'd had to make.

'What can I get you, sir, madam?' she asked, almost bowing, her hair the ubiquitous Soviet do: a solidly glued orange shape on her head.

Mo wasn't sure about 'madam'. She was only just twenty-three and planned to look twenty-one for a further decade or so, but she understood that reverence towards stupendous wealth was the order of the day.

She went into her compartment and sat down on the bed, unwinding her scarf and pushing her boots off. Pavel leaned in politely, smiling at her as though she was a little girl doing a jigsaw or something, and then he kept on walking. She realised that consummation might not be going to happen – separate bloody compartments. It flashed through her mind in a magazine-article way that he had a bit of a Madonna/whore thing going on, but she failed to take this thought as seriously as might have been sensible. She often thought in brightly illustrated soundbites, probably something to do with Eli, but she failed to give the right amount of attention to the really important ones.

The whistle blew and the train pulled slowly out of the station leaving waving families standing in the tight icy Moscow night air while inside the train they began to boil, the heating on a generous full and the atmosphere dense. Mo wiped a clear patch on the window and watched as the city receded incredibly quickly, giving way to the absolute darkness of forest and deep, solid snow between the trees, the occasional wooden house coughing out smoke and glowing soft yellow from the windows. She realised, making an 'oh shit' face to herself, that she was wearing socks with Snoopy on them. She held her feet out in front of her and wriggled her toes, accepting that she would have to go with it, unsexy as it indubitably was.

'Pavel, I've got really silly socks on!' she shouted into the corridor, taking off more and more clothes until she was left in a cream long-sleeved thermal vest and jeans. She hoisted her hair back into its ponytail and sat back down again.

'What?' Pavel wanted to know, coming into her compartment with a hamper now. This was more like it. 'Oh, silly socks. Yes, you have. Is that a dog? Or a beaver, or what?'

'A beaver? What have you been doing for the past twenty-five years? It's Snoopy!'

'Oh. Snoopy.' He nodded, as though he had understood something important about the universe. 'What have I been doing for the past twenty-five years? Well, perhaps I will tell you a little bit. And perhaps I will not.'

Mo, familiar enough with Russians getting confessional and spewing their endlessly bleak stories about the general grimness of life at her over vodka, didn't feel that this was all that attractive an offer. 'Oh God, please don't. Honestly, I've heard enough "I had a really shit and unbelievably violent time in the armyslashprison" stories to give me nightmares until I die,' Mo complained, having been relieved over their slightly strange and formally intimate dinners that he had mainly asked her about herself.

'I could give you nightmares even into the next life,' Pavel laughed, kneeling on the floor by Mo's feet and opening the hamper which was too big to go on the table. He picked a foot up to take a better look at Snoopy and then kissed him gently. 'I like dogs,' he said. 'I bought a puppy.'

'Really? When? Can I meet it? I've never even been to your flat. Oh God! You're married, aren't you?'

Pavel laughed loudly and got the champagne out. Moët. 'No! I am not married. You'll be the first to know,' he said, pulling out the cork with his teeth in one of the few little moments she'd seen where his background, his extremely working-class Russianness showed. He didn't know how to open champagne and there was something about this, weirdly, she knew, that turned her on. And then, worse, he took a swig out of the top.

'I will not be taking you for dinner with the Queen,' she said. 'You can't go around swigging the bloody booze out of the bottle, you know. What are you? Some street thug from Tomsk?'

'Yes, I am.' Pavel smiled again, pouring the golden bubbles into the train tea glasses.

'Oh, good.' Mo smiled back at him and, before they clinked glasses, he kissed her gently on the mouth.

'Pavel?'

'Yes.'

'We are going to have sex now, aren't we? Because otherwise it's getting a bit weird,' she told him, the train deep into the countryside now, the lights dimmed for an overnight journey, Boris probably already fast asleep.

Pavel put a jar of caviare, a pot of sour cream, a spoon and a packet of ready-made pancakes on the little table and sat down next to her, his broad shoulders seeming too big for the little compartment. He smelt of lime.

'Do you want to?' he asked, taking her hand and examining it, as if to check for blemishes or, perhaps, to make sure it was real.

'Well, whenever anyone asks me I'm suddenly not sure, but I've definitely spent the past few weeks wanting to! I've even stopped flirting with Bob at work.'

'Bob?'

'Oh, he's a producer. White teeth. From Illinois. I don't really fancy him.'

'But he is in love with you?'

'God, hardly.' Mo was tickled by the very thought of Bob having emotions beyond mild lust and the desire for another coffee. 'Anyway, why? Do you not want to?'

'I do. But I don't want to fuck you.'

'Oh.' Mo was vaguely disappointed. She went to bed with someone at university once who explained that he wanted to 'hold' her. It was the most boring night of her life and there was plenty of competition for that title.

She spread a pancake with caviare and sour cream and ate it, beaming. 'God, that's delicious. That's just the most delicious thing ever,' she gushed, swilling it down with some Moët. 'So who did you lose your virginity to?'

She thought she'd better keep the conversation on sex without letting him get too sincere, and she always liked these first-time stories about older seductress girls or first loves, embarrassing nightclub knee-tremblers and whatever. Little, of course, did she know.

'Actually, Boris was there. It was his idea,' Pavel began with a deep sigh.

'No way!' Mo laughed, thinking that was terribly strange as the men didn't seem close at all, not in anything but a dependant and employer type of way. And the thought of Boris having an actual idea was plainly absurd. But by the end of the story tears were streaming down Mo's face and she wiped them and her nose with the back of her hand, imagining the room, the apartment, the smells that Pavel described. She turned her face away from him towards the window feeling that she couldn't possibly touch him now, couldn't begin to do something with him that bore any relation at all to what he and the others had done to that poor girl.

'Mo,' Pavel whispered, touching her shoulder, trying to get her back. She flinched. 'Mo, please. I was fourteen. It was a long time ago.'

She turned to look at him now, her face smudged and stunned. 'Sorry. I know. I know. It's not that I blame you . . . It's just so sad and awful. I can't bear it.'

Pavel held both her hands and kissed her knuckles in the near dark. 'This is why I don't tell you about these things. You shouldn't know. It will change you and you must stay just as you are. I don't want you to change.'

Mo looked down at her hands in his and began to understand why they only talked about her. He laughed when she talked about school and smoking in the loos and Saffron, whom he remembered, and her make-up bag. He liked hearing about her dad and how she met Eli, about Frankie and the flat and her hamster. He wanted to know what she wore at university balls and what they ate, who her friends were and what they talked about. He was interested, genuinely, she realised, but only because he needed so badly not to think about his own world, even with all the wealth and apparent glamour of bodyguards and French champagne.

'I just . . . Sorry. I know I'm naïve. I just feel so sorry for her,' Mo said and started crying again.

'She's OK now. She lives in a beautiful place up in the mountains, with a swimming pool and a sauna and nurses . . .' Pavel tried to explain, the train rattling now across the steppe, snow dust flying up at the windows and turning all the landscape into a swirling white blur.

Mo was taken aback. 'Does she? How come?' she sniffed, trying to get a grip, for God's sake. She didn't even know this person, after all, and the world is full of horrors. But somehow his description of it, what it had obviously meant to him, had struck her hard, in the face.

'Well, Mo, I put her there. My mother, who is disabled, lives there also. I fund the place. It is a good place. There is an orphanage attached to it and for all the people with nothing, they can live there, free of charge. Not to me free of charge, but to them,' he laughed, always acutely aware that you don't get something for nothing, not that he knew the expression.

'That's amazing. Pavel, that's really amazing.' She smiled openly into his face, her eyes shining in hopeless admiration. This is the kind of thing that lots of people think they would do if they were rich but that not many people do actually do. 'That's amazing. What happened to her dad?'

Pavel looked hard into her eyes as though trying to decide something. It didn't take long. 'I had him killed,' he said, standing up and getting his cigarettes out of his coat pocket, putting two in his mouth and lighting both before handing one to Mo. Staring down at her lap and her stupid fucking socks, Mo took the cigarette and looked back up into his face.

'Good,' she said, jutting her chin up, her eyes filling with tears. 'Well done.'

Pavel took one deep pull on his cigarette and then stubbed it out in the thick steel ashtray in the train wall. Then he let Mo take a drag on hers before extinguishing that too. With his eyes locked on hers he put his hands inside her top and round her waist and pulled her towards him. He smiled. 'Would you like to have sex with me now?'

Mo could hardly breathe. 'Yes,' she said. 'Yes please.'

It was forty-eight hours later that they arrived in Tomsk, a bright sunny morning, the air and ground freezing, the morning rush-hour bustle somehow disconcerting after so long in the hot train. At first Mo counted the orgasms she had on the way, but gave up at thirty-one, feeling that they were somehow running into each other as she'd heard contractions do before people give birth. Perhaps it was all one long orgasm. Pavel had pulled the black-out curtain down and locked the door and they had, basically, made love all the way in the most astonishing extravaganza of swimming lust that Mo had ever experienced. Not, she realised, that she had experienced much.

A man wearing a lot of fur and driving a Hummer, which was parked outside the station as if the parking regulations could not possibly apply to a car like this (and it was probably true, they couldn't), met them off the train, carrying Mo's vast suitcase and Pavel's small leather doctor's bag. Boris seemed not to have luggage. The windows of the Hummer were blacked out and there was a bar inside which Pavel immediately opened, bringing out Borjomi mineral water and offering miniatures of all sorts of crap that Mo hated. Drambuie? No, thanks.

'I have to go to the plant for a while, but I'll take you to the dacha,' he said, instructing the driver accordingly. Mo, happy and exhausted as if she'd been skiing for a week except better, sat back and shut her eyes, not even looking out of the windows at a city she'd never seen before. She got the picture. Big Soviet city, grimy with winter, trams, idyllic but impractical, buildings bleak but imposing, the occasional pre-Revolutionary wooden mansion with soggy sagging balconies and eaten-away porticos. Who needed to actually look? She ached all over in fabulous muscular bliss.

The dacha, where she was hurled out of the Hummer into the harsh real world of no Pavel and a lot of very very cold air, turned out to have been built perhaps yesterday. Eli would bark a headline like 'Rich Russian Builds Naff Palace' and Mo smiled to herself, standing on the doorstep or, rather, on the ornate steps of the towering entranceway to what looked like something on Bishops Avenue, except it stood completely alone behind white slab concrete, fencing in the mud and slush of Nowheresk.

A woman in a French maid's uniform opened the door. 'Oh dear God,' Mo muttered to herself as the woman, knowing her name, welcomed her into the skin-searing heat of the 'dacha'. Now Mo had always thought dacha meant little wooden hut, climbing with honeysuckle, with old crone inside peeling apples for preserving. In this dacha the hallway had a gold statue of a naked woman in the middle of it, a fountain bubbling up around her, perhaps erotically. Everything was made of marble and, when her feet began to seriously sweat, Mo realised there was underfloor heating. The stairs, a curved staircase coming down on both sides of the hundred-foot-high hall, was carpeted in maroon and a huge skylight above it showed snow. Probably ten feet of snow that would sit there blocking out the light until when? April? No, this was Siberia. Probably June.

'I'm Varvara,' said Varvara, wiping her hands on her frilly white apron. 'I'll take you to your room. Then perhaps you'd like some tea.'

Mo nodded, wishing Pavel would come back. 'I'd love some. Is there a phone in my . . . ?'

'Yes, of course,' Varvara confirmed. 'You are fully equipped.'

Fully equipped? What did that mean, Mo wondered, following the maid up the stairs and dragging her stupid suitcase.

What it meant was a cinema screen on one wall and floor-to-ceiling videos to choose from, an already heated sauna in the en-suite bathroom as well as plunge pool, robes, wooden slatted loungers, the biggest bed she'd ever seen, piled high with pillows and duvets, a zinc-topped bar with drinks cabinet behind it and a selection of elegant slippers laid out by the wardrobe door.

'Fucking hell,' Mo whispered to herself.

'The telephone's over there.' Varvara gestured. 'I'll get you the tea.'

Outside, past the mega-sealed double glazing, Mo saw an expanse of snow that stretched to the horizon, punctuated only by the spindles of bare trees and, nearer to the house, a lake of slushy mud that had frozen against the concrete fence.

Inexplicably, Mo felt very frightened.

'I'm at work,' Eli said importantly. 'Not all of us have gazillion-aire boyfriends to bankroll our expensive lifestyle.'

'Shut up,' Mo told him. 'I'm in fucking Tomsk! We screwed all the way here and then he just dumped me at this mansion that was obviously finished yesterday and is like . . . it's like . . . I don't know . . . like a hotel where Saudi men might bring Russian prostitutes or something. And it's nowhere. Just nowhere. No road, no nothing. A bloke in a Hummer brought me here and there are cameras all over the place and this maid . . .'

'This is gripping stuff, Mo, but, seriously, I'm with a client—'

'You're too junior to be with a client.'

'And yet, nonetheless . . .'

'Oh, God . . . OK. Listen, I'll call you back.'

'Keep safe,' Eli said, making her feel even less safe.

'I'll try. Thanks,' she said very quietly and then sat on the very edge of the bed as though making herself comfortable would result in instant electric shock. She must at some point, after tea and *When Harry Met Sally*, have fallen asleep because she woke up to hear Pavel's footsteps on the stairs.

'You look like an angel,' he said, coming over to kiss her, and she had the disconcerting feeling of being absurdly idealised again, something she was hoping they had done away with on the train.

'Well, I'm not,' she said, kissing him back and hanging round his neck. 'I am fucking starving though.'

Pavel went into the bathroom and splashed his face with water, coming back into the room with a towel in his hands and a startled look. 'Good, because we're going out for dinner.'

It was that command thing again that sounded like an offer, but, fine, she'd said she was hungry, hadn't she? She pulled her clothes on, jeans, T-shirt, fleecy thing, and announced that she was ready.

He looked disappointed and she would soon see why.

The Hummer, and Boris, of course, swept them into the centre of town to a big Georgian restaurant with red lights and lanterns and a velvet cordon outside. Surprisingly, there were quite a few other Hummers ridden up to park on the pavement (all the rage in the regions, apparently) and people were scurrying in, a woman in white fur, the requisite big blokes with big necks. Pavel took her arm as though she were a grand duchess and escorted her inside, past the coat check where a woman in belly-dancing gear emerged from behind a dark curtain to take their stuff, and into the gold and red interior where long tables were laid with vodka, champagne and food, the air was swirling with cigarette smoke and the eastern tinkling music was loud. There must have been two hundred people in here and, as Mo and Pavel stood at the top of the steps about to descend into the dining pit, all two hundred of them stood still, stopped talking and looked up. The music stopped and the lights came on full.

Pavel raised his hand to everyone and they all clapped, reverently. 'OK, let's eat!' he shouted and the lights went down, the music started and the chat re-erupted.

'Why didn't you tell me?' Mo whined, escorted to the top of the head table by an Aladdin-trousered waiter.

'Tell you what?' Pavel asked, shaking hands with every man he passed as people craned to touch him.

'That we were attending a banquet held in our honour? Oh, and not to wear jeans?' She sat down and stretched a smile across her face. 'Hello. I'm Mo,' she said to the skinny and very depressed-looking bloke to her right.

'It's just a few friends. Calm down. We won't stay long,' Pavel explained and instead of sitting with her he carried on his tour of the tables, shaking hands with the men.

'Andrei. Andriusha,' Andriusha said, grimacing up at Boris who had taken his place behind Mo but who kept his eyes firmly on Pavel, his hand poised on his gun.

'This is incredible. I've never met any of Pavel's friends before,' she said, sipping at a strawberry drink she'd been poured from a huge Moroccan gilt jug. There seemed to be as many waiters as guests.

'He doesn't have friends,' Andriusha hissed, lighting a cigarette. 'These are just the main TomStal people. Those that are left.'

'Oh, right,' she said. 'And do you work for TomStal, Andriusha?' She was trying to be polite and was acutely aware that she should be wearing an evening dress like all the women here, pearly eyeshadow, glossy lips, shoulders on display. A lot of glitter.

'No,' he said, putting his cigarette down in the ashtray with a shaky hand and lighting another one.

'You've still . . .' Mo was about to point out, but quickly understood that this man wasn't well.

'I don't work. I used to do . . . I mostly stay at home,' he shivered and Mo, who had had enough freaky experiences for a day or two, turned to the other side where a lovely girl, who said her family owed their lives to Pavel, was sitting. Mo listened to the story of banishment, prison and then a new dawn with well-paid jobs at the steel works for all, including an on-site doctor's surgery and hospital, nursery and primary school. When Mo looked back Andriusha had gone and Pavel had sat down next to her and when he squeezed her hand under the table somehow everything began to seem normal again.

'There's a calm surrender to the rush of day
When the heat of the rolling world can be turned away.'

Elton John, 'Can You Feel The Love Tonight'

Chapter Twelve

Pavel sent him home: decommissioned, useless, defunct, over, dependent on his mother like a toddler shitting in a nappy. Andriusha was unable to bear the voices in his head, the ghosts of all the dead who knew him; he looked out of the window at the street that might as well have been a hologram of a street, so little did it have to do with him. His body felt immensely heavy, though his mother said he looked like a bag of bones. He sucked hard on his cigarette, feeling his lungs fill with stinging, acrid smoke and celebrating with a slight twitch of a smile on his sunken face that at the moment he was at peace, with no sense of the spirits he knew would swirl round him and drag him screaming to the ground when the sun went down. He wore only his father's pyjama trousers, tied tightly with a cord from his dressing gown to stop them slipping down over his jutting hips, an emaciation that pleased Andriusha, who felt that the less of him there was, the less the demons could consume. His long pale feet were cold on the ragged brown lino and his toenails thick yellow claws with which he was able to lash out at them from under the bed when he needed to. They always wore exactly what they had worn at that last moment, the same leather jacket, the same chain round their wrist, the same bleached jeans from Finland.

His mother scuttled in the kitchen, like thousands of cockroaches, he thought as he watched the boy with the kiosk across the road arrange his bottles of beer, vodka, fruit brandy and Georgian cognac. He had a gun shoved into his trousers at the waist and big coloured tattoos all over his tanned and muscular torso, some of them from prison, some of them not. His white-blond hair was shaved army short to his head; he wore a cigarette behind his ear and a silver dog tag round his neck. He played loud rock music from a giant black stereo with twin speakers that sat on the back of his stall and one of his eyes was closed by a raging scar that looked as though a small purple jellyfish had been thrown at him, had splattered into his face. Yesterday Andriusha had noticed a love bite on his neck as he'd snatched a bottle of the cheapest vodka from his hands, almost certainly home-fired samogon from Mrs Smerdyakova whose husband and two sons were all doing time together up north for murdering the next-door neighbour who said they'd raped his daughter.

'You should look after yourself, mate,' the boy told him every day, handing over the bottle and blowing smoke benignly into his face. If you had any idea who I used to be, what I used to do, Andriusha thought, but he didn't speak, afraid that black demons might fly out of his mouth and needing all the power left in his body to grip the vodka, to hold it tight to his chest without shaking so that it might get back upstairs to the flat intact. Sometimes, he needed to take a swig right there in the street, while the sun seemed to tear strips off his skin as he fumbled, cold and sweating, with the lid. He thought about Katya in Moscow, how shameful his behaviour had been. Unworthy. He always thought about Katya.

Andriusha's mother paid Igor, which was the boy's name, to water the vodka down. Igor, a robust blond angel with skin like butterscotch, had played ice hockey at school, had loved his time in Kazakhstan with the army, catching fish and eating caviare right from its belly, and who was in business now, enterprising, taking advantage of the brave new world just like Katya had seemed to with her modelling all that time ago. It was dangerous, of course – he was lucky the knife hadn't reached his brain – but a net will catch more fish than a pole can. It was a shame about Andriusha, everybody said so; the rot had set in when he fell in with a bad crowd, starting drinking.

Andriusha waited until the street had emptied out a bit, until the girls with cans of fizzy drinks and hot dogs from the kiosk next door to Igor's had gone home to their mothers and the boys who sat around the statue kicking beer cans and idly fighting had followed them, coaxing, shouting out, pleading. He pulled on his mother's heavy winter coat with the lily-of-the-valley brooch on the lapel, and shuffled out of the apartment on to the stairs where graffiti said 'Fuck' in English, Russian and what he thought must be Uzbek.

When his mother had told them off, the kids who loiter here with cans of spray from the car factory, one of them held her against the wall while another urinated on her shoes and stockings. She told Andriusha this matter-of-factly, the kettle screaming on the stove, a salami on the chopping board and a copy of *Rabotnitsa – Working Woman* – on the table with a scythe-wielding woman on the front in a headscarf as though the Revolution might still bear fruit. Her stockings were soaking in a plastic bowl in the bath and her shoes were polished, waiting for morning on a sheet of newspaper in the dark hall. She hadn't needed to say, 'Andrei, pull yourself together and protect me like the man your father was before.' That night, whimpering under the bed as the sharp fangs tore into what remained of his flesh, watching his accusers name him from the grave, he was certain that this time morning would never come, that this time the ghosts would at last take their proper revenge. But, sure enough, when the room filled with yellow light, strained like tea through the ochre curtains, his mother's swollen feet emerged in front of his eyes, heading for their pink fluffy slippers, the backs squashed down where her wide cracked heels had pressed on to them over the years, and the fronts grey, with bald patches now.

'Good morning, son,' she said as she always did, knowing that he would creep out once she had left the room and make straight for the vodka he thought she didn't know was under the bath. Or perhaps he would shamble, his fingers reaching out for the thin walls to support him, to the one he thought she didn't know was in the cupboard over the loo with the bleach. Sometimes, God help her, she almost hoped he would mix them up. Sometimes, God help him, he considered it.

He made his way gingerly downstairs, remembering how he had once run and jumped down them, dashing in his grey socks and Pioneer scarf, to meet Katya out by the statue when she threw stones up at the window even on the days when the air was so cold your spit froze. It was impossible to imagine now that his joints had not been painful and lumpen, that his breath had not been short and sharp as icicle points, that Katya had been just up the road and had loved him even, perhaps. Though the heatwave had been burning since the rouble crashed, the steel banister felt cold to Andriusha and gave him goose bumps, even in his mother's woollen coat. His flip-flops felt slippery and unstable on the concrete and he worried he might not make it to the warmth and relaxation of Igor's vodka.

'You should look after yourself, bratok,' Igor told him. Andriusha shuddered and pulled his lips back in an effort to smile, sending a shard of pain slicing into the nerve of the rotten tooth that threatened to drop out. His mother had sent for the healer. It was, he knew, her last resort but it was, he also knew, useless. Nobody knew what he had done and he could tell nobody, not until he told God himself.

The healer, Praskovya, was born with the gift. Her grandmother said so. Her grandmother had lived in one of the very few wooden houses left in Kirgask, near the railway station and just north of the big meadow. Was born there, in fact, in that very house on the day the last tsar was crowned and the whole family had said that this was a special child, a child with a gift. As it turned out, she had spent fifteen years in prison for her gift, denounced as a witch and a counter-Revolutionary by a woman who worked at the chemist and didn't like to see good Soviet business undermined by the loony who made potions out of the mushrooms and saw spirits that every good Communist knew didn't exist. (It was true that Praskovya the elder had slept with the chemist's husband also.) But Granny survived to see her grand-daughter have her first vision and she had taken the girl's plump hand in her wizened and tattooed one and told her to heal people, no matter whether they are wolves or chickens.

Today the cats were restless. She shushed and cooed at them but they writhed around her legs whining and moaning, moving from table to window ledge with a mewl and then leaping down, dissatisfied, pacing from room to room. Praskovya knew why. They were afraid for her, going to see the mad boy, the son of the Jew's widow. If the truth be known, she was afraid for herself; she had to give herself a talking to in the mirror while she cleaned her teeth with bicarbonate of soda, pinned her thinning grey hair back off her face with metal grips and washed her big hands under the cold tap. She nodded at her reflection, told the crone she barely recognised as herself that it would be fine, that nobody else would help the boy, that her powers would not desert her. Not even a boy any more, she sighed, moving through the ocean of pleading miaows, pushing the animals gently aside with her feet, pulling her headscarf down off the peg, preparing her box of candles, matches, herbs, though she doubted she'd need them. People liked her to have tools though, she found. They believed in her more if she did something, if she didn't just sit there like a fool in church. The boy was possessed by demons of remorse. That much she knew, and she would have to be strong. It might be her biggest test yet.

She took the tram from outside her building, newly painted blue, creaking and complaining as it stopped, Lena in the driver's seat, right where she'd been for thirty years or more, smiling out of her orange lipstick and even oranger hair. 'Seeing the spirits, Praskovya Lvovna?' she laughed, checking Praskovya's pensioner's pass as though it might have changed or expired or something since yesterday, might have been swapped for a brilliant forgery. Did she still not trust her, in God's name? Even in school she'd been suspicious of her.

'Yours will haunt me when you're gone, Elena,' she told her, shuffling to the nearest seat.

'Too right!' Lena answered, laughing even louder.

They could believe or not believe. When they needed her they came. You should have seen the Jew's widow standing on her doormat that day, bowing her head in humiliation at what she'd come to: begging the town's witch for help that no psychiatric hospital was ever going to provide. Oh, she knew what they said. But she was pleased she'd come at last. She had lured her here with spells when she'd heard – can you imagine what would happen to him in an institution? Drugged up to the eyeballs, rocking in a corner in a straitjacket, taunted by the nurses. No, the mother did a good thing knocking on the door that evening in her neat coat and her jingling brooch, tiny silver bells shaped like flowers that rang as she shook and cried. Her husband drank himself to death too, they said, kicked out of the Party, kicked out of the brick factory, a shadow of a man. And now the son.

The tram stopped by Togliatti's statue, arm outstretched, reaching for the future that wasn't going to come now, a few drunk boys with no shirts on jostling around him listening to the music, if you could call it that, from the kiosk across the street. She'd heard rival gangs were firebombing each other's kiosks around here, one boy stabbed in the eyes ... even though they imprisoned her grandmother, at least the Communists kept the streets clean and the children occupied, she thought, crossing herself at the same time in the Orthodox fashion as punishment for her unworthy thought. Shame on you, she told herself.

The entry system didn't work at the Jew's building, hadn't worked, in fact, since 1979, so Praskovya walked up the four flights of stairs slowly, holding on to the banister as Andriusha had done coming down, and pausing for breath on each landing. At her age everything seemed to take twice as long. The stairway smelt bad and there was writing on all the walls. When she arrived at the door, adjusting her scarf nervously, clutching her props close to her for comfort, she felt suddenly cold and afraid. They were in there and she would have to face them; even though others didn't see them, she could feel them, the murdered souls, and it made her blood run cold.

The widow came, the nurse for the schools, and welcomed her in, offered her tea as though that's what she'd come for. Although it was midday and the sun was white hot in the sky outside, Praskovya froze and the apartment seemed as dark as the grave. She could hear the chattering and screaming, but she knew they were not with him yet, they were lurking, seething behind curtains and furniture, the vengeful dead. They would wait until nightfall. That was their way.

'Thank you, madam,' she said, taking off her scarf and accepting tea in a china cup with a saucer of strawberry jam next to it (not homemade, she noticed). She'd put on the slippers she'd been offered and put her wooden box on the table, stating that she meant business with a reassuring clunk, no need for words.

Andriusha's mother remarked to herself that cat hair was woven into the cloth of the psychic's skirt. She should not, she thought, have invited her here, answering an advert in the paper, one of hundreds for spiritual healers, psychics, mediums. If she'd known when she was a girl, could have seen herself knocking on a stranger's door, begging for help for her son, desperate, wild with grief, she would have built a different life than this, she would have started again, twenty years old, standing outside the institute with her certificate and her hair blowing in the wind, eager for the life that would betray her, a pattern of forget-me-nots on her blue skirt. The woman could be anyone, in God's name.

'Shall we start?' Praskovya suggested, taking a candle out, putting it into a square wooden candlestick and lighting it with a violent strike of a match. She scrabbled around in her collection of polythene sachets for some rosemary and, when she'd found it, took a pinch and threw it into the flame. One blade lit, and dropped burning to the table where it turned to ash. The rest just scattered with the noise of pine needles falling to the forest floor.

The widow went for the boy and there was a muffled commotion in the bedroom before Andriusha crept slowly into the kitchen and sat down opposite Praskovya at the table, his long fingers, painfully thin, tapping at the plastic tablecloth and his eyes darting about the room. He wore a dressing gown and pyjama trousers, no shoes. A thick sweet smell of vodka and the sweat of sickness surrounded him. He seemed close to death though he was not yet twenty-five. He sat shivering, his spine jutting out in a skeletal semicircle as he crouched at the table, a cigarette quivering in his lips.

Praskovya reached her hand out and put it over his, trying to offer him some of her warmth, a physical proof of the help she promised to provide. Andriusha didn't move his hand away, but he seemed barely to notice her touch, his eyes flashing around the room looking for danger, every pore in his skin oozing vodka, his mind a rush of terror, his heart swelling.

She stared at him and was afraid. She scrabbled for the spirit of her grandmother, for the grandeur of her inheritance, the old brass samovar that had bubbled on the porch in summer with a gypsy scarf wrapped round the leak, the cut-crystal glass and carved board that had terrified visitors by spelling out the names of the spirits present, the love potion she'd helped make as a girl in ribbons, dropping in handfuls of rose petals from the garden and screwing her eyes tight shut for the magic; the whole whirling celestial grandeur of her destiny was here. She had never seen anything like this, as bad as this, though it was beautiful in its malignant glory. The boy had done terrible things to these poor lost souls. She would tell him straight.

'There are holes in your spirit. A million little pin pricks in the golden gossamer wings that should protect and surround you. I see them and I see black smoke blowing out of them. It is through these holes that the demons of the dead come. You have made the holes yourself, Andrei. You must purge them with good deeds. You must keep them out, send them slinking back to hell.'

She muttered all this quickly, simply stating the truth as she saw it. Then she threw back her head, palms flat on the table and closed her eyes.

It was at this that Andriusha's eyes began to spill hot fat tears, splashing on to the tablecloth, his body coughing up grief, his face crumpling, his hands curling to baby's fists, nails digging into his palms. She had told him, in some way that touched him, that showed him what he must do, the truth that he worked so hard to crush and dismember. A part of his mind – the remaining knot of flickering signals not yet extinguished, that perhaps, understood what was going on both inside and out – didn't want to get better because it didn't want to admit that he had wasted his life, that Katya was gone, that he was a pathetic, raving alcoholic like the bomzhy the police used to pick up off the streets and cart a hundred miles out of town, leaving them by the side of the road in the snow to die in piss-soaked trousers, icicles on their moustaches and beards. That he was, in fact, a mass murderer, however much his victims may have deserved it, however much he would have been killed himself if he'd disobeyed. For he'd done it for money, money that was spent now, money he had never really needed.

In this woman's truthful gaze he saw himself. The dark, engulfing cloak of madness that seemed to attack with such vengeful spite in reality protected him from the dreadful truth and he knew it. She had come to save him, but the message of her salvation was that nobody could save him but himself. He wiped his tears with the backs of his hands and looked into Praskovya's face, the first time he had truly seen a person for years.

Andriusha's mother, peering through the crack between the kitchen door and its hinges put her hand over her mouth. How could she have imagined for a moment that this madwoman might have something to offer her boy? Look at the state of him now. Why hadn't she just taken him to the hospital? It was absurd, ridiculous; Dima would have laughed his head off – calling in a psychic to cure a mental illness was as likely to work as a crayfish whistling on a mountaintop. This was how desperate she had become. And yet . . .

Andriusha was smiling, his eyes fixed on the psychic's open mouth as though what she was doing had some meaning. He saw plumes of black smoke now himself, coming from every corner of the apartment, dancing, swirling straight into the old woman's throat, like millions of dark butterflies, arguing with each other in high-pitched wails.

The next morning, having slept for eighteen hours on the divan in the front room, Andriusha showered, shaved, drank a big mug of instant coffee with three sugars in it, ate a slice of black bread with smoked fish and went down to the kiosk, feeling dizzy and nervous, his trainers tight and constraining after so long in bare feet and flip-flops, the air sharp and new in his nostrils. Igor was asleep, slumped in the corner on the floor, drunk, one hand on his gun, the other draped round the young girl slumped next to him. Andriusha knocked to wake him and bought a packet of cigarettes before walking through town on a dusty summer morning to make an appointment with the dentist. If you can choose life's turning points, he had chosen, he thought. He had been a slave to Pavel Ivanchenko since he was a teenager. He had handed Katya to him. Things were going to change. Perhaps it was too late to become the person he might have been, but it wasn't too late for others.

He would begin to make amends. Properly.

'The road to tyranny, we must never forget, begins with the destruction of the truth.'

Bill Clinton

Chapter Thirteen

All the money in the world didn't help at the British Embassy. Mo cringed for Pavel as he was insulted and humiliated by the consul's questions about his intentions. Britain would be bloody lucky to have him, spending his money and spreading his wisdom, she thought, hating that he was sitting in that Portakabin being harangued by a bloke called Derek. It wasn't right.

When they got back from Tomsk Mo thought things would definitely change, that she might stay the night at Pavel's flat, meet his friends, eat crisps and watch telly, that kind of thing. But, weirdly, they went straight back to the formal dating they had been doing before. A restaurant twice a week (nearly always the same restaurant, actually, and Mo found she was eating less and drinking more in frustration, and understanding that, really, she had nothing more to tell Pavel about herself), a kiss in the car and a chivalrous drop home.

'When are we going to have sex again?' she asked him on one of these dark journeys that tonight had ended at the office where she was doing a night shift. Everyone was talking about Mo's rich boyfriend with the bodyguards and the blacked-out Merc, little did they know who it was though and she wasn't about to tell them. Some part of her knew that Pavel must stay a secret.

'Is that all you ever think about?' Pavel asked, taking her hand.

She was sure this conversation was supposed to go the other way round. 'No, but it's weird. It was so amazing on the train and at your house and now we're like an old married couple or something.' She assumed that the married were chaste, it's what everybody said.

'Take me to your house in London,' he said, as if it had just popped into his head. At the traffic lights a child tapped on the window and he zhuzhed it down to hand fifty roubles over. This was a huge fortune in pocket money at the time, not that the child was likely to see a kopeck of it.

'No. I can't. I haven't got one. You don't want to go to my mother's flat.'

'Yes, I do.'

'Well, you can't. Nobody has ever been there. I don't want you to come.'

'Then I want to come even more,' he said.

Eli was taking against Pavel in a big way. They still hadn't met face to face since 1986 and he didn't like the way Mo was so obedient to him, Mo who never obeyed anyone, who was obstinate just for the sake of it. And now she was pulling out all the stops to get the guy a British visa just to take him to Frankie's flat where he himself had never even been.

'It's just bizarre,' he said, straightening his tie in front of the mirror.

'I know it is, but he's not English,' she answered, feeling cagey like she never normally did with Eli.

'"Brainwashed Girl Found Dead in Hummer",' he said, shaking his head.

'Don't say that,' she implored, but without any kind of conviction.

'Well, you know he's a criminal,' he said, sifting through the world's most enormous heap of legal documents, none of which had anything to do with criminal activity of any kind.

179

'You know perfectly well he isn't. You're the Soviet law expert and he didn't break any.'

'Technically, perhaps.'

'Technically, in law, is all that counts and it was you who told me that.'

Eli snorted in immense irritation. 'They all knocked a few people off on the way, of course. Everyone knows that, Momix,' he muttered.

Mo froze in anger. 'No, Eli. All Russians like to think that so that they can call them criminals and hate them for being capital-ists. If they went around murdering people don't you think someone would notice and put them in prison?' She was very cross, partly because she knew he was right and yet wrong. It wasn't what he thought. What Pavel had confessed to was honourable and right. Wasn't it?

'No. I don't think they would,' Eli said, and walked briskly out of the flat with his briefcase leaving a stale atmosphere and a bitter taste behind him.

The road where Frankie still lived contained the furniture of Mo's dreams. The row of shops with the flock-wallpapered Indian restaur-ant that served grapefruit juice and omelette and chips as an option, the newsagent's where she'd bought Frankie's fags for her ('Twenty Piccadilly and a box of matches, please.'), the bric-a-brac place that sold chipped china with small rosebuds on it and the old-fashioned bakery that only did sliced white loaves ('Anythin-kelse?') and perfectly square cakes with lurid icing on them and which smelt, slightly, of toilet cleaner, all churned around Mo's head, half-real and half-imaginary, as if standing for something in her mind but too blurry and obscure to show exactly what. Seeing them, as she did now, pulling up in a violently shampooed hire car with flimsy controls, Pavel sitting – not meekly surely? – at her side, she was surprised they really existed. She was sure she'd invented them to represent some kind of horror or unreality or lack of control.

'Here we are,' she sang, feeling uncomfortable, as she had since they got in the car. He'd booked them BA first class and the stewardesses had flirted and fawned; he'd hired them the car and it was waiting at Heathrow. But then his power sort of evaporated, his protective aura seemed to slide off into nothingness. He didn't have a British driving licence and had never driven on the wrong side of the road before. Boris was left behind to guard the empty apartment and Pavel looked now — standing by a car he couldn't drive, under the thick grey sky and against the sharply defined corners and miniature feel of everything here — smaller, paler, less sure of himself.

'Great,' he said, not willing to ask questions or appear uncertain, and this made him seem even more questioning and uncertain. Suddenly Mo wondered if she knew him at all.

Frankie lived still, would probably always live, in the dark flat opposite the parade, behind a kind of mock dry-stone wall and in a heavily pebble-dashed Victorian house that would never have got any light anyway but was all the more obscured by an odd tree with a dark purple trunk and leaves that Mo had never seen the like of anywhere else in the world, as though it was a fairytale thing like Baba Yaga's chicken-leg house.

'I hate that tree,' she told Pavel and he blinked at it, bemused.

'It's just a tree,' he said.

'No, I know, but . . . Never mind.'

The other houses on the terrace had, bizarrely, been gentrified. Only Frankie's building still contained flats. All the neighbours had knocked floor into floor and room into room to recreate one large family home with rediscovered fireplaces behind the chipboard and electric-bar heaters; they had uncovered tiled floors and lovingly restored them with the help of a new tile shop that had opened in the area especially to cater for people who were tearing up thin nylon carpet and jagged strips of razor-embedded cardboard stuck down with sticky black foam tape. The area had upped and come, leaving Frankie besieged by affluence in her smoky lair, the salvaged iron baths and reinstalled sash windows creeping up on her to expose her as a relic of a bygone age when you could smoke on a bus, offer a guest a can of beer and not have your teeth fixed.

There was a Somali family living in the flat below Frankie now and students upstairs, the pounding music and fug of marijuana smoke a strange memory trace of Frankie's earlier life. Standing on the pavement outside the house, Mo felt a shiver of fear creep under her clothes and settle there, where it could be assured that, like a flea on a dog, at least for the duration of her visit, it belonged. Pavel touched her shoulder impatiently but he couldn't help her here.

Mo held the keys in her tightly clenched fist and wondered whether to use them or to ring the bell. Use them and Frankie would shout, 'You frightened me half to death! What are you trying to do to me?' Ring the bell and Frankie would shuffle downstairs, complaining, 'Lost your keys, have you? Don't mind me.' Rage or self-pity: interchangeable, unpredictable but, ultimately, both, in any one visit, inevitable.

'Are we going in?' Pavel asked, gripping the handle of his small suitcase, flashing his eyes around to take in the foreign street.

Mo put her key in the lock, an action so familiar it gave her a sick feeling in her stomach as though the floor was slipping away from under her. She pushed the pizza delivery and airport-taxi fliers out of the way with her foot, scraping them across the bristles of the mat, and walked across the dirty lino under which careful Victorian patterns lay invisible, to the thin, white front door that had been slapped up at the bottom of the staircase, a Yale lock gleaming halfway up it, a bit too low, the locksmith measuring it out wrong in his careless hangover that day in 1971. It was the noise his handiwork made that would signal to Mo, lying up there in bed a weekend a month, as though it were a rickety ship's cabin in an apocalyptic storm, that Frankie was home and that she was safe. Well, everything's relative, she thought now, smiling to herself as she climbed the shabbily carpeted stairs. 'This is it,' she said to Pavel and he made a noise of acknowledgement in his throat but didn't speak.

Frankie was in the bath.

'Frances?' Mo called, holding on to the glossy painted banister and letting Pavel walk in behind her, overtly Russian, alien in the Englishness. She couldn't begin to imagine what he'd think, here now in the flat that had seen so many dreams of him, of just a Russian boy who represented escape and could have been anyone.

Someone, Mo thought, would strip the paint off this banister one day, chipping round all the twisted curves to reveal the wood to be varnished. 'Look, Seb! It's beautiful!' Up with the carpet, in with the sander. Mo didn't dare to admit to herself that it was a lovely flat with big rooms and high corniced (if nicotine-stained) ceilings, the kind of place she would live when she came back to London, herbs in the window boxes, magnets on the fridge. For her it must remain a dank, dark, smoke-billowing cave where vapours rose from the ashtrays and corners hid decay, otherwise her memory was wrong and she was mad, her childhood dreamt and fading.

'Christ! You terrified me!' Frankie squealed from the steam and gushing water, the frosted glass in a pane on the door showing her in pink, tatty-edged silhouette, swinging a towel up on to her head, a fag burning in her mouth.

'Sorry. I did tell you we were coming. I didn't want to ring the bell . . .' Mo said, not expecting to be heard, beckoning Pavel to follow her and walking into the sitting room where she slumped into an armchair, picking the horsehair out of a hole in the arm like the bored child she'd been for so long. 'How are you?' she shouted. 'All right?'

'What?' Frankie yelled back, opening the bathroom door now and letting out a cloud of damp steam whose smell crept through the flat and would probably cause mould, Mo thought.

'Are you all right?' Mo shouted again. Frankie poked her head round the sitting-room door. 'No need to shout. I'm right here,' she said. 'Did you hear about that bloke who they've all accused of raping them? You know, the presenter of that thing with the fat woman? I was just listening to the radio. Apparently he anally raped the girl with the—'

'No,' Mo said. 'We've just got off the plane . . .'

Frankie suddenly caught sight of Pavel and rushed in, excited, kissing him on both cheeks but carrying on with what she was saying. 'Amazing really. A fancy-dress party at his house. A lot of cocaine. He was dressed up like Fred Astaire. You know? "Siiiiinging in the rain . . ."' She began to dance, looking flirtatiously as Pavel with every step, smiling to let him in on the joke.

'Isn't that Gene Kelly?' Mo asked, straining round to meet Frankie's eyes, always shocked that she was real, like the parade of shops, a person staring back at her, resolutely in the room now, wearing a see-through kaftan, her jagged bones like a wire hanger inside it.

'Christ. You don't change,' Frankie sighed, still now, taking her fag out of her mouth after a big drag that hollowed out her cheeks and made the end burn bright orange.

She walked barefoot over to the window and glanced out as though she was waiting for someone, Pavel still standing, adrift. Mo wondered if, after all, she had been waiting for someone all her life, looking down at the empty, rain-drenched street where a cat dashed out from under a car to hide in a better place.

'I just . . . No. You're right. It's probably Fred Astaire. I've got no idea,' Mo said, looking over at Pavel, embarrassed, as if to show him that this was why she never had anyone round here. Pavel, she knew, would be appalled that Frankie hadn't even interrupted her train of thought to speak to him. He was used to banquets in his honour, for God's sake.

Frankie laughed bitterly. Not a laugh. A noise faintly resembling a laugh but expressive of derision, despair, rage, contempt. Mo knew she had said something wrong. But she knew also, at last, that there wasn't a something right. That was her only consolation.

'No! Not your era. All right. I get it. I know how old I am. Ginger fucking Rogers. I did what Fred did but backwards and wearing high heels. And you probably don't even know who Ginger Rogers is. Is that what you're trying to say?'

'God, Frances, no! I just . . . I have heard of Ginger Rogers . . .'

Frankie laughed again. 'Of course you have! Oxford University. You know bloody everything. I bet you think you're clever now, don't you? Does she do this to you too, Pavel?'

At last she had spoken to him, but only to try to get him on side. He might as well have been a green alien.

Only a few years ago Mo would have burst into tears at this point. Run to the loo, had to sit alone for a bit before going back in. Now she just sighed and longed for the sharp looming shapes and chaos of Moscow, wanted to make Pavel take her in his arms. It was stupid to have come here. They would stay in a hotel tonight. Frankie was drunk.

'I didn't mean . . .' Mo began, but gave up, her mind and body immediately defeated.

Noticing this, Frankie perked up even further, flicking a quick glance at Pavel to make sure he was listening, that he was with her. He looked baffled, stunned, rooted to the spot, his watch too flashy, his clothes too pressed, everything wrong.

'You used to love watching all those old musicals. Do you remember? The two of us curled up on the sofa, laughing our heads off at . . . what's her name? Doris Day. You loved Doris Day.' Frankie was blazing fury.

'I don't know . . .' Mo said, and it was true. She didn't remember at all, though she sent a search party deep into the frozen ravines of her brain. Had they sat laughing together? Why had every trace of the experience been obliterated? It was this certainty of Frankie's, this ability to provide information of which Mo had no recollection, that slowly slipped the fabric of sanity out from under Mo's feet.

'You loved her,' Frankie said again, though Mo couldn't even name a Doris Day film and had no interest in the actress whatever or, for that matter, in any old films really.

'Your father telephoned, incidentally,' Frankie added in the same tone, as though the two pieces of information went together. 'He wrote a while ago. I did send it on, I think.' She looked up at Mo expectantly, waiting for her comment. Her mascara had run in the bath and it was a tragic appeal this look, the make-up as black and as ill defined as her thoughts, a cry for help.

'Pavel and I thought we'd just . . .' Mo tried once more, tried to get her mother to focus on Pavel, to speak to him in a normal hostess-type way. She knew these mascara-drenched appeals, though she had never known what they were appeals for, and she was ignoring this one, jutting her chin and sliding her gaze away from her mother and towards the bookshelves, lurid paperbacks, shambolic, tumbling.

Mo felt her grip on reality dissolving and Frankie sighed, 'The number's by the phone.'

'Dad's number?' Mo asked, reaching out to Pavel in a gesture that was supposed to invite him to sit down but which he ignored. It was at this point that a man walked in and interrupted any clarification there might otherwise have been.

A man with a beard. He was fattish, fifyish, with a towel round his waist, stretched round a white and pink tubby belly with tufty hair in a stripe from stomach to chest where it joined the straggle of pube-like curls that covered his face and neck. He was blotchy from the steam and he held a tumbler of whisky in his right hand.

'This is Bosh,' Frankie said, blowing a plume of smoke out, her weight on one leg, hip thrust triumphantly out into the room. A spider plant lurked next to her on a tall bamboo plant stand, throwing its shoots optimistically out into the atmosphere, oblivious to the fact that nothing, surely, could thrive here. 'We're going to start a B and B in Ibiza.'

'Bosh?' Mo asked, staring at the man as though he too were an apparition, hoping, perhaps, that he might, indeed, turn out to be.

'Bosh,' Bosh confirmed, smiling and holding out his free hand to Pavel first so that his towel fell off, revealing the fleshy clump of his genitalia.

'I'm so sorry. I told you it would be awful,' Mo said, sitting across the table from Pavel in the Waldorf bar. It was the beginning of December and a huge tree twinkled behind him. They had been silent all the way in the car, Pavel staring out at London and Mo wondering what was going so horribly wrong. She felt she was supposed to look after him but had now idea how. It had always been his job.

'It's not your fault, Mo,' he said simply, but she felt she'd lost him without knowing why.

'Look,' she said, pulling at her hair. 'I know you don't feel . . . yourself here, not since we landed, but give it a chance. It's only been a few hours and my mum's from hell. We'll go out and eat Chinese and everything will—'

'I've never eaten Chinese before,' Pavel stated, swirling his cognac around in his glass and looking angry, truly angry. The manager rushed past. A crisis somewhere.

'You'll love it,' Mo told him, wanting suddenly just to go up to their room and burst into tears, having no idea how this situation had happened, this silent rage of his and this apparent demand upon her to do something about it. She had imagined being in London as wandering around galleries, sharing an umbrella, eating curry and Chinese, explaining the idiosyncracies of the British, whatever they might be. He'd wanted to come here and now he was acting like a lion, sedated by a stun gun on the savannah and forced into a circus, snarling, uncertain, terrified. 'Please, Pavel . . .'

Without warning, in the middle of a London hotel's festive atmosphere – tourists with bags of shopping coming in from the rain, laughing, the Christmas soundtrack playing lightly in the background, the grand piano covered in a felt shroud – Pavel smashed his glass in his fist.

'Jesus!' Mo said a lot too loudly so that people looked round.

A big shard of glass stuck out of Pavel's palm, blood dripping down his wrist and on to the white tablecloth, the ice melting on the carpet and the cognac making a dark pool.

A waitress with a lip stud came running over. 'Oh God! Are you all right, sir?' she said. 'I'll get the first-aid kit.'

Pavel was completely still and his face was cold as Siberia in January. Mo was transfixed by the look of him, her insides solidifying with fear.

'I was going to ask you to be my wife in London,' Pavel said, his voice tight and strained. 'But I now see that this is impossible. So I will say something else; I am getting married.'

The waitress was back and opening a green plastic box, kneeling next to it on the deep carpet by the spilt drink. 'I've called a doctor,' she said.

'You what?' Mo asked, stunned, utterly baffled. 'Jingle Bells' was playing.

'I am getting married. Goodbye.' The waitress looked at each of them in turn, her mouth hanging open.

'I was born in 1953, a child of the Cold War era, raised amid the constant fear of a conflict with the potential to destroy humanity. Whatever other dangers may exist, no such fear exists today. Mine is the first generation able to contemplate the possibility that we may live our entire lives without going to war or sending our children to war. That is a prize beyond value.'

Tony Blair

Chapter Fourteen

The day after she chased him out of the Slavyanskaya he showed up on her doorstep with a puppy, standing there with snow on the shoulders of his coat holding this tiny black dog with this huge bodyguard (who turned out to be Boris, of course – originally from Kirgask and they knew a couple of people in common), standing behind him.

Olga started screaming, she hated dogs, and Katya took the thing from him and walked into the basically all-white apartment.

'What am I going to do with a dog, Pavel?' she asked him, her eyes laughing.

'You are going to love him,' Pavel told her, looking at her as though commanding her to love them both.

Olga ran into the bedroom and shut the door, sending out a puff of her perfume like talcum powder into the room, and Pavel put down a thousand dollars in cash on the table. 'I don't want you to see anybody else,' he told her and, taking the dog from her and handing it to Boris, he led her into her bedroom and pushed her up against the door.

'I am going to fuck you so that you will never fuck another man as long as you live,' he said, pulling her skirt up around her waist and kneeling on the carpet between her legs, as if sex, given what she was and what she did, could ever matter a feather to her.

He came round every day and he stayed most nights, Boris

becoming a permanent fixture on the stairs outside her front door. In some ways she quite liked him. He reminded her of home and the bull-shouldered boys from school who you knew would never leave the army after conscription.

But two evenings a week, she wasn't stupid, Pavel went somewhere else, always arriving at her door by eleven, always smelling of the same perfume: Paris by Yves Saint Laurent, floral, sweet, girlish. Katya never said a word because she knew that a man like him would take time to win. She knew where he came from and how much he suffered, knew that asking would mean not getting.

In the long nights they spent together he talked to her about his childhood, about his brutal father and the horrific suicide, a punishment for him and his mother and brother, right in the apartment just after his mum got home from work, and he and Gleb were staring at their homework, chewing the pencil tips in unison, back when they were two halves of the same egg. He talked about the smell on his dad's breath when he beat him and he talked about his mother and how she let herself rot on the sofa, not caring any more, not about him or Gleb or anything at all, just staring at her nails. Katya thought he could talk the house down, whispering and whispering strange and cruel things that were so familiar to her, that were like the soundtrack of provincial Russia, a tragic, brutal story that anybody could tell their own part of, as though there was a whole snowdrift of misery out there, everyone throwing their flake in, the same as the others but different because it mattered to them. She stroked his forehead and kissed his temples and held him to her breast like a baby, though he never shut his eyes.

'Sssshhh,' she whispered into the sex-heavy air night after night. 'It's all over now.'

When her mother got ill Pavel took her home. They flew from Moscow on a tiny plane that he hired just for them, landing in Tomsk and driving in an enormous black car from America, like a tank, into Kirgask and to her mother's apartment.

She had chosen in the end to starve herself to death in her bed, the birds singing in the birch trees in the yard, Katya bringing her soup to refuse at mealtimes, begging her, coaxing her like a sick sparrow, as though she might persuade her back to health with the promise of Moscow with fur coats and pretty shoes, as though Katya might reverse her mother's decision with her own need.

There was a level on which, Katya could see, she enjoyed the pain of the tumours devouring her from the inside out, as her skin turned wax-paper yellow and her cheeks fell in, the smell of her breath fouling the tiny bedroom with the stink of rampant decay. Did she think it served her right for hoping for a better life, for whispering in the dark with Konstantin, for going to Moscow with dreams of Mosfilm, a Leningrad apartment and a white mink? Or did it serve Katya right, for her beauty and her gangster boyfriend and her sable? Perhaps though, in the end, it served her dead husband right for giving her the life of a brick-factory slave, with grubby slippers, cabbage boiling on the stove and a ring of red dust round the bath that made her curl up and weep on the spotless tiles with its persistence and its clearly written statement about who she truly was, whatever hopeful photographs might stand in the display cabinet. For it didn't matter much at whom the revenge was directed, it was a vengeful, cruel death and Katya was there for it, holding her hand at the very end.

In any case, it was how her mother wanted to go and go she did. As light as a dead bird she was when Katya lifted her off the bed and on to the paramedics' green canvas stretcher to be taken off to the morgue. One of the porters was smoking as he carried her downstairs, cigarette jammed into his mouth, eyes screwed up against the smoke, past a little girl who flattened herself against the wall and screamed, her school rucksack emptying itself into the stairwell.

Now she was an orphan, maybe a bit old for the term, but an orphan nonetheless.

Pavel went backwards and forwards between the flat and his dacha, with bodyguards and an air of tension that followed him everywhere, sometimes coming to sleep on the divan with Katya, but mostly returning to his fabulous mansion outside Tomsk, built recently, only just finished, and with a fountain in the foyer, a statue of a naked woman who was supposed to be her (he'd given a photograph to the sculptor).

Andriusha surprised her by coming to the funeral where he stood at the back of the hall, gaunt as a skeleton himself, triumphant under his invisible pall of gloom – until he saw her with Pavel. He seemed to collapse at the sight of them, but afterwards, when she joined him on a bench outside in the snow, clapping her hands together in her gloves because he looked so cold it was infectious, his clothes too scant somehow, he said he was glad to have introduced them and hoped they would be happy together. It was choked out and insincere, she thought, like the beauty contest runner-up congratulating the winner. Katya, in fact, had almost forgotten that he had introduced them or, rather, she thought, forced her to go and meet him as some sort of favour.

Though her hand felt heavy with the weight of the twisted pearl and diamond bracelet Pavel had finally bought her (the first proper gift, given a whole four months into the relationship and only reluctantly after she asked why he didn't buy her things), and though she smelt of Serge Lutens un Bois Vanille and wore vintage Dior sunglasses and carried a small white Chanel clutch, there was no question that when she was here, even with Pavel, Kirgask claimed her, ignoring the trappings of elsewhere, and told her, with incontestable certainty, that this, for all her pomp, was where she came from and where she must return. In some ways she liked it, and in all ways she liked that she shared it with Pavel, who knew for certain that he would never escape from his past, not with all the money in the world.

Amazingly, Vasily Vasilich himself was there at the funeral that day too, grey and bumbling, barely scraping by now on his pension, cooking kasha in a pan on his stove for supper and allowing himself a small glass of vodka with it. He nearly reached out to touch her from under his broken-spoked umbrella as she brushed past on a cloud of wealth, but she moved quickly away, whispering to Pavel who turned round and looked at him with contempt. That look, for Katya, was enough revenge on Vasily Vasilich for all his revolting lechery, but she kept quiet. A fly can't get into your mouth if it's shut.

For today, life, at last, was paying her back.

Katya wriggled her toes and the woman who was painting the nails pale pink stopped and held the brush in the air, dripping a glob of varnish on to the tiled floor.

'Sorry,' Katya said, laughing. 'It really tickles.'

She lay back on a slatted lounger in the cool room of the Turkish baths, steam billowing under the doors and Olga fast asleep next to her, her varnish drying. Pavel's mum, who had taken to referring to her son as 'my little Pavlik' at every opportunity, like a cuckoo in the woods, had been lifted out of her wheelchair on to a hot marble slab where her back was being massaged by a strong lady called Valya who took no nonsense and used to be a tank driver. For his part, Katya knew, Pavel was sickened that she was using his dad's nickname for him, the name of his vodka business (still running actually). She never said it to him when he was genuinely little, never said it before the money hit her account.

Today, this day, Katya was getting married to the richest man in Russia. Actually, to call a radish a radish, that was not quite true. She had got married to him yesterday in the Tomsk house of weddings with Boris, who she thought was a gentle soul really, as the witness. But this afternoon the old Epiphany cathedral, rebuilt with Pavel's money and renovated just as it had been under Nicholas II, would be full of people and she, Katya, would walk down the aisle in a diamond and ruby tiara that had once belonged to Grand Duchess Xenia Romanova, wearing a white satin Vera Wang backless sheath dress and an ermine stole, thank you very much. No really – thank you.

It had taken a long time to get him to propose and Katya strongly suspected that she had fought off competition, though he never mentioned it and she never asked. It had happened in a hurry, after a business trip that had brought him back to her with a wounded hand like a bear with a thorn in its paw. This injury and the urgency of his proposal made her heart start to thaw, even though she knew from what life had already taught her that this was usually a mistake where men were involved. As it would turn out, this was no exception.

She shook the thoughts out of her head, determined to revel in her day like the puppy, a proper dog now, who bounded around the gardens of the sanatorium where she was staying in the build-up to the wedding, while the dacha was being prepared. This was the day she had always known would come, this was the day her father had told her to be ready for and ready she was. Or, at least, she would be when the varnish dried. Olga stirred under her towels and grinned when she saw Katya's face looking down at her.

'I don't want you to move to London!' she cried.

Katya laughed. 'I'm not going until after we have a son, for God's sake. It could be years! I wish I'd never said anything. I just . . . Pavel wants his son educated in England. An English gentleman!' Katya imagined a young man bowing to ask her to dance like an officer at a ball and shook her head. Really she longed to go – clean wet pavements and hot toast, dogs on leads and bright green grass like a cartoon – though having a child seemed a distant and unlikely future.

'What are you going to do about that spot?' Olga asked her, re-assured, sitting up now, concerned as only a good friend could be.

'I am going to wear make-up. It's my wedding.' Katya laughed. 'Anyway, he never seems to notice what I look like – I mean, apart from the clothes. He sort of peers inside like a fox at chickens.'

Olga looked down at her nails. 'I like this colour,' she said, blowing them though they were already dry. 'Do you love him though?' This was not the first time Olga had asked her this, but she was never satisfied with the answer.

Katya clucked and pointed a finger over to where Pavel's mother had drifted off to sleep under the wide hands of the masseuse. 'What are you talking about?' she whispered. 'You mean like in a fairy-tale? You are such a goose, you know. Look at the facts. He is rich. Really rich. And he understands me and he needs me. If you ever hear of a better relationship than that then let me know.'

Olga laughed. 'You are hard as a brick from the factory,' she said. 'I want to fall in love.'

'Then go to Hollywood,' Katya advised, standing up now, seeing the hairdresser waving at her through the edge of the door.

While she sat at the dressing table in her room having her hair carefully piled up on to her head a lock at a time, pulled, blow-dried, thickly sprayed, tightly pinned, Pavel knocked hard on the door and came in. A blustery feeling of rage coming in with him. He was wearing a pale blue suit with a white rose in his buttonhole and he looked at her, in her sanatorium robe, with hard eyes she hadn't seen before, his scar prominent, his broken nose a sign today of thuggery rather than ancient pain. Something was coursing through him like oil through a pipeline.

'Is your mum ready? Liuba is pushing her today, isn't she?' she asked, hoping she was wrong about his mood, his look, wanting to keep things normal. She loved Liuba, whose brutal story she'd heard, whose hand she'd held and whose hair she had stroked. Sometimes she came to read her a story, the kind of story nobody had read her as a child, though child she remained.

'Yes, they've already gone to the cathedral,' he said. 'Did you invite the Andriusha cretin?'

Ah, this is what it was about. He wasn't jealous about any of her clients from Tokyo to Tallinn, whatever revolting and bizarre things they had wanted from her (one had asked her to 'give birth' to a real Fabergé egg he had bought that day at auction and that he wanted to see emerging from her cunt – he came on the spot) but her old friendship with Andriusha, his employee after all, though God knows he couldn't work for anyone in the state he'd been in, tore away at him like a vulture on a desert carcass. She had no idea why. She thought it was precisely because she had never had sex with Andriusha, he really had been her friend once, and this, in Pavel's warped mind, gave him a power over Pavel that Pavel couldn't stand.

Katya raised her eyebrows at herself in the mirror and the hairdresser backed off, fiddling with her clips and brushes, leaving a sprayed lock dangling in Katya's face. She had tried to show him the lists months ago, but he left everything to her, including even the security – tight.

'Why cretin? He's not been well, certainly, and I'm sure he might not always have been good at his job for you, but—'

'No. He was good. When I used him he was good.' Pavel seemed to spit the words out like the husks of the sunflower seeds they used to sell on the summer streets in twists of newspaper.

Katya sighed. 'Yes, I invited him. He is my oldest friend. You know that. And, after all, he introduced us.'

Pavel paced the room, glancing out at the garden that was beginning to come alive for spring but not really seeing it, the

198

atmosphere raging inside with his inexplicable anger as though a ringmaster was slicing an invisible whip through the air.

'Introduced us?' He grabbed her wrist and she stared at his hand, uncomprehending, as his fingers dug into her flesh. 'Introduced us? You know what I used to say to him, do you? "Find me the best whore in Russia," I used to say to him. You call that introducing someone?'

Katya pulled her arm out of his grasp, still feeling the pressure of his grip, and looked back to the mirror, making a show of pinning the hair up herself, pretending that this wasn't happening.

'Well, we met, didn't we?' she said, as though calming a child in the throes of a tantrum. 'None of us is perfect, OK, Pavel? We are all grown up, doing what we have to do,' she went on softly, aware that something was going on that would spoil her day today but not knowing what it was.

'That guy, that fucking scumbag has been threatening me, Katya,' he said, his lips an angry line, veins in his neck throbbing. 'Threatening me.'

Katya laughed. The very idea of poor Andriusha, half-destroyed he'd been, being a threat to anyone. Maybe, maybe when he first started out working for Pavel as a schoolboy, when the world was anyone's. But not now. Now it was all over – there was a clear winner.

'Laughing! You're laughing!' Pavel shouted and the hairdresser dropped her box of tools on the floor and shrieked. Pavel looked at her. 'Get out,' he said, and she ran out of the room, very frightened. Pavel, though not really a big man, seemed to fill the room with impending violence.

'Look. I didn't mean to . . . It's just that he's so . . .' she started.

'Do not laugh at me,' Pavel said, calmly now, pulling her out of her seat by her shoulders and standing her in front of him. He brought his face near. 'Do not laugh.'

She barely recognised the man, blurred as he was by hot proximity, with cigarettes and coffee on his breath and she was so staggered by what was happening, was slightly hungry with nerves, slightly high from the sauna and the excitement, the tiara on the dressing table making patterns on the walls in the scalding light, that he seemed absurd and, despite herself, she burst out laughing even louder, hysterically, unable to stop.

Pavel let go of her so that she collapsed back into her chair, tears streaming down her cheeks, laughing in fear and misery. She put her hands over her face and Pavel wrenched the chair out from under her so that she fell to the floor and then he kicked her hard in the stomach. She didn't make a sound.

'I'll see you at the cathedral,' he said, and thundered out.

This was what marriage to Pavel would be, she saw that now. The long years of her life stretched out in front of her like a sentence for an unthinkable crime.

Katya drew herself up to crawling and, as she vomited on to the synthetic blue carpet, she thought about Olga asking her, only an hour or so ago, if she loved him. She didn't realise it at the time, but she saw now that perhaps she had done, perhaps that feeling of hope and security, of a safe future and a deep mutual understanding, perhaps that was love. She had loved him. But not any more. Hardening herself into steel, into all the steel in the world, she thought, now owned pretty much outright by Pavel, she stood up and went to the bathroom, where she fetched a towel and cleared up her sick on her hands and knees. Then, one arm holding her stomach, which was in enormous pain, she went over to the door and called for the hairdresser to come back.

The girl had been hiding round the next corner and came running eagerly. 'Are you all right, madam?' she asked, scuttling in and busying around. Violent men were two a kopeck out here, after all, money or no money.

'Yes, fine. Everyone's nervous,' Katya said, and she lit a cigarette, trying to stop herself from the uncontrollable shaking that gave her away. 'Sorry,' she said. 'I think I'm going to be sick again.'

The wedding was everything she could never have dreamed of. A white limousine drove up into the hills to the sanatorium to fetch her and the chauffeur wore a white suit with gold braid. The car was packed full of roses and had a satin ribbon on the bonnet. At the cathedral the traffic had been stopped, cordoned off with metal stands and plastic tape, and a traffic policeman ushered her car through into the surrounding empty streets. The sun was shining sharply and there were green spring buds on all the trees. Olga, beautiful, sweet, loyal, clueless Olga linked arms with her at the grand door and they walked in together as the choir burst into celestial song (at least, Katya assumed it was celestial song, having, in truth, never actually been to church before coming to see the priest a week ago). The air inside was thick with incense and the sunlight through the glass made the dust sparkle like glitter above everyone's heads, everyone she'd ever known and an awful lot of people she didn't know. She looked desperately around for Andriusha but he wasn't there. And for the first time, even given everything she knew about Pavel's life and the way the world works, she was frightened.

She went through the motions of matrimony like a zombie, smiling at the photographers as if she were an advertisement for Siberian honey, bowing her head meekly towards the priest's blessing, holding her candle with something like reverence, walking out into the showers of petals and rice, her arm in Pavel's, kissing big Boris on both cheeks before she got into the limo, extra security flicking their eyes about for an assassin who, little did they know, lurked within. In the car she was silent, her hands clasped in front of her, and Pavel looked out of the window, drawing in his breath now and then as if he was going to speak, but never managing to get the words out.

If he said he was sorry, would she forgive him? She couldn't imagine what it would take, her heart was as bruised as her stomach and she had read, she remembered, that brains flash with pain when they are reminded of an emotional injury. Hers would surely flash for ever, like a satellite in black space.

Tomsk rolled by and they arrived at the dacha, strewn with ribbons, marquees in the garden, black-and-white-uniformed waiters and waitresses everywhere. She had hired half the city to do this reception, vats of caviare, vodka on ice, a string quartet from the conservatoire and later a jazz band from St Petersburg, money no object. But now it was all ruined, blanked out by the truth. The truth was – she was not going to shy from it like people who shied from everything in life, like her mother, like a coward – the truth was that she had just married a man who kicked her and knocked her off her chair.

Nothing now seemed real, not the gold statue draped with garlands of orchids, nor the cars parked up the road for miles, the sniper on the roof, the tiara which she reached up to touch, but which was cold and sharp – just a lump of money in the end.

Olga was in the car behind her, in the Hummer with some other girls from school, and she rushed out in tears to hug her friend as soon as the car stopped, holding her dress up out of the spring mud so that her white knees looked like a bird's legs, vulnerable and frail.

'God, it was so wonderful,' Olga gushed, kissing her. 'And this! Look at this!' It was the kind of house anyone would long for, Katya knew. She had suggested the underfloor heating herself and she had loved wandering around in her underwear and watching the snow-fall outside.

Katya tried to smile as she took her friend's hand and grabbed two shots of vodka off the tray they were immediately offered as they bent to come under the archways of flowers.

'To love,' Katya said, throwing the drink down her throat.

Then she bit the inside of her mouth until it bled, something she had not done for a long time.

'To love,' Olga repeated.

Katya would have liked to drown herself in the whole trayful but she didn't, because she felt blood start to drip down her legs. She had not know until then that she was pregnant.

'We are hurtling back into a Soviet abyss, into an information vacuum that spells death from our own ignorance. All we have left is the internet, where information is still freely available. For the rest, if you want to go on working as a journalist, it's total servility to Putin. Otherwise, it can be death, the bullet, poison, or trial – whatever our special services, Putin's guard dogs, see fit.'

Anna Politkovskaya

Chapter Fifteen

Eli and Mo were on their way back from the place he rented out at Peredelkino, the real Chekhovian deal with a deep paint-peeling porch, lace curtains on the windows, an overgrown garden leading down to the lake at the back where there were raspberries in the tangled darkness at the beginning of summer and blackberries at the end. Every now and then they dragged the corpse of a drunk out of the green water, vodka oozing out of his pores, a tattoo across his shoulders. Drinking to coma and then going in for a dip was the same Russian insanity, in Eli's view, that led them to sell off all their assets like maniacs, giving rise to the need for good lawyers and making him an incredible fortune.

'"Don't Drink and Drown",' he said to the car's interior as they passed a group of boys with towels over their shoulders and bottles in their hands heading in the general direction of water.

Mo was living in London now, in Frankie's flat, since Frankie and Bosh had gone off to start a new life in Ibiza, but her paper quite often sent her to Russia to write features about oil and gas and other gripping things that set the hearts of their readers racing. She hadn't seen Pavel since that terrible day at the Waldorf and he hadn't contacted her. For a while she expected Boris to show up at the door or someone with flowers and a devastated apology and, for a couple of months before she went back to London, she scoured the audiences at her gigs and half expected a surprise lift home. But she read about his wedding in *Moskovsky Komsomolets* and saw the photo, not for a moment connecting this astonishing goddess, who looked like a supermodel with a tiara on her head and swamped in roses, with Katya from the Ukraina Hotel when they were fifteen. She was familiar, sure, but the spectacularly beautiful all look a bit the same, especially dressed up like that. She bothered to note the irony of the tiara and remembered that he'd once told her she'd look like a provincial beauty queen if she wore one. Not in that one she wouldn't. She remembered tossing the paper aside and feeling a bit small and strange and uncomprehending. For she was extremely well aware that to have announced just like that he was getting married and to have done it so soon afterwards meant that he was seeing this other woman all along. Not that he would have minded or asked if she'd seen other people too, but, the thing was, she hadn't. He had been her boyfriend and all the while she had not, in fact, been his girlfriend. Perhaps it was for his bride – the dog he told her about that time. And it certainly explained why he was none too keen to fuck her mostly. I mean, look at what he was going to bed with. Well, it was a long time ago now. She scratched a mosquito bite on her leg. Say what you like about the Chekhovian idyll, but it wasn't half mosquito-infested.

'Did you see they're going to get TomStal for tax? Your old mate Ivanchenko's going down,' Eli commented, reading her mind, rubbing his hand through his non-existent hair, the glamorous Isro now shaven off to diminish the effect of catastrophic balding. She could always tell when Eli was dying to tell her something. He went all sort of springy.

'I was just thinking about him,' Mo admitted, lighting a cigarette as the countryside turned into the Moscow ring road and then the centre of town. 'They'll never get him,' she said, sure that he was indestructible. At least that was how she remembered him.

Eli shook his head, straightening his glasses. 'Look at Khordokovsky. And Ivanchenko's got a much murkier past.'

'Oh, you always said that.' Mo laughed. 'You were just jealous.'

'Speaking of which' – Eli smiled, taking her hand and telling the driver not to take Kutuzovsky – 'we mustn't keep Gilda waiting.' They were nipping back to the flat before flying to London together, she home, Eli for some big self-congratulatory work bash.

Mo hadn't met Eli's new girlfriend yet, but she was waiting for them, sitting on the sofa drinking a gin and tonic, when they came in, all the windows open, the summer pukh flying in and the *FT* on the table. She was an economist for a bank, German, six feet tall, blonde, blue-eyed and a religious Catholic. From Bonn.

'God, I should have known,' Mo laughed when he described her on the phone. That that was what he had always wanted, his sick fantasy.

'If you can't beat them, join them,' he argued. 'These are people I want on my side. I mean, look what happened when they weren't.'

'Eli, you're off your head,' Mo pointed out. 'We did beat them and even if we hadn't that's not an argument for fucking them.'

'Momix,' he sighed. 'This tiny weeny Jew does not need an argument for fucking this gorgeous giant of a shiksa.'

'Hi!' Gilda exclaimed, leaping up and hugging Mo spontaneously. 'I'm so happy to meet you. Eli talks about you all the time! Here, let me get you a drink.'

She ran off to tell someone to bring more drinks out and then came back into the room, smiling.

Mo started asking her some boring questions about an oil company she was writing about and that Gilda knew about and the maid came in with a tray, glasses, ice, lemon, tonic.

'Brilliant isn't she?' Eli beamed. 'She's from Godknowswheresk, a billion miles north of nowhere.'

'And I thought you were supposed to be left wing,' Mo laughed, pouring herself a drink while Gilda talked oil.

'Can't I be left wing and rich with servants?' Eli wondered, taking off his glasses and blowing on them, wiping them down with a corner of his shirt.

'No,' Mo shook her head.

'Anyway, listen.' Eli held up his hands to stop all other conversation. 'Before Mo and I leave for the airport I want to tell you both a story about Ivanchenko which will be particularly interesting to you, Mo. She used to go out with him a few years ago,' he explained to Gilda. 'How many years ago?'

'Loads,' Mo nodded. 'I last saw him with a big piece of glass sticking out of his hand in the Waldorf.'

'Jesus,' Gilda exclaimed, jumping on to an armchair and folding her legs under her. 'That's very extreme. What was he like?'

'Oh. Well, you know. Strange. Very Russian. I mean, *very* Russian. It was all rather formal but I think he was already engaged to the woman he married, actually. I should have known. I was very naïve.'

'And now?'

'Still very naïve. *And* single.' She laughed, mussing her hair, feeling a bit scruffy and silly in Eli's posh flat with his high-powered girlfriend. Actually, Mo had only just become single. She was going out with a newsreader for a bit, who took himself very seriously and said his job was a 'fur-lined handcuff' and complained about how hard he had to work all the time which, frankly, didn't look all that hard to her. He liked porn and fast food and it didn't work out. She only did it because he smelt nice and she was absurdly lonely.

'Anyway.' Eli was bouncing with excitement. 'This is why I got my flight changed to come with you. We can discuss it on the plane, but it is huge. *Huge.*'

Mo, always nervous about discussing Ivanchenko and slightly bored by the fact that so far, having had a rather short, weird and not that nice relationship with him, it was still the most interesting thing that had happened in her life and the only thing anyone ever wanted to hear about. She watched the slice of lemon bubbling to the top of her glass, shoving the ice cubes enthusiastically out of the way. Eli budged her up on the sofa as though they were about to watch his favourite film (*Zelig*) and have a popcorn fight, the mood boisterous and light, stinging with excitement, antiseptic before an injection.

He took a long slurp of his G and T and screwed his face up. Drinking, he'd always claim, didn't suit him, being Jewish. Still, in her experience he'd seemed to manage a fair amount of it.

He picked up a peanut and threw it into the air, catching it in his mouth and smiling, pleased with his trick.

'Jesus, Eli. WHAT?' Mo asked eventually, exasperated.

He began. 'So, I'm sitting in the office and this guy comes in, henchman type, obviously lowly, shoulders, you know?' he explained, flexing his neck muscles and sloping his shoulders in a bodybuilderish pose in imitation of the Russian ex-army fighting-bull look. 'Says he's got an offer for me. The boys frisk him and what have you, even though he'd obviously already come through the detectors downstairs, but what do they know, and he sits down right in front of me and slaps two cheques on the counter. London bank, sixteen million spondoolies each.'

'Someone gave you thirty-two million pounds?' Mo laughed, thinking that that was precisely the kind of luck that made Eli's life what it was. 'Hey! It wasn't Boris, was it?' she wondered, remembering so well Pavel's lumbering bodyguard and the story of how they'd gone to the disabled prostitute.

'Wait!' Eli commanded. He loved to have a good story. The sky was going deep orange outside as the heat and pollution merged into the perfect postcard sunset over the Kremlin, a view that doubled the price of any property in the downtown area as if it were the Champs-Elysées.

'"What's this?" I ask. The bloke shrugs and wants to know if I can be trusted with it. I say, "I don't know what I can do with it. This is a law firm, not a bank." Anyway, he wants me to put them in a vault in London, as a sort of personal favour, clear it with the government and then . . .' He took another sip of his drink. 'This is the good bit.'

Mo already hated this whole thing, nervous that Eli had been chosen and fearing, rightly as it would turn out, that it had something to do with her.

'He says I've got to cash them immediately if and when . . .' Eli paused with a big smile, his punchline well on its way, fizzing with expectation.

'If and when?'

Eli looked dramatically round the room as though the walls have ears, which they may well have had, and announced, 'If and when they nail that murdering so-and-so Ivanchenko and send him for all eternity where the sun doesn't shine, and, let me tell you, the sun really doesn't shine in those prison camps in Magadan. Or, obviously, if, and almost certainly when, someone else shoots him first, which, given the number of people who would like to shoot him, is my best bet.'

Mo was stunned. 'What are you supposed to do with the money? Why would he give you a gift like that, for Christ's sake?' she asked, slamming the door on all the thoughts and feelings clamouring to leap out, second-class passengers on the *Titanic*, gated in below deck.

'It's not a gift,' Eli explained. 'I have to start a charitable foundation with it. Keep funding his existing charity projects in Tomsk and around, start any others that might be appropriate, pay myself a modest salary.'

Gilda laughed at this, presumably the idea of Eli having any clue what a modest salary would look like if it jumped up and poked him in the eye was hilarious.

'Wait!' Mo shouted. 'You didn't take the money?'

Gilda shook her head, as if knowing her boyfriend better than to suspect him of that.

'Yeah, sure I did. Bold as brass. I just shoved them in Gilda's bra drawer and told him I'd think about it. Are you INSANE? Who would get involved with that guy? Well, you know, who normal?' He looked around to make sure everyone had understood his point. That Mo was a psycho.

'"Small Jewish Man Does the Right Thing",' he added.

'And what are you suggesting I do with this information?' she asked, turning to face him, understanding that he had somehow expected her to share in his enormous joy, to help send Ivanchenko down into the fiery abyss of hell with righteous judgement from above and, of course, a little shout of glee.

'Duh! Are you insane? What do you think I suggest you do with it? Publish it, for God's sake. It's brilliant. Proof at last that he's screwing Russia over just like everyone knows he's always been doing. He knows they're on him for tax and he doesn't want the country to get a brass farthing. Come on! This is the first time anyone's ever been able to pin anything on the murdering bastard!'

Mo wished he would stop saying that. It made her teeth hurt as though some chemical process had stripped off the enamel and made them hyper-sensitive to saliva, to oxygen, to skin.

'Hey, guys,' Gilda said, in that way that foreigners do. The kind of people who, if they were American, would never say 'hey, guys'. 'Your flight? The car's here?'

Mo could see that she was the responsible one, booking, checking, sighing about Eli's hopelessness. She went over to kiss her. 'It was lovely to meet you,' she said.

Gilda smiled. 'You too. Really great. Lovely,' she corrected her American English and added an English English 'lovely'. Americans never say 'lovely'. Mo wasn't sure what Germans say.

'I hope we can get together properly one time. Do you ski? We could all go skiing? What do you think? Easter, maybe?' Gilda asked.

'Eli doesn't ski,' Mo told her, wondering how this had escaped her notice.

'Oh, he does now,' she said, shaking her blonde mane.

'I do,' he admitted. 'We spent some time with Gilda's relatives at a lovely little resort in the Black Forest, perfect for beginners, actually, and lovely people, Aunty Gretel and Uncle Hansel—'

'You know that they are not called that,' Gilda complained, shoving him out of the door with his suitcase. 'Bring me back Marmite.'

'I promise,' Eli said, kissing her. 'Isn't she perfect?' he asked Mo on the way down the stairs.

'You know, I think she is,' Mo agreed.

But Eli did not give up. Swinging through the Moscow streets with the heat pounding in the open windows and the driver playing an Eminem CD, he continued his onslaught on Ivanchenko and how Mo should stitch him up. The fact was though, she couldn't. He had, she knew, actually confessed to organising a murder in her presence, confessed to her that night on the train. But she felt he had been right, not wrong, and that he knew the difference. The world he grew up in, the world he fought in was different to the one she and Eli knew and she didn't know how to describe that without sounding like an idiot.

She tried the lightly persuasive approach saying, as they queued at Domodedovo passport, control, fishing in the pocket of her leather jacket for her passport, 'The thing is that Ivanchenko has not, in fact, broken any laws, either Soviet or contemporary. The big natural resources giants got tax breaks that were agreed by the Kremlin at the time in an attempt to revive the economy. He persuaded people out of their privatisation vouchers in, perhaps, not the most ethical imaginable way, but it wasn't illegal. It was the Wild West. It . . .'

She stopped because Eli was looking at her as if she was talking about her passion for Jesus and how he lived yet in the body of a charismatic cult leader to whom she had just given her life's savings. His face was expressionless and slack but only for a second.

'Well,' he began, shouting after her as she handed her passport over and obeying the not-crossing-the-yellow-line rule, 'since you are obviously working for Ivanchenko's PR department, which persistently claims that somehow murdering people was not, for a brief period in Russian history, breaking the law in the strictest sense of the word . . .'

Mo could hear Pavel's irreverent laugh in her mind, dismissing these ravings as opinions that came from another planet, the place he had always accused her of landing from.

'Look. I doubt he has murdered anyone,' she lied, 'but if he has, it was probably someone who was trying to murder him.'

'Well, that's OK then.'

'Eli, you are a *tax* lawyer. Stop.'

They were still arguing in the duty free shop where Eli bought some batteries and Mo bought two hundred Marlboro Lights and a bottle of scotch. They were still arguing as they walked down the corridor to the plane and they were still arguing when the engines started to roar.

'Sure, he has plenty of enemies,' Mo agreed. 'And there's no shortage of people who want to believe he hit out at some of them. But you're being gullible. I can't believe you've been sucked in by the government's smear campaign. They're after him and they'll say anything to get him in prison and the assets in their hands. Or, apparently, your hands.'

'Hold up, Goebbels!' Eli said as the back wheels left the ground. 'Are you saying that it was the government who sent Big Thug Man round to see me with billions of dollars in order to frame Ivanchenko?'

Mo sighed. It seemed unlikely to be sure. She ordered a Bloody Mary from the nice stewardess (they were always nice in business class). She wanted not to be shouted at any more. She was looking forward to getting back to the flat, which she'd had painted, the floors stripped, the banisters varnished, all those things she predicted someone else would do one day. She'd also managed to get the council to cut the creepy purple tree down and she had put a herb box on the window sill. The students were long gone and the Somalis were dream neighbours, Ola bringing big pots of stew round for her whenever she came in late from the airport.

There was a woman sitting across the aisle from her with a toddler asleep on her lap. She had her sunglasses on and her hair in a lavish blonde ponytail; she wore a lot of expensive jewellery and was wrapped up in cashmere of different shades of grey. The child wore a Ralph Lauren jumper with the American flag on the front of it and was holding a second-generation grey elephant whose seams were coming loose. Mo kicked Eli hard in the shin.

'It's thingy,' she whispered to him, knocking her drink off and causing a big commotion as the stewardess came to wipe up the tomato juice that looked like a haemorrhage on the grey nylon of the plane's floor. Thingy, and Mo was certain it was her, did not look round. Perhaps she was asleep.

'Who?' Eli asked loudly, craning round from the window seat to see who he recognised on the plane. There were always a few. The community of regular Moscow–London travellers was small enough that you could usually find a friend. 'Where?'

Mo spoke like a ventriloquist. 'Right next to me. There. I know it's her! She looks just the same. Svyeta! *No.* Lena! No. Katya. It's Katya. Remember? The prostitute that Hepburn fucked that night when I met Pavel. When we met Pavel. You must remember. She was fifteen, you know. The most beautiful woman in the world. You were terrified.'

'I was not,' Eli claimed. 'Oh God, Momix, you're right though. That is her. And I'll tell you who else it is as well.'

'What do you mean? You know her son? You can't do.'

'No. She's Ivanchenko's wife. I'd recognise her anywhere. She did a huge shoot for Russian *Cosmo* after they got married and it was pinned up on the board at work. It's her.'

'That's insane!' Mo shouted, such that at this point Katya lurched into life and pushed her glasses back on to her head, looking straight over at them. Given that she was less than a foot away and looking straight at her with eyes that were orange, or maybe honey-coloured, there was nothing Mo could do but talk to her. Even in nice class planes are cramped enough to force intimacy if it catches you at the wrong moment. Mo coughed a bit, and smiled.

'Sorry. We woke you up. Um. We recognise you.' She waved at Eli, feeling her face go redder and redder and hotter. Perhaps it wasn't bloody her after all. 'Do you remember us? Mo and Eli, from the Ukraina Hotel about a hundred years ago? We were fifteen? You and I exchanged addresses and, actually, I must have written to you a thousand times, but you never wrote back. Umm. How *are* you?' She was relieved to have finished, as if she'd been doing an audition for a part she'd never in a million years get. Medea, say.

Katya looked at her and then at Eli who was leaning into the conversation idiotically, entirely uncomprehending for what seemed like forever, and then she broke into an enormous smile. 'Sorry,' she said. 'My English is not good. I need to process in my head.

Yes! I remember you! I wrote to you too, but in Soviet times, I guess it does not always happen as we plan it . . .' And she reached over to touch Mo's arm. 'You look just the same.'

'Oh God, no, no I don't. But you. Look at you! You look if anything ever better. And a lot richer!' Mo babbled, aware that Katya might think she was being rude. But Katya didn't. She laughed.

'My husband is rich,' she stated with a big shrug that said a lot.

'Actually' – Mo decided to go the whole hog – 'Eli here says he thinks you're married to Pavel Ivanchenko. He saw your photo shoot after the wedding.'

Katya screwed her face up. 'Oh, that was horrible. I looked awful. Those clothes! I thought they were so glamorous at the time. We didn't know anything in Russia. All that gold and sequin . . . I am so embarrassed,' Katya wailed, acknowledging that Eli had been right. This was the woman who had stolen her boyfriend. That was something she thought she probably wouldn't bring up. Eli, desperate for some attention, tried to order a bottle of champagne.

'I'm afraid we only have the small ones, sir,' the stewardess apologised. 'But I can bring you some nice glasses and keep topping you up if you'd like?'

This suited them fine and, five miles above the earth, Mo chinked glasses with Katya whom she'd met all those years ago in a country that no longer existed.

'And me!' Eli demanded, leaning in again. 'I'm part of this reunion too, you know!'

'Yes, darling,' Mo comforted him, patting him on the arm.

He nudged her hard. 'Aren't you going to say anything?'

'About what?' She turned to face him, wincing at the light from his window reflected hard off the clouds.

'About going out with her husband, stupid?' Eli was outraged that this was going to be brushed over. He was a bit of a stickler for truth.

'You are seriously disturbed,' Mo told him and turned back to Katya. 'Did you really write?'

Katya laughed. 'Yes! And the KGB come to my house. My dad punched him,' she mimed a punch. 'And . . . Well, yes, I wrote!'

'God.' Mo sighed, thinking about how she'd waited, and her posters of Lenin and how happy she would have been.

'I even asked you for help. To invite me to London,' Katya smiled, her son waking up, woozy and bewildered. 'This is Vanya,' she told Mo, stroking his cheek.

'Hi, Vanya.' Mo smiled too, feeling quite freaked out to be meeting an ex-boyfriend's son. It had never happened to her before and she didn't like it, though the child himself was lovely.

'Well, you don't need us to invite you any more!' Eli said, raising his glass.

'No,' Katya agreed, hauling Vanya on to the seat next to her and getting some brightly coloured plastic cubes out of the seat pocket in front of her for him to play with.

'Are you going on holiday?' Mo asked, feeling a bit sad to be making at-the-hairdresser's conversation with someone she had thought about and longed for, someone who had once represented something important to her. Escape!

'No, actually. We are moving there,' she said. 'Here. I've never been before. You will help me?'

By the time Pavel decided they were at last moving to London Katya had become a different person from the woman he married, a suit of armour with nobody inside like the ones in the exhibition at the Kremlin that she'd seen years ago. She no longer expected that she and Pavel would travel together, or make any informal joint arrangements, for she had a separate security brief and never asked him about his travel plans or his business – she had come to know better. She took care of herself and she had now put all her hopes into Vanya, her third-time-lucky baby, freezing herself against her husband whose attempted apologies for the unbearable blood-soaked horror of their wedding day had taken the form of glinting pieces of jewellery that she didn't want and hadn't asked for.

Of course Katya wasn't really asking for help. She was being polite, Mo understood.

'I bought a house on Cheyne Walk. Is this good?' Katya was eager to know.

'That explains the goon with the cheques. He's bailing out but without the assets,' Eli muttered so that only Mo could hear. She kicked him hard with the heel of her cowboy boot. 'Ow,' he said.

'Well, if you've bought a house on Cheyne Walk, I don't think you'll need any help at all!' Mo told her. 'Yes, it's very good. It's lovely round there, actually. Near the river, lots of shops and restaurants and probably nice nurseries for Vanya.'

Katya looked nervous at the mention of nurseries. 'Well, we have a lot of . . . We have to be very careful,' she said, looking behind her in explanation. The two seats behind Katya contained her security billet. 'Normally I fly in our plane. But Pavel moved me today. Only told me this afternoon,' she said, raising her eyebrows as if Mo would understand how difficult men are, always restricting your use of the private jet when you least expect it. 'I have a dog in the hold.'

'How annoying,' Mo agreed. 'I mean, not the dog . . .'

'Yes, it is,' Katya said. 'But what can you do?'

She got up to take Vanya to the loo and Eli bounced up and down in his seat, already on his third champagne miniature. 'I told the goon I was on this flight! I told him I was going to London! I'm telling you, Mo, Ivanchenko's up to something. He must have known you'd talk to her.'

'Oh shut up, Eli,' Mo snapped. 'That's absurd. We are talking

218

about fuck all. You are completely mad. You'll be claiming it's some global anti-semitic thing in a minute.'

'It might well be.' Eli nodded sagely. 'It might well be.'

'I'll tell you what this is,' Mo turned round properly to face him. 'It is a *coincidence*. They happen all the time. When was the last time you got this flight and didn't run into some long-lost someone?'

'When was the last time you got this flight and ran into Ivanchenko's wife in the same week he tries to get you to launder billions of dollars for him so that Putin won't get his hands on it?'

Katya returned to her seat and Mo ignored Eli for the remainder of the flight, chatting to Katya in what became an almost normal way, about London, about Moscow, about men, though it was true that Katya knew an awful lot more about them than Mo did. 'Everything they say is a lie,' Katya stated and Mo had no reason to disbelieve her.

Looking back, both women agreed they'd needed to send out messages in bottles to an imagined soulmate as far away as they could imagine, to another planet really, a screaming SOS of animal stickers and Kirgask stories that helped them both to believe in their lies. Mo could cast herself in the role of the fortunate girl on the right side of the curtain where freedom and joy reigned, who might help with an invitation to London one day (God forbid Katya would ever see her flat) or who could offer to send marvellous riches unheard of in provincial Russia. And then she might momentarily ignore the truth of her situation, as terrified, terrorised and helpless as any cowering Soviet citizen.

And for Katya, perhaps it was a way of idealising life in Kirgask as she knew she should, and the lake and her parents, and the Communist dream of the brick factory: the very foundation stones of life produced by her own father! She didn't need to mention that the man who ran the beauty contest she won had sexually abused her and essentially sold her into prostitution in Moscow where she ate only grated carrot for about three years and picked up fat old apparatchiki in the less nice hotels. Because somewhere in the world there was a Katya from Kirgask who rode horses in summer and whose mother was nearly a film star, living a parallel life in the imagination of an English girl with bouncing curls who walked through London in the rain.

In some ways it didn't matter that the letters hadn't actually arrived. They served their purpose anyway. The women kissed and exchanged phone numbers before getting off the plane, agreeing to meet up in London soon.

'Oh, come on! Take my number too. You have to. If you ever need a lawyer, you know . . .' Eli interrupted. 'I mean, I only do tax, but I can always refer you if it's . . . you know . . . if you've been shoplifting or something . . .' Katya passed her little blue suede address book over to him with a soft smile.

Mo noticed that Katya smelt of lemons and worried that she smelt of stale sweat, having not washed for ages and still wearing the same white(ish) shirt, jeans and boots that she'd arrived in Moscow in days ago. That rich Russian composure that Katya had nailed was something to which Mo aspired without remotely believing she could ever attain it. The perfections seemed to involve remaining almost motionless at all times, not something Mo was good at. She looked down at the piece of paper with Katya's number on it and her own bitten nails.

'You'll never call her,' Eli said, pulling his briefcase out of the overhead locker.

'I will. No, I will. It's just . . . you know. I don't want to get into the whole thing . . .' Mo explained, wishing that she had never had anything to do with Ivanchenko and could therefore have a glamorous Russian friend who lived on Cheyne Walk. Katya was busy with Vanya and the security blokes and all their stuff, so Mo and Eli got off the plane and left her to it.

Mo looked around the arrivals hall when she picked up her case, wanting to say goodbye again, but by the time she caught sight of Katya she was going through passport control, her trolley piled high with Louis Vuitton luggage, Vanya sitting with his legs dangling on the front, and Mo couldn't catch her. She found that she reached out her hand to wave all the same.

'Whoever does not miss the Soviet Union has no heart. Whoever wants it back has no brain.'

Vladimir Putin

Chapter Sixteen

Katya allowed the switchboard girl, buried deep in the cellar of Oxley House, to put Andriusha's mother through this time. London did not free her from Kirgask, or from the spectre of her disappeared friend. Andriusha had been missing for two years now and Katya tried to blank her mind to the possibilities, probabilities, hoping simply that he would come home, healed of his troubles, perhaps by a hermit-like sojourn somewhere warm, in a southern republic. Hoping against hope, for she was well aware of what had likely happened. She was drinking coffee in her room and watching an old Soviet comedy, *White Desert Sun*, on the plasma-screen thing that took up most of one wall.

'I know,' she sighed as Andriusha's mother wailed. 'I know. We all miss him.' She did not allow the choking sob of the truth to get any further than her stomach.

Today Katya was going to meet the woman from the concierge service. So far, London hadn't been easy. Her horrible secret, her need to keep her domestic life out of the world's glare and the good excuse of security concerns meant that she was left in desolate loneliness. Pavel wouldn't even have any non-Russian staff, so, really, she and the baby had ended up in a kind of Moscow prison in London. God only knows what he was doing the whole time, but it seemed to involve trying to become an apparatchik, a British one, but they were the same the world over in her view. The establishment was the establishment and she didn't trust it.

She'd heard about the concierge service from a fox-faced girl she met at one of these horrible functions where the Russians stand around feeling insecure and appearing too vulgar and so, to cheer themselves up, bitch about the appalling shabbiness of the English who come to nursery open days with their clothes covered in dog hair, grey showing through at their roots and mud behind their fingernails.

'The women all look fifteen years older than they are and have the most enormous yellow teeth which they bare without caring a cucumber,' Fox Face said to her in a low whisper. Katya laughed because it was true. She was trapped by an elaborate display of lurid flowers and next to an austere painting of a kind of military person with a moustache and red uniform, talking to Fox Face who was actually the twenty-year-old wife of a shipping magnate from Archangel she called herself Antoinette, though Katya was sure that was her working name from when she was doing the men from the dockyards; she could detect a strong whiff of Svetlana about her, whatever she might claim now that she was encrusted with ice. An Englishman with a fawning kind of gay-type manner, like all those people she met at these stiff yet drunken functions, came over smiling broadly. How did they do this, she wondered? In Russia something is either formal or people get drunk and have fun. Here the English get very drunk but nobody ever relaxes. She shook his damp hand and he twisted his face into some strange contortion of intimacy, knowing that the real thing would never be. 'How do you find London?' he asked both ladies.

Katya smiled, seeming to slightly frighten him. 'It is a very beautiful cultural city,' she said, and was considering elaborating (she had been to the opera with Pavel who fell asleep – they were invited by an important MP) when the man's wife, one of the yellow-teeth and dog-hair brigade, pulled him away.

'How can he be married?' Antoinette said. 'He is gay.'

'I'm not sure,' Katya said because she wasn't. 'I think maybe they are just like that.'

'They are just like that because they are all gay,' Antoinette argued and Katya had to admit that no other explanation would properly account for the manner of Englishmen, especially at these charity functions. It had not taken Pavel long to understand that charity was the fastest route to respectability, social money-laundering of the most effective kind, how to give it away was, in the end, as important as how to make it.

'You're probably right,' Katya sighed, wishing there was music or dancing or something other than this standing and talking. What was wrong with these people? Pavel was in a corner with someone from government.

'You should sign up with this concierge thing. They do everything for you. Staffed our whole house and' – Antoinette lowered her voice to a conspiratorial whisper – 'found this student who comes round to teach me about art. Speaks Russian. Klyova!' she said, giving her age and background away immediately with this last adolescent exclamation of excitement, never mind that she'd sat next to the Prime Minister at dinner twice in the past month and had Englishmen project qualities like 'enigmatic' on to her when she couldn't think of anything to say and her swamp-green eyes glazed over in something between a coma of absolute tedium and genuine intellectual panic.

'That sounds good. You know, I love my house, but there is nothing to do here,' Katya agreed.

'We should go out? Me and you? Come on. We'll ditch the bodyguards and go to a club and dance!' Antoinette was obviously desperate to act her age and was probably only waiting for the four years of married life to elapse that had to elapse before she would get a really good settlement. And she'd have to have a baby too,

Katya thought to herself without judgment. Good for her, was her heartfelt view.

'That would be nice,' Katya said, and it would have been, but she would never call her. She had never called Mo either. She had too much to hide now.

'I'm going to start an art gallery. Since they all think we're so mysterious and that,' she went on. 'You could do it with me? Do you want to?'

Katya smiled softly and didn't answer.

So, on this bright English day when the sky is eggshell-blue and tiny woolly clouds flit anxiously across it (she always wondered why even the sky is small in England), Katya called the service Antoinette had recommended and she spoke to a woman with an aristocratic title of the kind with which the English are so obsessed. The woman invited her into an office where she was given champagne by a fat girl in trousers and where everything she said was greeted with avid interest and simmering excitement as though she were a Party leader with tickets to Moscow up his sleeve and tickets to a labour camp in his back pocket.

The countess had dyed her hair very blonde and then tucked it, straggling, under a blue velvet hairband. She wore big pearls in her ears and round her neck and the pale pink frosted lipstick she chose to wear showed the dark yellow of her higgledy-piggledy teeth to its most hideous advantage. Katya wished she had someone to laugh with about her and the whole silly business. The countess's husband did not approve of the concierge service she had started but she didn't care, he could stuff it, because he was having an affair with the woman whose dogs pick up at the game shoot and don't think she didn't know it perfectly well.

It didn't matter that Katya gave a false surname. Carstairs. This was a pretence that her husband was English. Well, it was possible. A lot of Russian girls in London had English husbands. It was all the rage. Perhaps they met while she was translating for his business trip to Moscow and he had taken her for a drink in his hotel and put his hand up her skirt? Today she had refused to let security follow her upstairs ('Stepan Arkadych, I don't care what your orders are. Wait here. I will be fine.') and she had not yet given the countess her address, saving that step until she felt sure she could trust the woman, sizing her up like a chicken on a slab. Katya could tell by the dark flush that was rising up from the collar of the aristocrat's shirt and into her slack jaw that she had smelt the money, a pig on a truffle, frantic with excitement, hunger, the assurance of reward. Her rose-gold rings were a little too tight on her fingers and Katya was aware that this was the type of Englishwoman who wears her grandmother's moth-eaten fur coat and thinks it's glamorous. They even turn up at parties in them. This stunned Katya as much as seeing men walk in first, letting the door swing into their wives' faces.

The countess explained to Katya, sniffing the air of fabulous wealth that travelled with Katya everywhere she went, that they would find her suitably discreet staff, plan her opulent parties and dinner parties, buy thoughtful and awe-inspiring presents for her friends, have all her laundry and dry cleaning done off site, supply her with, essentially, anything she might want including fitness instructors and, if she felt . . . less than confident at Downing Street suppers, lessons in British politics from Oxford graduates.

Katya had all the staff she could stomach and had no interest in learning about politics. She had learned everything she ever wanted to know about politics from Vasily Vasilich. 'What I would like,' she explained, still and composed in her suit of cashmere armour and using her best English grammar, 'is a yoga teacher.'

'I believe we have the perfect man for you. You don't mind a man? Some people prefer a same-sex instructor?'

'Either is fine,' Katya said.

The yoga teacher in question's name was Tyrone. The countess had done the vetting herself, prised out the character references like winkles from a shell. He was wiry, muscular and tight as a drum with a leather thong round his neck displaying a mystic eastern charm, a colourful tunic over baggy linen trousers and brown sandals on his veined feet: the epitome of a yoga instructor. He had scrubby hair the colour and texture of the fields after they'd been scorched and he wore silver rings on his fingers as though he might wave them in the air to conjure up a genie. He arrived three days later.

'Mrs Carstairs?' he said to her that first time, eyes wide with the apparent effort of absorbing this level of wealth, even though the countess said this wasn't his first customer from concierge. Everyone was like that when they first came here, she knew, but why should she hide it? It was so English, she had learned, to apologise for everything, especially money.

'This is the first time I've had to sign confidentiality forms and produce police clearance before a class,' Tyrone laughed as she shook his hand. 'Incredible place. And, yes, I'm white!'

Katya had no idea why he would say that, not having expected anything else.

She could imagine, though, how he viewed her, how he viewed the house and the security. She remembered a time when she too would have found it weird, not so long ago really, but a world away.

In fact, he'd got off the tube at Sloane Square and followed the directions he'd been given, two purple yoga mats rolled up on his back, incense sticks in a plastic sachet in his rucksack and his *Sounds of the Soul* CD at the ready. He walked past the glossy black door in the ancient red brick wall four times before he realised it must be his destination and, indeed, on a tiny brass plaque above an even smaller entry system it said: 'Oxley House'. He pressed the buzzer and chewed the skin around his thumbnail, always nervous about new clients and whether he would succeed in getting them relaxed enough, enjoying the positions, working hard, especially in their homes where half the time children would run in covered in crap or, now that he was on this concierge list, servants or someone would have some ridiculous question. If he was lecturing about globalisation nobody would interrupt like that, but people just didn't have the respect.

The door opened with a sharp click and Tyrone found himself walking through a metal detector just the other side of the wall and putting his bag in the dark hole of an X-ray machine as though he was about to get on a plane and the airports were on high alert. A guy the size of a brick shithouse frisked him, looking at him as though he were, in fact, a piece of shit, and practically hurled him out the other side of the booth on to a vast gravel driveway in front of a stately home surrounded by bright lawns that swept away from the house towards a lake on one side and some trees on another. He was pretty sure he saw a peacock.

'Holy fuck,' he muttered to himself, noticing now that there were quite a few blokes in black looking heavily armed and prowling about the place. A door opened at the front of the house and an old woman in a maid's uniform with a white apron waved him in.

'Khello,' she said. 'Wait here.'

It was cool inside, black and white marble on the floor and two imposing busts on columns either side of the front door, huge paintings on the walls, all of them probably worth millions of pounds, he thought, though he didn't personally recognise any of the artists. He saw a camera shift its angle to capture him and sensed, perhaps from the barely perceptible shufflings around him, that the house was full of people, all of whom would probably slit his throat if he made a false move. He smiled to himself at the thought of having his throat slit for wobbling a little in warrior pose (not that he would).

There was a padding from the main staircase and the most

staggeringly beautiful woman he'd ever seen in his life came down, pink cashmere socks on her feet and grey cotton sports wear wrapped gently round her body. She had her hair up in a messy ponytail and she seemed to be the colour of sunlight.

'Mrs Carstairs?' he asked, aware that he was about to sneeze; minions from enormous vases of lilies had already entered his nasal cavity to check in for sensitivity: high.

'Katya.' She smiled as he sneezed. 'Na zdorovye,' she said, and he recognised this phrase as meaning 'cheers' when Russians were drinking. He had a friend who was a doorman at Annabel's and he'd been sent on a day's course with all the staff to learn a few Russian phrases. One of them was 'na zdorovye'.

'Spasibo,' he smiled back at her, the only word he was confident about saying in Russian. Apart from, you know, vodka and tovar-ishch and stuff like that.

That was Katya's life as seen from Tyrone's point of view, Vanya upstairs with the Siberian girl, everything in its place.

'We'll go to the gym, OK?' she said, leading the way down a long art-infested corridor with floor-to-ceiling windows out to the back garden where beds of roses fought to be more noticeable than the heli-pad, though Katya liked the heli-pad with its suggestion of escape, not that she was able to avail herself of that option. They went through to the extension: the more modern bit of building by a large bleach-smelling pool with retractable roof and a proper gym with a dance studio and a separate fitness area; all the machines gleaming their constant readiness. She had liked the house from the brochures she was sent, mostly because of this section: modern, heated, secure, equipped, like the Tomsk dacha that she still missed, for all the wedding-day misery.

'Here OK?' she asked him, throwing her arms out to the dance studio with a nervous smile.

'If there's a CD player?' Tyrone nodded, busying himself with a long rummage in his rucksack and then sitting on the floor to take off his sandals and flex his feet.

He laid out the mats, lit the incense, asked Katya to turn the lights down. Then they faced each other cross-legged for the Om.

Over the next few months Tyrone, as Katya had known he would, almost tiresomely predictable, became consumed with Mrs Carstairs, finding that she dominated his dreams and presented herself to him, soft and naked, every time he closed his eyes, her flesh quivering in front of him, begging to be touched. Trying to maintain a state of penile flaccidity for a whole two hours at a time in her presence, while they stretched and breathed and writhed alone in the near dark, was often more than he could manage (though fortunately his trousers were baggy enough for this not to be too much of an issue) and Flavia, his girlfriend, told him over a large mixed bean salad that he had 'mentionitis' and had better not be fucking this Russian billionairess.

'If you went to that house once a week you'd be mentioning it,' he told her, hiding his obvious guilt in the truth like a pearl in an oyster.

Katya was partly relieved that her effect on men had not been diminished by her marriage and that perhaps not all Englishmen were as gay as they seemed. It was pathetic, she knew, but her yoga lesson was her favourite part of the week, weeks that otherwise seemed to roll by like pukh on the steppe. The nightclubs and parties, functions and balls that were forced upon her by the role Pavel wanted to play in this country (the role of not getting extra-dited back to Russia and being allowed to keep his wealth here tax free, let's call a radish a radish) held absolutely no interest for her because she was there with Pavel and she knew what he was capable of. She shook hands with politicians, royals and footballers with absolute equanimity. In any case, Pavel was almost always 'out on business', a phrase that exempted him from any further explanation, the message being: 'You like the money, put up with the deal.'

Tyrone, Katya noticed, watching the screens as he arrived, had made friends with Boris, who was now frisking him more gently and almost offering a smile. He'd learned how to say 'zdravstvuiye' and had tried it out on Boris. Boris smiled his strange grey teeth and slapped him on the back so that he nearly fell over. Tyrone interpreted this as social success and smiled back, hopefully.

'Tyrone,' he said, pointing to himself.

Boris nodded. 'Boris,' he said, and smacked the side of his own head so hard that his earpiece fell out. Boris, from his initial position of superiority over Pavel, back in the old life in Tomsk, had quickly come to be bullied by him on account of the stupidity for which Boris was already famous. The euphemism was 'sportsman' though, in fact, Boris was not skilled enough to be particularly good at sports; he was, however, the strongest person for miles around and could lift a Lada Zhiguli clean off the ground. He was useful in life because people found him scary to look at, and he was good at breaking arms in one clean snap, but he kept grey rabbits in his uncle's garage. Once the tables had turned Pavel used to say, 'What's wrong? Got a bear in your ear, Boris?' and he would reach up to smack him round the side of the head. Sometimes, when he introduced Boris to someone – a weasel-faced thug who sold girls in the lorry park up by Marxism-Leninism Street, say – after he'd taken control, he would whack him round the ear and say, 'This is Boris.' After a while Boris, who noticed it got a laugh, started doing it himself.

Katya wished he wouldn't. But Katya wished a lot of things. One of them involved Tyrone.

* * *

Last night they went to a party at a footballer's house in Virginia Water, where a lot of Russians live. There was massive security and stickers to put in the car window, a metal detector, the whole deal. Katya was bored, picking at the food that kept coming round on trays held high above the waiters' heads. A famous chef had made it, a model in a red basque told her. Ice-cream in a test-tube that tasted like caviare. Who on God's earth needed ice-cream that tasted like caviare? Katya wondered.

'Search me,' a black footballer from Venezuela replied, falling in beside her.

In the car on the way home Pavel worked himself into a rage. First he was slumped, drunk and leaning against the window. Then he seemed to come round and started ranting about her being a whore and all this stuff that he said nowadays.

'Pushing yourself on that nigger,' he said as they turned off Chelsea Embankment towards home. He slapped her in the car but saved the rest till later.

Today was a sharp sunny day and Katya knew what would make her feel herself again. Vanya was with the sweet nanny. She kept it to the one girl because of what her mother used to say: 'A house full of nannies and a baby without eyes.' She didn't understand it but it had always frightened her. Today was the perfect opportunity.

She came down the stairs to meet Tyrone, her eyes blazing and her whole body fighting inside her tight clothes. She flicked her head towards the corridor and he followed, meek and rather afraid, as she strode down to the gym as if someone she loved were imprisoned down there and she had just found the key.

'I will pay for this lesson in sex, OK?' she said, taking her clothes off as though suffering a violent allergic reaction to them, not caring if he saw the bruise on her neck and the imprint of Pavel's fingers.

'Umm . . . if you think . . .' he mumbled.

'OK?'

'OK,' he agreed, clearly wondering if he was also supposed to take his clothes off. She did it for him and she pulled his hand towards her breasts and the other between her legs.

Life would pay her, she was sure of that and, as she watched him fall into her thrall, hypnotised by lust, she bit the inside of her cheek until it bled.

The next week, Tyrone did not show up. He did not show up the week after that or the week after that and in the fourth week Katya confronted Pavel, just before an important ball at the Dorchester where London's mega-rich Russians would be fêted yet again. She smoked a cigarette first, slowly and quietly, alone in her white-swamped bedroom, and then she walked down the corridor and pushed open the door to his study. She wasn't scared of him and never had been because she knew he wouldn't kill her. He needed her too much.

'What have you done to Tyrone?' she asked him as he hunched over his computer, watching the money roll in. Pavel turned round in his chair and laughed. He was drunk and he had aged since they came here, the pressure of pretence. He looked less coiled, she thought, more resigned. At home the thugs got rich and everyone respected them for it, but here you were supposed to be genteel as well. It didn't come naturally. She walked right up to him and leaned into his face, challenging him to do what he would surely do. 'Where is he, you bastard? Did you kill him?'

'We are in England, Katya. You can't go around killing people.'

'Oh! But in Russia you can?!'

'The rules are different. You used to know that. When I met you.'

'Your rules are different to everyone's. Where is he?'

'He will be fine. But he won't be coming again. If you want to go back to work don't do it from my house.'

'This is my house too.'

'Really? You are a street slut from Kirgask. Don't get any ideas.'

Katya spat in his face. 'You bastard.'

He rose slowly with a menace that had become almost idle, predictable, but no less real.

'I never worked the streets,' Katya said before he hit her. She was proud of this fact.

When his attack let up Katya dragged herself to her feet and stumbled into a run, hurtling to the nursery to grab Vanya, the girl looking at her as if she was mad, and flying into the nearest bathroom. He probably wouldn't bother to follow her. His heart wasn't even in his jealousy any more. He was just going through the motions. Katya locked the bathroom door and leaned against it, hugging Vanya to her chest and understanding, as blood dripped from her face into his cobweb-soft hair and on to one tiny clenched sea-urchin fist, that this was not the life she had meant for him. His breathing slowed down with hers, and she loosened her grip on his thigh, adjusting to the relative safety of their slate-grey cocoon, small spotlights strung on a wire across the ceiling casting a pinkish light over the deep rectangular basin, flattering the person in the mirror, erasing fine lines and blemishes like an advertised cream. This was a guest bathroom, where all those people who had so longed for invitations to this well-patrolled Chelsea mansion would go to stare at themselves and wonder if they were real – if they, an ordinary person with congestion-charge fines and a recycling bin, were actually dining with Ivanchenko, flushed from champagne, gorged on money, and softly lit in the bathroom mirror.

She heard the front door crash back into its frame, setting off a brief scream from the alarms, and she heard the anxious first steps of Varvara, the housekeeper, flying into action, her big cabbage-picking hands lifting up the larger pieces of glass, her soft Siberian voice whispering instructions to more junior staff and, probably, her bloated heart waiting for Katya and the baby to creep out of their hiding place and translate the incident into something manageable, a marital row, just one of those things a woman must live with. Then the young ones could text (illegally – Ivanchenko's privacy contracts were a feat of British legal prowess) a coherent if flurried story to their friends and families, closure injected by Katya's strength and determination: crisis over like a slick news item after a disintegrating tragedy.

Katya looked at herself in the mirror, one hand over Vanya's cheek for now, not wanting to put him in the picture. Pavel's ring, a stupidly pretentious gift from her before their wedding, had cut her just above the eyebrow and what he said had shredded her insides to ragged ribbons. Blood was coming thick and fast, seeping through her lashes and on to her cheek, giving the hideously phantasmagorical illusion that she was weeping blood, which, of course, in a sense, she was. Her nose was not broken but it was bleeding and the taste was sharp and sickly in her throat, metallic, throbbing, the taste of a car crash. Her bottom lip was cut and had already swollen to the size of a summer slug, the fat blistery things they would find near the lake when the shimmering hot days had exploded into thunderstorms and she and Andriusha ran for cover with their towels and picnic, laughing away the fear as dogs cowered and children screamed, the sky erupting in groaning violence.

'All right. All right. We'll be all right,' she told the baby who wasn't crying, reassuring them both with a voice so calm that it made her reflection seem all the more grotesque. It was an eerie calm, like the still of the dawn before an execution. She would make even this OK. She dragged some tissues out of a silver box and started to dab at her face uselessly, the tissue sticking to the wounds, blood drenching them immediately they came close to her skin, she knew that action was important nonetheless, however futile. Keep moving and he won't have won.

Balancing Vanya on her hip now, Katya took off her jewellery with one hand, a ridiculous ensemble of heavy diamonds and rubies that made her look like an eighty-five-year-old duchess in one of those sepia photographs of the Romanovs that a certain type of patriot so loves to display, as though by having this image on top of the television they are not actually on the twentieth floor of an estate outside a provincial town where the lift doesn't work and the gangsters have long since taken control.

She wiped the blood off an earring like jam off a spoon. Pavel loved her to wear this stuff, to stand next to him dripping his wealth as if he'd taken some expensive picture with him to the Raisa Gorbacheva Foundation Ball at the Dorchester and not an actual person, forcing it to sit next to him through an evening of tedious speeches and the displays of Cossack dancing that people seemed to think Russians would like to watch.

Let him stuff his face with sycophancy without her, everyone grovelling for some cash like wolves at a corpse, the English passing off bizarre behaviour as a baffling riddle from the mysterious depths of the Russian soul and interpreting the most rudimentary politeness as an act of exclusive intimacy and potentially life-changing promise. Party-givers endlessly assumed that Russians were addicted to caviare, blini and vodka – if they weren't before they arrived on the London charity scene they soon would be, as sure as eggs and love were only good fresh.

Tonight there would be crystal bowls of sharp glistening black eggs on every table of the Dorchester ballroom (the English, a little afraid of it, overcompensated by slopping large spoonfuls on to their plates with red-faced enthusiasm) and condensation-gleaming ice buckets with vodka and champagne, delved into unceremoniously quickly by shaven-headed men from the airless depths of Butyrka prison, stuffed into designer dinner suits, prison tattoo hidden under a Rolex, gasping with the relief that only alcohol would bring them.

There were women who, despite all the money in the world, still went back to the Ukraine to have their work done, mouths fat and gleaming, faces taut and matt, breasts round and tight as unpicked melons and their minders flinching along the walls, terrified that it would be their principal whose necklace would be stolen on the dance floor, ensuring a swift exit back to Tambov and a night job in car-park security if they were lucky or forcing old ladies to sign over their flats for care if they weren't, and the predictable, if tawdry, murders that must follow the signature. It was one thing fighting in the train station underpass, another squeezing the scrawny neck of a urine-smelling crone who remembered the Revolution and had made love with her sweetheart in the cornfields before collectivisation.

And tonight nobody would be sitting in front of the neat piece of cardboard on which a public schoolgirl with a secretly pierced belly button whose mum was the party planner, had penned with exquisite calligraphy in Latin and Cyrillic lettering: Ekaterina Maximovna Ivanchenko. The top table would have a gaping hole in it, nobody to sit next to Mikhail Sergeievich himself, though she was almost tempted to go, her face pulped, her pale grey taffeta stained with shame – this is where his money comes from, she would say by her terrifying presence, a ghost at a banquet. But she didn't, because revenge, she knew, was a gradual process to be thought out and planned, to be executed in a myriad of different ways, like piecing together a chandelier that, only when complete and risen triumphant into the centre of a ballroom ceiling, can dazzle to outshine the sun.

She took off her high heels and put Vanya on the floor where he patted the tiles with fat hands and shouted at them while she washed her face in cold water, clearing her mind with the painful splashes as though slapping the cheeks of a fainted girl in a crowd. She, as ever, both the fainting girl and her saviour. Then she scooped him up, opened the bathroom door and called out for Varvara, who had, of course, been busying herself less than five feet away, awaiting her summons. Katya handed her the baby and then sat by the hallway phone, the folds of her dress rustling as she crossed her legs, dried blood on her shoulders, an actress in a gory film, making a call between takes, the painstakingly applied sanguineous make-up bizarrely out of place as the stills photographer caught her off duty, covered in ketchup and cochineal.

She called the doctor, a Russian, Dr Lyuda, who did everyone Katya knew, and who would come and stitch her face up, stinging antiseptic, jabbing local anaesthetic, flicking thread as she chatted about her cats, the catastrophe for Britain that was the blacks, Muslims and Jews and how much better life was in Leningrad, before. Before. Before was a big thing for the older Russians. An Elysian time when salami hung from trees in bunches and bread popped out from the bushes, steaming and fresh. Katya wondered why they romanticised like this. Didn't they remember how their feet hurt after a day in the grinding queues, how the blue-grey clouds of exhaust fumes dry your throat out, how the slush of utter despair swills even into the cleanest homes, how the men are dead of drink by fifty if the camps don't get them first?

She thought about the lemon smell of her mother and the brick dust in her father's ears and was homesick for somewhere that didn't exist any more, actual nausea rising in her throat. What, she wondered, was she doing sitting in this Queen Anne stately home, hidden behind red-brick walls, peacocks strutting the lawn, helicopters out the back, a kitchen garden that the chef had made into a business (Oxley jams and sauces with the house crest on them, sold to a market that had no clue who actually lived here), wearing a ball dress that cost more than a car, having her face repaired by this thieving witch . . . She missed the simplicity of summers and winters and Andriusha. Real tears now splashed on to Dr Lyuda's hands because home, if that's what it was, was the past, the taste still livid as mustard on the tongue but forever as elusive as a dream.

'Don't worry, nearly finished, chicken,' Dr Lyuda said, breathing supermarket microwaved meatballs into Katya's mouth, the pores in her skins wide as craters on the moon. 'Nearly done. You need to be careful on those stairs.'

She wanted to call Olga and hear her laugh, talk about the old days, hear about her clients and the weird stuff they wanted her to do, but she worried that Olga wouldn't believe her story, wouldn't be able to imagine that someone like her had got herself into a situation like this. Didn't they know men? Couldn't they wrap them round their little fingers like Chinese noodles round a fork? And in the end she dialled a number so familiar to her that it felt like something chimerical, something only she could know, from the very beginning of life, her mother's voice in her ear, the soft blanket of her cradle. She wanted to talk to a woman who loved her.

Andriusha's mum had plagued her with calls, each one a little stab at Katya's conscience, a reminder of pain that ought to be felt. Every time she checked her messages there would be the plaintive voice, accusing her with its gentle tone of abandonment of having dug a hole with her fingernails and escaped alone. And what was she, Katya, supposed to do about it? Send money, paste lost notices on trees? One day, they would find his body and say it was suicide though perhaps only she, Pavel and whoever he'd paid to do it would ever know different.

She was shackled to the richest man in the world as though he held her from behind by the hair, more forcefully than any client ever did, than he ever did when he was a client himself, when she was in control, kept the goods he once had to pay for, a man whose yachts now hit the inside pages of the British tabloids for their sheer opulence. The English called it 'a gilded cage' but that wasn't right because a bird lives in a cage and birds don't suffer like this. For all the magnificence of her material life, she would rather have rowed out into the lake and stuck a net in the murky water any day, sitting late under low stars, eaten alive by rampant mosquitoes, grilling fish over a small fire, singing Joni Mitchell songs, terrified the trees might hear and report them for anti-Soviet activity.

"Allo?' a voice answered and already Katya was in their apartment, dumplings frying in butter in a big black pan, jars of pickled tomatoes along the window ledge and that horrible old sofa with hard-rimmed cigarette burns speckling the arms where Dima had forgotten them, drunk.

She smiled and winced as the pain shot through her stitched lip, reminding her who and where she really was as the chock of the helicopter sounded loudly overhead and a siren wailed on Cheyne Walk.

'It's me. Katya. I'm sorry I haven't called sooner. We have a complicated security system and . . . Anyway, I just wanted to see how you are . . . whether there's been any news.'

But there was no sobbing, no sighing, no crackle of a long pause down the long-distance line. 'Katenka! What a joy to hear your voice – the first lark of spring! Andriusha is here. I'll fetch him. He will be so happy to talk to you . . .'

Andriusha hadn't spoken in the car as he and Boris thundered across Russia in a journey that seemed to take weeks. His hands were tied behind his back but if he'd had the will he might have been able to escape. Boris was a brute but he was no expert. He drifted in and out of sleep on the back seat, never given a share of the food and drink Boris bought, the empty packets and cans tossed backwards with a burp or a snort. Somehow Andriusha knew they were near like a dog who senses its owners coming home: the landscape flattened into tundra, no other cars on the road, the kind of thick grey light that barely changes with night and day, the white blanket of ground stretching for ever.

Boris got out of the car and pulled him out, scrag that he was of a person, with one strong hand. Then he spoke. 'Cunt, it's cold,' he said, stamping up and down and pulling a revolver out of the waistband of his trousers. 'OK. Run.'

Andriusha, who hadn't eaten for days, who was so thirsty he felt like a vobla, a dried salted fish that old women sell outside stations, who needed a drink like a dog needs a bitch, whose lips and fingertips were blue, whose body wouldn't withstand a gust of wind, raised his swollen eyes to Boris and said, 'What?'

'Run,' Boris explained. 'Boss's orders.'

Boris helped by giving him a push. Andriusha fell face down into the snow at the side of the road and Boris dragged him back up by the scruff of his neck, half choking him on his own shirt collar. He put the gun to his temple. 'Fucking run, mate. OK?' he suggested, and gave him a gentler push this time.

Andriusha staggered, slipped, shuffled towards the line of the horizon and, perhaps when he was far enough away that Boris didn't have to think of him as fully human, the guy fired two shots, cracking through the frozen air, at his back.

Did he miss on purpose? Who knew. Who, indeed, cared, because he knew himself he wouldn't last long. Half an hour, maximum.

He woke up lying on the hot metal floor of a tank, his arse and shoulder blades burning, almost on fire, his face and fingertips frozen, perhaps frostbitten. There was a guy standing over him. A guy who had a tattoo of the word 'PRICK' on his forehead. Even Andriusha recognised this as inmate prison punishment, but he didn't think he was in prison.

'Shit,' Prick said. 'I was going to eat you if you didn't come round.'

He held out his hand to Andriusha who weakly raised his and

was brought to his feet as part of the handshake. He stumbled and broke his fall with the pipe of the stove, burning himself viciously. 'Ow. Fuck, fuck, fuck!' he shouted, clutching his burnt hand, banging his head on the roof of the tank as he jumped in pain, collapsing to the floor again.

Prick laughed and held out a bottle of vodka in one hand and a radish in the other. 'There are a lot of us out here. Deliveries come. You'll be fine, son. Fine,' he explained. And he was. One of the escaped convicts of the northern tundra for more than two years, but now he had deemed it safe to come back. Or, that is, Prick had, dropping him off on the far edge of town where the ice begins to thaw.

It seemed to take him a long time to come to the phone. Katya was stunned, paralysed.

'Katya? Hi. Sorry – I was just doing the window boxes,' he said. 'Hands covered in dirt even though it's the middle of the night. Mad, I know. How are you?'

If she hadn't just been punched in the head she might have thought it was like being punched in the head. In fact, she had an ache in her jaw as though a tooth had come loose.

'Andriusha! Is it really you? Oh my God! And I thought . . . Never mind! You sound good. You sound different . . . like you've got a mouthful of mustard. When did you come back? Where were you?'

'You don't want to know.' He laughed, sounding for all the world like he used to, like when they were really young, before he ever met Pavel and long before she did.

'If I didn't want to know, you onion, I wouldn't ask. Where were you? We all thought you were dead.'

'I should be. I nearly was. I had to let him think I was. We can't talk about it over the phone. There are things I need to tell you whenever you're ready,' he said, serious now, no need to say who the 'he' was. She didn't say a word and there was a long silence before Andriusha broke it: 'Katenka. How are you? I'm sorry it has taken me so many years to ask.'

'I don't know . . . We have this strange life here really . . . It's . . . I have snipers on my roof!' she said, and started to giggle.

Andriusha started to laugh too.

'It's . . . I have a son. And my husband just beat me up because I accused him of murdering the yoga teacher I was fucking . . . Well, not murdering. I don't know. Getting rid of. You know?'

'I do know. You're fucking your yoga teacher?' Andriusha laughed. 'My God. It has come to that! I see you need me.'

Katya was laughing uncontrollably now and Varvara looked confused as she put a silver tray down next to her with steaming pale tea in a paper-thin china cup and Russian sweets on the saucer next to it, incongruous somehow. Katya nodded her thank you and chose a lemon one to unwrap with one hand while she held the phone in the other, the wax paper thick between her fingers.

'That is NOT the point and you know it,' she said. 'Oh, Andrei. Come over. Please. I'll have the plane fetch you. Will you come? Have you got a passport?'

'No. I belong here. But I will wait for you here. When you are ready.'

'I am going to start an art gallery with a girl I met. And I'm going to get divorced,' she said, the decision taken in a glorious instant. Luckily, she knew a lawyer who would help. She had his phone number in her address book.

'Good for you,' Andriusha told her. 'Me, I'm going back to my geraniums.'

'This is not a clash between civilisations. It is a clash about civilisation.'

Tony Blair

Chapter Seventeen

T oday, however hard he tried, Pavel Ivanchenko had not felt lucky at all. Things were getting bad. Some makeshift bomb had been detonated at the office, stamped near Tomsk where his earliest enemies still lurked. They got him down to the mail room to have a look and he'd leaned down to peer at the pitifully rudimentary engineering. It would hardly have grazed him if he'd opened it untreated. Compost-based like the things they used to teach the Soviet soldiers to make during the war, pathetic weapons that the Germans could deactivate by pissing on them. But it was a reminder, like he needed one, that people were out to get him. Well, they could keep trying.

As if it wasn't enough that his wife was screwing around. He watched the grainy tapes in Boris's hut, heard her moan and groan, writhe around, watched that wiry little pederast thrusting his dick into his wife, his hands on her arse, his face contorted in ecstasy. Strange how much like pain it was, like dogs in an alley they were, and now the death threats were coming in like fucking charity-ball invitations. The Russians were trying to extradite him, the British weren't that happy to have him (some prick from the Foreign Office had come round 'for a chat' the other day, wearing those stupid pederast shoes with patterns punched into the leather and a yellow tie) and the embezzlement writ that he'd been dodging for months had finally been served. They couldn't pin it on him, but the fact they dared to try meant things were shifting.

And then the terrible thing that hung over him now like a blanket on a corpse. All because of his kindness. He went out to eat by himself at the geisha place that was a secret to all but around ten men, all Russian. It was hidden behind a red lacquered door in Knightsbridge and the girls were all flown in from Japan on massive salaries by a wizened crone who knew a business opportunity when she saw one. Pavel liked the sashimi and the tight cunts of the girls, enthusiastic little nymphomaniacs. He left the security outside and was settling down on some cushions when the text came in, vibrating in his pocket.

I am still alive. I have been to visit Liuba. You can't run for ever, Pavel. Turn yourself in.

For a second Pavel felt a real chill down his spine. How could the fucker have survived? Boris took him out on to the steppe and shot him in the back. Pavel believed him unflinchingly. Even if he had somehow survived the gunshots the wilderness would have killed him; nobody in the area would take him in without Pavel finding out. He changed his mobile phone once a week. There was only one place Andriusha could have got his number.

And Liuba! Why her? Why that murder when it was the one that was a good deed? A favour to the girl. It was because Liuba's father, that evil motherfucker, was the first person Andriusha had killed for him that he'd got fixated on him. Pavel remembered describing it as 'a big favour' and told him he'd be paid beyond his wildest dreams if he took the girl up the mountain to the sanatorium afterwards, settled her in.

He knew he would have to get out of the country for a while, go and face the demons.

He sat on the floor now and smoked a cigarette in the dark. A red light flashed above the door confirming what he already knew, that he was safe in here. There was no need to be in the dark or to sit on the floor, but both suited him for now. He drew the smoke in sharply, the slight pain as it hit his lungs telling him that he was alive. Yet he was still as a dead man, though his knuckles were flayed and his head throbbed at the temples with the acknowledgement, the traces of what he had done. He could deny it to himself, sometimes he did, because there was some truth in the explanation he had once offered to Katya, years ago when there was some hope left, perhaps, after that first time in the sanatorium: that he was overtaken by something, by some other personality, a rage that swept through him sending his brain a violent red and forcing his body to obey it. He couldn't help it, perhaps, but whatever he might claim it was still him, not somebody else. Maybe, indeed, it was a purer essence of him than he ever displayed when he wasn't fighting, like home-brewed vodka, the kind he'd traded in the old days. Before.

Afterwards he felt how he always felt. Like this. Something inside him was better, he thought as he heard the policemen leave, defeated. They wouldn't find him. Called the police? Who did she think she was? She would be in a hard labour camp for thirty years for all her illegal activity – prostitution carried heavy sentencing in those days. A hooker called the police! The rage was gone, the burning wild thing that gripped him by the throat desperate for escape and insisting on satisfaction was extinguished, but then he was weak and desolate, a blackened empty building, annihilated but still smoking, for something inside him was worse. Then he needed a woman to look into his eyes and take him in her arms, soft and wet and good, someone who wouldn't try to escape, who wouldn't rather be dead than stay with him. He thought of Mo, the English girl from long ago, and of a time when he thought he might be able to wrap her dark warm skin and black hair around himself for good, nothing cold or Siberian in her, only the warmth of places where olives and oranges grow and the air smells of spices. Baku, Yerevan, Samara. He thought of taking her to those places and hearing her laugh, watching her eat baklava with pistachios in it, drenched with honey, tasting the honey in her mouth. But she hadn't understood, could never understand in the way he'd hoped Katya might. Katya who had seemed for a while like salvation and, if she hadn't known that dirty scumbag Andriusha, maybe she could have been. If she hadn't invited him to the wedding. But she did, and the marriage, the hope died before it even began. That was life, of course, and, in the end, she was linked to the side of him he wanted to bury for ever and so he could never shut his eyes with her, never lean into her golden skin and be still.

Here in the dark he felt as though the world was finally closing in on him as he'd been born and swaddled in the bleak Dom Roda knowing it would. His father would splatter himself across a wall, his mother would fall through the night, he would be alone and scrabbling up to the top of a heap of scrap metal dragging Gleb with him. The slag heap at the factory was what he imagined when he was little, hardly knowing then how literal he would make his fantasy: his scrabble to the top where he might be able to breathe, where he wouldn't need anyone, only be needed.

And if Katya didn't survive this time? But she would. She could survive a nuclear attack, that woman, he thought, wondering why she cared so much about a yoga teacher she'd only been fucking as revenge against him anyway. She knew the risks. He told her back in Moscow that he wouldn't tolerate rivals. He had paid her to get rid of them.

Kindness didn't get you anywhere.

When the house was quiet and his head had stopped spinning with grievance Pavel stood up from the floor and punched in the code that would release him with a buzz and a long high beep. He squinted in the bright light and ruffled his hair, realising as he did so that he had a lot of blood on his hands and on his shoes. Jesus, he thought, he had overdone it this time. But she had asked for it, said she'd call the police, accused him of all kinds of shit she'd never find any proof for. And, if it did come to it, Boris would go down for him, because, after all, it was his thumb prints they'd find embedded in the yoga teacher's flesh if they ever looked. Or they would have if Boris hadn't sliced all his prints off with a whittling knife. Pavel smiled to himself.

He went upstairs and walked across the deep white carpet of their bedroom, leaving bloody footprints behind him like a polar bear dragging its kill across the ice. He showered in the vast cubicle, planting his feet on the black slate and letting the water hit his back, a thousand hailstones bashing the crap out of his life so that he would emerge renewed, like the nutters in the wilderness who follow gurus and later die out there in the ice, baptised in the summer, plunged into the river near where the old Town Hall used to be, saved. Pavel knew for sure that only money can save you from what they are all trying to get away from: a life without hope in the Siberian provinces.

Soon, he thought, soon he would have to act, before they all got to him. If only the Jew would take those cheques after all, he could have made sure Putin never used Ivanchenko steel for his pseudo-Communist dream. The Jew was the only one he'd dared ask so far, but he'd do it. He could do it. He had got a kick at the time out of shoving Katya on to a flight with Mo and her Jew friend, wondering if they'd see each other, speak, wondering if Mo would understand that this was the woman he'd left her for, that this creature was the one he was fucking while she whined at him about sex in a way no Russian girl ever would – Russian girls pretended they were doing you a favour even though you knew they wanted it. Mo asked him directly. It turned him on and revolted him equally.

'Varvara,' he shouted out of the bedroom door. 'Can you tell Slava I need to go to Tomsk, immediately.'

He was at the Tomsk sanatorium gates within six hours of leaving Oxley House and, breathing in the familiar forest air and planting his feet on home soil, he had no thought of visiting his mother.

The woman on the desk practically fainted. 'We had no warning, sir,' she complained, rushing off to make sure everything was in order, making sure everyone knew Ivanchenko had arrived, could get their fawning faces on. He marched down the luxurious but institutional corridors that smelt thickly of cooking oil and lilies and straight into Liuba's little room where he found her painting a picture, big yellow sunflowers with fat green stalks, her face concentrated, her hair hanging forward. A nurse stood by her, encouraging, drinking a glass of tea. It was dark outside, late.

'Please leave us alone,' Pavel told the nurse and Liuba, noticing him now, looked frightened, stood up and put her brush down.

'Is Katya here?' she asked. She adored Katya. Everyone adored Katya. Pavel was amazed she remembered her after so long. Pavel was not going to play games with her. His life, his livelihood were in danger, everything he had ever worked for might be taken away because of this fucking moon-faced girl he'd saved out of real remorse.

'No. And she's not coming. Listen, Liuba, a man called Andrei Klyzhenko, Andriusha, has been talking to you,' he told her.

She nodded, looking at the floor, twisting her hands together and wriggling one foot out to the side. She was older now, of course, but she still had the mind of a child.

'Don't talk to him again. He wants to kill Katya,' Pavel lied, aware that for Andriusha to pull this off, and he wouldn't, he would need Liuba to make a statement and he would need her to make it to someone who wasn't on the Ivanchenko payroll. Unfortunately there were more of them than he'd like these days.

'He brought the police. They were nice. They gave me choc-olates,' she said.

Jesus Christ, he'd already done it, Pavel realised, feeling the anger rise in him like a hard-on, feeling the walls close in and his head start to boil.

He looked at her in rage and revulsion. He lit a cigarette, took one long drag and then went over to the window, opening it and flicking the cigarette out, watching the orange glow fly through the dark sky to the ground.

'Your testimony won't count. You are a moron,' he said, mainly to himself, but with a seething anger that felt like a need to vomit. It was Andriusha, not him that she had seen kill her father. Then it was just his word against Pavel's and Pavel would make sure he didn't last long enough to give that word.

Liuba laughed, the sound as grating as an alarm clock in his brain. 'I'm not a moron! You are!' she said playfully, her lips curling up. This was too much for Pavel and he lunged at her, out of control, pushing her back on to the single bed and pummelling her face with punches. She made no sound at all, just went completely limp in defeat, shut her eyes and seemed to die under him. And he, remem-bering or regressing into the terrible dark of the past, found himself tearing at her nightdress, pulling her pants down, holding her down by the neck and fucking her, properly this time, once and for all. When he had finished he found his own face was soaking wet with tears.

Afterwards he told her to get in the shower and to tell the nurse she slipped over. If she spoke to Andriusha again, he told her, he would kill her. She walked very slowly over to the shower, treading on her painting on the way and making multi-coloured footprints on the tiles as she went towards the toilet before sinking to her knees.

Pavel stayed the night alone at the dacha, no staff and no heating, just himself in the dark, sickened by the terrible thing he had done.

The first time he had abused her he was a boy whose heart filled with pity. He had rescued her and done her the favour of having her father's brains blown out. And this is how she repaid him. And that was how he had repaid her. Things were unravelling. He felt it in the pit of his stomach.

'We want good relations with Russia. But that can only be done on the basis that there are certain shared principles and shared values.'

Tony Blair

Chapter Eighteen

The restaurant was vast, stark and white, an old warehouse near Smithfields where the staff wear pristine starched butchers' aprons and neat-toothed smiles, striding about the enormous space with glistening bottles of wine and big medical corkscrews. It was a relief to be here breathing easily in the squinting light, facing an old man in a three-piece Savile Row suit, a public schoolboy (you never become a public schoolman) who still played fives for his old house every Thursday evening and who loved offal. This place was famous for its offal.

'There are so many men in here!' Mo said to the waitress, ordering a glass of Sancerre and goat's curd with a roast onion and rye bread.

The waitress had long blonde hair pulled into a ponytail and silver rings on her fingers. She was Australian. 'Tell me about it!' she said conspiratorially, delighted to have found an ally.

James from the office leaned forwards slightly, a habit he'd probably picked up in MI6. 'He's trying to get citizenship, you know. Thing are coming to a head for him.'

'Who?' Mo asked, looking around, as though Rupert Murdoch were perhaps sitting behind them.

'Ivanchenko. Wants to buy a football club or some such. Legitimacy. Brought the missus over a couple of years ago. We hear he's planning permanent exile. Thinks Putin's got it in for him. Probably right.'

He spoke like a telegram, as though code was safer, Careless Talk Costs Lives.

Mo raised her eyebrows, stalling for time, already understanding what he was going to commission her to write and not looking forward to it any. As if she didn't know he lived in London with his wife and child. She lived here too. She hadn't been hiding under a rock or anything. She wondered what 'some such' could possibly be. Either he was buying a football club or he wasn't. There weren't many things that could be described as similar. She noticed the pointed 'we' James often used, blurring the distinction between a few newspaper executives and the secret service, though, in fact, he often meant he'd read it on Reuters.

She glanced down at her phone to read yet another text from Eli about Gilda. It was what she loved about him – that he was so excited about life, that he thought every tiny little thing that happened to him was unique to him and unexperienced by any human being before him. When he first got a girlfriend he thought he'd invented sex and now he thought he'd invented marriage.

She wouldn't do it again last night, Mo. What should I do? Is it my technique? Is she a lesbian? Help. ASAP.

Every time he looked at another woman he worried he was a philanderer and his whole life was going to crumble to nothing. Eli Zinn would never accept that, in the end, he was just human. And so was Gilda.

She texted back under the table. *Definite lezza. Will call you later. Xx*

She knew, because she knew Eli, that he would never stay faithful for ever but she hoped that Gilda would have him back when it happened. Because, well, there wasn't anyone better than Eli. She smiled to herself and tried to focus on the matter at hand.

She was already writing a big piece about Ivanchenko and had been digging away at the business stuff, guarding his secret, of course, about the Down's girl's father, not because she should, she hated 'should' and 'ought' and all that crap anyway, but because she wanted to. 'Should' and 'ought' were always excuses to do what you wanted to do in any case, the persuasive argument you'd offer to someone else who didn't agree with you. Anyway, now James was going to hassle her into doing a face-to-face interview and she wasn't at all sure that she wanted to jeopardise the piece. She might — let's face it — she easily might, be lured into a flattering description of a courageous businessman who had made good in no-holds-barred Russia. She was fairly sure she was close to smelling the breath of proof that he had murdered at least one business rival and had effectively stolen the country's largest steel mine from its doughily naïve new shareholders; it was a question of persuading people to go on the record, to sign up to truth in a national atmosphere of adhesive deceit. Now officially the richest man in the world, rumours darted around Ivanchenko like shadows, licking up against him everywhere he went, never proven, never properly denied, shrouding his business dealings and endangering the lives of anyone who got too close to him. Three of his senior employees had been wiped out in professional hits this year, slumped in Moscow doorways in dark pools of blood, neighbours deaf, blind and dumb. Not that he'd ever met them personally, probably. He probably told world leaders that his businesses really ran themselves these days. That had always been Ivanchenko's brilliance: to delegate and thereby to remain squeaky clean.

And he went everywhere surrounded by a swarm of armed bodyguards, snipers prowled the roof of his villa on Rublyovskoye Shosse and he lost a driver in March when one of his cars was blown up in an assassination attempt, its shell smouldering by the side of the road, gaping, jagged, for days afterwards.

'Why are you doing this, Mo?' Eli asked her, a baby in his

arms, a muslin square on his shoulder. 'She won't let me have her circumcised!' he hissed when Gilda went out of the room. They lived in Hampstead now, back from the dangerous glitz of Moscow to the comfortable glow of affluent London, where shelves of erudite books decorated their front room (Gilda was retraining to be a psychoanalyst, sick of money and its sullying brutality – 'Can you imagine? There you are, fucked up, Jewish, and you go into the bloody shrink to be faced with vast Nazi. You'd never get over it,' Eli explained. Gilda shushed him and took her glasses off with a deep sigh).

'I thought it was only boys you circumcised? What are you, some Ethiopian villager? I'm doing the piece, of course, because everyone should know that these people – I'm going to call them oligarchs, what do you think? – these oligarchs just surrounded the last tsar—'

'I'm confused. I thought the tsars were all murdered in a cellar in Yekaterinburg?'

'You *know* who I mean. Yeltsin. They were like courtiers, creaming off the whole country's assets in return for loyalty. And given the country, those are quite some assets. And now Putin's trying to get it all back.'

'Mo,' Eli scoffed, wiping the sick off his sleeve with the muslin square and trying to pour himself a whisky one-handed. 'Are you seriously trying to suggest that Putin is a hero for the people? And what do you mean get it back? Back where? To whom do you, does your paper, believe it technically belongs? Putin is as big a criminal as Ivanchenko, but that's not the point. This is a legal point, not a moral one. A point, or various points, actually, of Soviet and Russian law. Ivanchenko actually coerced the business out of the voucher holders often against their will: illegal! Ivanchenko had a couple of his rivals murdered: illegal if unprovable. Ivanchenko didn't pay whatever it is . . . fifty billion dollars' tax to the Russian government: illegal! AND Ivanchenko tried to get the assets secured out of the country so that, should anything happen to him, Putin won't get the cash: illegal. I expect there's a greasy idiot sitting at his desk in London right now, rubbing his hands with glee . . .'

Eli, it seemed, had been doing some homework. Now, it seemed, he believed that Ivanchenko could be brought to justice by the law and it wasn't just a question of moral high-ground over murky dealings.

'Yes, but—'

'Oh, yes. Sorry. You don't care about any of that. You're just still pissed off he dumped you for a supermodel and you've been single ever since,' Eli said, sitting down now as his daughter slept on his chest.

'Well, there is also that,' she admitted. 'I have not been single ever since! There was . . . you know . . . thingy . . . I have just had a lot of work to do, OK?'

'Right. She called me, you know?' Eli announced as he quite often did, saving his big news for an ordinary lapse in conversation.

'Who did?'

'Katya Ivanchenko.'

'I did not know! Why would you not tell me this?'

'I am telling you.'

'OK. When? Really? Katya called you?'

'She called me. Wants to come and see me in a "professional capacity". I said sure, though, frankly, those are tax problems nobody in their right mind would want to try and sort out.'

'That's weird. Don't you think that's weird that she'd call you?'

Gilda came in with a bottle of Chablis and some glasses. 'Who called him?'

'Oh nobody, darling. Just a Russian supermodel multi-billionaire's wife . . .'

They all laughed, which was odd because it was true.

* * *

Mo got off the tube on the day of the interview at Green Park, solitary and purposeful, despite the jostling crowds of men in cheap suits eating sandwiches and women striding along as best they could in crippling footwear, their calves tight and muscular with the effort, plasters visible on their heels where the skin had blistered and bled. Thick grey clouds hung oppressively low in the sky but sharp light shone through them nonetheless and made Mo squint, looking up at the pigeons hopping sluggishly round the *Evening Standard* stall, ignoring the lush green of the park behind them for the trodden down splodges of chewing gum dotting the pavement. Traffic clogged Piccadilly, buses churning out exhaust into the walking crowds as they chugged, stationary, in the actually motionless rush-hour frenzy.

She smiled to herself as she passed the Aeroflot office, now neat and bright, offering competitively priced flights to China via Moscow and all the lures of first-class travel. Mo remembered, fondly now – that fondness of retrospect – the eternal wait in the rain for a visa, snarlingly issued from beneath a portrait of Lenin, the camaraderie of the queue whose movement was barely perceptible to the naked eye and then the shabby tin-can Aeroflot planes whose petrifying take-off and landing procedures were military in style and designed to conserve fuel, certainly not to reassure the nervous passenger. Going to Russia, she knew, had entirely defined her life, mostly in a good way, but certainly in a way that had saved her from her dad's desertion and from Frankie's mood.

Mo crossed the road with a shoal of sallow people who moved as one, obeying the lights unconsciously, their minds on other things or nothing at all, and she slipped up the steps into the golden wealth-glowing sanctuary of the Ritz.

She saw him straight away, and walked towards him smiling with her hand outstretched, not wanting to risk offering her cheek or taking his. A man reading a newspaper in a seat by the door flinched to attention, adjusting his earpiece with an attempted sweep at his hair that was far too bristling short to need sweeping. One inadvertently brisk move and she would be pinned to the ground with a Makarov 9 mm in her mouth, she knew.

Ivanchenko leaped to his feet, slightly knocking the low table on which his glass of champagne sparkled. He wore pressed beige trousers and a white shirt with thin red stripes down it, the uniform of the off-duty multi-billionaire who left Siberia behind him a very long time ago. He smelt subtly of Acqua di Parma and he wore a signet ring on his crooked little finger, a ring not handed down to him from his grandfather, and not embossed with the family crest. In fact it was a present from Katya, who had had their initials engraved on it in Cyrillic. Mo saw straight away that he was not the same man she had brought to London not really so long ago and who had rushed back the same day, unable to cope with the sudden loss of absolute control. He was confident here now, ruling his immediate surroundings just as he had in Moscow. He still looked like a Soviet propaganda poster though. A supreme chiselled Russian with ice eyes.

'Hello, Mo,' he said, beaming and clasping her hand in both of his in that presidential way that conveys warmth and security but also power and control. Mo shook her hair back and wished she was in a Chanel suit with sheer tights round slim ankles and flat shoes so that she might at least appear to any passers-by to be his equal, someone, possibly, advising him on a painting. As it was, she had the parasitic journalist look utterly mastered, and might as well have slapped a tape recorder on the table to complete the first impression, she thought. He had once found her scruffiness endearing or, at least, she'd thought so. Now they were both older and she was still scruffy.

'Thanks for doing this,' she said, sitting down and arranging herself like a self-conscious schoolgirl. 'The paper asked me to get an interview. I'm doing a big piece in any case.'

Ivanchenko smiled, bemused, sitting back and raising an eyebrow. 'Should I be worried?' he said, not looking worried at all. 'You look wonderful. Your hair looks nice.'

Mo knew by now that he always gave a compliment before he said anything else and that he'd probably chosen her hair because all her clothes were so crap.

Ivanchenko looked around and flashed a glance at a white-coated waiter who understood the command and dashed off to find a silver stand laden with cucumber sandwiches, miniature fruit tarts and warm scones. Another waiter brought champagne on a teetering tray, and cream and jam in heavy silver pots. It had taken Pavel years, but he had it down now.

'Are you ever worried?' she asked, not able to imagine him feeling threatened by a newspaper article.

'Not in that way. Cheers,' Ivanchenko said, leaning forward to knock his glass against Mo's, getting her on side, she thought, before she'd even asked a question, ordering for her in that unspoken gesture of massive power. He was issuing instructions with every movement: relax, trust me. Well, it's what they all do with foreign journalists, foreigners in general in fact, Mo thought. If she were some low-life from a southern republic running menial errands for him, he'd have a different air about him, she knew. You don't take over the world's steel industry with just one face, one laid-back lazy smile and a dollop of clotted cream.

It was hard to believe that she had been naked with this man, that, in fact, she had had more sex with him than she'd ever had with anyone else. And the best. Perhaps that was it. She'd been spoilt. That's why no other relationship had stuck.

He drank more than half his glass of champagne in a single, devouring mouthful, transporting both of them into a filthy Siberian cellar where black-toothed, big-handed men sat round with vodka and cards, always looking for a fight and always getting one. It made Mo laugh with its Russianness in this very not Russian place.

'Na zdorovye!' she said, taking a small sip out of her glass and looking at him to show that she knew, that she had smelt the Russian provinces, the struggle and the darkness, but now she saw what had changed about Pavel. His eyes had changed. He talked to her but he didn't want her to understand him. There was a pleading look that had now completely gone. He had, perhaps, given up.

'Listen,' she told him. 'I know it seems weird because of our . . . because of everything . . . but I am actually going to have to interview you about TomStal.'

She managed to choke out a couple of brilliant and piercing questions before Pavel said, 'I bet your husband loves the way you bite your lip like that.'

She laughed as though he'd said she had beautiful eyes, a crass chat-up line that nobody but an idiot would fall for, and then checked herself quickly. Why shouldn't he be interested in her, gentle with her, flirtatious and direct? He was sincere, so she answered.

'I don't have a husband. I don't even have a boyfriend at the moment. Men are scared of me, I think. Or I'm just ugly. Or, hey, both,' she said, shrugging and blushing a bit in a way that she didn't imagine was endearing any more – a blushing girl, maybe. A blushing woman, hardly.

'Ah,' Ivanchenko breathed, solemnity seizing his features. 'So you have nobody . . . to hold your paw.'

And Mo, completely without warning, having had no idea at all that she was even lonely, let alone that loneliness coursed through her like AIDS-infected blood, found herself ambushed by fat hot tears that were pouring down her cheeks. It was the word: he'd said it in Russian, 'lapa', paw. It reminded her out of nowhere of holding small hands up to people she longed for but who never held her, as a baby or a toddler, she couldn't even remember. She hadn't known tears were even in there, boiling wildly in their internal cauldron, bubbling over, spitting and hissing, let alone that it would take just one tiny infantalising word of gentleness to release them.

Pavel, who she planned to depict as the terrifying oligarch with unknowable wealth from the murkiest of sources, came over and took her in his arms, pressing his fingers into her back and kissing the top of her head gently as she let go of herself, cutting the invisible but agonising barbed wire that was bound tightly round her, holding her together. She felt as if she had been given a massive shot of valium, as though she was someone in seizure to whom paramedics came rushing. It was just that she'd been in seizure all her life and who even knew?

A waiter hovered for instruction. Ivanchenko nodded at him and, in the dim golden light with the pianist playing a West End musicals medley, a brandy was brought, as it so often is, to the tearful woman whose marriage is over, whose children are leaving home, whose daughter is getting married, whose long-term prognosis is bleak. Mo sat up and wiped her face childishly with the palms of her hands, leaning forward for the drink and smiling in mortified gratitude at the waiter with his silver tray and almost imperceptible forward inclination, verging on a bow. Ivanchenko gave her a stiff white handkerchief from his trouser pocket, the kind of accessory carried only by the arriviste, and she screwed it up in her hot hand but had no use for it.

'Sorry,' she said. 'I have no idea what's wrong with me.'

He moved back to his seat and waited for her to look at him.

Eventually, when the shame had cooled to a smoulder, she did. 'How's Katya?' she asked, meaning to reassure him that she wasn't expecting or asking for anything.

'She's well. She has gone into business with a friend. Our son goes to nursery. I hear she is well. She has ... Well, what can I tell you? She has moved out. I think she will ask for a divorce.

264

You know, she was only ever interested in the money. She never wanted a real marriage,' he said, looking at her in that way he had, as though he was sizing her up. 'Women!' he shrugged.

'Oh, I'm really sorry,' Mo sympathised, quite genuinely. 'That's sad.'

'I was not the best husband, I think,' Pavel admitted, looking resigned.

There was a long pause where Mo could hear people's teaspoons hitting the side of their cups, the piano seemed too loud and the volume of chatter turned up to maximum. The sound was dizzying. And then Pavel spoke.

'Listen, Mo. I have to leave for the South of France in an hour. Why don't you come with me, we can talk on the plane, have dinner. I'll have you back in London by tomorrow morning,' he said, a calmness in his voice that made it sound like a normal-type suggestion.

Mo, unsure of how to use this jelly-like body but certain that distance from Ivanchenko, on whose shoulder she had now cried, in whose arms she had felt able to close her eyes, would mean she was unlikely to be able to use it at all, nodded.

'I wish I had some kind of excuse to make that would make it sound like I'm doing you a favour. But I'm totally free and I'd love to come. I didn't realise until about two minutes ago how lonely I've been, though I know admitting that to a man is supposed to make them hate you.'

'I don't hate you, Mo.' Ivanchenko smiled. 'Your directness is . . . is what makes you Mo.'

Later, sitting on a beige leather seat and looking down at the clouds, she wondered exactly how he'd done it. He was asleep, face against the window, hands clenched into tight fists in his lap, looking like a little boy, someone who couldn't possibly persuade a grown woman to come to the South of France for the evening, who wouldn't have the confidence to reach across a plate of cakes at the Ritz and take her hand in his, stroking the back of it with his thumb, looking into her face as though only he could provide what she needed.

The steward, a handsome Siberian in neat jeans and an expensive shirt, asked her if she needed anything and offered blini with caviare, sushi, salade niçoise, crayfish-tail salad or French onion soup with fresh bread. He had vodka, water, tea or coffee but no champagne today; they were reloading in Nice. She ordered tea and picked up the phone on the wall beside her, dying to call Eli, though she knew him so well she could run the whole conversation herself.

'You're doing what? Going where? "Famous Journalist Abducted by Oligarch",' he would say, stunned by her audacity/stupidity and, though very judgemental about the quality of the man, keen to know what the jet was like.

Ivanchenko stirred and her tea arrived in a Versace cup that made Mo laugh with its brash declaration of fathomless wealth. He opened his eyes and, still slumped, raised a palm to her, like a bear rolling around in a forest. 'Are we there?' he asked her, straightening up and turning to look out of his window as they descended through the clouds.

'Ten minutes to landing,' the steward told them in Russian, collecting a spoon and a scrumpled serviette from Ivanchenko's table.

'I was dreaming about Tomsk,' he said, the word in Mo's mind still billowing with smoke from the stoves of wooden houses huddled together in clusters against the avalanche of snow that would pile up around them and sometimes engulf them entirely in the white eternity of frozen winter. She chose to ignore the other, less romantic Tomsk that she had actually seen, of grey tower blocks, toxic factories and cavernous mines where men lived and died in the choking dark. Never mind that naff horror of a dacha he'd built with the gold nude statue. 'Everything important to me is in Tomsk, even though

I live in London.' Little did she know then what he actually meant by this.

'Yes,' Mo told him with half a smile, embarrassed to admit quite how much she knew about him, things he had quite categorically not told her himself, snippets of information caught in the net she had cast out round the world, pieces that she would fit together to form an account of this man who threw his shadow about the imaginations of so many people, those who feared him, those who admired him, those who thought a bullet in the back of the neck too good for the crook who had plundered Russia's riches and bought himself an island in the Caribbean.

She could have said; 'Your violent father shot himself, your mother crippled herself in a survived suicide attempt and you left school to look after her and your brother. She's in a sanatorium, the sickly brother's a concert violinist whom you don't talk to ...' But, of course, he would have known all this and the violent rest that troubled Mo with its dark whisper, hanging in the dry air of the Gulfstream V, muttering round Ivanchenko's apparent innocence but refusing to break into a shout.

Passport control, when arriving in this blaze of superiority, had more the air of a waiter checking through a restaurant order ('Medium rare was that, sir?') than of an official procedure, and though the air was hot and dry the car was as cool as a cave.

'I love this!' Mo declared. 'I really must travel with the super rich always.'

Pavel laughed, apparently finding her endearing.

The security, which Mo remembered from being escorted by Boris, meant, obviously, that there was a threat and really shouldn't make anyone sane feel safe, but it did in fact make her feel escorted, cared for and ... well, secure.

'God,' she sighed into the balmy air of abroad. 'It must be so nice to be looked after all the time.'

Pavel looked at her as though she was mad, but Russians often did that so she thought nothing of it. Another car followed them off the tarmac and on to a palm-lined dual carriageway and Mo raised her eyebrows at Ivanchenko in acknowledgement of the absurdity of their motorcade. Nobody, she meant to say, was going to try and murder her for her Oyster card.

'You have no idea how many serious threats I get,' he shrugged, though, in fact, Mo had a fairly good idea if the truth be known. She could also have had a pretty educated guess at who was issuing them.

'And if someone's successful,' she asked, lurching into journalistic mode to protect herself from the fact of being in an oligarch's limousine in the capacity, basically, of a date, 'who gets the cash?'

Ivanchenko laughed and reached out to brush her arm with his fingers. 'Don't worry,' he said. 'You are safe with me.' He looked at her with a half-smile of sympathy and sadness, making clear that he recognised and pitied her and that he wasn't talking about the efficacy of his bodyguards. She knew she was being very elaborately seduced and was glad.

'My wife – probably ex-wife – gets an agreed amount. Not much,' he told her as the cars started to climb into the scrubby hills, heat shimmering off the road and glittering out over the sea. Mo put 'not much' at something under fifty million pounds. 'And I will find someone who will take the rest. I intend to donate it all charity, if something happens. A kind of charitable fund. I'm not letting Putin get his hands on it. On anything.'

Mo was stunned, thinking about Eli and the offer Boris had come round with. Ivanchenko had a reputation for being in with the Kremlin, which was why he wasn't in prison with the other oligarchs who allegedly hadn't paid their taxes, but she and Eli knew better, knew the Kremlin, and practically everyone else with a pulse, was out to get him.

'Eli told me you tried it on with him,' she said, not wanting any of this South of France business if it involved keeping quiet, pretending to be somebody else. 'Did you choose him because of me?'

'Yes. I thought he might do it because of you.'

'You don't know Eli then. But even if he had, if the cheques are in London, there's no way the British will let anyone cash them. Not if they represent seized assets,' she pointed out, amazed to be having this conversation with Pavel himself looking at the lines in his forehead that had appeared since she last saw him, watching the gates of exclusive hill-top houses wind past them, catching them on camera just in case, sprinklers shimmering over the emerald gardens, vulgar red and pink flowers drooping vaginally from the dark bushes, their lips splayed and swollen.

'Don't you worry about it,' Ivanchenko said, tapping on the driver's glass and whispering something through the intercom. 'Nearly there.'

It was much later, after dinner on a wisteria-hanging terrace with enormous pumpkins glowing fatly in the undergrowth of twisting roots, crickets singing in the black cypress trees and the yachts of the rich and famous, but mostly just the rich, twinkling out in the distant bay, that Mo reached into her pocket for her lighter. An old retainer called Valya had ruffled Ivanchenko's hair and lumbered out with plate after lavish plate of supper. A seafood platter on ice, oysters, lobster claws, mussels, clams and gigantic prawns. Grilled sole with melted butter, asparagus, sharp salad and fruit. Other staff lurked deferentially in the background, taking the plates from Valya as soon as she went through the doors and handing them to her just before she emerged, all chattering into walkie-talkies, clarifying the hierarchy, breathless with excitement that Ivanchenko was here, Mr Rochester coming home to Thornfield Hall. Mo cracked claws, wrenched open shells, sucked molluscs from their homes with hungry teeth and let the juices dribble down her face before she mopped them up, laughing, with a huge white napkin. Ivanchenko watched her with a smile.

Valya had a few key teeth missing and moved with difficulty on swollen ankles, but her love for her master was her very purpose, like the butler in *The Cherry Orchard* who gets locked in the house at the end when they've sold and abandoned the estate. She gazed, clucked and poked at him as though she'd suckled him herself back in the east wing of their own estate outside Tomsk, swaddled in the nursery until the snow melted. But, of course, Ivanchenko had not had an adoring Nyanya, nor anything else for that matter. So now he had bought one.

'I think,' he said, spitting out the stone of a date into his hand, 'that you are so used to being lonely that you have no idea what it would be like not to be.'

Mo breathed in the thick, drunken summer air of his words and fought the urge to hiss and sneer, to accuse him of a seducer's mendacity. They had had a lot of sunset pink rosé to drink and the sea blurred into the hot sky. For he was right, of course, but was he offering a cure?

'What would it be like? Sounds scary,' she said, leaning forwards on to her elbows, letting a bracelet slide up her arm.

'Not necessarily,' Ivanchenko offered. 'Sing to me.'

'Don't be ridiculous.'

'Why ridiculous? Don't be so English. Sing to me. I want to hear your voice.'

'Really?'

'Really.' He dragged the cushion off his wicker chair and put it down on the floor next to the table, lying down with his arms above his head and his eyes shut, tanned bare feet crossed at the ankle.

Mo laughed, took a sip of her wine and started to sing, softly and, perhaps, not brilliantly. 'Stars shining bright above you, night breezes seem to whisper, "I love you . . ."'

When she'd finished, Ivanchenko seemed to be fast asleep and Valya appeared with coffee.

'You've got a lovely voice, dear,' she said in Russian.

Mo beamed, as much with drunkenness as gratitude, and took a cigarette out of the packet on the table, digging into her pocket for a light when she could have used a candle as she'd been doing all evening until now. The familiar piece of paper fell to the floor and she picked it up and, perhaps because she was drunk, she stared at it now in the candlelight, the flames absolutely still, swollen in the heat, hoping it might reveal its meaning, give her some direction. Of course it was too late now to make up for the years of standing in the playground, glancing always over her shoulder with a flicker of hope that had finally been extinguished – a war of attrition between a child and reality. Reality would always win.

Ivanchenko flashed his eyes open and leaped up to standing as though he had heard the crack of gunfire. 'What is that? A ransom note?' he asked, leaning over the back of her chair and putting his arms all the way round her, the direction of the evening now unmistakable if it ever hadn't been. Mo felt his bristles against her cheek and tried not to think about it.

'It might as well be. My father's phone number. I've been carrying it around with me since that time we went to Frankie's. Do you remember? That awful day . . .'

Ivanchenko took the scrap of notepad out of her hand and scrutinised it. Then he held it to the candle flame until it was properly alight and dropped it to the floor, burning. When it was completely consumed, a wisp of grey on the brick tile, Mo could still see the scratchy figures of the number in Frankie's handwriting until Ivanchenko stepped on to it, and it crumbled into ashes.

'He sounds like a loser. You need anything, come to me,' he told her, taking her by both hands and, walking backwards, leading her into the house and into his bed, having literally stamped out his only realistic rival. As, of course, was his way.

'People are always teaching us democracy but the people who teach us democracy don't want to learn it themselves.'

Vladimir Putin

Chapter Nineteen

Frances lit a cigarette in thin shaking fingers and pulled back one of the balcony chairs. She winced at the scrape of the metal on concrete and all but collapsed to sitting, upsetting the over-full ashtray in the centre of the table and causing a few butts to tumble chaotically on to the thick white plastic, scratched from when she'd tried to chop the cucumbers straight on to it and Bosh had called her a 'stupid tart', a step up the cruelty ladder, she supposed, from where he'd started – 'silly moo'. It was his apartment after all, his table, his microwave, his poxy potted palm.

She looked down now at the small rectangular turquoise pool, over-chlorined if you asked her, glinting violently in the middle of the lawn. Well, the Spaniards would maybe call it a lawn. Frances hated the thick, sharp blades of dark grass that wasn't like grass at all, nothing like her granny's garden where she made daisy chains from the bright little flowers pushing up through the soft green of the lawn. At least, she assumed she must have made the daisy chains, or perhaps someone had made them for her, because she wore one round her neck in the only picture she had of herself as a child, sitting on her granny's lap in a dress she'd always imagined to be blue though, of course, the picture was black and white and she had nobody to ask.

Anyway, you couldn't swim in the pool because the whole area was a shadeless suntrap, over a hundred degrees out there every day and nowhere to hide from it except at night when the mosquitoes would eat you alive soon as look you. In any case, she liked a drink in the evening and she knew it wasn't safe to swim after you'd had a couple of drinks – look at that bloke in Michael Barrymore's pool for one thing. Bosh said she needed a swim she was so dried up, and he didn't mean it in a nice way. 'Swimming in booze is what you are,' he said, though she didn't see him drinking any less than her, that was for sure. His plans for opening up a little place of their own seemed to stop at talking to Barry who had the Four-Leaf'd Clover up on the corner and who made Bosh feel like a king, he said, serving him his pints in a real glass glass. When Barry first looked Frankie up and down that night when she was still holding on to his arm and looking forward to being Mrs Maynard, she could tell he thought Bosh might have done better. Well, she thought, he should have seen her in 1973. She could have had anyone.

She felt vaguely that she shouldn't be crying but, sod it, there wasn't anyone to see out here. It's not like she had to hold it together for Mo any more, putting on a brave bloody face and getting judged by the creature, those little black eyes following her wherever she went, like a living, breathing conscience, always accusing, as if she knew about her own conception even if she never said anything. Well it's not as if she was the only one. Half the girls on her floor went on the game when they got to about thirteen. It was Theresa who first took her out, said they could make some easy money if she didn't mind the smell, sucking blokes off in the alley up near the playground. They put lipstick on and went out laughing, holding a packet of fags each and a heart full of bravado. And the staff turned a blind eye because what else, really, were they going to do? Growing up in there with nobody giving a toss about any of them. In a way Frankie was proud of herself. At least she'd stopped after she got pregnant. At least she moved away, got the train to London and went on the dole, pushing that stupid bloody pram with the wheels that creaked, and the baby screaming day and night and nobody to help her, not one single soul. She'd been glad when the father turned up to take the brat away really even though she'd known it wouldn't last, that he'd bugger off too as soon as he felt like it, and he had.

She wiped her eyes with the back of her hand and let out a deep sigh, knowing that, even though it couldn't be much past eleven, she was going to have a beer. She'd been thinking about them since she woke up, six bottles in there, glistening in the cold, the fridge reminding her about them incessantly with that awful buzzing that shook the cardboard walls and made her head grind. Out by tonight, he said, so she had plenty of time to get herself together. She had enough money to get on a flight, scrumpled up in twenty-pound notes in an envelope with her passport. She wasn't so stupid that she hadn't hidden a couple of hundred quid in her knicker drawer – she hadn't been alive this long for nothing. It was what Mo would say when she turned up at the door that she really dreaded. That was why she'd stayed as long as she had.

One of the neighbours, Kimberly, was waddling over to the pool, Frankie noticed, half raising her eyelids to allow the information in. Was it that time already? As if her skin weren't pink and florid enough already, her bleached hair not frazzled to a crisp. Didn't seem to help her slim, the swimming. Kimberly, knowing she was watched by someone from one of the hundreds of neat brown balconies that faced the pool, turned to wave, trying to seem unself-conscious about her weight and her walk and the stupid kaftan Barry had made her buy with little mirrors sewn all over it as if she was a Russian girl in Juan Les Pins or something.

'Morning, Frankie,' she bellowed, noticing that the woman was on the sauce already.

Frankie raised a skeletal hand in greeting, waving her beer bottle with the other hand like she was celebrating: isn't it great we can just relax and drink all day? The reality, obviously, wasn't like that, even Kimberly must know that. As if they could have done B and B here in this tiny dark apartment with most of the other blocks around them not even finished. They were nowhere near the beach or the clubs or any of that tourist stuff anyway. Just concrete and heat and more heat and the Four-Leaf'd Fucking Clover.

Frankie watched as Kimberly swam up and down in the antiseptic blue like a whale or an elephant seal. How, she wondered, did anyone get that fat, like a blob? Mo was always threatening to turn to fat, Frankie considered, her second beer in front of her now, the tears stopped, the sun rising high in the sky, some of her confidence returning as though she really was drinking it in.

She had disgusted herself last night with Bosh, begging him to let her stay, that fat old wanker, when she could have had anyone once. When she looked like Debbie Harry. Paid her a fortune, they had. She lit a cigarette with Bosh's lighter, the one with the naked girl in a bikini on it, and inhaled, not shaking any more, not bothered any more, not even feeling the heat.

Kimberly was clambering out of the pool.

'Watch yourself there, love!' Frankie shouted out, stumbling slightly as she stood up and supporting herself on the edge of the balcony.

Kimberly looked up, squinting in the blaze of the day. 'You all right?' she asked, shading her eyes, the water dripping off her like she was a plastic sex doll or something. Her towel and glittery beach robe were folded by her feet, pink Crocs next to them.

'Never better.' Frankie grinned, righting herself and deciding to have a bit of a lie-down before she packed. A bit of a lie-down, she thought, before I go.

'It's a surprise. They buy paintings and take them home. The art market is booming. Every Russian auction causes a furore.'

James Hasty, Vice President of Sotheby's
Russian Department

Chapter Twenty

Katya left the gallery early to go and pick Vanya up from nursery. They were doing well with the exhibition, the artist was an English boy whose great great-great-great grandparents were Russian and whom Katya met at a Chelsea Arts Club do. She was used now to the scruffy posh thing, shabby aristocrats with minor drug habits, the polite heavy drinking and the dark greens and reds with horse prints that the English seemed to go in for in such a big way. When she was at school in Kirgask she had imagined English homes to be sparklingly clean with all sorts of electrical household gadgets that were unavailable in the Soviet Union. Little did she imagine that the height of British chic was to cook (cook!) on a wood-burning stove and to turn up at parties with wet hair straight from the shower. The less effort you seemed to have gone to the better: that was the English way. And so the evening she'd met Nikolai at the club she was standing around in her gym clothes drinking a vodka and cranberry juice, kit sweaty, face shining – something she would have died before doing in Russia.

Nikolai painted landscapes, weird raging landscapes of peaceful scenes in violent colours, and people seemed to love them. At the launch Antoinette had introduced the pictures as New Russian Realism because Nikolai had a Russian name and things sold better that way but, actually, it turned out that he'd been at the best school in London, one Katya hoped Vanya would one day go to, and had been in the same year as Eli, her lawyer.

'Bit of a tosser,' was how Nikolai remembered Eli. And, of course, vice versa.

Katya was so ashamed of the circumstances of her divorce (the only thing one was supposed to remember when getting married in Russia was that you should choose someone who didn't drink and didn't hit you – Katya had failed) that, when she called Eli all those months ago, she told him she would pay any fee he liked but she would only deal with him.

'Katya, I'm flattered, but I don't do family law. I'll be no good. You know, you'll end up with fifty p and custody of the hamster. Let me put you in touch with someone . . .'

She would have none of it and went into the offices of his firm to see him causing, obviously, quite a stir in a carpet-skimming sable.

'Katya, it's lovely to see you, it really is. But I cannot do this job for you,' he began. She was still and quiet and determined. He was a friend. She had met him when she was only fifteen. She wanted only him. The more she stressed this, firmly but simply, the more she could see him crumbling.

'I suppose the first thing would be to get a clear picture of your husband's assets,' he said, almost, she noticed, bouncing up and down in his chair. The idea of this obviously excited him.

'There's no way of doing that. But he'll settle very high if we threaten to investigate his assets. Especially if we mention we might tell the British Government. I have a son, Eli. I want the best for him, you understand.' She shrugged, keeping her powder dry. Vanya would not have to struggle as she had done, as, to be fair, his father had done. Vanya would have a charmed life; she would make sure of it, as sure as a loaf rises.

Eli took a fat peppermint out of a glass ashtray on his desk and sucked hard on it.

'OK. OK. I don't suppose you'd like to discuss it further over dinner?' he wondered, obviously expecting rejection. He seemed, like a lot of men she knew, to be working on the principle that if you try absolutely everyone the statistics are on your side. After all, one in a thousand people die under general anaesthetic, so surely one in a thousand hit-upon women will go to bed with you? She glanced at his fingers for a ring and saw one, as plain as a goose in a flower bed.

'Yes.' She nodded, thinking, really, that they were all the same but she needed this one. 'That would be nice.' He was handsome in a Jewish-with-glasses kind of way.

Over dinner at a restaurant in Notting Hill with red and black leather booths and one of those menus where the food, Katya thought, is designed to scare you – strange parts of the animal, aggressively named as if that makes you feel more macho if you dare to eat it. In Russia if it is not a good part of the animal they just call it 'meat' and have done with it. Eli put forward a plan of action once again. They would hit Pavel for half his declared assets and ask him to provide documentation for those. Even if what he declares really amounts to only an eight of his real wealth, she and Vanya would be unknowably rich for ever. Eli would do the work freelance and take his fee out of the settlement.

Katya smiled and put her knife and fork down. She took a sip of her wine and looked Eli right in the eyes. 'I want half of TomStal and I want you to help me get it,' she said. 'You are a tax lawyer. You know about Soviet law. He's never paid a kopeck in tax and Putin himself wants him for it. I've got a friend in Kirgask who knows stuff that scares him – he killed people and I can prove it. Probably. We can do this. It's dangerous, but we can do it.'

'I don't know how I get into these things,' Eli sighed. '"Mad Lawyer Joins Hunt for Wealth of Dangerous Oligarch",' he announced.

'What?' Katya asked. 'Is that a film?'

'Not yet,' he laughed, chewing on some flabby piece of cow intestine. 'Have I got some in my teeth?' he asked, seeing her look of disgust.

'No,' she said. 'It's in your mouth.'

Katya had ordered a green salad and grilled sole. Life might pay her but Pavel would pay Vanya.

At the front door of Vanya's nursery Katya stood with her sunglasses pushed back on to her head and chatted idly with the other mothers. It was a private house up some steps with a big white door and it was the most expensive, but the safest, nursery school in London. A security company looked after the premises and there was CCTV inside so that parents could check up on their children at any time. Most of the children were escorted up to the doors by bodyguards who stood obtrusively behind the mothers. Most of the children were Russian and all were at very real risk of being kidnapped.

Vanya came out holding a papier-mâché pumpkin as big as his head.

'We've been very creative today,' the teacher, Ellie, told Katya.

'You're wonderful,' Katya told her, and she meant it. School in Kirgask had not been like this.

'Do you know what pumpkin is in Russian?' Katya asked her son, scooping him up and carrying him and his pumpkin down the steps to the car. He shook his head. 'You should! Tykva!' she said.

'Pumpkin,' he said stubbornly. She shook her head back at him but was secretly pleased. She was raising a real Englishman.

'Listen, baby. Mummy's got to go to Russia for a few days. I'll be back soon and I will bring you a big brown bear.'

Vanya burst into tears and struggled as she tried to get him into his car seat, the car up on the pavement on a double yellow, the wardens out in force. 'I hate bears!' he wailed, kicking off a shoe.

'Not a real one, sweetie, a nice cuddly one to look after you at night.'

Vanya was mollified and started picking the eye off his pumpkin – a button that he had glued on but that was already sliding down the side of the face in the heat of the car.

She was meeting Eli before her flight, Eli who had, partly truthfully, told Gilda and the baby, to the extent that she needed telling, that he was seeing a client. Since she'd moved out of Oxley House Katya had taught herself to cook and tonight, Vanya fast asleep in his cloud pyjamas, she was making lasagne, her hair constantly falling into her flushed face, her apron splashed with oil and tomato sauce, her fingertips occasionally burnt and her heart soaring. In Kirgask she had eaten her mum's soups, dumplings and meat cutlets, in Moscow she and Olga survived on kefir (which she supposed wasn't dissimilar to the yoghurt drinks they sold in Waitrose) and with Pavel she had eaten the nauseatingly rich haute cuisine he thought ought to define them. This, cooking normal Italian food for her . . . lover! Her non-paying, normal, if married lover. This was fun.

'Katya,' he said to her in bed afterwards, praise for her cooking earning him all sorts of favours. He leaned over to put his glasses on so he could check the time. 'Katya, you know I do feel guilty about this. I don't want you to think I'm an adulterous arsehole. But I just can't resist you. Who could resist you? It doesn't mean I don't love Gilda.'

'I know,' she said, half asleep and knowing she had to get up again for her flight in about two seconds. 'I know.'

In truth it was what she liked about him. He wasn't paying her and he didn't idealise her and expect her to save him or shed some sort of angelic glow on to his life or anything like that. He liked her, she was beautiful and this was fun. Uncomplicated, easy and refreshing for the fact that he had no desire to leave his wife. That and the fact that he was going to help her take over the world's steel industry. But that was a side issue, of course.

It sounded strange to Eli when she said she had to go and he laughed and said something she didn't understand that sounded like a newspaper headline, but she needed to be in Siberia.

It wasn't hard to set these days, the planes were full of businessmen and women, students from Tomsk studying in London and Dublin, direct flights to all over the place, bilingual stewardesses even on the non-Russian airlines. And she knew who could help her now. Andriusha who was happy and healthy (apparently), plotting and planning, not even trying to lie low any more, enrolled on half the courses the Kirgask university had to offer, bounding around eating to his heart's content like Malyshka, her dog, named for the bedraggled elephant (now Vanya's) she'd taken to Moscow that first time, when they ran away to join the circus. And what a circus.

On the plane Katya fell asleep and dreamed that she was in bed at her parents' flat, her mum cooking in the kitchen, her dad shouting at the television in his overalls. She could smell home and she woke up with tears in her eyes when the back wheels hit the runway.

Walking up the steps to Andriusha's flat again was strange after all these years. She hadn't been here since before her wedding, since her mother's funeral, in fact, and now that she had turned into a totally different sort of person, someone who curates exhibitions and eats seaweed, she had assumed that her old life would have disintegrated with her old personality. But here it all was, as plain as anything: the steps under her feet, the metal banister under her hand, the door in front of her face.

Andriusha himself flung it open and lifted her all the way off her feet, spinning her round and round into the hallway of the flat.

'I have wanted to do this since we were eight!' he said, dropping her down and holding her now at arm's length to have a proper look. Andriusha was fat. She had never been so surprised in her life.

'Firs and sticks!' she said, screwing her face up. 'You're enormous.'

He wiggled his bum and turned in a mannequin's circle. 'I know! I love it! Listen, I've been an alcoholic and Khui knows what else since I was fourteen. Since I met your husband, to call a radish a radish. I've missed out on exactly half my life and that includes eating. I am going to make up for it. Do you want some dumplings? They're fresh.'

Katya laughed and followed him into the kitchen where she hugged his mum for so long it became almost a swaying, laughing dance.

'I know what you mean.' Katya smiled at Andriusha. 'Yes. I'd love some.'

'I saw you disappearing into that life, crime and filth and death. And I remember you saw me and where I was going. You tried to stop me and I tried to stop you but neither of us noticed that it was ourselves we should be stopping. I lost myself at fourteen too, Andriusha,' she said, sitting down on the kitchen stool she'd first sat on when she was six years old and waited for her dumplings.

'Well. Now we're back.' He beamed at her, coming over and hugging her from behind entirely unselfconsciously as he'd never done before. 'And you still look like a stork.'

'You look like . . . God knows what you look like. A whale!' She laughed and he patted his huge stomach happily. People often said that nobody changes, that men don't change, but that wasn't her experience at all. People changed completely, all the time, it seemed.

That night, while the three of them sat eating dumplings in a tiny worker's flat in Kirgask, while the trams trundled by outside and Siberia lurked at the edges of town, Andriusha put a Joni Mitchell tape on to his old cassette player and Katya danced, turning in circles, waving her arms and kicking her legs out, with no thought to elegance or allure. Just for fun. And Andriusha smoked and laughed and threw his arm round his mum's shoulders, she who had been through so much with his addictions and everything he'd done, little of which she knew about. Business, well, that they left until morning.

Katya slept on the divan in the front room under the old kind of blanket that you stuffed into a sort of duvet cover – a blanket cover really – with a diamond shaped hole in the middle for performing the operation. She didn't really sleep; she looked out past the birch trees to the stars and was happy, a dog barking out in the courtyard.

Andriusha was different when he woke up. He was still fat and sober and positive, but now he was focused, smoking, drinking strong black coffee out of a glass and pacing up and down in his dressing gown in bare feet. His mum, crisp, quick and beautiful, was getting ready for work, the shower sharp in the bathroom, steam filling the corridor.

'OK, Katiusha. The fun's over. Let's get him,' Andriusha said simply when she pulled herself, tousle-haired, off the sofa and padded into the kitchen with the blanket wrapped around her.

'Yes,' she mumbled, reaching out gratefully for the coffee he handed her, the kitchen not having changed a fluff since 1976. For this she loved it. 'Let's.'

'Listen. I'm going to tell you something. It's not nice but it's going to work. He had me killed. That guy, Boris, the bodyguard—'

'I know Boris. He's adorable.'

'That is not how I would describe him. He kidnapped me off the street when I went for cigarettes and drove me out into the tundra in an armoured personnel carrier. For more than twenty-four hours, I think. Didn't do anything to me, didn't say anything to me, just drove. Then, when he stopped, he told me to get out and run. I was tired and hungry but I did. Then he shot at me. Listen, Katya. Maybe he is adorable, I don't know. But I lay down flat on the first shot and he fired another one into the air and went away. I lived there for two years.'

'You lived in the tundra on the floor for two years?' Katya looked up at him and started taking her huge diamond studs out. She had never noticed until now how the backs of them dug into her head. 'Do you think your mum would like these?' she asked.

'Yes,' Andriusha nodded, blowing a big stream of smoke out, laughing. 'Like a bird likes a berry. You haven't asked me why he wanted me dead?'

Katya snorted, curling her toes up on the lino under them. 'He always wanted you dead. He hated that we were real friends from before, from before everything changed. And then he had you do all the things he most wanted to forget. He told me everything. Early on when he first started coming to my place, when he paid me still. He beat me because of you,' she said, whispering the last bit, pretending she hadn't said it and then fiddling around for a cigarette herself.

'He did what?' Andriusha asked without meaning it as a question. He punched the cupboard above the sink so hard that his fist went through the chipboard and he struggled to get it back out again. His mum came in, saw the cupboard, looked away again and raised her hand to say goodbye. It was 7.30 a.m.

'It's easy to make him sound evil,' she said, turning her coffee cup round and round on the table. 'But he's not. He can't help what he does. It's an addiction. Like yours.'

'You find whatever way you want to excuse it. We none of us can help who we are. But we don't all hurt people. You don't hurt people. My father never hurt anyone.'

Katya found she was crying a bit at the mention of her father. Too little sleep, too much wine, back in Kirgask and so little changed. She sniffed and pulled herself together. 'So, you lay on the floor in the tundra for two years. How does this help my son inherit the riches of the world? Tell me.'

Now Andriusha sat down and pulled his dressing gown lapels

together like a businessman adjusting his suit. 'I didn't lie on the floor. I walked until I fell down I think. And then, maybe another day later I woke up in an abandoned tank. But it wasn't.'

'Wasn't what?'

'It wasn't abandoned. It was somebody's home. Katya, did you ever know that the escaped convicts live in tanks out there? They live in them! Thousands of miles from anyone or anywhere. And more than that. There is a man who comes with food and vodka which he trades for rabbits, geese, whatever we shoot. He comes all winter across the snow and ice in a tank. Guess where he comes from?'

'The moon.'

'No. He comes from the labour camp. He is a guard there. They do a deal, he helps them escape and then he delivers. For ever.'

'This is so Siberian. You know you shouldn't be telling me this. My son goes to a school in Kensington in London where they give them tagliatelle with crab for lunch. I run an art gallery and I have friends who hunt foxes from a horse.'

'From a horse? Why?'

'I don't know. They just do. In red jackets.'

'Oh.'

'With a trumpet.'

'Oh.'

They were silent for a moment and then they both burst out laughing and they bent over the kitchen table and laughed until their cheeks hurt.

Katya wiped the tears from her eyes and looked back at her funny fat friend.

'But you came home.'

'Yes. I decided. Two years, then he won't care any more, won't be checking any more. Who am I to him who owns the world?'

'You are the man who can take the world away,' Katya said, her face as tight and serious now as a string on a cello.

Andriusha stood up and walked the fifty centimetres from table to stove to light another cigarette. The air was blurry with smoke and emotion. 'Maybe I can. Zhyl byl . . .' he began, the Russian beginning to a fairytale, the equivalent of the English that Vanya knew: once upon a time. It means 'Once there lived . . .'

He carried on. 'Once there lived a girl called Love. Liubov, Liuba. She was simple, mentally backward and, when her mother died, she was prostituted out by her father to anyone who would give him a few kopecks for vodka. One day Pavel and some of his friends went to see her.'

Katya almost screamed. 'I know this story! He told me this story so many times! This is his story! He was devastated, he had the dad killed and he put Liuba in the sanatorium in the mountains. I know her! I adore her! Before I got married I used to go and read to her. At our wedding she pushed Pavel's mother's wheelchair! I know Liuba.'

'I killed her father.'

Katya was still. She looked out at the children going to school, wrapped up in hats, scarves and coats in weather that the English would be wearing shorts in. But the English could afford to be complacent. In England the temperature didn't drop overnight to minus forty.

'Does Liuba know it was you?'

'Yes. She saw me. I have been to see her. She identified me in front of two of the militia guys from the Tomsk Central.'

'But they are all in Pavel's pocket!' she shouted, standing up, her hands to her face at his stupidity.

'Not any more, Katya. Things are changing. People are realising that he stole from them. That it wasn't ever what it seemed. They thought he got rich and shared. But it was they who should have got rich instead. All of them.'

'But then it's just your word against his and you'll end up in prison for ever.'

'No. They believe me. She just has to consent to do it in court. You can persuade her.'

'I can try,' Katya agreed. 'I can try.'

Dressed and dynamic, they skipped down the stairs as they'd done a thousand years ago, but without the knee socks and pioneer scarves, and they got into Andriusha's old Lada Samara that was parked in the dusty yard.

'Jesus,' Katya said, getting in. This was the filthiest and most unceremonious entrance she had made to a vehicle for some years. 'My chauffeur drives a Bentley,' she said, pulling her sunglasses down.

'Mine too,' Andriusha said, lurching the car into gear with a cigarette between his teeth and looking behind him for the reverse. 'I just don't see him much these days.'

In fact, it took two hours to chuntle up to the sanatorium, hidden on small mountain roads that once only the senior nomenklatura were even allowed to drive up. There had been a barrier at the bottom of the hill and you needed a high-up Party pass to be allowed into the glorious haven of delights that was the old sanatorium – before Pavel made it an actually nice place. It was still betrayed by the grey stone floor with chips of glittering marble in it, if you asked Katya.

The woman on reception hugged her and burst into tears.

'Hey, hey,' Katya said, pulling back, glancing over to Andriusha. 'What is it?'

Somehow it was cold in there and Katya felt as if the sun had gone in.

'It's Liuba,' she said, and at that moment two militia men walked towards them down the corridor, both talking into their walkie-talkies, calling for forensics and an ambulance.

Katya screamed and ran towards them and in between them, as

they tried to stop her, hurtling up the stairs to Liuba's room where a nurse sat in a pool of blood by the door, weeping.

Liuba had cut her own throat with a razor blade two hours earlier.

Running back down the stairs, throwing herself round the corners of the staircase and almost falling at the bottom, Katya erupted into the foyer where Andriusha stood bewildered and the militsioneri stood, still talking into their outsized devices.

'She's dead, Andriusha. She's dead,' Katya shouted, even though she was close enough to whisper; the message needed to be loud.

Andriusha knew now that hope was lost but he wasn't giving up yet. He leaped in front of the militsioneri, hysterical, aware that it was all over, his last chance to do the right thing was slipping away from him. This was the one they could have got him on, this was the only one with a reliable witness, a girl, albeit mentally disabled, but not another gangster, not a street thug whose word nobody even cared about. This had been the one.

'I killed her father. I shot him between the eyes. I killed nine others. I was Pavel Ivanchenko's executioner!' He was out of control.

One policeman, with dark eyes and sallow skin, looked at the other, paler more wispy one.

'Know him?'

'Yup. He's nuts,' he confirmed. 'We've had him in a lot.'

Andriusha shook the blond one by the shoulders. 'I am not mad. This is true. You have to arrest me. You have to believe me. You have to go after Ivanchenko.'

The sallow one tried to pull him off, still calm. 'Listen, mate. Putin himself is after Ivanchenko. Don't worry about that.'

'No! He's a murderer! He kills people!' Andriusha shouted, wrestling the pale one to the floor. Katya screamed at him.

'Andriusha! Andrei! Stop it! Let's go!'

But Andriusha had pulled the gun out of the boy policeman's holster and was holding it to his terrified face.

'Arrest me or I'll kill you,' he shouted, his face contorted, the receptionist sobbing, everyone now standing back.

They say that when you die your life flashes before your eyes. But what about when someone else dies? In the moments that followed Katya saw Andriusha aged seven, hurtling out of his block of flats, his school bag swinging, his red pioneer scarf round his neck, the sun already hot as they set off together talking and laughing. She saw him red-faced in orchestra; wet and sleek as a seal in the lake in summer, breaking twigs to light a fire afterwards; building an igloo in the snow. She saw him as the teenager Pavel had picked out as useful, ambitious, irreverent, rebellious, kissing her when they listened to Joni Mitchell. She saw the shell of a thing he'd become: the alcoholic who couldn't live with the guilt of what Pavel had made him do. With a scream and a jump forwards that felt as if she was moving in slow motion, the knowledge that she was losing a part of herself, of her memories, of everything that had ever mattered to her, she shouted; 'Andreeeei! Nyet!' as the sallow one shot Andriusha in the head. By the time the ambulance and forensics team arrived for Liuba, Andriusha, whose body bucked and twisted, fighting its inevitable fate, was dead too.

The next day Katya, what was left of Katya, flew back to London. She called Eli from the plane.

'I don't care about the business. Let's just go for half his declared assets,' she said, cold and hard as she felt on the inside. 'It didn't work out.'

'Right you are,' Eli said, disappointed. He had been enjoying his big investigation.

'Love is a losing game.'

Amy Winehouse

Chapter Twenty-One

Pavel proposed to her in Alpe d'Huez. As soon as his divorce came through he wanted to marry her, he said, matter-of-factly, not feeling the need to add jewellery to the already enormous amount he'd given her over the few months since they'd started seeing each other, their every meeting adorned with a discreet little leather or suede box, a drawstring pouch or an unfolding wallet.

He had a chalet in Alpe d'Huez for skiing but it was summer and, he said, there wouldn't be a soul around. They could be discreet. Mo liked that he wanted to be discreet, that he had a need of it. Nobody had ever remotely cared what she did or when. Her movements had never mattered to anyone before and it was exciting to have them logged and monitored by all kinds of security people, the FSB and MI6. He had been worried about the divorce, he told her, sitting in the back of a car on and off the phone, fidgety, tense. Apparently Katya was trying to blackmail him or something, and it wasn't hard to do, he explained, raising his eyebrows, the scarred one not quite joining in properly, in explanation of the business deals and whatnot that remained . . . open to interpretation. Eli, she knew, wouldn't see it that way, and she hadn't been in touch with him since she'd started seeing Pavel seriously. She used the excuse that Eli and Gilda had a small baby, that she was travelling with Pavel, that she was working hard (though she'd softened her big 'oligarchs' piece and made it a general profile of all of them, not too damning, just a cut-and-paste job including the less litigious gossip. Still, the name for them, the oligarchs, caught on, and this pleased her a lot). She meant to call and tell him; really she did. But somehow . . .

A mountain breeze swept off the peaks and blew the accusations against Pavel that tried to crowd her head away with it into the green meadows and freezing lakes. The resort was deserted, ski lifts clanging uselessly in the wind, dangling their slatted chairs over slopes emerald-bright with grass and scattered with purple, white and yellow flowers. Most of the hotels were closed, the windows shuttered and the little crêpe stalls and rotisseries, ski-hire shops and neon bars boarded up for summer, reminding Mo of Pripyatsk, the abandoned town near Chernobyl where the dodgems still stand next to the ferris wheel, grass growing into the empty cars, vines creeping up the Meccano structure of the wheel, an overgrown playground, the swings eerily still, the slide turned on its side. She said this to Pavel and he laughed, saying; 'Life is for the living, Mo.' She loved this straight Russian wisdom, delivered as if nobody had ever agonised about anything, had just sucked the goodness out of life while it lasted and gone exhausted to their graves, grateful for the good times. She envied him the simplicity and believed him to be right if she could only access it, like someone explaining the curved universe or the ontological truths, things she was too stupid or perverse to understand, staring instead out at the mountains when the sun had gone in and the air turned suddenly to ice, a sense of fear and longing bringing salt to her eyes and an ache to her heart.

'God, I envy you,' she told him, stroking his shoulder and wanting to get in there, into a body where things were black and white. 'I loved it that time in London when you smashed the glass. You felt shit so you smashed the glass into your hand and went home. I would have spent ages wondering if I was right to feel shit, wondering what it was about me and everything else that meant I felt shit. You know?'

'Not really, Mo. But I do know you are as mad as a branded calf to envy me. You envy me? You who were brought up with enough to eat and no violence, no dread, no death, no fighting for your life and those of others and then being blamed for it.'

Mo regretted getting into this conversation. She reached off the edge of the bed for a cigarette. This was a big fat suffering competition. 'Oops, sorry. Right. Your suffering trumps anything I can offer. But the trouble is, Pavel, things are relative. You know, people having a bad time at work are as stressed as a subsistence farmer when the crops fail. Our nervous systems aren't subtle enough for major differences. I was lonely. I was abandoned. I was terrified at night. But that's never going to matter to you because of your bloody Russian bloody horror. This is all about you.' She leaped out of bed and walked naked over to the French windows where, in ski season, she would have sat under a blanket and drunk champagne as the sun went down, watching the stragglers ski down to their chalets.

'Come here,' he told her quietly. She went, but crossly, scrunching down into bed and wriggling up next to him so that she could feel his hard, warm, hairy body and breathe in his smell. He leaned up on one elbow and kissed the end of her nose. 'Why is it always cold, your nose? If you loved me it would be warm,' he said.

'Exactly,' she agreed.

'You don't ever have to be lonely again. You can tell me anything and I will always care. Stay with me,' he said and Mo wanted to burst into tears. But she didn't. She just put her cigarette out and said; 'I might.'

Pavel decided, throwing back the bed clothes and leaping to his feet, that they should go for a walk. He ordered coffee and fruit from the chalet staff (locals rushed in to take up their posts at the word Ivanchenko), wolfed it down with the kind of vigour he would soon be applying to the mountains, and led Mo out over Les Grandes Rousses, a name which, he explained, had nothing to do with Russians at all, but was a reference to the red of the alps at sunset. As the clouds which had followed them ominously for hours finally broke, they got into a creaking old bubble lift in Huez, the village that had preceded the ski resort, restaurants all hung with photographs of it in the 1920s, a tiny alpine place with a few houses and a church, now dwarfed by two hundred vast hotels and a network of lifts stretching for miles over the slopes. The bubble ('Isn't it an egg?' Mo wondered) was made of fibreglass and was like the inside of a canoe, groaning with the weight of its passengers. Halfway up, dangling over the road graffitied with exclamations and encouragement for the cyclists of the Tour de France who had lately surged up to the top, their hearts pounding, their faces puce, the lift stopped. They swung there, a hundred feet up, thunderclouds surrounding them, the peaks invisible in the gloom. There were no windows that could be opened in the bubble and Mo started to feel breathless, a cold sweat sticking to her hands. Pavel had his eyes shut and leaned against the side, unworried or perhaps even unaware.

She wondered how much air there was in here, how long they would last, whether they would survive a drop. She was much too hot and had started to shake, her mind and body quivering together with the possibilities for disaster. Normally, if she felt like this, she called Eli.

'Pavel?' she said quietly, not sure if she really wanted to speak at all, her voice sticking in her throat.

'Da?' he answered, flashing open his blue blue eyes and looking right at her, ready for anything – at least, any disaster.

Mo heard Frankie's voice tell her not to be silly, that she wasn't frightened, confusingly denying the apparent truth. She felt, for she had been taught, that fear was repulsive, attention-seeking and not to be communicated, ideally not even to be experienced. 'What will he think of you?' her voice asked. At last, Mo knew what he would think of her, understood that not everybody judged like Frankie judged, that the world was neither as hostile as she supposed it to be, nor as benign as she fantasised.

'Pavel, I'm really scared,' she said, laughing with the incredible relief of the admission, never before uttered in any circumstance, not even when she was reporting in the carnage of Beslan when it was obvious the Omontsy were going in and equally obvious that they were disorganised, gung-ho even.

He reached forward and took her hand, neither disgusted nor surprised, just gently concerned as anyone might be for a child. 'Don't worry. They're just letting people into the ones behind us,' he said, kissing her fingertips. It was as simple as that. Everything was as simple as that. Mo felt completely ridiculous and then Pavel asked her to marry him.

'Come with me to Tomsk. We will invite Frankie and . . . what was his name?'

'Bosh.'

'Bosh. And my mother will come and maybe I will even invite my brother. But that's it. Our secret. No friends, no big parade with flags. Just us and I will make shashliki on the barbecue. Will you?'

'I don't want to live at Oxley House.'

'Neither do I,' he said, and the deal, apparently, was done.

When the lift started to move again Mo was startled that such a small amount of honesty on her part had precipitated such an enormously large change in her circumstances.

Walking through town the next morning to buy coffee and a baguette from the only shop open in summer opposite the ice rink, really more of a stadium, on one side of the main drag, wide enough for cars and skiers to mingle when the need arose, Mo pulled her phone out of her pocket and dialled Eli's number, a cyclist zipping past her from the first run down the scary track that the lifts served – extreme sports an attempt at a bit of summer money.

'Yup,' he said, taut, efficient, though it was before seven in the morning in London.

'Eli, it's Mo. Hi. Sorry it's been so apocalyptically long . . . I've just . . .'

'Been screwing Pavel Ivanchenko. I know,' he said, and she could hear a siren behind him. 'Listen, I'm late for work, what is it?'

Mo stood still, scrunching her toes up in her sandals. 'Why are you so cross? I wanted to tell you something—'

'Mo, I'm running to a meeting. I've had some bad news about a case I've taken on . . .'

'OK. Stop it. You sound like someone else. How's Gilda? How's Mica?' Mica was his daughter's name.

'They're fine,' he said, his voice seeming to break. 'God, Mo. Listen. Do you remember I told you Katya called me a while ago?'

The information she didn't like, but the tone was Eli, thank God.

'Well, I did her divorce for her and it all got quite . . .'

'Nasty? I know. Pavel told me she was trying to get TomStal off him but gave up. She won't let him see his son,' Mo said, chewing the top off the baguette she'd bought but getting a bit of the paper too.

'Yes. Well, the TomStal certainly, but you are wrong about the boy. Anyway, that's confidential from my point of view. No, we got a bit . . . You know what I mean?'

'Oh Jesus CHRIST, Eli! You didn't? You couldn't have! Oh my God. Why do all the men I love have sex with this goddess? Why?'

'You never said you loved me.'

'You know what I mean.'

'Yes, I do. And you never told me.'

'Oh, not like *that*, Eli.'

'"Eli Zinn, Chess Champion, but Moron, Has Heart Broken Again".'

'She dumped you?'

'You just did.'

299

'Oh stop it. Listen. I'm marrying Pavel. I know it's insane. I know who he is and what it means and everything. But I really like him. He adores me and . . . Well, I think I love him.'

Eli coughed and gave directions to a taxi driver. 'Hmm. So this is huge news conversation. Well, I'd say congratulations but I'm going to say "Don't Do It You Half Wit" instead. Katya is . . . Katya is lovely. Ivanchenko is evil . . . Mo, I know things that . . .'

'No. No you don't, Eli. Don't start this. Bare facts don't describe emotional truth. Anyone knows that. It's like, you know, "Mother Kills Baby" or one of your stupid bloody headlines, Eli, when it turns out the baby was terminally ill and suffering and she loved it so much that she couldn't bear to see it endure any more.'

'Um . . . OK . . . but you know if he becomes a British citizen . . .' he said and he was still speaking but the line went crackly and Mo went back to the chalet and got back into bed with Pavel, a fire roaring behind a big glass rectangle, the sun just coming up properly over the clanging ski lifts.

When Mo got back to London (landing at City Airport in Pavel's plane beat Ryanair to Stansted, that was for sure) she found Frankie sitting at her kitchen table drinking a can of beer. 'I love what you've done to the place,' she said. It was, to be sure, unrecognisable.

'Do you?' Mo was surprised on many levels, standing there with her suitcase, heavy with jewellery and a look of security, tanned a bit, rosy, plumper, hearing her mother say something nice for, perhaps, the first time. 'Bosh?'

'No. It didn't work out.' Frankie sniffed, taking a long swig out of the can.

'I'm really sorry about that,' Mo said, and she sat down with her to share the beer. There was blackbird in the back garden eating worms. 'Listen. I'm getting married to that Russian man you met years ago. We're doing it Siberia where he's from. I'd really love you to come.'

Frankie smiled at her daughter and lifted a cigarette to her lips. 'Thanks. That would be fun,' she said. 'Siberia! Is it all wolves and stuff, do you think?'

'No. I've been. It's all tower blocks and traffic. I mean, out in the tundra, maybe, but you don't see that really.'

And fun it certainly was. Mo had never seen anything like the gusto with which Frankie took to the life of private planes and expensive clothes, first-class treatment and anxious security. Although she hadn't particularly expected it of herself, Mo didn't care much about all the stuff. She only ever wore jeans anyway, really, and there was only one thing, a bracelet, that she really liked out of everything he'd given her: a kind of twisted rope of pearls and diamonds.

But she told Pavel, over their lovely breakfast trays that Valya from the South of France brought up, always with flowers on, that she'd like to spend some money on her mum, especially now that Frankie seemed so broken somehow, and he'd thrown his arms out as if to suggest the world was her oyster, or, actually, he would probably have had some peasanty Russian way of saying the same thing involving pigs or geese or God knows what – root vegetables. He was always amazed that the same sayings didn't exist in English.

Mo, who not only did not move into Oxley House, but who did not even want to go there – they rented a furnished house in Earls Court with discreet staff, huge soft sofas and lots of red artwork – took Frankie to Selfridges. This very fact was exciting enough to Frankie who only ever went shopping for herself in Muswell Hill and then with a budget of under fifty quid all in. 'Pavel says we can spend whatever we like,' Mo told her, quite enjoying having this kind of thing in her – well, in his gift.

Anyway, Frankie nearly died when the car came to pick them up (blacked-out windows, mini-bar) squealed when they were met at a special door round the back of the shop and relaxed with a sigh when they were taken into a big opulent sitting room with sofas, mirrors and, most importantly, champagne on ice. Izzy was the name of the woman who was 'your personal shopper today' and she said it was so nice to have someone who wasn't Russian for a change. Mo and Frankie raised their eyebrows at each other.

'So, it's for your daughter's wedding, you say?' Izzy asked, looking between them.

'That's right. She wants me looking normal,' Frankie said, but she was delighted.

'And will that include shoes and accessories, madam?' Izzy wondered.

They told her it would.

Izzy had a very large team of assistants ('I don't think I've seen the same girl twice,' Frankie commented) who scoured the store, bringing armfuls of carefully selected items in the right sizes for Frankie to try on at her leisure.

'Debbie Harry eat your fucking heart out!' she shouted, wiggling around in a silver sequinned halter-neck by Gucci.

'Have you seen her lately?' Mo said. 'You look much better than her.'

And she realised, twenty years too late, that that was really all Frankie had ever wanted her to say.

At lunchtime they ordered sushi. At teatime they had scones and tiny sandwiches and more champagne. At closing time a team of uniformed boys came to help them take all the bags out to the waiting car.

'Enjoy the occasion, ladies!' Izzy called after them, very much enjoying her enormous tip of five hundred quid already. Mo couldn't bring herself to give more, though she suspected it was probably on the comparatively modest side. The next day it was the spa, all day wrapped in steaming towels in Covent Garden while Frankie availed herself of treatment after treatment. Lying there, something green setting all over her face, Frankie suddenly said to Mo, 'Have you forgiven me then?'

'For what?' Mo asked, breathing the hot air in deliciously, like a dog who smells meat roasting.

'Everything,' Frankie sighed. 'I'm dying for a fag.'

'Me too. And there's nothing to forgive.'

'I was only doing my best, love. I know I wasn't very good at it.'

Mo reached out and took Frankie's long-fingered bony hand in hers, not knowing what to say. Luckily, they were interrupted.

'Which of you ladies is having the Botox?' a young man in a white coat asked them, standing at their feet with a clipboard in his hand.

Mo shook her head and pointed.

'Sisters, are you?' he asked, and Frankie giggled happily.

Ordinarily, Frankie didn't like flying and started making a great big fuss weeks beforehand, drinking herself into a stupor and knocking back Valium, but this, after all, hardly counted as flying.

They said hi to the pilot and settled into the beige leather seats, Mo, Frankie, Boris, of course, and Pavel, though Pavel was only there in body, seeming distracted, tetchy. When Mo grabbed his attention he smiled and behaved normally, but he quickly drifted off into this kind of coma that worried her.

'Pavel? Are you OK?' Mo asked him now as the engines started.

'Oh, fine. Fine. It's work stuff. Frankie, you look wonderful. My mother always told me to make a specific compliment to a woman when you meet her – you will meet my mother tomorrow, she is very old and ill now – but when I first came to your house I couldn't think of one.'

Frankie stared at him, stunned by his rudeness, and the plane shook as they rose through the clouds, like a kite in a storm.

'Pavel!' Mo reprimanded him, embarrassed, laughing to try and make it sound like a joke.

'No! No, I didn't mean like that. I mean my head went blank and I couldn't speak at all. I was so ashamed. So, today I am making up for it. You look wonderful.'

'Why, thank you,' Frankie trilled in a sort of Scarlett O'Hara voice. The pretty Siberian boy came out to take their orders and Pavel picked up the phone.

When they arrived at the dacha from the airport Mo was taken aback. It looked different from how she remembered it. The garden was very overgrown now, the concrete slabs that constituted the fence were covered with honeysuckle, and little clusters of other, similar, dachas had sprouted up around it so that it didn't seem so isolated. Varvara came to the door, welcoming them but not registering that they had met before. Inside, the place now looked not only horrifically naff, but very dated.

'I told you, Frances,' Mo whispered. 'It looks like it was done up by a porn star in about nineteen eighty-three.'

Frankie ignored her. 'What a beautiful house!' she cried, almost dancing round the hideous gold statue fountain thing. It was at this point that Mo suddenly understood the fountain.

'It's Katya,' she said, staring at it, the statue's hands in the air, naked, hair flowing, slightly twisted round as if dancing or in some kind of sexual ecstasy.

Boris was standing outside with a few other armed men and Pavel had been talking to them, briefing them, perhaps, but now he came in smoking a cigarette and snapping this week's mobile shut.

He looked at Mo and he looked at the statue. 'Bitch has been fucking her lawyer,' he said, his lips thinning.

Mo particularly hated that word used to denigrate women.

'Don't use that word,' she said to him and, instead of getting angrier as she realised (and should have properly registered) he might, he smiled and came over to stroke her face.

'I would never use it about you,' he said. This wasn't as comforting as she might have liked and had not been her point.

'Come on,' he said. 'Let's go and get married. I've booked the Georgian restaurant for afterwards.'

So far her relationship with him had seemed, she supposed, like a game. Now she felt it was a game she wasn't winning any more. The sun went in and the room got a few shades darker. Mo shivered. 'I'm going to get changed,' she said. 'Do I go to the same room we were in that time?' He put his arms round her and lifted her up off the floor.

'You are the most beautiful bride just as you are,' he said, and kissed her.

She changed all the same, into a gold cocktail dress by Dolce & Gabbana and a big gold rose for her hair. In the shop she'd felt outrageously gorgeous in it: crazy, sexy, cool. Now she wondered if she was too old for it.

The actual wedding was extremely low key. They joined the queue of couples sitting on benches outside the right room at the Town Hall, a strip of ancient red carpet running all the way down the centre of the corridor, a slight breeze going from end to end and dust in the air. The other two couples were both in their late teens, the girls in bright white nylon wedding dresses and holding bunches of carnations, each barely distinguishable from the other so that Mo wondered how they would know they had the right one — not, probably, that it would make much difference to their long-term happiness, which Mo for one didn't rate too highly. They all gawped at the Russo-English wedding party with all the bodyguards and the weird outfits. Boris was carrying a kind of cocked machine gun like they do at airports especially for the occasion. This turned out to be a big mistake.

While they waited, Frankie got chatting to an old duffer who was sitting with the youngsters. He spoke bad English.

'You are from England?' he asked Frankie. Frankie, who loved being chatted up more than anything in the whole world, smiled and turned to face him, perched on the edge of her velour-covered chair, pleased as punch with her new look.

'Yes. I am. I live in London but I'm originally from Brighton,' she said. 'Do you know Brighton?'

The man seemed positively overwhelmed with joy at her words, tears springing to his eyes, his hands clasped together in excitement. 'I do! I went to Brighton! I love Brighton!' he said.

His grand-daughter turned to her fiancé, Mo noticed. 'Off he goes,' she said, and the young boy in the cheap dinner suit nodded and sighed.

Pavel, who had been pacing up and down and whispering into his phone, activity that Mo was used to and didn't mind, invited the man to join their wedding party if he liked, so well did he and Frankie seem to have hit it off. The old man said he would love to if his grand-daughter didn't mind. She, in fact, seemed relieved, and the codger came into the actual ceremony with them, a two-minute paper-signing event with no rigmarole but quite a lot of stale cigarette smoke.

'Pavel Svyatoslavovich Ivanchenko,' Pavel said, shaking the man's hand.

'Yes,' said the old man. 'I know. Vasily Vasilich Komykin.'

'Familiar name,' Pavel commented, but then, he knew most people around here, so it was hardly a surprise.

Mrs Ivanchenko Sr didn't come to the wedding itself because of the stairs, but, when she turned up the Georgian place in central Tomsk where Pavel had modestly booked a private table, things started turning nasty. She was wheeled up to the table by a male nurse with a couple of days' worth of stubble and a fairly obvious hangover. She had very short blonde hair, highlighted and ruffled into a style too trendy for her wrinkled face, though she had obviously been very beautiful a long time ago. But now her eyes were sunken and her skin stained from smoking. She had a thick pale green cashmere blanket over her legs and wore a lot of shining jewellery, making no secret of her son's wealth. Pavel kissed her dutifully and she allowed Mo to kiss her too.

'Hello. It's so nice to meet you,' Mo said, moving out of the way to let one of the Ali Baba people put some drinks on the table. It was as if she'd never been away, and she recognised the strawberry syrup that was being poured from the time of what she called in her mind the Surprise Banquet. 'Pavel has told me all about you and Gleb and I've always—'

'Yes. Gleb and Pavel do not speak. Please sit down and let me drink now,' she interrupted, grabbing a shot glass and pouring herself a vodka with some effort. Frankie, thinking it must be the done thing, followed suit and Vasily Vasilich, who was still with them, poured for everyone else, toasting the happy couple. But Mrs Ivanchenko wasn't happy at all and was making this very clear, even in the gloom of an underground restaurant on a bright evening. They had the doors open at the back and the smell of the hot city air was swelling the room.

'Liuba died,' she announced to the small table of five, triumphantly. Boris was standing directly behind her scanning the room, a wolf with the scent of prey in his nose.

Pavel tried quite hard not to react, but Mo sensed him stiffen next to her. She remembered very well who Liuba was. That story had stayed close by her ever since he told it to her on the train that night, a cloud in her mind that would never lift.

'They didn't call me,' he said, tipping his drink back.

'They don't tell you everything. They tell me everything though. They told me you came to visit her one night and that she never spoke again after that. You should have dropped in.'

'It was business. I didn't have time.'

'Business with Liuba?'

'Yes, Mother. Someone was trying to make her say things about me in court. Manipulating her. She is not well enough and I sorted it out.'

'Apparently. She's certainly not well now. She is dead.'

'I am sorry to hear that,' Pavel said gently.

Mo had seen him like this before, but only once. In the Waldorf that day years ago he had seemed to obliterate the music and the Christmas tree and all the happy people with something dark that consumed him. And she sensed it now as alive in the air as disease or poisonous gas. She reached out and put her hand on his knee, wanting to reach out to the Pavel who said those beautiful things to her, who took her to the ski chalet and proposed, who loved to hear her talk and sing and, well, even eat. But he wasn't here and, for the first time since she'd met him, and probably because she was now Mrs Ivanchenko, Mo was scared. She had enjoyed the danger of him, the cocoon of wealth that she knew was threatened daily by all the people who would take everything away from him and see him rot in jail; she loved the ease of waiting cars, subservient staff, her wallet of new credit cards that were never refused. 'Insufficient Funds' words that would never touch her again. But she was becoming aware, as Eli would have pointed out in an instant, that there was a price.

'What are they saying?' Frankie asked.

Mo ignored her and Vasily Vasilich, who hadn't enjoyed himself so much since the end of the Cold War, wasn't up to it linguistically.

'Well, she cut her own throat, Pavel. She was my best friend,' Mrs Ivanchenko went on.

Pavel laughed, but it wasn't a real laugh, and a chef in a chef's hat approached the table with some kebabs on a tray that were still on fire. 'Your best friend? The girl was a fucking retard,' he said, and Mo winced at the words and what she realised were his real views on the subject, all the emotional drama of his rescue of Liuba perhaps for show. This language was his language and it came naturally out of his mouth in a way that Mo had not expected. Tomsk street life, she realised, was something she did not know very much about, however far in the past it might seem now that he was head of a huge international corporation, friends with British MPs, married, of course, to an Englishwoman.

'Shit,' Mo said to Frankie, about to burst into tears. 'I've just realised something.'

'What, love? What's going on?' Frankie wanted to know.

'I've just made him a British citizen,' she said as the world pulled into jagged-edged focus.

Mrs Ivanchenko was not finished. In fact, she had hardly started. 'Your wife came up to see Liuba too,' she continued, drinking her fifth shot.

'Not my wife. Mahogany is my wife.'

'Not this one. Katya. With her nice friend, the boy from Kirgask who used to come to the flat when you were a teenager. I think he worked with you on the vodka.'

'Klyzhenko? Andriusha?' Pavel whispered, understanding that the walls were closing in like a bad dream.

'That's right. He was so upset about Liuba that he attacked one of the policemen who'd come to see her body. And they shot him dead, right in the lobby of the sanatorium. Just like that.'

'And Katya?' he asked, not caring any more what Mo heard. She had long since moved her hand and her mind.

'She left,' Mrs Ivanchenko said. 'Said she needed to talk to her lawyer.'

It was the word lawyer that seemed to be the trigger for Pavel and he stood up and pushed the table over, knocking his mother out of her wheelchair and leaving her helpless on the floor with a serene smile on her face. He looked, in his tailored cream linen suit and new wedding ring, pushed on to his finger an hour ago by Mo who now barely even recognised him, as though he was going to kill someone, and the waiters and waitresses who could take cover ducked down behind the bar, the others froze to the spot like a party game, holding their trays and cutlery and napkins. It was too early for other diners. And maybe he would have killed someone, but he didn't get the chance because at that moment six balaclava-wearing men with machine-guns ran into the restaurant and made for Pavel. Boris, who was highly trained for just such an eventuality, shouted at Pavel, 'Go to the car!'

Mo, Frankie and Vasily Vasilich threw themselves to the floor and crawled on hands and knees in the direction Pavel had run, out the back door.

'Jesus, Mo. What is going on?' Frankie wailed. But Mo had absolutely no idea.

Boris opened fire and hot blood began to splash around the restaurant as the staff screamed. Outside, the escapees ran round the side of the building to the car that had reversed hard towards them. They clambered in as a few children who had been playing in the yard by the restaurant stared, open-mouthed.

'Take us to the fucking airport,' Pavel shouted, as they all tried to adjust themselves, tried to sit normally in what had become a getaway car, swerving round the Tomsk traffic, cutting across tramlines, the driver leaning on the horn. Frankie wiped a drop of blood away from her nose with her finger, looking at it in horror on her hand.

'Who were they?' asked Mo quietly, holding her own hands clasped hard together and trying to stop her lip quivering.

'Tax police,' Pavel answered. 'He's got me. Putin's got me. We have to get out of the country. Bitch must have tipped them off.'

'What about Boris? What about your mother?' Mo asked.

'What about them?' he answered her, looking shards of ice into her eyes. Mo understood perfectly.

When they got to the airstrip it was completely dark and none of the party was speaking. The car pulled up right at the steps to the plane and Pavel, glancing around him, said, 'Let's go. I thought they would have surrounded the plane but they're not that fucking clever. I need to get out of Russia now.'

Frankie whimpered, 'My passport. It's in my handbag at the restaurant . . . I haven't got a passport . . .' She burst into heavy tears.

Pavel looked at Vasily Vasilich. 'Take her back to the dacha, will you? She can pick the passport up tomorrow. I'll have her booked on to a flight,' he said.

Vasily Vasilich nodded obsequiously as though the Tsar had asked him to perform a special mission of delicate diplomacy. Frankie didn't stop crying. She had dirt on her white skirt from the restaurant floor and blood on her top and in her hair.

'Varvara will look after you,' he told them and grabbed Mo by the elbow. 'You must come with me,' he told her, and she realised that she didn't have an awful lot of choice. She was a walking passport herself now. This was quite categorically not the wedding day she had imagined.

Back in London, at home, newly married, Mo crept up the deeply carpeted stairs to the bedroom. It had a modern four-poster bed with brown curtains and a vast dark red and brown painting taking up the whole opposite wall. Mo had not chosen any of this furniture and did not know or like the area of town she now apparently lived in as Mrs Pavel Ivanchenko. She took off her filthy, disgusting, soiled and ruined clothes and dropped them on the floor by the bed. She stood in the shower for a very long time, using all the different Molton Brown liquids to wash every last inch of herself. She used black pepper shampoo on her hair, liking the sharp masculine smell of it and watching the white foam run down her dark wet body, feeling like a total idiot. She turned her face up to the hot jet and scrunched her eyes up. She was married to a violent gangster. And she had always known that's what he was on some level. It was why she had liked him, what turned her on about him – that he wasn't a fey public schoolboy with a joke and a wink and slightly camp manner, someone who would end up needing emotional support from her, offering only jolly companionship, if that. But she'd been hopelessly naïve.

The maid knocked softly on the door and Mo wiped her mouth and drew her breath in hard. 'Yes?'

The visitor who she was told was waiting downstairs, whom the maid had turned away a few times already when they weren't at home, who refused to leave a message, was not somebody Mo desperately wanted to see.

Stunned at the sight of him, and refusing to take him into her mind or house until he stood so close to her that the only alternative to embracing him was to stand back and let him further in than the hall.

'This isn't a good time, Dad,' she said.

'I left a message with Frankie a while back. I hoped you'd call. I got this address in the end. You're obviously doing well,' he said, looking around, cowed by the characterless opulence of the place.

'It's rented. Do you want tea?' she asked, not wanting to share her news or anything about herself with this man.

Settled into a deep maroon armchair and stirring needlessly his black, sugarless tea, he looked old, the bounce of cartilage between his bones replaced by some limp connection that dragged and tore, pulling him towards the ground. 'So, you're loaded,' he said, halfway between a statement and a question.

'My husband is,' Mo said, echoing something Katya had said on the plane that time, with Eli, not wanting to add any information to that bare fact. 'I hoped you'd call for about twenty years. Then I gave up. I'm not doing it, Dad. I'm not entering into this. Things aren't going well at the moment.'

He had no response to this and just mumbled his sympathy and moved awkwardly around in his chair as though there might be a position of comfort, it was simply eluding him for the time being but one more shuffle might produce the right words and take the static out of the atmosphere. 'I'm sorry,' he said again.

Mo thanked him and cocked her head sparrowish on one side waiting for whatever momentous news he had come to impart, what worm he might have to offer – something so spectacular that it might excuse a lifetime of songless silence?

'I had a heart attack a while back,' he began, pausing as if for laughter or applause, continuing falteringly when it didn't come, a comic whose first joke had fallen flat.

Mo registered that somewhere behind her armour she couldn't begin to care less.

'It was a bit of a wake-up call, you know?'

Mo didn't.

'And, anyway, well, your mother told me back then . . . You know. Scared me off. After I took you to the Zinns' that day?'

Mo understood what kind of thing he was talking about. What Frankie must have said to him.

'Did she?' Mo wondered, searching her mind for evidence but finding none, except that she really, really didn't look like the man in front of her.

'Well, you know what Frankie's like. She said some terrible things. I've . . . er . . . I've been in Norway.'

313

'Norway?'

'Making furniture.'

'Right. What about Terri and Zane?'

'Oh. Well, Zane comes over to stay a lot . . . In the holidays . . .'

It softened Mo, as though the coals had been scattered with water and the towels plumped up on the hot pine slats, to know that he had been building something, perhaps an oblique effort at reparation, making things, perhaps furniture for families to use, just not his family, or not this one.

'And . . . I wanted to say hi. And to see if . . .' He stopped and looked as though he might cry, his lip trembling with the effort of generosity and of holding back his river of sorrow. 'To see if you might like a table.'

Mo found that where he had succeeded, she failed, and she let the tears spill down her face at last, two decades' worth. 'I would love a table,' she said. 'Thank you.'

Later that same evening while Pavel was downstairs on the phone calling in favours from every politician and businessman in the country, trying to persuade newspaper editors to run anti-Putin editorials related to the attack on him in Tomsk by armed tax collectors, Mo called Eli. She wanted to tell someone about her dad, but probably not Pavel. Not today.

'Oh, Gilda, hi. I thought I dialled the mobile . . . Oh, I did. Sorry. Um, how are you?'

There was a long pause and Mo thought perhaps they'd been cut off, or Gilda had got into a lift or something.

'I tried to phone you,' Gilda said, eventually.

'Oh God. I'm so sorry. Everyone's having the same problem. I have to change my phone all the time now, and I don't know how to make sure the calls always get diverted. I'm crap at that kind of thing. Anyway, listen, I've got news and I really need to talk to Eli, to you both, because I need some help with this—'

Gilda interrupted her by bursting into tears. 'Eli's dead,' she told her, sobbing into the receiver.

Mo put her hand over her mouth and thought she might be sick.

'He was having an affair. Someone sent me a text to my phone and I confronted him. We had this terrible row, this huge fight, but I didn't . . . Mo, I would have forgiven him . . . But he . . . jumped out of the window of his office in Canary Wharf. Last night.'

'Gilda. Gilda. Can I come round? I'm coming round,' Mo told her and then she ran into the bathroom and threw up. She had been trying to avoid confronting the knowledge that she had been carrying around for two weeks now. She was pregnant.

'This time, the corrupt bureaucrats will win.'

Boris Berezovsky

Chapter Twenty-Two

Eli's funeral was at Golders Green cemetery. Mo didn't mention anything about it to Pavel. She just got up in the morning, put on her black suit and left the house. She took the tube as far as she could and then got a bus, refusing now to use any of Pavel's money for any reason. She didn't care if someone shot or kidnapped her very much, not at the moment. She was using her old bank account again, fished the card out of a box of her old stuff, even though there wasn't more than a couple of hundred quid in it.

It was raining and she dipped her head and shoved her hands down into her pockets, walking up Hoop Lane to the place, catching the burning stink of death in the air as she walked. She was late and the rabbi was talking when she walked in, so she found herself not arm in arm with Gilda but standing at the back behind amazing crowds of people. She hadn't known he had so many friends, was so popular. She had always thought she was his only real friend and maybe it was true. But who were all these people?

One of them, she quickly realised, looking sideways at her, also lurking near the back, was Katya, holding an old black Labrador on an orange leather lead.

Mo's instinct would have been to run away, but she was petrified by grief and unable to think clearly. Katya came straight over to her and kissed her on both cheeks as though they were social acquaintances.

'We have to talk,' she said, quietly, as the El Maleh Rachamim was being recited at the front.

'Katya, I'm so frightened,' Mo told her, not realising before she'd said it that it was true.

'Don't be,' Katya told her, putting an arm round her shoulders. 'Eli wouldn't like it. We're going to be fine.'

The 'we' startled Mo and comforted her. She hadn't expected to find an ally here – or anywhere. She started to cry.

'He makes you feel like you're on your own, Mo, with only him in the world. But you aren't.'

Mo turned and looked into Katya's golden face and she smiled, noticing as she looked at her that Katya was wearing a bracelet exactly the same as hers. She raised her wrist to show her and Katya rolled her eyes.

'He doesn't even buy it himself,' she whispered, and they both looked to the front where Eli's body was covered with a prayer shawl.

'He didn't kill himself. He would never have killed himself,' Mo said.

'No,' Katya agreed, and her dog stretched in a position that absolutely explained the name of the face-down dog yoga position. 'You can help me get him.'

Mo, whose rage for her best friend and her own utter idiocy could have blown the roof off the synagogue, felt her anger harden around her as molten lava turns to rock. 'What do you mean?' she asked.

Katya slipped her a card from a gallery in Chelsea with her mobile number on it. 'Be careful. He's listening to everything. I have police protection now,' she said, and slipped out before Gilda or any of Eli's family saw her.

Mrs Zinn, Eli's mum, carried her grand-daughter and held her to her chest, walking slowly and carefully in the delicate high heels she always wore, just like the ones she was wearing when Mo first ever saw her, when she climbed out of her dad's car to go and look at Eli's tadpoles, when everything seemed like it was going to be all right.

Mo couldn't go back to the rented house again, so she went to Frankie's. Frankie was still not back from Tomsk. She had called to say she was fine, that she and Vasily Vasilich were still at the dacha and she was going to make a little holiday of it.

'A little holiday of it? Frankie, we were nearly arrested by armed tax police at my wedding. Some of them are definitely dead. Boris is dead. You can't make a little fucking holiday out of it. Incidentally, I'm at your flat.'

'Be my guest,' Frankie said, a little terse, her parade pissed on. 'Boris is fine. He is here, actually. None of the officers was actually killed and he wasn't charged. They kept him in for questioning for two days and he's helping them with their inquiries. That's if I've remotely understood what Vaska is saying! His English is terrible!'

She laughed riotously and Mo put the phone down, couldn't bear to tell her about Eli, couldn't bear to say his name, to acknowledge that he wouldn't say some stupid headline to her again, tell her how insane she was and how misguided. It was only then that she saw the flashing light of the answer machine and played the message.

'Mo, it's me. Eli. Listen, I'm at the office. Gilda found out about Katya and we had a big bust-up. Anyway, I swear a car tried to run me over on my way here and . . . Look, I'm feeling very nervous. If Gilda knows, maybe Ivanchenko does. I know you're marrying him and all . . . Oh God, Mo. "Man Makes Big Mistake Fucking Ex-Wife of Oligarch".' And he rang off.

Mo was too upset to cry and too shaken to react. It's not that she thought it was safe here, but it was home and she had nowhere else to go. Because when she got off the W3 at the bottom of the road, braced against the rain, a car had ridden up on to the pavement and nearly hit her, racing off again, numberplates covered and windows blacked out. It was probably a thirteen-year-old in a car stolen from the manufacturer, but it might not have been. Mo piled furniture up against the door and went round locking all the windows. Pavel had no reason to want to hurt her, she knew, but he soon would have and she was anticipating the punishment.

Mo switched the television on and watched something about people decorating their houses so they could sell them for more money. When the doorbell rang she put her hand instinctively on her stomach, feeling mammalian in the protective gesture. She still hadn't told anyone. She looked out of the window and saw a couple of blokes standing against an anonymous-type car. Katya walked backwards to gaze upwards and Mo went down to let her in.

Her eyes were puffy with tears and she was shaking, but in complete mental control.

'Mo. You have to help me. He's taken Vanya,' she said, following her up the stairs. The policemen stayed outside, shaven-headed, vigilant, slimmer and slighter than the Russian bodyguards whose place they'd taken.

'Your son? Jesus,' Mo breathed. 'When?'

'Mo, I don't know. Today while I was at the funeral. The nanny said someone came up to them in the street and just grabbed him. The police are doing what they can but, you know, I think he's already not in the country. Mo, you're the only person who knows him like I do. You have to help. He's going to kill me.'

Mo took Katya into the front room and shut the curtains, not knowing what exactly they were hiding from or quite why. 'No, Katya. He won't kill you. He's a hard-nosed businessman and he wants to keep his money, but he wouldn't hurt us, women. Or Vanya.'

Katya let out a bitter laugh and sat down, crossing her very long legs and putting her hands on the arms of the chair. She told Mo that the police had suggested she go on TV, appeal to Vanya's kidnappers, do a big campaign, pull out all the stops, get his dad involved. 'His dad,' she told them, 'is involved.' They interviewed him this afternoon in fact, found him willing, open, but were convinced he had nothing to do with it. Katya knew different. She knew Pavel Ivanchenko.

'He used to beat me up. He enjoyed it. He raped a mentally-ill girl once and had her father killed afterwards, put her in a home where she killed herself. His business rivals drop like shot geese in one bizarre accident after another.'

Mo peered past the curtain just to check that the ordinary London street was still out there, that there were other things in the world but Pavel Ivanchenko and the havoc he had wreaked.

'I know that story about the girl. It wasn't like that. She was a prostitute and Pavel was sickened with himself afterwards and rescued her. She was abused by her father. He was a child.'

'Yes. That's the version he tells. Who really knows? Why did she kill herself just before she was going to agree to testify?'

'Testify to what?'

'It was a plan we had. I was trying to blackmail him into signing over half of TomStal to me and Vanya. It didn't work.' Mo sighed, beginning to understand.

'You know he tried to give TomStal to Eli once? Practically. He was so worried he was going down. That Putin was going to put him in prison for ever, for tax evasion, and he didn't want the assets to go to the government. He gave Eli these cheques to cash if he died...'

Both women were thinking along the same lines and their eyes met over the revolting spider plant that Mo had been unable to throw out.

'Do you think they are at his house? That Gilda has them?'

'I doubt it, Katya. He refused to do it... but...'

Katya banged her fist on the chair. 'Why didn't Eli tell me?'

Mo shrugged. It didn't seem complicated to her. It was just like Eli. He liked sitting on secrets and he never told anyone anything they didn't need to know. He'd been trying to help Katya nail Pavel and TomStal on tax, so he wouldn't have wanted her to think he had, or had ever had, an ulterior motive.

'Why don't we pretend we've got the cheques and say we'll hand them back if he hands Vanya over?' Mo suggested, almost afraid of saying the child's name, afraid for the child, afraid for both of them, feeling sure that Pavel and his monumental power would surely crush all of them.

'He doesn't work like that. I will have to kill him before he kills me. He knows me and Eli are wrapped up in the tax thing. He'll never be able to go to Russia again and he won't be able to stand that.'

Mo didn't mention the spot of bother they had just had in Tomsk with the tax police, but it confirmed what Katya was saying.

'Killing him sounds extreme,' Mo smiled, hoping without foundation that Katya had picked up the English sense of humour that manifested itself in wild exaggeration delivered as tedious fact. But Katya, as serious as a hanging judge, was not laughing.

'It is an extreme situation,' Katya said, lowering her eyelids as though closing her eyes to any other possibility, putting a lid of vein-throbbing skin over the matter. Mo could feel all the blood running out of her veins and into the black hole of fear that had opened up in the flat, like an abyss.

If there was a God in his Heaven putting snails into their shells and carefully ordering the chaos of the black void with omniscient pedantry, it would, Mo now supposed, have been at that moment that Pavel's fate was sealed, the decision that would hurtle along without them already taken, though she had no idea then that the slice of determination in the calm drink of Katya's eyes, might really result in a splash of bright blood in white fur and the hideous choke and gurgle of real death.

'I can't kill anyone,' she said, both hands over her tummy now, knowing that she couldn't be a murderer and a mother at the same time.

'You don't have to. I'll do it. You just have to help me,' Katya said. 'He would kill you and not think twice. If he had to.'

Mo's mind and body fought this idea with all their strength, a tiny rebel army of fantasy armed with stones and Molotov cocktails rising up against the mighty hi-tech stealth-bomber power of the truth.

'He would think about it for ever,' Mo concluded. 'He would regret it for ever and it would eat away at him as everything eats away at him. But he would do it if he had to. You are right.'

And all of a sudden, sitting in the same front room to which she had returned from her first trip to Moscow all those years ago, with the Che Guevara poster she hadn't been able to remove in her redecorations (though she framed it) and the misted-up mirror, looking at Katya with her legs crossed and her eyes intent, Mo remembered the first moment she'd seen Katya and she had thought to herself: that is the kind of girl people kill for. She just hadn't thought it would be her doing the killing.

In Hampstead, Gilda came to the door holding Mica asleep on her chest. 'Oh, Mo. It's good to see you. I'm sorry you couldn't make the funeral . . .' she muttered. 'Let me get you some wine.'

She hadn't even seen Katya, who stood like a goddess of light or something behind her.

'I did come, I just . . . You know. I couldn't stay. Gilda, listen. This is Katya,' she said, presenting her.

'Why are you doing this, Mo?' Gilda asked, her eyes filling with tears and a flush rising from her neck and overtaking her face.

'I'll tell you if we can come in,' Mo said simply, coming in and beckoning Katya to follow.

Gilda was too weak to resist and she let them come in, but took them into the kitchen which seemed somehow more businesslike than the lounge. Mo noticed that she, like Eli's mum, had a roll of kitchen paper that matched the units. It made her smile but only because she wanted to point it out to Eli. Mo sat down at a big cherry-wood table and Katya stood, her hands folded, calm, swathed in linen that didn't crease on her as if by some magic. Her policemen were outside.

Gilda leaned against a unit, a look of blank defeat on her face.

'Katya was Mrs Pavel Ivanchenko when she met Eli. He was doing the divorce for her because all three of us – actually, all four of us – met in Russia when we were fifteen and Katya trusted Eli. There was a degree of trying to stitch Pavel up to get her the settlement she wanted.'

'For some people, nothing is ever enough,' Gilda said bitterly.

'No, Gilda, listen. I don't know if Eli told you . . . before . . . Before. But I was seeing Pavel and we got married a week ago in Russia, in Siberia where he . . . Never mind. But Eli always said I was stupid and that Pavel was evil, and I realised while we were there, anyway . . . Oh God . . .'

She stopped, drew breath and started again. 'Pavel has kidnapped Katya's son now and he is dangerous and we need to do something. We think he killed Eli too. You know he would never have jumped.'

Gilda put her hand up to her mouth at the thought of what might have happened. 'But I found out about his . . . about your . . .' she said, holding out a hand, her other wrapped tightly round Mica. '. . . affair.'

Katya looked down, trying to seem apologetic, but really, how could she be thinking of anything but Vanya. She was calm for him, because if she lost control she could not bring him home safe; so she had to stay calm, but inside there was a raging sea.

'Come on, Gilda! You know what Eli would do about that. He would say, "Fair cop. 'Small Jew Caught out by Wronged Wife'," or something like that. He would buy presents, beg forgiveness, explain that nobody would pass up a chance to be in bed with Katya . . .' She couldn't bring herself to tell them about the message on the machine.

Mo realised she had gone too far and stopped, but Katya and Gilda had started to laugh, and Mo started too, mad, hysterical, desperate laughter that ended with them all sitting down over a bottle, two bottles, then three bottles of wine, and planning the death of the oligarch.

'Yes We Can.'

Barack Obama

Chapter Twenty-Three

The women checked into the Grand Hotel Europe on the Nevsky Prospect for the day, Mo exaggerating her tiny bulge, Gilda clinging to her daughter in mild hysteria. In the end, Gilda, who was to have had such a key role, was never even needed. Katya did not have her child in her arms, but she longed for him like a swallow longs for summer.

Mo hadn't been to St Petersburg for years and she looked out at the view from their top-floor suite in awe. The canals were half frozen even though it was barely winter, and the twinkling domes on the church at the end of the street looked like something in a fairytale: edible, sinister.

The most ridiculous and audacious part of their plan was already enacted. Katya had called Pavel on the phone and told him that Vanya's disappearance had made her realise how much she still loved him, that she missed him and that she wanted to talk to him about getting back together.

'That's absurd. He'll never believe you,' Mo said to her, eyes wide, when she suggested it.

'He's a man, Mo. Men believe you still love them even when they murder your best friend and your lover. Especially this man,' she said with a slight smile.

In fact, he fell in with the plan without any flinch of suspicion, agreeing to meet in St Petersburg which Katya had chosen because, she said, she wanted to be in the most beautiful place in the world when she did the most ugly thing in the world.

'That is very Russian,' Mo said, but Katya did not understand what she meant.

Mo was nervous. 'So, we tell him Gilda has the cheques he gave Eli ages ago and that we'll give them back to him when he tells us where Vanya is?'

'Exactly,' Katya confirmed for the millionth time, brushing her teeth vigorously in the bathroom and coming out with foam dribbling down her chin. 'Then, after he's told me, I give him a glass of wine, all seductive like this,' she said, pushing her hips forward, 'and it's over. When he's dead I put a gun in his hand and call the tax police. They'll pile in guns blazing. There's no way they'll notice he's dead until he's pumped full of bullets.'

It sounded good to Mo, but it also sounded sort of unlikely. 'And if it doesn't work? If he really doesn't know where Vanya is? If he cancelled the cheques years ago? If . . . you know . . . if he doesn't die. If he does die and they arrest you. Us.'

Katya was calm. She wanted Vanya back and she wanted to murder the bastard who'd taken him. She hated him for so many things, but mostly she hated him for making her love him.

'They were actually bonds,' Gilda said, breastfeeding in the window seat. 'They don't date like that.'

'I don't know,' Mo said, lying down on the thick carpet and staring up at the ceiling. She was in a world of her own but Katya brought her back to this one.

'You don't know? You don't know? He kicked me in the stomach on my wedding day when I loved him and I had a miscarriage.'

Mo sat up. Katya was shouting.

'He had Boris hospitalise my yoga teacher. He had Andriusha shot and left for dead out on the tundra. Boris again. He beat me up so often and so badly that the Russian doctor near our house told me I should go into a refuge. Russian doctors never EVER say you should take any help but theirs. We all know he had Liuba's dad shot but we don't know how many others. He told me once but I wasn't listening. All the lowlifes who gave him money to buy out the steel works, one by one they disappeared. Mo, HE HAS MY SON,' she said, turning and walking back into the bathroom to put the toothbrush down and wiping her mouth with her hand.

Gilda spoke more quietly. 'He killed Eli.'

Mo stood up now, planting her bare feet in the carpet and looking out at the grey horizon. 'Yes,' she said. 'Let's do it.'

It was early evening when Katya left the hotel and walked the short distance to the restaurant, pulling the collar of her white mink coat up around her neck. Mist rose from the canals and slipped around the ankles of the scurrying people like a thousand cats; maybe, Katya thought, the souls of all those who had died in the swamps building Peter the Great's mad Venetian-dream city, a place that would become synonymous with madness. Katya hired an upstairs room in a kind of restaurant/brothel that one of the girls she used to know from the Moscow beat now ran. It was in a discreet courtyard off the Nevsky, opulent and beautiful with gypsy dancers, Eastern food and lanterns hanging from the walls. Katya hugged her friend and paid her the money, cash to leave the premises and stay away for the night: ten thousand US dollars bound up in an elastic band. She climbed the stairs carefully in her heels, throwing her hair back behind her shoulders, confident and serene. They had left food and champagne out; Katya tipped a tiny amount of almond-smelling cyanide into a glass and topped it up with the champagne. She flicked on the music from an iPod in a stand, some sort of Spanish guitar music, and she waited.

Pavel arrived on time and discreetly, ducking under the heavy curtain and smiling at her, sure of himself, with two bodyguards who at first stood against the wall. Katya was on her own.

'Hello,' he said, which was unusual in a way that Katya was unable to pin down.

'Tell them to wait in the car,' she said to him, lying back on a low sofa as if to suggest that sex might be on the agenda. He was, she thought, truly the only man in the world who could believe that a woman whose son had been missing for over a week might feel like having sex. It was as absurd as chicks in December. But he went for it. And it all might have gone according to plan. If he hadn't been thirsty. He had a lot of information to cough up before he went dying on them.

He looked different, Katya thought, dishevelled, strange. Perhaps he had reached the end of the line too. His clothes, normally so perfectly tailored, didn't seem to fit properly and there was something, something misshapen about him that she couldn't pin down. He didn't tell her she looked wonderful either, and yet she did.

Pavel would talk and talk, or pace up and down or try to make love to you, but he never took a drink until everyone else was drinking, so she was surprised when he not only lifted the wine glass immediately but drank the whole glass in one shot.

'Nyet!' she tried to shout, but the word stuck in her throat and, by the time he looked at her, she could see he realised and the whole hideous, phantasmagorical scene unfolded. He rushed at her, murdered now and murderous, and Katya stood and shot him as he lurched, ending up on top of her in a hideous parody of sex, blood leaking out of him and his mouth spitting bile. Mo burst in as he fell and, unexpected, as if from nowhere, Boris the bodyguard appeared from behind the curtains as though to help, but help who? And in the end he just stood, stood and stared, not protecting his principal and not helping the women, just standing. Chasing Pavel

330

out into the street, genuinely afraid now that he was immortal, magical, that he wouldn't die, Katya watched stricken as he leaped into the cold black water of the Neva and was gone.

Afterwards Katya went back to the hotel, the doorman gently bowing to her as though she had been out for a stroll, and, indeed, she turned her coat inside out and held it folded over her arm, a swan gliding across the water but underneath frantic and kicking with anxiety about Vanya. The plan had not worked and yet . . .

'Katya! Katya!'

She heard her name called and she glanced around the lobby to see an old man stumbling out of an ornately upholstered gilt chair towards her; next to him, also rising and approaching, was a woman. A woman holding Vanya.

She hurled herself on her son, grabbing him and holding him to her as tight as she could before taking in anything else about the strange couple. He reached his arms out to her face and smiled.

Shaking and crying with joy and relief and all the horror that had gone before, she whispered in his ear, 'Baby. Hello, baby. How are you, pudding?'

'Auntie Frankie and me made biscuits,' he told her.

The woman spoke to her and Katya looked into her face, somehow so familiar and yet unknown to her.

'Are you better, dear?' Frankie asked.

'Am I what?' Katya asked her, blinking. Behind her an American couple were checking in at the grand reception, the top-hatted doormen billowing around in their cloaks with brass stands of luggage.

'Better? You were in hospital, Pavel said. Oh, perhaps it was a secret . . .' Frankie trailed off, wondering if she was being rude. Katya realised quickly what was going on.

'Oh my God,' she said in Russian over and over again.

Frankie put her arm round Katya's shoulders. 'Are you all right love?' she asked. 'I'm Frankie. Mo's mum. Did he not tell you?'

Katya shook her head and collapsed on to a chair near a low table where someone had abandoned a pot of tea, slices of lemon on cocktail sticks lying on a saucer.

'We've had a lovely time, haven't we, Vanya?' Frankie said, leaning forwards to stroke the boy's cheek as Katya snatched him out of her reach.

Vanya laughed and nodded.

'Uncle Vaska!' he shouted and Vasily Vasilich stepped forwards and smiled.

'Hello, Katya,' he said.

Katya looked up at him in stunned disbelief. 'What the hell are you doing here, you revolting old goat?' she choked out at him.

Vasily Vasilich shuffled on the marble floor a bit. 'Well, I . . . Frankie and me . . . We've been staying at Pavel's dacha outside Tomsk for a bit and looking after Vanya and . . . Well, he asked us to bring him here today but there was nobody to meet us and he didn't have a room booked, so we've just been . . .'

'Firs and sticks,' Katya said finally, shaking her head and kissing Vanya again on the cheek. 'I love you,' she said, smiling at last.

'I love you, Mama,' Vanya told her, struggling to the floor so that he could run around the lobby.

Mo couldn't believe it was only yesterday. It already seemed like a hundred years ago as she lay there, letting the bathwater go cold, thinking about Pavel and death and meeting Katya so long ago. The fact that it had led to this. She listened to the radio like she always did in the bath, just as if she hadn't been involved in the murder of her unborn child's father, as if everything was just the same. And it did look the same. Barack Obama talked hope and change and enablement. Mo understood the words but the meaning washed over her.

When the doorbell rang Mo got out of the bath slowly, ready to face what would need to be faced, knowing now that she had all the time in the world. She pulled on her dressing gown, blue and white striped, that was hanging, that always hung on the hook, and took a deep breath. She padded to the door, making wet footprints on the tiles downstairs.

But it wasn't Interpol or MI6 or the local police even. It wasn't a journalist or a TV crew come to ask about her wedding, had she heard, what did she think. It was Gilda.

'I thought we weren't going to see each other,' was the first thing Mo said, reaching forward anyway and giving Gilda and Mica a big joint hug that made her cry. Gilda had a pale cashmere jumper on and it stuck to Mo's wet cheek a bit as she pulled away.

'It's OK. Boris went into the police station in Petersburg and just confessed. Apparently he'd dished all kinds of dirt on Ivanchenko when they took him in after the tax police shootout . . . Oh, of course, you were there, sorry.'

'No. It's fine. Come in,' Mo said and they went upstairs to the flat. In the new atmosphere of the flat, somehow calm and placid like a very deep lake, Mo thought: It really is all over. A story that started so long ago, on that first trip to Moscow, was finally over.

'Anyway,' Gilda said, settling down and accepting the offer of wine even though it was eleven in the morning and she was breast-feeding, 'he might even get a suspended sentence. He's been a big informant over the past week or so. A lot of old crimes solved. I think he probably committed most of them.'

'But not this one,' Mo said. 'So it's good of him. That sounds absurd. But, you know. It is. "Big Bad Man Does Good Thing".'

Gilda smiled and her eyes welled with tears, not needing to artic-ulate her grief for her husband since Mo so clearly shared and understood it. Mo smiled sadly at the thought of her lovely friend, Gilda's lovely and stupidly unfaithful husband. Though his point about not being able to resist Katya was a good one. Surely nobody ever had.

'I think Boris would do anything for Katya. She says he must have watched what Ivanchenko did to her on the security screens, you know?' she said

'Yes,' Mo answered, finding it strange to be accepting his new name, his surname, when she had whispered Pavel to him so many times, had felt so close to him. It was frightening how far away it was possible to feel. 'How do you know all this anyway? When did you get back?' Mo asked, crashing around in the kitchen for the glasses, opening and shutting cupboards that all her life had contained the same things – suddenly unsure of everything.

'Oh, I stayed the night. I just got home an hour ago. I came straight here. I have news. No. Two pieces of news. The first is that Vanya was with your mother.'

'What?'

'Pavel flew him to the dacha and this old guy, who Katya knows, apparently, and your mother, looked after him. Thought they were doing Katya a favour while she was in hospital. So it really was just Pavel trying to frighten her, I suppose. Amazingly cruel ... although ...'

'Don't,' Mo said, 'Wait. My mother was looking after Vanya in Tomsk. This is insane. She didn't call to tell me. She didn't think it might be worth a mention?'

'Apparently not. Anyway, Ivanchenko brought them in with Boris to Petersburg to surprise her. Boris had been at the dacha too. It's all too surreal.'

'Katya must have been quite surprised to see that lot.'

'I was upstairs. I never got the text from you two to show up with the bonds so I was watching Al-Jazeera English all evening ...'

'God. So, he's OK, Vanya?'

'He's fine. And I have other news.'

'Christ, Gilda. I am a bit fragile,' Mo said, sipping her wine and drinking the courage in to hear yet more news. She picked a bit of horsehair out of what had become her favourite old armchair, sitting forwards on the edge of it. Gilda, moving Mica from one breast to the other and looking as if she was about to say something about a new nappy rash cream she'd found, spoke, looking Mo right in the eye.

'I really do have the bonds. I thought it would put you both in danger to know. Eli and I hid them in my bra drawer for ages while we decided what to do about it. We cleared them with the Foreign Office years ago. We are allowed to cash them now that . . . I mean, we have to do all the charitable stuff, but there will be quite a lot spare for . . . a salary?'

'You have thirty million pounds in bonds?'

'Yes. Well, no. Not any more. The bank does. I thought we could split it?'

'Thirty million pounds?'

'No. More like ten after we've . . .'

Mo collapsed backwards, throwing her head against the soft back of the chair, and she burst out laughing.

'A mysterious Russian billionaire has trumped his big-spending rivals and broken a world record by splashing out €500 million euros (£392 million) on one of the most sumptuous villas on the French Riviera.'

The Times

Chapter Twenty-Four

Pavel Ivanchenko woke up and told himself he was lucky. He was sick of the view out of the window. He was sick of the grey courtyard and the dog shit, sick of the woman who came round constantly, begging to be let in, pleading to know why. She had long straggly hair and huge puppy's eyes that had melted into a vast spring lake of sorrow when he had pushed her away from him in revulsion that first day when he was stale from the plane and the anguish. She had sat, shivering, outside the door for nearly fifteen hours (he had little to do but count them) and the woman across the hall brought out hot sweet tea for her and a slice of some repellent-smelling piece of crap, had sympathised and been sure they would soon make up. He was appalled to be linked by anything whatsoever to this bedraggled specimen. He was used to having a racehorse on his arm, a goddess, the honey-gold lioness or the lovely gypsy with the flashing eyes and the sharp mind.

The stringy woman spoke to him through the door when she came (less and less now as the months went by, but God, she was persistent) like someone at their mother's grave, weeping, relating news, reminding him of their love. He learned that she was a cellist and that she was turning down work to stay by his side until he got better. Got better? The only explanation this weasel-faced woman could think of for his not wanting to see her was that he was ill! Only once had she caught him on his way out of the building but he darted past her and she was too slow, though she screamed after him through the Novosibirsk traffic, baffled, desolate.

He watched the footage of his own murder with detached interest as if the coverage applied somehow to someone else, which, of course, in reality, it did. He read the sanguineous splashes of news pieces and then, later, the slightly more measured obituaries, all, he noticed, rehashes of the piece Mo had written long ago, in another life. It made his fists clench and his teeth hurt to know that they had all betrayed him. Boris, his wife, his ex-wife. He saw pictures of Oxley House on the news, Oxley House where he would never go again as long as he lived, a place that had been home, not that he had a real understanding or feeling for that concept, so beloved of other people. Nobody, out of all the people he'd helped and paid for, nobody had stood by him in the end except Gleb. Poor Gleb who finally paid his bloody dues, finally stood up and took the flak for everything he, Pavel, had done on his behalf, finally paid him back.

It had been pathetically easy. They'd done it all the time at school, until Gleb started insisting on growing his hair like a girl and Christ knew what. Nobody had ever been able to tell the difference just by looking, not when they were little, not unless they spoke to them and saw Gleb stuttering and cowering like a cur being kicked by a gang of schoolboys. And now he was waiting, growing his own hair, waiting for the money to come through, what he hadn't given away so that they wouldn't chase the rest, just enough to start again in style, just enough to get the hell out of this shit-hole. He'd put in an offer on a place in France. He didn't know how Gleb could have stood it here in the back of beyond in this flat, wall to wall CDs, tapes and records, sheet music heaped up everywhere, all over the piano and at least four violins, one of them, he knew, fantastically valuable in Gleb's terms. In most people's terms. The Aranyi Stradivarius, in fact.

This morning a journalist had stopped him on the doorstep, a blizzard sweeping through town, whistling through the grey high-rise blocks of flats as though it could flatten them, leave the whole place white as girl's skin with only the black railway snaking through to Moscow, three days and a universe away. She was pretty, hiding under a black woollen hat and a big fur collar on her coat.

'*Kommersant*,' she said, naming her employer. 'We're doing a profile of your brother for Saturday. Does the death of this oligarch mean the death of the oligarchs? You know? How do you feel about his murder, Gleb Svyatoslavovich?'

Pavel stood still for a while, absorbing his new identity. This was the first time he had been addressed by his new name, not counting the sad mad girl with the big-eyed grief. They hadn't actually said it at the airport, not out loud like this: Gleb Svyatoslavovich. Forever.

Pavel let some snowflakes melt on his shoulders and then he shrugged and said what he supposed Gleb might have said if he'd known what he was really being used for, if he'd had the choice. Pavel had simply called it 'a favour', had described 'a bad situation with women', had said he was 'desperate for help' and asked Gleb to pay him back for the years of financial support, for his upbringing, for everything.

'He had it coming to him,' he said, smiling at the pretty girl with the big job, whose cheeks were pink as summer apples and whose eyes were green as moss.

'They say you were in Petersburg only days before it happened?' she smiled back, looking like a spoonful of cream on a pancake.

'Maybe. I don't know the times,' he told her truthfully.

'You've cancelled a lot of concerts. When will you play again?' she asked, stamping her feet up and down in the snow in front of the doorstep, her hands deep in her pockets. An old man was failing to start his car, half buried it was, over the other side of the court-yard; another old man come to offer fur-hatted sympathy rather than help. The car yelped, scraping metal on metal.

Pavel thought about this and would have experienced, perhaps, a twinge of sadness for all the lessons and the wailing nightly practice in the tiny flat, the dreadful tunes echoing into the universe with their desire and their potential future, their mother's tight-lipped hope and Gleb's star-faced look of faraway joy when he played. Would have, if the guy hadn't been such an utter arsehole.

'I won't be playing again,' he said. 'In fact, I will be moving away. Changing my life.'

'Me too!' the girl said, her head on one side, allowing him to think for a moment that they might change their lives together, that he might show her another world of . . . But no. He shook the thought off with a shudder and smiled.

'Goodbye,' he said. 'Good luck.'

And that night he let the weasel-faced woman in and made love to her, safe in the knowledge that only their mother had ever known the difference for sure. Only Pavel had a mole on his left ear.

maxi   echo
oscar   kenco
otto   herbie

casper   huntley
rufus   honey

vorg   flynn

rusty

archie

Rebel Heiress

Fiona Mountain

'Wonderful . . . haunting . . . One of the best historical novels
I have read' Alison Weir

'Completely engrossing, a must for all who enjoy historial fiction'
Choice magazine

Born into a world seething with treachery and suspicion, Eleanor
Goodricke grows up on the Somerset Levels just after the English
Civil Wars, heiress to her late mother's estates and daughter of
a Puritan soldier who fears for his brilliant daughter with her
dangerous passion for natural history.

Her reckless courage will take her to places where no woman of her
day ever dared to go. Her fearless ambition will give her a place in
history for all time. But it is her passionate heart which will lead her
into a consuming love – and mortal peril.

'Wonderful . . . A read I will never forget' Emilia Fox

'Rich and brilliant . . . Fiona Mountain is an exceptional
storyteller' *The Lady*

'I was gripped from beginning to end' Katie Hickman, author of
The Aviary Gate

THE POWER OF READING

Visit the Random House website and get connected with information on all our books and authors

EXTRACTS from our recently published books and selected backlist titles

COMPETITIONS AND PRIZE DRAWS Win signed books, audiobooks and more

AUTHOR EVENTS Find out which of our authors are on tour and where you can meet them

LATEST NEWS on bestsellers, awards and new publications

MINISITES with exclusive special features dedicated to our authors and their titles

READING GROUPS Reading guides, special features and all the information you need for your reading group

LISTEN to extracts from the latest audiobook publications

WATCH video clips of interviews and readings with our authors

RANDOM HOUSE INFORMATION including advice for writers, job vacancies and all your general queries answered

Come home to Random House

www.rbooks.co.uk